D1071302

arded
SCC

Books by Daniel Stern

The Girl with the Glass Heart
The Guests of Fame
Miss America
Who Shall Live, Who Shall Die
After the War
The Suicide Academy
The Rose Rabbi
Final Cut
An Urban Affair

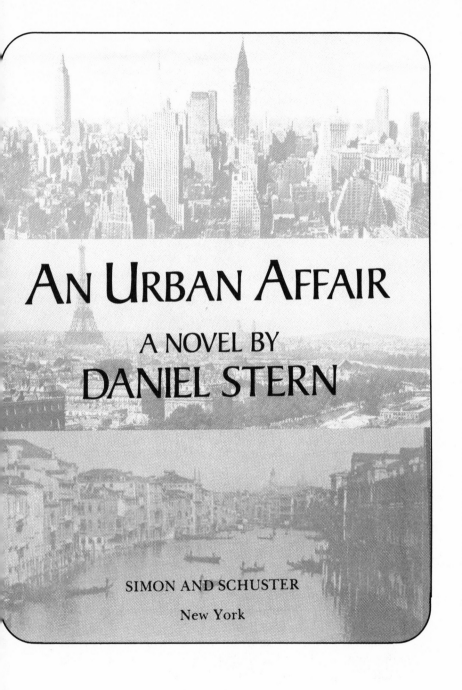

An Urban Affair

A NOVEL BY
Daniel Stern

SIMON AND SCHUSTER

New York

COPYRIGHT © 1980 BY DANIEL STERN
ALL RIGHTS RESERVED
INCLUDING THE RIGHT OF REPRODUCTION
IN WHOLE OR IN PART IN ANY FORM
PUBLISHED BY SIMON AND SCHUSTER
A DIVISION OF GULF & WESTERN CORPORATION
SIMON & SCHUSTER BUILDING
ROCKEFELLER CENTER
1230 AVENUE OF THE AMERICAS
NEW YORK, NEW YORK 10020
SIMON AND SCHUSTER AND COLOPHON ARE TRADEMARKS OF
SIMON & SCHUSTER

DESIGNED BY GLORIA ADELSON
MANUFACTURED IN THE UNITED STATES OF AMERICA

1 2 3 4 5 6 7 8 9 10
LIBRARY OF CONGRESS CATALOGING IN PUBLICATION DATA
STERN, DANIEL, DATE.
AN URBAN AFFAIR.
I.   TITLE.
PZ4.S838.Ur   [PS3569.T3887]   813'.54   80-15495
ISBN   0-671-41226—4

Photographs from The Granger Collection, New York.

Portions of "Hearing of harvest rotting," "Paysage Moralise," and "In Memory of Sigmund Freud" were taken from *W. H. Auden: Collected Poems* by W. H. Auden, copyright © 1976 by Edward Mendelson, Executor of the Estate of W. H. Auden. Reprinted by permission of Alfred A. Knopf, Inc.

"Notes Toward a Supreme Fiction" from *Collected Poems of Wallace Stevens* by Wallace Stevens, copyright 1942 by Wallace Stevens. Reprinted by permission of Alfred A. Knopf, Inc.

"Fourth of July in Maine" from *Near the Ocean* by Robert Lowell, copyright © 1963, 1965, 1966, 1967 by Robert Lowell. Reprinted by permission of Farrar, Straus & Giroux, Inc.

For Anäis, Jim, Jules and Sue—who left too soon.
And for Benjamin, Doreen, Jay Daniel, Rachel
and Stephanie—
who arrived exactly at the right time.

AN URBAN AFFAIR

Part One

PROJECT
SIMON

Sad is Eros, builder of cities,
and weeping anarchic Aphrodite.
—W. H. Auden
"In Memory
of Sigmund Freud"

1

He was often "just back." Just back from Japan: the city of Kyoto must be expanded. There was no way, he told them, dazed with fatigue and slatted sunlight, no way to expand the city of Kyoto. Just back from Paris, from Cleveland, from Pittsburgh, from cities that must be saved from growth, from themselves.

She was often "just leaving." Just leaving for a travel agents' convention in Geneva. (The most boring city in the world, she said. A week in Geneva is like a month in the country.) Just leaving to lead a tour of sociologists to Kenya, to Kuala Lumpur.

"You have a very elegant trade," he said.

"Ah, my customers, my children," Sarah said. "Elegance is beside the point. It's their innocence, their love for new sights, new experiences."

"And you—don't you like to travel, too?"

"I'd go away with you, tomorrow."

"I can't go away tomorrow, or the day after tomorrow, or the day after that."

It was a test of sorts. Her face did not cloud; her mouth did not turn down. She was not going to be a spoiler. They

13

were going to make each other happy. They were in it for happiness.

She lives on a city block that is like no other: Fifty-seventh Street between Sixth and Seventh avenues. In spite of its scraggly, fenced-in trees, it is essentially a place to work, not to live. Yet here Sarah lives, in a building fronted by a blue awning. On the gray concrete of the façade hang gold and silver nameplates. M. ROSENTHAL, LUTHIER. A luthier, she explains, is a violin-maker. But they make few and mostly buy, sell and repair. Sometimes, as one waits for the elevator, there are confused, lovely sounds of violins and cellos to be heard. It is a building with a dentist, with many offices with milk-glass doors shielding the interiors from view, with ambiguous names like Acme Corp., Inc., and one with Gothic lettering that reads Trans-World Publications; behind this door the light is, strangely, never on. Only ten people make their homes here. All of them appear to live alone. Sarah is one of them. The block is bounded on the west by Carnegie Hall, on the east by a Horn & Hardart Automat, a street of art galleries, of music, book, record and pet shops, of old buildings and remodeled apartments with large floor-to-ceiling windows, some of them duplexes, which look down over the crosstown traffic. In one of these Sarah lives.

It is an apartment that was once part of a larger unit. The front door opens directly into the living room; couches, chairs and coffee table proclaim it a living room. But there is a kitchen, without a true door, in full view. To the left is a bedroom with an enormous bed, covered by a feather quilt. (Simon had never seen a bed of its size.) Just outside the bedroom door is a staircase that leads upstairs to a study, full of memorabilia, and second bathroom. The walls are covered with posters: shining suns from Provence, blue waters from Tahiti. Tapestries weave their way across one wall. Everything, except perhaps the great bed, speaks of travel.

14

Simon let himself in with the key she'd given him. These were evenings condensed by the pressure of a false ending. Five hours: all the time in the universe. Still, how to structure a life in those hours? He would always arrive first, directly from his home or the library. It was spring and travel agents, it seemed, worked hardest in the spring.

He dozed in the bed, rolls of feather comforter providing comfort and too much warmth for April. Next to him, on the end table, four-color brochures promised happiness via new places.

In his half sleep, he was a tourist only of the evening, a tourist of the three-room apartment, of the five hours, planning pleasures.

Simple pleasures: sometimes she would wake him and they would discuss the day's developments over a drink. Other times she would tiptoe in, carefully undress and reach across the enormous sea of that strange bed to fold her slender self into his arc, their fishbellies glowing in the semidarkness of the room, with the window open to the honking and hissing of buses, like angry geese, the blare of horns, the roll of spring thunder in the distance, the undefinable myriad noises: cracks, booms, sharp crashes, all merged into that city noise she jokingly held him responsible for.

"The thunder?" he whispered.

"Isn't that yours, too?" she said softly, and fell asleep for a few moments until the telephone jumped.

"Oh, who . . . Yes," she said, irritable with sleep. "Oh, Daddy, what is it? What's the matter?"

The matter was some friend of Sarah's father who wished advice on where to go for a convalescent cruise: his wife had died and he had undergone major surgery. Where should he go? How should he spend his time, his money, his unfocused attention?

"You're like a priest," Simon said.

She reached across him for a white plastic bottle of lotion and rubbed it into her hands.

"Priestess," she said, "with chronic dry skin."

15

"People come to you for a solution—"

"A temporary solution."

"All solutions are temporary." And he chanted: " 'Travel is a good thing . . . it stimulates the imagination. Everything else is a snare and a delusion. . . .' "

"You're quoting," she accused.

He admitted it. "It's a failing in my craft. We're always quoting literature."

She settled lightly into the curve of his arm, hair tickling everywhere. She said, "Actually, you're quite useful. Every time you fail and cities become more and more impossible, people turn to me to get away."

"The way I turned to you."

"No," she said, "that's different," and she thrust herself between his legs like a force, a surge of nature, her long legs embellishing the blocks of his thighs, her splayed hair adorning his chest, hair long enough to entwine his thighs, her hands suddenly at play, her breath accelerated beyond hope of control. They were in each other's hands.

On impulse, they decided to go to dinner in Chinatown. It is a quiet but large decision: risky even though his wife is away. As they were leaving the apartment he almost fell over a shopping bag stuffed with records.

"Someone left it at the agency," Sarah said through a curved mouth being painted in the hall mirror. "Months ago. Rameau and Brahms—all of them. But only things like Brahms serenades and Rameau operas. Forgotten music." She laughed.

Simon poked through the bag. There must have been twenty albums. "It's going to be a Rameau-Brahms spring," he said.

It might, it turned out, be a Brahms, Rameau, umbrella, textbook, dog spring. People were always leaving things at travel agencies: umbrellas, books, records, scarves, animals, birds in cages, purses. Sarah would wait a decent interval—at least a month—and turn over the valuables to the police. From the rest she would take what appealed to her.

Out, then, to the chancy dinner and into the rain furiously promised by the earlier thunder.

By the time they finished dinner the rain was gone, everything wet, the streets streaked, the evening almost gone. But they had made love first, had made their twilight tour of each other, leaving a touch of extra time to tour Chinatown. They found an unexpected little park bridging the Chinese and Italian sections, round, with a dry fountain at its center. Chinese children bounced balls while old Italian men sat in stone groups, as if they had always sat on those same benches in the same attitudes of age. They ate sandwiches out of brown paper bags and a mysterious unlabeled bottle circulated among them.

Sitting on a bench in that park, he told her of the chaos, the anarchy and misery, of his early years.

"But the strange thing," he said, "is that I've found I can't do without happiness now. Most people can spend months, years; I've got a friend, Linc Aaron, who's spending his whole life without it. And I had a friend who died without having much of it. My two best friends had absolutely no gift for happiness. But I can't do without it, even for a short time, anymore.

"Is that why you're here with me, on a bench in Chinatown?" He lifted the hair that hung heavily on the nape of her neck and held it in his hand. It was pleasantly coarse.

"Because you make me happy," he said. "Because I need to be happy."

"Or just because you need *not* to be *un*happy?"

"It's like a drug. Once you've had one kind of happiness you have to find other kinds, new kinds."

Cool, tasting falsely pure, the night breeze blew through the piles of green-bagged refuse that fringed the little park. Still, it smelled sweet, redolent of unsifted city perfumes: traces of gasoline fumes, park grasses, distant oily

17

food being cooked, moist flowers, Sarah's soap-and-cologne odor; a city wind, odorous, beneficent.

"And what if I make you unhappy?"

"I'll leave you like a shot," he said. They were still new enough for him to make such jokes with ease.

"You didn't leave your wife when there was trouble."

"That was different."

"Ah, it begins."

But it did not begin. There was a purity in their concern for each other's happiness; a sense of the importance of the absence of pain. They were like survivors of a train crash. Survivors of their own earlier life, they were fragile, and respected that fragility.

2

HE HAD ALWAYS ASSUMED, simply, naturally, that he would be among those who would rebuild the world. As Dante had built the city of Hell and Heaven, he would build the city of man. After postponing real life for years ("I fell asleep for nine years," he told Sarah later), he'd graduated from the Yale School of Urban Affairs in 1963. The cities were burning. Apocalypse on its way. It was no longer the poets, the writers, the historians or philosophers who would take the essential part in such matters. Utopia, salvation, had passed from the domain of the imagination to the actual. The architects, the urban planners, would save or lose the world. That is to say, the cities.

His thesis at Yale had been entitled:

"On the Possibility of Human Happiness in Large Urban Environments of the Future."

"Professor Aaron told me I'd added a new dimension of *chutzpah* to urban theory."

Sally laughed. "It's what I like about you."

"Nerve?"

"Call it confidence."

"Call it nerve. I never had it," he said, "before I was happy."

3

IN THAT FIRST ENCOUNTER she came toward him, tall—easily five feet nine—a beautifully put together ensemble of imperfect parts, her long, slender torso swathed in black hair far too long for someone her age: perhaps thirty, perhaps thirty-two. Her calves were stocky, while the rest of her willowed out. She stood before him, feet planted robustly apart, chewing on a pencil point, then, thrusting it behind her ear into a tangle of hair and smiling at him, said, "Yes . . . ?"

He was there on impulse; back from Chicago only three months, but the winter was already cold and long. There was a mysterious on-and-off pain in his right hand, yet he didn't want to see a doctor. The city was getting to be too much for him, even for him. His wife would be returning soon, after a two-week professional visit to Montreal. He wanted warm amnesiac travel plans, a bright new idea. But he forgot it all in that moment.

She had an eyebrow like a quick stroke of charcoal; she had a round face that glowed with health, later glowing in much the same way when suffused with grief. She had a voice pitched low, a pointed sound, independence condensed into the timbre. She appeared to be happy. Yet her eyes would fill up as swiftly as an allergic nose. As if unknown to her, emotions fled through her pores, into her eyes and down her cheeks. It was a dramatic contrast to the independent style she sported: very much her own woman—except when she wasn't. She was chagrined by this. "I never cry," she would say for the fourth time that month.

4

APRIL: TWO DAYS of steady rain had softened and
cleansed the air—made it what the weather bureau called
"acceptable." They accepted it. The car radio warned of a
hot summer for which the city was not prepared: all sorts
of essential services might have to be curtailed unless Con
Edison reformed at once. In the meantime it was a perfect
spring night; until somewhere around DeKalb Avenue.
Movement slowed down to a crawl; exhaust fumes turned
the acceptable evening air acrid. Horns flashed their irritable Morse code.

But Simon and Sarah's good humor prevailed. He told
her a little about his project for redesigning large cities
into smaller units to avoid such experiences. She was in an
amused, amusing mood and preferred to tell him precisely
when she had become convinced that his precious cities
didn't work. She told him, as they inched forward every
few minutes, of her love affair with an older man—a man-
ufacturer of children's clothes with a special interest in
travel. She had arranged a sales meeting for his company
in Japan. The relationship developed in quick steps: a
passing acquaintance, a friendship, an affair and, at the
last, a passion. He was a good man: very much the survivor
of hard knocks who has not allowed those knocks to
toughen or coarsen him. Still, they were overwhelmed by
the difference in their ages. (His daughter was eight years
older than Sarah.)

Sensibly, they had stopped, pursuing their absence with
all the seriousness and intensity with which they had pursued each other. No phone calls, no letters, no subtle hints
to mutual friends: silence. And what she found so strange,
so insupportable, was the fact that they never caught sight
of each other by accident. Yes, her complaint was essen-

20

tially mathematical. His office was only two blocks away, as it had always been. The Chinese restaurant where he lunched at least twice a week was still around the corner from Rockefeller Center and from her travel agency. Yet the brutal massing of so many people in one area called a city had so raised the level of randomness, of chance, as to make it next to impossible to run into someone, someone for a glimpse of whom one felt one was dying. That was what Simon's cities had done.

Sitting there surrounded by breathing metal, muttering gas fumes, stuttering engines, he did not dismiss her complaint lightly. He went along with her ironies about cities while she clearly enjoyed her life. But the murderous numbers he had to cope with in structuring and restructuring his cities, real and imaginary, depressed him more than she knew—more than he was ready to tell her. The tale of Sarah and her older man fused with the endless line of cars poisoning the soft evening.

In the next week he ran into Sarah three times. It was as if he had been designated by some unknown authority to make up for past pain. The third time she was on her way to the bank with a deposit. They laughed at the impossible encounter and touched hands in the gloom of a cloudy day and went to her apartment to make love. By the time they'd straightened the sweaty sheets and dressed for the day again, the banks were closed; but life seemed a little more open to benevolent accident. For one dark spring day they seemed to have repealed the city's law of averages, to have invented a new mathematics of love.

5

IT TROUBLED HIM some days—in Low Library at Columbia doing research, or sitting with Matthew in the playground in Washington Square Park. Why now? Why in the fifth year of a second marriage, at age forty? He had gone to Chicago with grand hope. The time had come to deal with the megalopolis; to use all the lessons learned in the Japanese failure, to make the accidental city into one in which people could live. The money was there—two grants in addition to the city funds. But the project had died in ten awful, smoggy months, Matthew sick with false asthma, Alex restless, edgy—her famous Eastern poise and self-possession infected by the strangeness, the incorrigible Middle Westernness of the place. And the immense plans, the money already spent, the hopes of the Yale Foundation, everything finished in one final Götterdämmerung: a city council meeting and a riot in a usually tranquil park. The groups had too many letters to make sense. Finally, acronyms were gibberish. What the rioters had in common was the desire that Simon should leave their neighborhoods alone, let the city continue to grow at random, the garbage uncollectible, the schools unfit, the air unbreathable. The rocks they threw all had invisible notes attached to them, a reverse echo of all those open-air protest gatherings of the sixties: Watts, Detroit. Then it turned dark with pressing bodies, Simon struggling with two men and a woman, his right hand jammed painfully against a great rock—the park had been full of rocks, large and small.

Yet the night before, after his initial presentation to the city council, which had gone so well, he had been made welcome by the city of Chicago at a dinner. Perhaps "welcome" was too unambiguous a term. The atmosphere had been heavy with the losses and cancellations of the past year. Talk about growth and change was now muted; the assorted planners, architects, government officials and foundation executives were stale with repeated defeats. No one knew quite why they were there—except that Simon seemed about to pull off a coup none of them had been able to accomplish for some time: get enough support for a try at a city planning project in one of the toughest cities in the country.

22

He was feverish, incubating a cold or flu, a little dragged.

At the same time it was exciting. Jane Jacobs was there.

"I'm honored you could come."

"I've read your stuff on Japan. You're doing the Lord's work. . . . You see that fellow leaning against the wall?"

"With the cigar and the hat?"

"Right! I came to keep an eye on him for you."

"Who is he?"

"Murphy—an alderman. One of Mayor Daley's duly elected goons. Watch him," and she was gone into the crowd. It was not the kind of conversation he'd have imagined having the first time he met Jane Jacobs. But it gave him a charge.

In fact, he was all charged up, in spite of the confused signals he'd been getting ever since his arrival in Chicago.

It was not his fault that the country could not exorcise the ugliness of death in Asia. Spontaneously he ignored the speech he'd written and tackled the federal government. If this country wished to express its humanity, why not begin with Washington itself?

"Buildings sit, in Washington, like monsters on their separate blocks, as isolated from each other as warring nations." If neighborhoods were the answer to salvaging cities, why not start with the neighborhood of the federal government? Make the institutional complex livable—encourage street-level uses of buildings. Create natural trystoriums in and around public buildings: libraries, coffee shops, plaza parks. Rediscover scale in cities, starting with the capital. He'd gone on weaving a crazy spell, the madness of which was lost on no one. Didn't he know that government programs for the cities were being cut back —abandoned, in fact? He knew—and threw in a surprise curve: a suggestion that government funding was not the whole answer—that the neighborhoods themselves had been mobilized before and could be mobilized again, bringing out their own money, brooms, cans of paint, planting their own trees, cleaning up buildings.

23

It was a great success. The kind of magnetic exhortation that had helped him move forward so swiftly. He had fallen asleep for nine years; to catch up he'd needed to develop special stratagems. Today's improvisation was one.

Over coffee afterward, a tall, tweedy man took him up.

"Good remarks," he said. "I'm Cappy Kaprow. Office of Urban Redevelopment. That was not the usual brand of bullshit."

"No," Simon said. "My own brand." He was wary of bureaucrats. Kaprow laughed nervously. "If you want to develop that into a proposal, I think I can get it to the President. Or pretty close." Cards were exchanged. Kaprow said, "Everybody's bitching about no money for cities because we have to wind down the war. But you sidestepped all that. Humanize the cities—the President will like that."

But all this was the night before. The day after was something else.

It began with a deceptive success.

In Room 436 of the grimy city hall Simon mounted a slide show with such eloquence that all factions were swept along with him—for the moment. Slides of neighborhoods appeared on two sides as if by a magic benediction. Trees blossomed, mysteriously, in granite beds; streets that ended in brick walls opened, as if by divine edict, onto sunlit vistas, framed by plazas harboring fountains and playgrounds. Bus routes developed extraordinary reach and flexibility; ethnic neighborhoods were preserved, yet were brought into subtle connection with their neighbors. The awful unyielding rigidity of the city's interior grew soft and pliable with possibility.

When the lights went on the audience blinked with wonder. Who was this prophet from New York smiting stone and bringing forth water? That lasted about thirty seconds. The "audience" broke apart into the collection of special interests that it had been before Simon's magic lantern show. How did Mr. Shafer propose to do X without impinging on Y? Why was more money and attention not being allotted to Q instead of to B and C? His proposals were biased in favor of whites, in favor of blacks, in favor of income levels over fifteen thousand dollars a year, sentimental about the poor who were destroying the tax base with their welfare habit. . . .

Other speakers supported Simon and at last the meeting was adjourned until the next day—when a plastic model of the entire project would be unveiled in Grant Park at a noontime rally. Simon was elated, still; he was used to opposition. It came with the job.

Standing in the far corner of the room, wearing his hat and his cigar, Alderman Murphy smiled patiently.

There was the familiar discrepancy in estimates of the crowd's size. Afterward the rally's organizers claimed two thousand, the police said eight hundred. The sun shone untroubled by clouds; the groups gathered peacefully; their varied signs made up a continuous poem: NORTH/SIDE/CITIZENS FOR URBAN REFORM/LEAVE/OUR NEIGHBORHOODS/ALONE/NORTH/SIDE/BLACK/CITIZENS/SUPPORT SHAFER/PLAN. . . .

One group straggling at the outskirts held up a sign: OUT OF VIETNAM—NOW! Everything was pertinent; everyone had a voice!

Beyond the outer rim were blankets and radios; Thermos bottles and beer cans were passed from mouth to mouth. Simon Shafer Day in Chicago was beginning in festive style. As the public address system was being tested and someone was checking the stand on which the model unit stood, Simon stood at the edge of the platform. A smog haze merged with the motes of sunshine at the horizon. He had the sense, for a quick moment, that those towers trembling in his sight were his to do with as he wanted: that his vision could make these seemingly intransigent materials—glass, steel, concrete—fluid, workable. That the dividing lines between where people lived and their actual lives could be made new; that desires and

25

boundaries could be merged, for once, instead of existing in their traditional opposition. It was an easy, good moment. Not a rush-of-power moment. Rather a moment promising that whatever changes were begun on this sunny spring day five weeks before his fortieth birthday might last in the flesh and spirits of all these people for generations.

It lasted about ten minutes.

It was impossible afterward to pinpoint who started the rock-throwing, or, in fact, precisely why. A troubling editorial in the *Chicago Tribune* suggested that such an ambitious project simply entangled too many constituencies: you can't satisfy everyone, the newspaper concluded. At which point Simon murmured to Alexandria, "But you have to start by pleasing somebody!"

Somebody who was not pleased began the catcalls after Simon had done a simulated runthrough, using the model for a giant three-screen multimedia show. Somebody who was still less pleased threw the first rock. At this point the milling about commenced on the platform. Below it, Alex was standing next to Simon. "I told you not to do this outdoor dog and pony show," she whispered to Simon. She had, indeed, worried about the notion of too much drama. But it was exactly the drama Simon had thought he needed to unite support.

Two policemen flanked Alex in true Chicago macho style; in an instant Simon could no longer see her. He couldn't see much as a mass of bodies flowed onto the platform and rocks clunked against his precious model. Sirens cracked the air and another policeman commandeered the public address system, shouting unintelligible orders at the crowd.

Somehow all of the planning commission ended up struggling together toward the exit where cars were parked. But Simon was separated from the rest by a black man and a woman.

The man had sleek, shiny black skin with pockmarked

cheeks; his eyes were pinpointed with blood at the corners; he grimaced with rage; spittle sat in the corners of his mouth. He wore a bandanna around his forehead; it gave him the style of a bandit chief. The woman was white; she wore, eerily, a flowing white dress. They pressed Simon and finally the man shoved him against an enormous boulder; Simon's hand was caught between his hip and the rock, with the full weight of the bandit chief pressing down. The pain was electric.

Simon never knew how he got to the limousine. He was seated next to the man Jane Jacobs had warned him against; plump Alderman Murphy, still behatted, smoking a cigar that threatened to make Simon vomit right there in the back seat of the Cadillac. He gazed straight ahead. Even as Simon wondered where Alex was, he was surprised at the alderman's silence: he expected some apostrophe, some summing up of this extraordinary occasion. After a few moments it came.

Removing his cigar from his incongruous Cupid's bow of a mouth, Murphy muttered the judgment of nations.

"Asshole," he said.

The next day his fever bloomed and the flu struck. Simon slept around the clock. Around the centuries, too, since he woke from a dream of Huizinga's Middle Ages— ever the urban scholar—with bells in his head, his ears, his memory.

The illness lasted for weeks. He seemed unable to shake the weakness; Simon, who was never ill. Also the bells. Orange peels on the bed blanket, a half-capped thermometer, glasses of water heavy with motes of dust: magical objects, each with a message they were forbidden to reveal.

Not that Simon could have handled any revelations. He was troubled enough about the visions and the voices. Then came the flutes. Sometimes they accompanied the bells, sometimes not. Once Simon sprang out of bed to see if the radio was on; it was not, but the flutes fluted anyway.

His friend Ben Demos came often to visit, even though he was dead. He would stand and pace nervously by Simon's bedside.

"Well," Ben said. "The natives didn't seem to know if you were Cortez, Hitler or a combination thereof. It's a dangerous thing to extend your hand to the people."

"Ben, do you hear bells?"

"I always hear bells. You can't go by me."

"How about flutes?"

"Flutes I only hear sometimes."

"How about right now?"

"Sure. Right now."

"But from where?"

"The question of flutes is independent of where."

"Since when, Ben? It's okay for you to talk that way; you're dead. But—"

"Don't talk like that!"

"Like what?"

"About being . . . 'dead.' "

"Why?"

Ben shivered and cracked his knuckles. "You think I'm used to the idea?"

"You think I am? It happened so quickly. And you're the first of my friends to go. How come you're back?"

"That's better. Use euphemisms, like 'go.' I'm only here as a messenger. Maybe that's why the flutes and bells."

"Maybe? How can it still be maybe?"

"There's always a maybe."

"What's the message, Ben?"

"It was delivered."

"When?"

"Yesterday."

Shit! Simon thought. Ben was gone; it might have been a dream. Simon felt stupid. Dreams like that were the small change of a nervous breakdown. And yesterday's message was clear—as mud! "Get out of town. Give up. Cut your losses." Orange juice bit his tongue but failed to clear his mind.

There was always a reasonable explanation. Ben had been a nay-sayer. That was his style. A Brooklyn boy saying yes to food and no to the possibilities of life. (It had been Ben, all right, plump, waddling; death did not seem to be dietetic.)

In a circle of wild intellectuals ready to conquer the world, quoting, writing, playing, pushing, painting, exhibiting, Ben had pushed only privacy.

"If I can play the piano, why does it have to be for three thousand people in Carnegie Hall?" Why indeed, Ben? Your brother a deaf-mute, your father mad and silent in the living room while you played.

"It is a dangerous thing to extend your hand to the people." A quotation? Or pure Ben Demos? (Ben's education, like his life, had been a ragged ripping away, without system or plan. Except for the music with which he'd made his fragile living.) Was it to confuse him with cryptic remarks that Ben had come? Or was his presence, real or imaginary, a reproach? Private Ben versus public Simon. His hand hurt. At least that was real. To hell with flutes and bells. There was always pain to hold on to.

For Simon, the way to handle pain was action.

Amid the confusing mélange of bells, fever, flutes and disillusion, he remembered fragments of the conversation with Kaprow. Alexandria was eager to leave as soon as his temperature was ninety-eight point six again. But something kept Simon back. He jotted down notes; notes which soon became an ambitious letter to the President. The bitterness of the recent fiasco faded under the grandiosity of words. It was like writing fiction to heal the pains of reality. reality.

> . . . It is time for the President to lend his prestige to the humanization of our cities. Cities are made of generations of use, an accretion of history, years and events which have made their corners, parks, bars, restaurants personal to people. It may seem strange to personify cities, to speak of them as having years of life, but think about a public clock

one used to meet under [Simon and Alex had met for months under the clock at Penn Station], a favorite corner. In a transient society such places become even more important as ways of maintaining our sense of identity, of continuity.

"You schmuck," Ben Demos said. "That hit on your hand must have affected your brain. Nobody gives a damn about humanizing cities. This is 1971. Every man for himself. Your wife is worried about your sanity. The people don't want your neighborhood revival and they told you so with rocks. Go home!"

This time he didn't even stay long enough for a reply. Still, Simon *knew* it was a fantasy; but no less essential for being one.

The final fantasy took the form of a recommendation for a federal Office of Urban Design—but one that would mobilize neighborhoods as much as funds, individuals as much as groups.

"A sixties sonata," Ben Demos said. "You've got a tin ear."

Simon thought, feverish and exhausted, writing to the President of the United States is no stranger than talking to dead friends. He mailed the letter. That night, his right hand still cradled in a sling, he began to organize his papers. Project Chicago was off.

Simon the savior was finished, too—for the moment. He and Alexandria were once more "just back" from another city that would not be saved. Back to a low-key life, teaching one class at Yale. They had not given up the apartment on Riverside Drive. It was only a question of moving back light furniture and such movables as disappointment and disillusion. Matthew was only three. In a year schools would have been a problem.

But, for the moment, the problem was Simon's sense of being becalmed, bereft of projects for the first time in years. There were a thousand errands to be done; lamps to be fixed that had been damaged in transit; books to be found that had been thought lost. Like the convalescent he was, he slept and read. Lying late in bed, for the first time in months he read for escape: his old love, Shakespeare, first. Favorite plays not read for years: *Coriolanus, Othello.* But the second Sunday after returning, the apartment overheated for spring, Sunday seeming to stretch endlessly before him, orange peels and plastic toys on the quilt, Alex busy in the kitchen with Matthew, then on the phone with old friends, suddenly his escape route closed. It struck him that his reading had only been continuing his inner argument on different terms; Othello and Coriolanus shared a monumental ambition. And as for escaping from cities—what was Othello without Venice or the angry emperor without Rome? He might as well be rereading Mumford's *The Culture of Cities,* which had to be done to prepare for his class anyway.

The city as an idea was under attack. Half of his students wanted some kind of utopian commune; the other half simply enjoyed basking in the phosphorescent glow given off by decay.

Aggression in the classroom thickened in the air like paste before he entered the room. One toughened stump of a young man, red beard, red-rimmed eyes glowing fanatically:

"Professor Shafer, how do you reconcile belief in the city as redeemer of civilization with the student movement in Russia? After the burning of Moscow in 1812, they said that 'Communion with God lies in the wilderness. The Redeemer comes from the hills and silent places; Satan is on the boulevard.'" He wore white pukka shells around his neck and a bracelet of bells on his wrist.

Ah, dear God, a religious nut; just what he needed. Calmly, answer calmly.

"The major portion of our political, social, intellectual and artistic history is that of the great cities from Rome to Byzantium to Leningrad and New York. The Augustine sense of the human condition is crystallized not in the holy mountain of God, not in the desert of His burning bush, but in the City of God—*De Civitate Dei.* We segment our

31

image of historical epochs—medieval, Renaissance, Baroque—according to the rise and fall of representative cities. . . ."

He was interrupted by a supersuave young black woman who had made it to the heaven of New Haven from the Pittsburgh ghetto:

"Take a walk through the downtown section of any major city. You've been judged; we're just waiting for the sentence to be passed. Your City of God is not doing too well by His children."

Simon's right hand throbbed. The pain was imminent. Bad woman, he thought. He'd confided a little of the Chicago experience to her during a private interview; now she was using it against him. Or was that only his current paranoia?

"The megalopolis," Simon said, "is not the only possible model. That's what we're here to discuss." And he shuffled some papers on his desk, wearily; he was preparing to end the class early.

"Aristotle said that no city should have a circumference exceeding that in which a cry for help, wherever uttered, cannot be clearly heard at the outer gates. That is not the answer today. But it may be the paradigm of the question."

And he turned away, angry at himself. The joint between the index finger and the thumb was jabbing him with pain. Unfair, he was being unfair to the students while tormenting himself.

"Hey," Ben Demos said. "Do yourself a favor and cut the urban-pastoral bullshit." Round face and frizzy hair counterpointed dry disillusion.

"Why talk when you should sing? Don't fake them out. Sing, Simon, sing:

From this the poem springs: that we live in a place that is
     not our own . . .
And hard it is, in spite of blazoned days."

6

ONE FELL IN LOVE after disappointment: when self-esteem was at a low ebb, when illusions were in short supply. He began to tell this to Sarah when he realized that neither of them had ever mentioned the word "love." It was a day of blazing sun at the central rink of Rockefeller Plaza. They had stopped to gaze at the tacky imitations of French cafés below. Sarah was bending over the rail, having handed him a package to hold for her. He saw the back of her head, cocked sideways, the outstretched leg behind her, in a lovely arc, still for a moment, forming a frozen question it was much too soon to ask. He changed the turn of his sentence in midair and said, "I guess I'm talking about public ambitions and private happiness."

"Oh?" she said, and turned back from the railing. "I thought you were talking about love."

"I started to."

"We're not in love."

"How do you know?"

She waved a disdainful hand at the people below them, standing in line on a warm April twilight, waiting to get into a fake French café for fake French food, and said, "We satisfy each other. We make each other happy. That's all."

She specialized in minor and major mysteries: a minor one was the package he'd carried home for her. It was another of those *objets trouvés* left at the agency. But unlike the Rameau and Brahms recordings, she refused to reveal it to him, placing it deep in a linen closet instead. When he asked about it she changed the subject abruptly.

"Tonight was the first time you walked me home from work. Weren't you nervous?"

"A. Alex is out of town. B. You could be an innocent companion: a dispenser of foundation grants, an architect . . ."

"You're so academic. A . . . B . . ."

She was undressing, by chance in front of the mirror above the bureau that faced the bed. Her head escaped a blue turtleneck, then she stood for a moment bare-bosomed, her breasts half cups: curved inward above, outward below.

"This is our third time alone together," Simon said. "You're not shy in the slightest. Why won't you show me what you brought home? Is it something obscene?"

"I don't exactly know."

She examined herself thoughtfully in the mirror. "I'm not shy with you because *you're* not shy. The first time you were naked in a minute."

He held her, half naked as she was, feeling the weight of all his clothes against her flesh. Then he kissed her and reaching under her skirt, put his finger inside her. A moment later, when he brought his hand up and held her again with both arms, she held his wrist and put his moist finger between her lips and they kissed mouth, finger, tongue all at once. "I like to taste myself on you," she said. Some chaos of his nerves erupted at this: a stretched string of passionate feeling that broke and let him fall, defenseless, to the bed, carrying her with him.

"Why am I naked and you still half dressed?"

"That seems to be the way it turned out. It's temporary. Either I'll get undressed or you'll get dressed." She propped a pillow under his head, covered herself with half a sheet and smoked silently.

"I never saw you smoke before," Simon said.

"I don't often."

"Sarah: creature of small and large surprises."

"Small?"

"Smoking, suddenly."

"Large?"

"That wanton move."

34

"Which?"

"Tasting yourself on my fingers."

"Ah, *that* wanton move. Name me another small surprise."

"Hiding that object you brought home from the agency."

She turned large eyes in an open gaze on him. "You're one, also, you know."

"One what?"

"An object found and brought home from the travel agency."

"No one left me there. I brought myself."

"Was it very bad, the Chicago thing?"

"It left me a little shook up. Now I'm taking a long look, that's all," Simon said. He settled his head on her breast. "Maybe it's time to think historically. It's 1971. Not 1771 under Thomas Jefferson or George the Third, not 1871 under Andrew Johnson or Louis Napoleon. In ancient times people took their lead from leaders."

"What does that have to do—"

"Just that there are times that feel properly public and times that feel private. I took my master's and doctorate in wildly public times. Maybe now it's time for personal happiness—not rebuilding cities, saving worlds."

"So that's what you meant about disappointment and love," Sarah said. "I refuse to be an alternative to your career."

"You should meet Linc Aaron, my friend from Yale. Discuss my career with him."

"I refuse," she said, "to be explained away by theories of disappointment and work."

He had been watching their reflection in the window, a peculiar monster composed of sheets, limbs, pillow, clothes, invented for the day. But the window had grown first blue and then opaque and he could not see it anymore. When he felt the tremor of her body under his head he knew she was not laughing but couldn't believe she was crying.

35

It stopped as quickly as it began: a spring tear-storm characteristic of Sarah country.

"All this refusing," he said, rolling onto his side and placing his hands over her wet eyes. "I was hoping you would refuse me nothing. Not even secrets in closets."

She slipped out from beneath him and began to strip off the clothes that Simon still wore. His shirt, his tie, his undershirt . . .

"I refuse to lie in bed with half a man," she said gaily. And when he was as naked as she, slid herself into the crevices created by the angle of his arms, legs, neck. "Someday I'll show it to you," she said, her long black hair drowning his mouth, her breasts squashed against his chest, one of her hands reaching down and cradling his testicles gently, the middle finger pointing tenderly between his buttocks. "Someday," Sarah said, "when I know you better."

She slept: the radium-lit clock face was so bright that Simon could make out the titles of books scattered on the end table. He saw Virginia Woolf's name, and Emily Brontë. Was Sarah a feminist? He did not even know if she had sisters or brothers. He'd never had a clandestine affair, with its necessary restrictions of time and information. When did you find out all those essential facts about the other lover? Or was having an affair a way of testing how crucial all the biographical debris actually was? Marriages were novels, full of data. Affairs must then be short stories, by contrast: condensed, allusive. Or perhaps poems: images and emotions, abstract because of limitations of shared time, contact. So much had, of necessity, to be left out.

One of the bedside books was by a man. *South Wind* by Norman Douglas. But was Sarah reading it for pleasure, or was it background for booking a tour of Capri? There was something sensual about speculations while Sarah slept at his side: private afterplay. Sarah's mouth, his finger, his lips and her moistness, his thinking about her: everything had mingled, was mingled, still.

7

WALKING THROUGH the orthopedist's office was like a trip through Lourdes. A baby with a tiny leg in a miniature cast; an old man encased in plaster from the shoulders to the jaw; a young woman on crutches, swinging a plastered weapon as she walked.

Dr. Rowan had been recommended by one of Simon's students. A fanatic of bone, Dr. Rowan was; the student had suffered a ski accident, and Dr. Rowan was the plaster saint of skis, the knitter of bones. Dr. Rowan is also, it turns out, over six feet tall, with blond eyebrows and white hands, pale white fingernails, trimmed short, beneath which gleams pink-white flesh.

"You've got some bone chips in this wrist area here," he says, tracing along the x-rays with a fingertip.

"Would that cause the pain?" Simon asks.

"Amazingly, yes. Look at this network here: they look so delicate. There are two hundred and eight of them, you know; no more, no less. One cubic inch of human bone can stand a weight of two tons, yet they wear away, in unpredictable places and times: it's only one of many mysteries. These little carpals in the wrist, for example—" Simon is forced to interrupt. He likes the idea of being treated by a fanatic of bone, but the rhapsodizing makes him nervous.

"Would these chips cause the pain, now?"

"We call them joint mice. Of course they hurt. They're alien bodies where they are, floating loose. See here: these shadows. That makes two hundred nine and two hundred ten—and the extra two were not planned for. How long have you had the pain?" Simon told him of the panicky moment in the park; the hand crushed against the rock. "About four months."

"No," Dr. Rowan said, "that wouldn't do it. This is the kind of thing you get from long, repeated wear on the same joints. Usually years and years. What do you do, Mr. Shafer?"

"I'm an urban planner."

"Does that mean you draw plans—physically?"

"I used to be a draftsman."

"That could do it."

"But there must be something wrong. It began exactly that day in the park—that moment—and it's stayed with me, on and off, ever since." Dr. Rowan shook his head, dismissing irrelevancies. "No, this is the kind of thing you see in women who have done sewing all their lives, don't you see? One trauma wouldn't do it."

"Then why wouldn't I have had it before?" The tall wraith of whiteness loomed over the light box and the x-ray of Simon's hand. "Look," he said, tracing a thin pale finger along the bone map. "Capitate, lunate, hamate, pisiform—all carpals of the wrist so elegantly made that it would make a Swiss watch look like a clumsy mechanism. All tiny tough live tissue we call bone—manufacturing blood cells, holding everything in its place. Made to wear until they dry out in old age and grow brittle. But these little shadows"—he straightened up, tall, impatient— "they have no place, no connection." There was no way to deal with a fanatic of bone except to say, bluntly, "But you don't know why they should have worn off now?"

"No, I don't know."

That was a kind of victory, getting him to say "I don't know." Still, the doctor had the last words. He had the hypodermic syringe filled with cortisone to be injected into the joint; he had the prescription for Butazolidin and the Ace bandage. And strongest of all, he had the threat of an operation which contained the promise of relief from pain.

"How old are you?" Dr. Rowan asked.

"Forty."

"The operation might be a worthwhile risk."

"Is it a simple one?"

"To be fair, no. You can see the complexity of small bones in the wrist. On the other hand, if you can live with the pain . . ."

He lived with the pain. There were whole days without it. On other days—and nights—it was a constant: every time he opened a door or grasped a pencil or held any large object in his right hand he was reminded of the exquisite miracle of bones he was carrying in his wrist, a miracle flawed. He could not give up using his right hand. Hardest of all to give up was the connection between the pain and what had happened to him, to his life. To bear a wound directly related to the failure of his grandest project, his largest hopes, gave it point. Otherwise, something foolish called joint mice—and purposeless pain.

8

"CAN'T WE GO away somewhere?"

"No."

"Why?"

"Married men can't just go away somewhere."

"Some can."

"Then I'm not your first?"

"No. It was awful. I swore never again. He told his wife."

"That *would* be rotten. Not me!"

"Ah, 'not me.' "

"Don't you believe me?"

She had a subtle way of turning themes toward Simon and away from herself, whenever past personal events were on the verge of becoming present conversation. They'd jousted over a late brunch on this chilly Sunday morning full of the yellow freedom of sunshine trickling through green curtains. He was there on a lie, of course: his wife was to have been at home, he was to have gotten away—pretext of a professional meeting with his old teacher Linc Aaron. Actually, Alexandria was still gone. Simon was quite free. But he did not want to be, as yet. He had no idea what he was up to with Sarah; he just knew it was best to be as married as possible for the moment.

Last-minute arrangement though it was, she greeted him as if he'd been expected all week. The robe pink and soft, the table set with a fresh rose in a bud vase at the center. Instead of making him feel guilty for his deceit, it made him press her harder. New as it all was, he wanted to know more: the short story could become at least a novella.

"Oh, there's nothing to know about me," she said. She'd said it, or a version of it, so many times. This time Simon did not let it pass. "Everybody has had a mother, a father, the whooping cough, an education, all kinds of things."

"I never had the whooping cough. I had measles."

"Why do you put me off like this?"

She looked at him gravely, taking a full beat as if to tell him she was absolutely sincere, and said, "You don't want to hear that stuff about me."

"You mean no man you've been involved with has ever gone into the usual things?"

"Taking a history, like a doctor?"

"Learning about you, like a lover."

She shook her head. "Not really; no. Do you want some more coffee?"

While she poured she stared straight at the thin blue-patterned cup and said, "If you were a little more like Sherlock Holmes you'd realize how much I've told you already."

"Like what?"

"Well, you were lying next to me when my father called, so you know my father's alive and living in New York. You know I have a travel agency; that I once had an affair with a much older man, and once with a married man who told his wife and made an ugly mess; that I like books." (There were books everywhere, it was true: in wall bookcases, on the marble coffee table, on the hall table beneath the mirror.) "Your eyes tell you I'm about thirty, that I like the colors green, blue and yellow. I like Brahms and Rameau . . . that, like a certain Simon Shafer, I want to be happy . . . and that I don't think men really want to know all about a woman when they ask deep, deep questions: they just want to know something pleasant and untroublesome." She leaned back in the curve of his arm, waited till he put the coffee cup down and kissed him: a period to the run-on sentence. "Elementary," she said.

"You're throwing all that at me, instead of any one thing."

"What one thing?"

"Any one. I'll take any one."

"And if there is none?"

Why the probing? The wonder was almost enough to make him stop—but not quite. Was he so interested in the private detail because he'd failed miserably in the public detail? He'd had an awful fight with Alex just before leaving Chicago. At the core of it had been the question of how private and how public a man he really was. One of those evenings in married life in which things were said that had the hard, crystallized shape of eternal statements. Things that would always linger behind the sound of a familiar voice, no matter if the voice spoke tenderness or sensuality: the casual poisons of intimate life.

The words had been so simple. "Don't forget," she'd said. "Behind all those grand ideas, all the great plans for ripping out a city and starting all over again—underneath all that you're really a politician and a businessman."

Perhaps his startled silence had enraged her further. Or (the indeterminacy of unpleasant memory) it might have been the smog-induced sinus infection which had been driving her wild. But all at once she had clutched her handkerchief to her nose and from behind it, shouted at him—his Alex, bereft of her Vassar cool, of her good taste, crying out: "For God's sake, Simon, you're *not* Lewis Mumford, you're *not* Jane Jacobs, you're *not* Paolo Soleri. You tried a big scheme and you lost because of money and politicians. If you could see that . . . Oh, damn it."

Falling into Sarah's trap, he began to tell her about that evening. Again, she surprised him.

"I don't want to know anything at all about your wife," she said.

"How about me? Do you want to know about me?"

"Yes."

"And my child, little Matthew. Shall I tell you how smart he is?"

"That's fine. That you can tell me."

He held her dark face between his hands.

She did not look away; her gray eyes stared him down. Not cool, they spun a gaze that took him in while the mouth below curled in an expression of such rue that he was still held off. "I'm just me," Sarah said. "Is what happened to me me? Is that it?"

"Part. Everybody is part biography, part history."

She took her face back from him by lighting one of her rare cigarettes and standing up. "You've left out a few: demographics, topology." She swirled suddenly and ran to the bookcase to pull out a blue-bound book. Simon cradled his right hand in his left. It was a technique he'd developed to lessen the pain. On occasion it worked, sometimes it did not. Today was a good day.

"Here," Sarah said. "This is me." And before he had time to be literal—as he would have been in a moment, suspicious of a novelist lover who had written about her —she read to him.

It was a poem by Auden; the cadence told him that. But as soon as she began to read, Simon blocked out the sense of what she was saying. He was struck by wonder that he should be struggling so with this young woman for a touch of her past.

The first night he'd gone out with Alex, they'd stayed

up until dawn in an orgy of what she called "the thens."
Then I gave up ballet. . . . Then I flunked out of college.
. . . Then . . .

> ". . . Knowing them shipwrecked who were launched for
>   islands . . .
> Where love was innocent, being far from cities.
> But dawn came back and they were still in cities. . . ."

It had been Simon's joke that he'd married Alex because
he was sick of "the thens," could not go through one more
first date. He was going to have a mimeographed sheet
made up and mailed in advance to all prospective girl
friends: "Then I switched from architecture to urban
planning. . . . then I got divorced. . . . Then I spent a year
in the army." It would save time and endless repetition.

It seemed to him that he lived in a world of people only
too desperate to lay their "thens" on your back, on your
soul, on your doorstep, in your bed. Sarah was unique;
oddly at home in physical gesture and metaphor alike.
Anything but literal statement of personal historical fact.

She was crouching at his feet, unaware that he was not
really listening. Her tone told him that the recitation was
ending.

> ". . . And we rebuild our cities, not dream of islands."

She smiled up at him; her robe winked open over long
thighs. Suddenly Simon seized her by both arms and
pulled her up in front of him. He shook her angrily, surprised at his own rage. Had he fallen into an affair for the
first time, just to be put off with lines about islands and
cities? He felt foolish, too. Was that all he wanted for
them: to be like everyone else, lying in bed, she full of his
semen, a Kleenex neatly tucked in to save the bed sheets,
the two of them telling each other intercoital sad stories of
the death of love affairs, marriages, parents, pet dogs . . . ?

Still, he said, "I asked you about yourself."

"No you didn't. You asked about things that happened
to me."

43

"The same thing."

"No. Things that just happen don't matter. So there's no big point in remembering and talking about them." He held her, trying to control his anger. He was damned if he would point out that he was happening to her, that they were happening to each other; one of those things that apparently happened and didn't matter in Sarah's universe.

Sarah was in his arms, between his hands, at least; only this time being pressed in a different kind of passion. Surprisingly she was passive. She seemed to understand his rage. Her stillness gave silent approval to his complaint, her face flushed, a rose push of blood visible under dark skin.

In the face of such acquiescence only chance could save him from feeling foolish: apologies, the bright thrust of the afternoon dwindling in a long detumescence. Chance turned out to be the ring of a doorbell. Startlingly loud, it seemed, until Simon realized he had not heard it from the inside of the apartment before.

Sarah scrambled to her feet and into the kitchen to murmur questions and reply into perforated metal.

Simon sat on the couch; rage gone, arms and legs heavy with confusion. Crazy bastard, he thought. What do you want? Still undefined, his fall into Sarah's arms had no shape, no cause, no destiny. He had no idea of how far he wanted it to go. The unspoken assumption was it was to go nowhere. He had wandered into a travel agency one day, restless, looking for guidance. That guidance was not expected to extend beyond travel. His wife and child were in Canada, while Simon lingered in the aftermath of their "troubles." (You didn't leave your wife when there was "trouble.")

Why, then, press poor Sarah for her Life and Times. The rage was as much against himself as against her. It was unfair all around. This sunny brunch, this tourism of the senses of past weeks, this visit, was a temporary, passing place. A place in which he was putting his head, spirit

44

and body back together after a bad time. All the more reason not to come on like Tristan to a reluctant Isolde.

It was Sarah's mother. No warning phone call; no warning at all to Simon that Sarah had a mother in the vicinity. It was, in the flesh, a piece of the past Simon had been pulling at. In the fur, actually.

"It's turned cool," Rachel Geist said. "People forget April is often quite a cool month in New York." She sloughed her mink onto the couch.

"Mother . . ." Sarah began.

"I tried to call. The circuits were busy. For an hour. Not your number—isn't that something?—the circuits for this whole area. This city doesn't work anymore. I dialed and dialed!"

And accepted a glass of tonic water.

Sarah's mother looked fifty but must have been sixty: a good-looking woman with a fleshy face. She smiled without warmth; austere. A quality that, diluted in Sarah by a generation, showed in the younger woman as that sense of being one's own woman, pleasantly aristocratic. It was interesting to see the derivation and the difference.

"I wanted to warn you, in case you see Edmund, that he may not be in good shape. His friend Blau died a few days ago. They were very close." To Simon: "I'm sorry for intruding."

Simon murmured the offhand, forgiving sound that was called for. Mrs. Geist would not sit, strolled restlessly around the room smoothing her hair, brushing her hand across the dull bronze statuette of an Indian dancer. She paused and traced the curve of the figure—some goddess or other, one leg raised in a sacred dance.

"I remember when you brought that home from India. Not long before Jephtha died. I remember thinking: Sarah's only eighteen and she's wandered across India alone."

"Were you proud?" Sarah asked.

"No. It was just a kind of being startled that such a young woman could do that."

45

Sarah stood, quite still, in the center of the room. Her flushed face was tranquil again.

By the time Mrs. Geist was gone—only about five more minutes—the air in the room was different: a different electrical charge, an absence.

"Your mother has presence," he said.

"Ah, presence. Mother has presence, yes."

"You don't believe that, about all the circuits being busy?"

"I do, yes. Mother doesn't lie."

Simon drew Sarah down to the couch next to him and tried to kiss her. Her face was damp with perspiration. All that time she'd been standing, poised, calm, in the middle of the room, her mother pacing, Sarah had been sweating.

"Listen," she said. She turned her face away, moist stray hairs grazing his lips.

"I don't want to listen now," Simon said. He reached for her again. "I'm sorry about before. It's just that I want to know about you. Simple as that."

What he did not say was: not today, anymore. Hence the kiss and what might follow, to still conversation.

But it was a restless Sarah now, on her feet, circling the sofa. No kisses, but no evasive poems either. He could have what he liked, it seemed: brandy, more coffee, a special blend made with cinnamon. Anything but kissing or silence.

"They're divorced," Sarah said. "Edmund and Rachel. For a long, long time."

"Edmund is your father? All these first names."

"Yes. And Blau is a doctor friend who came to this country with him, oh, back in the twenties. It was my parents' divorce that set me off."

The new, mercurial Sarah disappeared into the bathroom for a moment, leaving Simon to sip cinnamon-flavored coffee. It was a strange taste in coffee; as strange as hearing about the family of a young woman he was sleeping with. It had taken years—at least three—for him to realize that Alex's mother and father were anything

46

more than strangers, connected to him by their daughter and his wife, who happened to be, by accident, the same person. It could not be done again in an afternoon. He was not ready to take in all these names: Edmund, Blau, someone named Jephtha who had died.

Sarah reappeared, rubbing lotion into her hands. "Winter dries them out," she said. "By summer I'll have smooth, lovely hands. In the meantime, sandpaper." She rubbed as she spoke. A sweet smell arrived in the air.

In a last effort to distract her, Simon said, "I could see in that kind of imperious manner of your mother's a little of that reserve of yours. What I complain about and like, too." It didn't work. In secrecy or revelation Sarah was equally determined.

"I was in college when it happened. It made me unique among my friends. We had Vietnam dropouts, dope dropouts, radical dropouts. I was a divorce dropout. I ran away. I didn't want to be a member of the divorce. So I took my third year in Paris."

He knew he should be quiet and listen. But anxiety about finally hearing a history of Sarah pushed him to interruptions.

"As an escape?"

"And when the year was up I took a long, long vacation."

"A long escape."

"This is *my* story. No moral judgments. I went to North Africa, the Middle East . . ."

"Sarah in Egypt."

"No titles, either. And from Egypt I worked my way— figuratively speaking—across the subcontinent to India."

"Sounds long. How long?"

"By this time I was missing part of my senior year. Much moaning and groaning from Rachel and my father."

"Jewish guilt over the divorce."

"You don't know them. That's what I was trying to provoke. But they wouldn't buy it. They just waited. Patiently. Separately."

47

"And patience paid off."

"Now you're trying to write the ending. You really don't want to hear the story, do you?"

Simon settled back on the couch and closed his eyes. Happily, Sarah kissed him on the mouth and said, "There's a surprise ending. You'll like it."

"I hate surprise endings. They're too banal. Like life." She placed a hand over his mouth. "Cheap epigrams won't stop me, either. Where was I?"

"In India."

"I'll skip the affair with the pilot; the one that began the moment we got off the plane."

"Please . . ."

She is gay, younger than he's ever seen her; silly. Simon drifts with her. The taste of cinnamon in coffee adds to the strangeness of being there.

She tells him of her travels. Six months stretches into a year, a year into a year and a half. Exotic place names float in the afternoon air. Teheran: a harbor and a party at which some unexplained violence threatens, then dissipates; Oran: a cemetery on a hill, an aging ex-radical friend of her father's, turned homosexual and print-maker; Hong Kong: and an affair with an ex-marine, now lawyer, who, it develops, is a C.I.A. agent; or is that suspicion only an excuse to break it up and move on?

Data flows by Simon, oddly impersonal, like a slide show of a journey shown too quickly. Letters from parents grow impatient. In response, Sarah's arc of movement curves toward home. An abortion is performed in a Havana hospital by an enormously fat doctor with rings on every finger; a gentle man: was his name Blau? Or is Simon drowsing defensively under the flow of words? His eyes remain shut.

"Is that the happy ending?" he murmurs.

"Coming soon." Her tone is no longer playful. Endings, happy or otherwise, were apparently serious matters.

"I found my calling then," she said.

Simon looked up. Something in her tone disturbed him.

She was gazing out at nothing, chewing on her lower lip. He knew what it was: it was the temporary loss of irony. This enforced autobiographical spree was not without cost.

"Maybe it was post-abortion depression. I came home from Havana to New York as if I'd been away for a decade. It was only a year and a half, but my friends had all graduated. Some were married. It was 1960. My sister, Jephtha, died in a bad way three months after I came back. The summer of '60 was the hottest summer I can remember. And I'd just been in Tangiers and Havana. But those are not actual cities. Really hot summers in cities are hell with a capital H. That summer was. Jephtha and I never got along, never knew each other, truly: we were like all sisters, except those who know and love each other. Rachel and Edmund got together for a few weeks after the funeral. But Jephtha was nobody's fault, so they couldn't paste it together with atonement and all that stuff and they gave me the keys to the house on Fire Island and after five days alone in a place called, of all things, Lonelyville—place names get to be important when you're involved in travel; it's between Ocean Beach and Fair Harbor, Lonelyville, and you have to use rain water because there's no town water—after five days I knew several things. That I was an undomesticated animal; not as bad as Jephtha, but I knew I was not going back to college, not going to have the usual kind of professional life, not going to have a husband and children in the usual way or the usual time. And most of all I knew I had discovered Travel.

"I was picking shells on the beach, on the fifth day in Lonelyville, a hot, dry Fire Island day, nobody else on the beach; I remember there was straggly beach grass and a trail of footprints suddenly stopping in the middle of the beach, crazy driftwood, shapes like people's heads or birds, and a line of real birds, sandpipers, at the water's edge."

Sarah walked up and down in front of Simon. She was

49

excited and her pink velvet robe flapped open as she walked, then closed again. The orange peels curled on blue-patterned plates, danced in spring sunlight slanting lower through the windows. It was midafternoon; the light was less intense. But Sarah's mood was brilliant. She seemed a little crazy, as people do when they unexpectedly try to communicate something impossible: a moment that made one the person one is. Simon watched her, interested, fearful.

"I'm telling you the details of the scene because it's important to understand. Everything seemed super real and super strange. I'd smoked some grass the night before and maybe that was still with me . . . and I was still high from a year and a half of travel and low from Jephtha dying like that—sometimes we were terribly close, terribly intense with each other—and I was still a little shaky from the abortion: they weren't so slick then; and when this black dog trotted onto the beach and began following me while I walked, I suddenly saw—as clearly as I can see you against the window with the tower of that ugly building behind you—I saw that the dog was exactly there, on that beach with me and nowhere else, while I was in so many places, yet as much on the beach as the dog was . . . and without really thinking with my head, I understood how travel, the very existence of travel, calls up the whole problem of having a body, a physical self, and therefore having to be in one place, only, at a time, when there are so many other possible places in which to be.

"Animals are always in one place only. So you see, travel raises the basic question of the human imagination—and I realized this with such excitement, as if it was why I'd had to travel around like a loony for so long while my parents got divorced and my friends got married and my sister went off the deep end, just to learn this simple thing everybody knows: that travel equals imagination."

She knelt before him for the second time that day. People act out who they are or want to be. Did something in

50

Sarah want to kneel? But she knelt in her vivid mood, eager to impress on him what she was saying, to be closer to him.

"I'm here," she cried, "but ah—I *could* be there. You're surrounded by green swollen hills of Vermont, but ah— you *could* be on blue water in Kenya or on slate-covered sand dunes in Fire Island. Travel is what makes us human, because it lets us imagine something else. I was a maniac prophet of travel for one morning, following that black dog, getting too sunburned because I hadn't expected to stay out until noon, and I knew that I was going to do something marvelous with travel. . . . It changed my life. I never expected to tell you all this, Simon, you make me a little crazy, Simon, I'm not this way with other people the way I am with you." She wept, her head on his lap. Simon, double-hearted for the moment, was moved by the way Sarah was moved; at the same time, stroking her hair, hoping she would stop crying quickly, he thought: Too much, it's too much; I'd better tell her I have to get home. Too much.

The bright-red drops on his pants were shocking. Then all at once her head was thrown back in an attempt to stop the sudden nosebleed.

"Don't worry," she said, and fished up a handkerchief from a pocket in her robe. "It's a thing I have. When something gets to me, my nose bleeds. It's a hazard in my occupation." She laughed from behind the stain on her reddening stancher. "I have bled all over Japan Air Lines; I have bled in the snow on Mount Kilimanjaro."

In a moment, a surprise to both of them, they made love on the floor, orange peels, bloody handkerchief, red-stained robe, ruined trousers and all. In the middle, she cried out, "Simon, Simon, you make me so crazy. . . ."

They were standing at the door and he was saying good-bye when, as if on a jag and unable to stop, she said: "I came down with a fever the day after that beach day. Aftereffect of that rotten abortion in Havana. When I got better, I decided I wanted an equalizer, as a woman, if I was going to build my life on travel."

Then, in the most surprising act of a day of Sarah surprises, she grasped his hand. She held it hard and he felt a shock of pain. She leaned back against the wall of the foyer, spread her legs and gently put one of his fingers up, up, still further up, all the way up inside her, wet and open from sex, her eyes closed not in sensuality now but in private revelation, and murmured: "Feel it—do you feel it? You can't touch the coil, that's up too far, but you can feel the little string that tells it's in place; do you feel it? The equalizer? Do you feel it?"

9

SIMON HAD TOLD SARAH ABOUT LINC. Which is to say, he'd warned her. It was hard to know where to begin. He picked traits, that was easiest; told her of Linc's unpredictableness, his pleasure in arbitrary reversals; his background as an actor in England, an American teen-ager of often-married parents, touring in Shakespeare—a style that carried over into peculiarly Lincolnian rhetorical flights, particularly when he was high. High on liquor, more often high on pot, high on pills (at a difficult period after *his* first marriage), and high on politics for the longest, most troublesome period: almost a decade.

"Linc is a force of nature," Simon had said, in the cab going across the bridge to Queens. It was late in the afternoon, the sky stacked with disapproving clouds. He was crazy to be taking Sarah out, as if Linc did not know Alex. But he was applying simpler tests, these days, to actions. The idea had made him happy when he'd thought of it. That was reason enough.

* * *

"Don't bother to explain how it failed," Linc said. "You never have to explain failure—only success. It failed because it failed: because it was ambitious; because it was a belief in new ways to make a city, to live in cities. It's easier to get rich by saving them from drowning." He spoke past Simon; at Sarah.

"Are you going to get rich on this one?" Simon asked.

"I'm going to try. Why didn't you answer my letters? I mean I was asking you to do nothing less than help me save Venice from drowning . . ."

They were sitting on the floor sipping coffee out of plastic mugs. It was only four-thirty, but through the wall-sized windows the sky threw more shadows than light. There was a heaviness in the air: impending rain.

"For God's sake, I'd set out to build the New Jerusalem and all I had were black-and-blue marks and a miserable wife to show for it. Then Greer calls me and offers me a chance to build a New Town in Georgia, in Montana, anywhere I want. Also, at least fifty thousand per."

"Greer is a schmuck!" Linc said.

"Some people say he's the wave of the future."

"Who? Alexandria?"

"No. She just wanted me to settle on something sensible and stay with it. Greer seemed sensible."

"You could have told me all this in a letter, or on the phone."

"I was freaking out."

"Then you could have just said no or yes! You didn't say yes to that Greer New Town garbage."

"I didn't say no, either. I still have to decide. May first."

"Why are you holding your hand like that?" Linc asked.

"Sometimes it hurts. . . . Do you ever think of Ben Demos?" Simon asked.

"Poor Ben. Not much. I didn't know him as well as you did, even when we were all bumming around together. Maybe it's because I don't have as much feeling for music as you do."

"Maybe."

"And he was too cynical for me. Not just unpolitical; he didn't think anything was worth doing. Not even playing the piano as beautifully as he did."

"No, Ben was more for being than for doing."

Simon prowled restlessly around the great table on which Linc's complex model designed for the Lagoon of Venice sat; while Linc offered Sarah more coffee and Sarah refused him even that. Simon examined the sunken caissons more closely. Linc apparently made a more attractive offer: the curious burned-paper smell of fine hashish filled the damp, close air. When Simon joined them again, a bottle of wine was open. Sarah passed him a joint as if they'd been smoking together for years.

Sarah had become a challenge to Linc. The hash only reinforced her mood. She smiled a beige smile when Simon spoke, then sipped some wine.

"Something's puzzling me," Simon said to Linc.

Lank, lean, gangling like his namesake, Linc leaned over and refilled Simon's glass. "Puzzle away," he said.

"Why are you in caissons and water tables and mechanics? Things any good engineer can handle?"

"Because the big and beautiful words didn't pan out. Urban renewal—Negro removal, the comic says. Drug reform—replace heroin deaths with methadone deaths, the comic says. . . ."

"Fuck the comics," Simon said.

"Easy, easy. Hash is supposed to not rile up the blood like alcohol does." It was a mistake, Simon knew, to have come to see Linc in the middle of his downs in the middle of Simon's new ups with Sarah. He had put himself into Linc's hands, of course, by bringing Sarah along. But that was no problem. He could imagine no contingency in which Linc would betray him to Alex. Still, an involuntary reference, a too stiff response to a question . . . There was no way of being certain that Alex would never know, except by sealing himself and Sarah off in her bedroom, in Chinese restaurants no one he knew would

54

ever frequent, and in other carefully chosen temples of happiness.

Simon sat down, alone, on a bamboo mat near the floor-to-ceiling window. He preferred the late afternoon shadows there. Let Linc loom over Sarah, casting his shadow for the moment. Let them murmur their pot talk. (He'd only smoked about a half dozen times in his life, but he knew that anything memorable was rarely said.) He had a dread of falling into some sentimental musing aloud to an old friend about what could not actually be spoken. Simon had not answered Linc's letters offering him a job because he could not bring himself to put down, in clear, cool words, the difference between creating something and shoring up ruins, however magnificent those ruins might be. Simon's head sank on his knee; he felt alternately tranquil and nauseated.

He had no idea how he had come to be lying next to Sarah, with Linc now looming over *him* delivering a wine-hash peroration:

"He's too decent, your friend, to speak of the *gigantic* gulf between us. Look at your prize package. Still, after everything that's happened he has the courage, the determination—nay, the desire—to be what I trained him to be. An impossible being, part architect, part philosopher, part politician, part historian, part mathematician—a man who must know the poetics of line and height, and the arithmetic of the sewage system; a man who can persuade a sculptor to capture the spirit of a city square and persuade a city council to float a water bond issue that will make the whole thing a reality. A man who can have the guts to ignore the impossibility of street life in cities built for one third of their present population, and who must also have a whole other set of guts—to ignore the kickbacks under the table to the contractors without whom the roads will not be paved."

The few pot puffs hit. Simon wondered why he was on the floor, Linc so far above him.

"Here you see us," Linc said, "two angels in our fallen state. Only I deny it, ignore it, bail myself out with machines of water. You're only in hell when you *know* you've fallen."

He pointed, dramatically, at Simon.

"*He* knows. Comfort him, Sarah Geist. Comfort him."

As if Sarah had obeyed, Simon's head was in her lap; her hand fluttered at his hair. A crack of thunder struck at the air. There would be rain.

"Don't give me that crap about fallen angels," Simon said. "You've given up."

"I've learned."

"You've given up."

"I've accepted reality."

"Given up," Simon murmured.

He was determined, stubborn as a child. And, like a child, consumed with the injustice of it. You *could* not train an army for war and then desert.

"Don't you understand?" Linc said. "It's too late to play God in cities. We've become curators of past glories. Preservers of wonderful and awful ruins."

Simon struggled to his feet. Sarah stayed stretched out: Odalisque on Queens Loft Floor. But between Simon and Linc parity was needed: some last words of clarity that required a face-to-face position.

He shook his head, at the same time to clear it and to say no.

" . . . Nothing against saving Venice . . . trained for bigger things." They were in the streets. It was as sudden as that.

"Ugly, ugly Queens."

"When was the last time you were in Queens, Sarah?" Linc asked.

"Years. You don't go to Queens. You go *through* Queens."

"But look at this bridge," Simon said. "Nothing connected to something so beautiful can be entirely ugly."

Drunken, half stoned, they did tourist things. They took

the Circle Line's last boat trip of the day around Manhattan Island. The city slid by them in a haze of twilight, funnel smoke and silly laughter. Disembarking, Simon and Sarah grew less festive with every step; they went to the top of the Empire State Building. Only Linc retained the purity of his "up." (Simon speculated that he might have been well "up" before they'd arrived.)

"It's twilight," Simon said. "*Crépuscule,* the French call it. The time of possibility: day gone, night not heard from yet." A group of Puerto Rican children herded by a man in yellow trousers and a yellow shirt peered into telescopes and chased each other around the rooftop. The unstable weather appeared to have discouraged everyone else. One boy carried a transistor radio from which poured, surprisingly, an aria from *The Magic Flute.*

It began with Simon. "You're offering me nostalgia, that's all, with your Venetian restoration, your ecology; nothing new, just nostalgia."

"I'm offering you fifty thousand bucks a year—and more. More than Greer."

"I could use it. Chicago left me broke." Simon thought it best to deescalate. "God or somebody made the world. I just want to make it work better."

"Don't give me that mock humility. You want to write your own book of Genesis."

Pink paint spread across the edges of the horizon: a spring sunset. Sarah leaned on a telescope and pretended to search in her purse for a quarter.

"The trouble is," Linc said, "you're *from* the city—an urban product to the marrow of your Jewish bones—so you have to take it over. Yes, don't look offended at me. Take it over! Nothing as modest as modifying it; nothing as commonsensical as starting fresh. Take it over! That's the scale of your ambition. A Balzac without a pen . . . a Marx without a philosophical system . . . a Lenin without an army."

Linc waved a military arm out over the city sinking into twilight, laced with lights, ambiguous. "Don't forget all our nights in the gardens of Yale. I know the size of your need for heroism. I know. When you were born the gods stamped it on your rump: Project Simon. From that you projected outward. Project Simon—a never-ending building and rebuilding of the outside world."

Exhausted, Linc slumped against the wire-meshed balustrade. He turned his beak profile to Simon and Sarah. "Better protect and restore the past," he said quietly. "Nobody ever died from nostalgia—and it never broke anyone's heart."

Sarah ended the long silence. She asked, like a doctor taking a history from a hysterical patient, "Are you married?"

"I was married," Linc said. "For seven miserable years. Doomed."

"When did you first know?" Sarah asked.

"Before I married her and every rotten moment thereafter. That's Aaron's Law. Everybody knows right away. The rest is just patchwork and Band-Aids."

"For seven years?"

"For seventeen or seventy."

A thousand feet above street level, Simon marveled at Sarah's ability to reverse ground; to take the general and move it to the personal. She had startling gifts, not least the lovely gift of surprise.

10

LATER, ALONE IN THE STORMY NIGHT, in her apartment, the heavy air on their bodies like blankets, they made love. Simon was, for the moment, a heavy lover. He was worn out by the day's dialectics, by iron clashes of old, rusting friendships.

But Sarah was perversely inspired. The residue of the

hash? The strangeness of being "outside" with Simon, meeting his friend as if they were a couple instead of a forbidden adventure?

"Touch me there."

"There?"

"Yes. Not hard."

"Like that?"

"Now harder. Yes."

"Oh. Turn over."

"Yes . . . wet your finger."

A presence invisible to him; a presence to be mounted from behind, abstract, no greater commitment possible for him at the moment. A ride, lightly tossed at first, Simon taking his cues from Sarah: contradictory, provocative.

"Too deep. Now. Ah, deeper, deeper."

He was simpler than the afternoon's arguments envisioned: Simple Simon, without expectations, without heroism. He rode his chance-encountered steed in their field of sheets, deliciously mechanically, posting, galloping; imagining himself in tune to some unspoken words thrown at him by her shadowy, hill-curved rump: Ride me, ride me, though now she was silent except for breath and throat murmurs.

Afterward he lay collapsed on and in her, the hunt over, the quarry—each other—exhausted, trapped.

"I haven't had the air conditioners put in yet," she said. "I didn't expect it to be so warm. It's only April."

"I like sweat."

Still later, smoking one of her rare cigarettes, she lay on her stomach again. She looked up at him, sideways, and said, "You know why I like it that way?" (Never, Alex had said to him early in the game, before they'd married, never tell people your sexual fantasies. It spoils everything.)

"Why?" he said.

She turned her eyes away, then her slanting head.

"I like the feeling—just for a few minutes—that I'm being used; that you're *using* me. Do you understand that?"

59

"Is it so hard to understand? Especially for a few moments?"

"I mean, do you understand it from *me?*"

He thought a moment. Then he said, "No, I guess I don't. If you mean would I have expected it."

"That's not what I meant." She stood up, folded a hooded red velvet robe around her and said, "You don't have to understand everything, *now,* do you?" Simon finessed that one. "I'll bet," he said, "there is not a globule of sweat on you that isn't mine."

"I don't sweat," Sarah said. "Not even in the summer." She went into the bathroom and came out performing her lotion-rubbing business.

"Dryness is my problem," she said, "not wetness."

"That was splendid, the way you suddenly asked Linc if he was married. Right in the middle of the Declaration of Independence."

"He's funny, your Linc. Project Simon."

"What?"

"Project Simon. His summation of your life."

"Like all summations—"

"Not true?"

"True and not true. Just because I like to play at making and remaking places to live. It's not such a big deal. People aren't what they do anyway; they're what they are."

"Is *that* true?"

"I don't know, now that you ask. But I don't know much these days."

"You know when you're happy."

"That's not knowing; that's feeling. I'm happy right now."

"Too easy. *Omne animal post coitum . . .*"

"Yes?"

She finished her hand-rubbing and sat down on the bed, naked and sweet-smelling. "I forget the Latin word for happy."

"It doesn't matter. The word in the saying is *triste.*"

60

"Is it? How could I have got that wrong? Anyway, you don't look so damned *triste* to me."

"I'm not," he said. But a paralyzed feeling took his mind and body. It was true that he felt like nothing, like exhaled air, when he had no overriding concern, no large Project Simon. He'd never learned the knack of just living. Alex had laughed at that in him and had quoted at him: "As for living, our servants will do that for us." Alexandria was good at living. She was the first person he'd known whom he could take seriously and who had "hobbies." On their first date, rained out of a performance of *Henry V* in Central Park, they'd walked out of the wet grass and downtown. Thinking to make first-date small talk and knowing about his work—(Linc had introduced them—she'd asked him about hobbies, about spare time, about things done lightly.

His pause, his confusion, made her laugh.

"I never thought about that. I mean, I don't *have* spare time. There's always too much to do, to read, to plan, to put into action." She saw him as some kind of sacred monster. The Man Who Had No Hobbies. Alexandria, too, had been intent on her career as an architect. But she played golf, sewed, had once played the harpsichord; watched birds with binoculars in city parks.

"If you did any of those things it would threaten everything," Alex had said that first night, drawn to him and afraid of the ambitious young man already touching her responsive hand. "You'd make it Project Golf, Project Harpsichord. My God, you live in a world of projects!"

They'd both forgotten that conversation until eight years later, when the biggest "project" of all was falling apart—and they appeared to be falling apart with it.

With that banal prescience new lovers and long-married couples have, Sarah asked, "What *are* you going to do now?"

He looked down at her on the bed, eyes glancing off his

own nakedness, penis pleasantly limp. "You mean now that I've had my way with you?"

"I mean now that you don't have a Project Simon?"

"I've got an appointment next week to see what Greer is doing and give him an answer."

"Isn't it nice how everybody's making you offers?"

"Everybody?"

"This Greer, Linc . . ."

He filled in her pause. "You."

"Me?"

"Don't I have a standing offer to run off to France with you?"

"Not standing. And not running. Which will you take?"

"I don't know. It would be nice to do what I do again."

As if sorry she had made him so thoughtful, she said, "I like what you do very much."

"Have I made you happy?"

"Yes," she said. "Now I've made you sad."

"Maybe the Latin has it right. *Omne animal post coitum* . . ." They were poised, she sitting on the bed facing him, legs slightly spread beneath the red robe, hands modestly folded over the separation between her legs, he standing looking down at her, then past her at the clouded window. Flutes played lightly somewhere. It was a moment waiting to go beyond itself. They had passed a certain amount of time together; had spoken a certain number of words; they could open toward each other, close off or stay suspended in silence. Simon found that he could say nothing.

Filling in his silence, she jumped back to her old theme. Couldn't they go away somewhere together? Just for a week? The world was full of so many magnificent places. And it was April. April and May were marvelous everywhere except Africa, and it was not Africa she had in mind.

Not waiting to hear once more about how married men could not just go away somewhere, she littered the bed with brochures. He still naked and sweaty, she robed and

62

dry, they sprawled among the color photographs while she told tales, as to a child.

Once upon a time there was a race of warriors who inhabited a town high in the mountains above Provence. They were so fierce they were nicknamed l'Aiglons: the Eagles. Their town was later destroyed by orders from Paris—the reward of fierce independence. The ruins were carefully tended as a tourist attraction, complete with three-star restaurant. It was called Les Baux. Bauxite came from there. And, according to Sarah, a unique and eerie tranquillity could also be extracted from a visit.

Outside, afterthoughts of the thunderstorm rumbled; thunder being universal, it contributed to the sense of placelessness and timelessness. The story of the city to which Sarah was proposing a trip was about other people in another time. But it threatened the happiness Simon was feeling at that moment.

In self-defense, he played games.

"I didn't know travel agents traveled."

Sarah wilted; her eyes were closed. "They don't much," she said flatly.

"But you do. You run."

"I'm different."

"Yes, I know. Will you run from me?"

"Should I?"

"I would guess so."

"I'll never run. I wouldn't admire myself. I'll walk, if it comes to that. I like to admire myself."

"Not always. I have to force you to look in the mirror at your own body."

"Ah, my body. That's not myself." Her eyes were still shut. She was angry. She said, "What did your wife say about your bloodstained pants last week? Did she think I was menstruating or did you tell her it was a nosebleed?" Startled, caught in the lie of his wife's presence/absence, all he could think of to say was, "I thought you didn't want to talk about my wife."

"I don't!"

He reached across the mounds of paper to touch her. But she was gone into the living room, padding barefoot and swift, eager to be away from him. It happened so quickly that he was left half fallen on his stomach, an arm foolishly outstretched toward . . . nothing except the telephone. Which chose that moment to ring. Simon was so taken by surprise that he picked up the receiver; as much to stop the unpleasant sound as anything.

It was the international operator, then, one-two-three, a French operator and finally a man's voice: "Sarah, darling?" Even with those two words the voice carried a foreign accent. Simon hung up instantly. But not before Sarah had picked up. He lay there for the next ten minutes listening to the distant murmur of her voice from the living room. Then he got up and put on his clothes.

She stood in the corner of the living room near the window. One hand was thrust into a pocket of her red robe as if she might be concealing a weapon. She'd drawn the red velvet hood over her head, for no apparent reason. To lighten the moment, Simon said, "You look like Little Red Riding Hood."

"Oh?"

"I didn't listen," he said. "I hung up right away."

"Would you like to know who it was?"

It was Simon's turn to refuse. "No," he said. There was in her tone the promise of ugly revelation. "I don't want to know who it was."

"It was my husband," Sarah said. "He lives in Monaco."

11

When Simon left he walked into a night still rumbling with distant anger, air still damp and close on the skin. In front of the Great Northern Hotel, an old woman with dyed blond hair walked a dog under an umbrella, though no rain fell. The indoors scene played and re-played in his mind while he walked past the woman and the dog, past shops shuttered for Sunday, locked iron gates at Brentano's bookstore.

Sarah's statement was one of those outrageous impossi-bilities that instantly had the sound of truth. It was the way she pronounced that name, out of a musical comedy—pronounced it correctly, with the accent on the first sylla-ble, *Mon*aco—that had made him believe her at once. Now, thinking it over, he realized that of course, in her job she would know how to correctly pronounce place names far more exotic than that.

"Why didn't you tell me you were married?"

Her defiance fled, air from a balloon. "We're not exactly married and we don't live together."

"*Are* you married or not, Sarah?"

At this solemn, stuffy, anguished question, which they both realized should more likely have come from Sarah—it was clearly the wronged woman's question—they both blew up into laughter. There followed alternate apologies: for bad tempers, for undue pressures, for evasions, for the catastrophic idea of the Linc Aaron visit . . . for run-ning from bedrooms . . . for picking up telephones. . . .

There were piles of garbage in plastic bags in front of the Russian Tea Room. Two cabs waited near the entrance steps to Carnegie Hall. A few tired-looking teen-agers sat on the steps beneath a poster announcing that night's pro-gressive jazz concert. Instead of taking one of the taxis home, as he usually would, Simon walked north toward Central Park. He walked bemused, neither thinking nor feeling; only remembering. There are some experiences that cannot be assimilated by analysis, by examination, but only by a kind of dumb repetition. And so, playing and replaying that one theatrical moment ("It was my hus-band. He lives in *Mon*aco."), Simon walked and walked.

There was not one perfectly safe block to be crossed on foot until he reached home.

The air was still wet; it clung to the skin like a presence.

Central Park was a tropical jungle; under the shifting clouds the shadows of damp trees, perfectly still in the windless night, loomed over the shadows of sprawling rocks. Simon walked north, the path curved; there seemed to be no one else in the park on foot. The yellow beams of cars slid by every few moments. For the most part the night was without moonlight; the clouds that had created the afternoon thunderstorm still hung, plump and listless, in the sky.

Once he was well into the park he turned south and looked at the random scrawl of the skyline against the horizon. It was a mysterious calligraphy, the signature of his buried life and ambition. He was not a New Yorker; as a child his eyes had known this outline only from movies and books. But now he knew it well. The only other city he knew as well was Paris, and that not from its skyline, but from lower down: bridges, street turnings, parks in which he had chased and cajoled Ariel, his poor mad first wife. Unexpectedly, the moon pushed aside a cloud and lit up the uneven building line. The myriad dots of light were suddenly surrounded by clear vertical and horizontal building outlines. The Chrysler Building winked at him and anonymous apartment buildings rimming the park; far below, he knew, the World Trade Center pushed up at the sky. For some reason he felt calmer.

Alone on damp Sunday streets Simon Shafer walked uptown through neighborhood after neighborhood.

"What do you think you're getting into?" Ben Demos said.

"I don't know yet."

"It seems she's married."

"I'm not sure. Besides, so am I."

"She's much younger than you."

"Only a decade or so."

"You're not cut out for this secret life."

"Ben, you always think things aren't worth doing. She makes me happy."

Ben Demos, Greek angel of the negative, accompanied

Simon as he walked home. The early dead of Simon's life, he had even interpreted his work in cities in the light of death. What amazed him about people building cities, Ben Demos had once said, was that they were all going to die. To build a house was one thing. You needed it to survive the elements for the time that you were alive. But no one man or woman needs a city. Only the insane notion of enduring, surviving as a species—as a group—could justify cities. A hive, an anthill, yes, for insects. But individual men know the city will outlast them, that they will die with some part of the place they call home unvisited.

Perhaps that very part of the city in which they might have been happy.

12

HE WAS ALMOST ASLEEP, worn out by passion that confused as much as it satisfied, when the phone rang. It was Alexandria.

"Did I wake you?"

"Yes."

"How's your hand?"

"Comes and goes." He did not mention the proposed operation.

"We had a snowstorm."

"We had a thunderstorm."

"You do sound sleepy. I didn't call so late to talk about the weather."

"It's nice to hear your snowy voice," he said. "Why *did* you call so late?"

"Because I was too nervous to call earlier. I want to apologize."

"How's Matthew?"

He has a cold and he gave it to me. But he has a puppy and he's happy."

"And you?"

"I'm going to be miserable until I can apologize."

"For what?"

"For running away to Canada. I know myself, and I was about to come on very heavy about which job you should take. So since I knew I couldn't shut up, I ran away. Do you miss me?"

It had been a while since they could say things like "do you miss me" easily. It didn't come out easily this time. Neither did his: "Of course."

"Of course is no answer," Alex said, with a try at a laugh. "But it'll do. Will you forgive me for running away?"

"I'll forgive you for apologizing," Simon said. "How's that?"

"That's good, too. My God, Simon, I can't believe our last conversation before I left was a fight about your never knowing how to set the table."

Pause.

"Oh, shit," Simon said. "How'd we get into this?"

"It's how we get out of it . . ."

"When are you coming back?"

"When do you want me back?"

"Are you ready to exchange snow for rain?"

"How are you doing without me?"

"I'm a convalescent, like you. Post-Chicago blues. My classes are rotten. How's your conference?"

"Nothing much that's new. I was going to stay away till May first."

"I can decide with you here."

"Have you decided?"

"I saw Linc—I'm seeing Greer next week. But I'm not in such good condition for decisions."

"Then it will go by default."

"You know how those things are. There's always a little more time."

"Except when there's not."

Simon imagined Alex, dark skin with white robe, or nightgown or pajamas or dress. White was her color. He tried hard to remember her perfume, but could not. He wasn't sure one *could* remember perfume. He tried to recall Sarah's, but that didn't work, either. Suddenly it seemed a good idea that his wife and child come back quickly. Whatever he was getting drawn into, he could do with a safety measure. Life, he'd told his students in defense of the urban existence, is best lived in a resisting medium. Man is a hard-weather animal.

"Come back," Simon said. "I want you to come back."

A few days later the spring began in earnest. It was April, but without the rains. Hard, chilly sunshine lit up the far corner of Sixth Avenue, where the health food store and flower shop garnished the sidewalk with jonquils and daisies and boxes of granola. The Four Seasons Record Shop filled the late afternoon air with Vivaldi violins, and the sidewalk outside Paul and Perry's Pet Place became a menace to strollers, with its pyramids of birdcages and a marmoset on a long leash. Winter made the city block a prison; spring made it a neighborhood.

Alex and Matthew were home and it was as if they had been away for years. The strangeness between Simon and Alex was stronger than before. Perhaps because of Sarah; perhaps because of distance and time spent apart, and resentments undiscussed. Sarah and Simon ate dinners at little Village restaurants that offered inexpensive pasta dressed in a variety of sauces; that offered a below Fourteenth Street safety—or so Simon hoped. (No people he or Alex knew were downtown people. There was always the random possibility of exposure, but the likelihood was small.) Once he and Sarah ate in a restaurant and before they could order dessert had touched each other in places and in ways that made it necessary for them to leave the restaurant quickly. They had eaten fish, delicately broiled, and drunk a Tuscan fish wine that came in a green bottle shaped like a fish, and Simon took the empty bottle with him to place on Sarah's mantel as a memento of hasty passion.

Now it was Sarah's turn to be nervous about being out in the world with Simon. When his wife was away he'd lied to Sarah and said she was home. Now that she was back, he often lied and said she was away. It took pressure off Sarah and she was happy.

13

RIVERSIDE DRIVE was knife bright in April sunshine, clear and cool. The bad weather had ended with Alexandria's return. Simon had to walk down eleven floors; the elevator was broken for the thirty-second time since they had moved into the old building, full of style and cockroaches. The roaches had left, mysteriously, one winter; the style was crumbling rapidly: chipped cornices, gargoyles with missing ears.

Simon stood at the corner waiting for a taxi, hesitated: perhaps a bus. Money was going out, none coming in. A cabdriver made his decision for him. If he didn't go quickly he might not go at all.

"My father's birthday party," Sarah had said. "Come with me."

"Unwise."

"What's so wonderful about being wise?"

"If someone sees us together."

"No one who could possibly know you will be at the party. They're all analysts, over seventy mostly."

"I'd better not."

"Edmund wants to meet you."

"Oh? What does he know about me?"

"Just the bare facts. That you make me happy; that you're married. Things like that."

"And will it make you happy if I go to your father's birthday party?"

"Yes."

Edmund Geist was small with years, plump, vested and watch-fobbed. He looked very nice surrounded by the Upper West Side kind of German refugee paraphernalia, even though it was Greenwich Village and he had emigrated from Russia in 1925. Simon was glad he'd come. It was a change from circling Alexandria and fighting the hand pain—wondering if he dared turn a doorknob with his right hand or pick up a pencil and write, if he dared speak to his wife without grand tremors from either of them.

"This is myself and Sarah's mother shortly after I arrived in America to make the Marxist revolution"—Dr. Geist pointed at photographs and bobbed his head in small, quick movements; he turned to Simon and grinned, looking suddenly much younger—"with the success you see all around you," he finished.

He did, indeed, look like old photographs of Trotsky: a dark, serious, Sephardic Jewish face framed by wing collar, bushy mustache and the derby of the period. They wandered down a long foyer to which Dr. Geist had directed them immediately. The other guests were arriving and clustering in the dining room, where Sarah played hostess.

"And this is Sarah's sister, Jephtha." A beautiful face, shy blue eyes, heavy-lidded, hair down to her shoulders, something surly, wild in the turn of the mouth.

There followed group photographs of the executive committee of the American Communist Party and the first faculty of the New York School of Psychoanalysis.

More input, Simon thought. Thank God for computer terminology. Not information: input; not knowledge: input. Information and knowledge were subjects to which you stood in some relation. The young woman in the next room, making drinks for middle-aged psychiatrists, making small talk with aged psychoanalysts—she stood in no relation to Simon. Listening to the old man, he was oddly grateful for his own sense of detachment, of unreality. These people were nothing to him: a woman he slept with

71

but did not love; her father, a stranger like her. Better a bitter fight with Alex than this drifting in and out of lives, people telling him tales about sisters who had died, husbands they might not be married to, revolutions that had not succeeded. Happiness was, for the moment, forgotten.

The photograph-lined foyer gave onto a study, also choked with memorabilia. There was also, mercifully, a drink from the hand of the old man. Raising his own glass, Sarah's father said:

"To Sarah."

Curiouser and curiouser, Simon thought, and drank the toast.

"I hope there will be no analysis, Dr. Geist."

"Ah, I am only lately an analyst. Only for the past forty-five years. What I am truly is a failed revolutionary, a Bolshevik *manqué*." Simon heard Sarah's "ah" in Edmund's voice. "Not to worry. There will be no analysis."

"You asked Sarah to bring me today."

"Yes, it was my request."

"Why?"

"I'm seventy years old. My best friend died two weeks ago. And they're making a big fuss over this birthday because I've been sick. But I wanted to tell you . . ."

"Tell me?"

". . . about Sarah."

"Yes?"

As if summoned, she appeared, red dress, white swirled top, dark skin glowing.

"What's the conference?"

"A quiet drink, Sarah darling. How are the guests?"

"Waiting for you. What are you telling Simon?"

"Everything. You interrupted."

"Don't let him talk too much," Sarah said. "Years of listening does it. An occupational problem. Is Mother coming?"

"Later, for the cake—in fact, *with* the cake."

The doorbell rang and Sarah was gone. Dr. Geist stood up, drink in hand. Simon caught a whiff of his breath; it was ripe with alcohol. Had he been drinking all morning? The despair of age sometimes flowed through bottles.

"No way to tell you straight—the partial facts. No, only to tell what it was like, oh, about fifty years ago, coming to make the revolution—not alone: Blau and the others. What a time, what a joy, staying up all night at meetings, bringing sandwiches—fish mostly, I think—then riding the Fifth Avenue bus back home—double-deckers they were then—back home to the Bronx. A furnished room . . . wonderful view of Woodlawn Cemetery . . . still small then . . . planning . . . plotting . . . to build a new world on the bones of the old. Eating . . . my God, how we ate while working out ways to feed the masses of the future. And drink . . . whiskey—nobody drank vodka then. Police, too . . . the police took an interest in those days: it was not entirely academic. But hope needs food and finally we starved . . . the movement died."

"Of . . .?"

"Malnutrition of ideas, premature rigor mortis. But I was only twenty-eight: all that passion to live out, all that life left to get through . . . grand visions die hard. Blau never gave up; keeled over after a meeting on West Ninety-sixth Street. His heart gave up, but not Blau."

"And you?"

"I thought I would die . . . I wanted to die. You can't stop making new worlds so easily . . . a tough habit to get rid of. You get used to that first moment of the day when eyes open up, and you are not alone: you are sharing that moment with the people. Nobody can understand the intoxication of those words: 'the people.' Even when you closed your eyes at night, you closed them with 'the people.' "

Simon sipped vodka and closed his eyes. He intoned: " 'It is a dangerous thing to extend your hand to the people.' "

"Who said that?"

"A Greek friend of mine. I think it's a quotation."

"It's worse to withdraw your hand. What do you do with

it?" The old man dangled a hand, puppetlike. "Useless. I wanted to ensure the happiness of generations to come. Ecclesiastes in reverse. Instead, I turned to individual happiness. Not my own . . . no knack for that. Patients. I lost patience with the people . . . as a reward I received patients." He laughed behind his glass; teeth clicked. "But now it is a sunny Sunday afternoon fifty years later and I am drinking too much for a Sunday afternoon. No more whiskey: vodka . . . now we drink vodka. I will embarrass my guests, my wife (no longer my wife), my daughter Sarah, whom I love and wish happy. Tell me: you and Sarah, are you happy together?"

"When we're together, yes."

"And when you're apart?"

"Then we're apart. And being happy together is not the question. Until the next time we're together."

"Sarah seems happy now. Happier than before."

"She's made me happy."

Geist swerved. One of his old man's unprepared changes of subject. "I'll tell you the first time I was truly happy after I left the Party. It was my First Patient." He announced it like a theme. "A young woman. *Everything* was wrong. She was anxious, obese, couldn't work—she'd been a fine teacher—hated her mother (who loved her), envied her father (who'd beaten her). But worst of all, she hadn't slept more than two or three hours a night in ten years."

"Pills?"

"Didn't work. Such anxiety you've never seen. Tense as the E string on a violin. So—we worked. Ignorant young Dr. Geist, the former hope of the masses, and his first patient.

"Remember, I'd been desperately unhappy myself all this time—between the death of my revolution and the birth of my first patient. I carried a rock in my chest; I learned to breathe around it, but it never budged. I was close to 'taking a window for a door,' as someone once called it."

"What stopped you?"

"One day my patient came for her hour and announced that she had slept for nine hours the previous night. Her eyes shone, her skin looked fresh. I knew that if I were close enough to her, her breath would smell sweet; she was a child of morning, bright and clear and ready for life. I had, it seemed, created nothing less than sleep. Can you imagine how that felt? The rock moved, lifted and never returned. Apparently I had decided that if I could create sleep in one human being I could bear to go on living. Ach"—Dr. Geist lapsed into a heavier accent—"never mind awakening the masses. Better let one tortured woman sleep."

During the recitation Simon had lain back on the long lounge and set his drink on the floor. Now he sat up and realized that the lounge was actually Dr. Geist's analytic couch; on the opposite wall shimmered the framed bona fides granted by various institutions. This was Geist's office. Simon stood up quickly and finished his drink.

"What happened to your young woman, finally? How about her other symptoms?"

Dr. Geist bowed. "So, you suspect. And correctly. Not only did the other symptoms not budge; the insomnia came back worse than ever. She had to be hospitalized, the sure sign of failure in psychoanalysis. But by then it did not matter."

"Didn't matter?"

Dr. Geist put his glass down on the floor next to Simon's. Hands free, he turned them outward in a gesture of innocence and said, "I had been saved."

"My father used to say: In every relationship there's one who is saved and one who saves."

"Who's going to end up saving who—with you and Sarah?"

"I'm married and so is Sarah. We've *been* saved."

"Sarah is not exactly married. And if you'll forgive me, you don't appear entirely saved. There's something you should know about Sarah."

75

"You're ruining the party." Sarah had appeared in the doorway again. She carried a tray of hors d'oeuvres. "Aren't you finished yet?"

"Watch her skin," Dr. Geist said.

"Yes?"

"I said *watch*, not look!"

"Why?"

Sarah did her disappearing act, taking long black hair and the hors d'oeuvres tray with her. She was angry. But it was unclear at whom. Simon felt his own taut violin string unwinding within him; the unaccustomed vodka at 3 P.M., perhaps. At the same time the pain in his right hand spoke: the first time that day. The joint mice, nibbling again.

It made him impatient to be gone; impatient to get back to being alone with Sarah, to the pleasures of touch, of movement, of exhaustion; to the happiness of being encapsulated. He cradled his right hand in his left.

"What is it?" Simon asked. "What do you want to tell me about Sarah?"

"She's not the way she seems. One day you'll notice that lovely dark skin is turning yellowish. That's the sign."

"Of what?"

"Ask Sarah—"

Simon was irritable, interrupting, "About her skin?"

"About the pills. She'll tell you, if you handle it right. She's different with you. Different than with her junkman. You of all people can ask her about the pills. Come; now we go to the party."

But before Simon could speak or Dr. Geist could move, the party came to them. Sarah had grown tired of waiting. A flood of doctors—Dr. Tauchnitz, Dr. Barclay, Dr. Eisenstein—inundated them. Sarah deposited a great baroque cake on Dr. Geist's desk. She smiled at Simon. (Had she, in fact, been angry?) He saw her father's wide-set eyes, open and direct in her face. She was simple, straight, happy: Sarah at a Sunday afternoon celebration. Slim in her red party dress, long black hair trailing below her shoulders, she seemed more desirable than ever. For a moment Simon could hardly believe his good fortune. She was his consolation. Let her save him. They were not in love. She'd told him that herself, that sunny day in Rockefeller Plaza. To be in trouble but not to be in love—and to take such secret pleasure in a young woman; that must be what happiness is! Next to that simple definition, the minor mysteries of secret packages in closets, a life history full of contradictions, even lies, and strange paternal warnings—all seemed trivial.

As for pills: all Simon could think of was the biting joint mice in his hand and the little pills the doctor had given him for pain. He'd taken none, afraid to find that they didn't work; that he was condemned to an inevitable operation. Better vodka in the daytime, he thought, and the ambiguities of Sarah's skin. He refilled his glass as the party guests sang to the man who had come to save the people and had himself been saved. To the old man they sang loud and sentimental verses in German:

> Ein prosit, ein prosit,
> Lang sich sie leben,
> Lang sich sie leben. . . .

14

SARAH LIES STRETCHED OUT before Simon, on the brown velvet couch in the living room. She is naked from the waist down, her legs spread first in a wide V, then arching out into angular parentheses. He kneels in front of her, enclosed between her legs, kissing and licking and drinking and looking. One of Sarah's arms dangles next to him near the floor; the other arm is thrown across her eyes.

It had happened quickly. They'd arrived back at her

apartment, light-headed in the aftermath of song and alcohol. More music seemed in order, some "forgotten" records of Rameau. Then an impromptu tour of Sarah's
travel mementos. Impromptu is the watchword of the day.
It is a small apartment, but Simon has learned the bedroom, only, by heart. Upstairs, in the study, suddenly a
thousand lovely things crowd his eyes. If he is looking for
distractions, they serve.

"I picked this up in Vienna. The most beautiful clocks
in the world are not Swiss, they're Austrian." It was black
and gold and crowned with a plump naked cherub.

"Do you know," Sarah says, "that Austria has the sec-
ond-highest suicide rate in Europe. Twenty-two out of
every hundred thousand people kill themselves."

"You're a fine and lovely guide," Simon says. "Full of
information."

"This tapestry is from Hong Kong. I didn't buy it. It was
a gift from a man who wanted to marry me."

"An ex-marine, wasn't he? Turned out to be C.I.A.?"

Sarah looks puzzled. "No," she says. "He was an airline
pilot. He turned out to be a homosexual."

Do not place statements side by side and compare. An
affair is not a truth-or-consequence game. He glances at
his watch as surreptitiously as he can.

"Are you late?" Sarah asks. "Do you have to go home?"
Her eyes are blank; determined not to appear troubled.

"Not yet," Simon says. "I'm sorry about the watch-look-
ing."

"I've read novels about affairs," Sarah says. "They always look at their watches." She smiles. But the fine post-
party mood that had led to the gay little tour of her collection of artifacts is turning fragile. They have not spoken
of her father; of his absurd warnings; of anything except
the carefully arranged debris of Sarah's profession which
decorates the apartment. There follows, swiftly, blue-
veined porcelain from France, a miniature stove from
northern Italy, gypsy candelabra from the caves of northern Spain, a Kenyan fertility God. He has been concen-

trating so much on Sarah's hidden treasures—the secrets of the body, secrets in closets—that he has not noticed the visible treasures all around.

But soon what began spontaneously turns mechanical. Something has dimmed the guide's enthusiasm. Simon's glance at his watch; the oxidation of alcohol; something . . .

"I found this on a trip to . . . this is the only one of its . . . a copy of . . ." The impromptu trip has turned too real. Sarah is now playing the game of guide; a role no longer impromptu. Simon senses the mood will collapse, the questions will return.

"Sarah," he interrupts her.

"Yes?"

"Lift up your skirt."

"What?"

"Raise it!"

Surprise works. Awkwardly, hands holding the cloth to her waist, Sarah moves next to Simon, standing near the couch. Suddenly he kneels, waves of will and submission moving between them, kneeling in temporary control. He removes the dancer's leotards she wears each day. Then, surprising himself as much as Sarah, Simon gently moves her legs farther and farther apart.

"No," Sarah says. But she is a lovely flesh stabile: as rooted to the spot as a statue. Her "no" is as cryptic as statue language. It does not mean stop; it does not mean continue. It is a word meant for herself only, mysterious as the languages children invent. Simon continues to move her legs wider and wider, until the angle reveals, between the dark, curly hairs and brownish flesh, a delicate rose flush. In his supplicant position, yet still in command, he can use only his left hand (the right hand gripped in pain). He presses one fold of flesh to the side, like drawing a curtain aside. For a long moment he looks. Close up, slightly angled from below, he sees an oval shell, whorled with textures, a cave within a cave, crested by a tiny tuft, pinker than the rest, shadowed at the center where it leads within; all of it moist and lighter in color than anything in range of his eyes. In contrast, her thighs show map tracings of blue veins beneath the skin, like the French porcelain she'd displayed earlier. He gazes, dazed, aroused. Nothing less ambiguous can be imagined or seen in the entire world. It is an end to speculation; it is itself, entrance to Sarah, her cave of flesh, convex, concave, curving under his fingers touching ridges of flesh, and then under his tongue and lips. It is there.

Sarah falls, seems to float but falls, backward on the couch. Her legs extend back to the natural V that welcomes Simon in. As if starved, he begins to devour; he sucks in as much as his mouth can hold, then gradually raises his head so that the captured flesh, top ridge and all, slides out slowly; but he keeps his lips tightly shut and his teeth almost closed; the flesh slides out, back to itself, gradually, scraping gently against the gates of teeth, then recaptured again by the sucking mouth. He allows himself to notice only Sarah's murmurs of pleasure. It is a feast of close attention. Nothing else is available to his consciousness. Later he will remember that the long, slow looking gave him particular pleasure, perhaps because Alex could not bear being looked at there. Later he will remember that the elegant sounds of Rameau underscored the hungry passage of the lovely flesh in and out of his mouth. Later he will even remember a French philosopher's definition of prayer as merely an extreme form of attention.

But for now, devotion is complete, attention is total. It is something he is doing utterly for its own sake. His mouth is wet, alternately full and empty, his tongue grazes the four compass points, his eyes now closed, now open, but seeing little because too close. In this absorption, he is surprised when Sarah speaks.

"What . . . what are you doing?"

"Don't you like it?"

"Oh, yes, yes. I just . . ." She subsides.

He returns to the innocent, pink, convoluted shell set before him.

Again: "But . . . Simon . . . what are you *doing?*"

The pure attention broken, he understands that her question is not general, abstract, troubled. It is literal. *What,* precisely, is he doing?

"What do you want to know?"

"How . . ."

"Why?"

"In case . . ."

"In case . . . ?"

"Once . . . I didn't quite know what to do. I kissed and fondled, but . . . I didn't know what to *really* do."

"First this . . ."

"Ah . . ."

"Then this . . ."

She whispers, "Almost sharp, almost hurting."

A breath. "But not quite. Then . . ."

Sarah trembles, her legs and her stomach contract, convulse. But for Simon, the chalk-talk demonstration has made passion subside. The moment has become oddly innocent; sweet, not intense. A *way* to do something, not a reason for doing it. A mechanism for pleasure, not a way to happiness. When he gets to his feet they are unsteady. The direct simplicity of the act is gone. In its place has appeared still another surprise. The surprises which gave him such happiness at first have become anxieties. Leaving Sarah strewn on the couch, her rumpled skirt above her waist, like a large, half-dressed doll, he goes into the bathroom. The heated air is redolent of sprays and lotions, all sweet and natural-smelling. He begins to rummage in the medicine cabinet, clinks bottles and vials and drops a bottle of iodine on the floor. He is enraged. Too many questions! He wants answers. He can begin anywhere; he will begin with the pills. What he wants is any unusually large bottle of pills. Any collection of drugs that would require explanation. His heart is beating faster now than when he was lying before Sarah's double cave of flesh. He has never noticed before how loud a noise bottles can make when bounced against each other.

"What are you doing?" It was the third time she'd asked him that in the past ten minutes. Even when people shared the same room, their actions were never, it seemed, quite clear. Everything had to be explained. In unexpected protest against this, Simon closes and locks the door.

"Simon, what are you looking for?"

"Answers!" More vials clink; glass against glass, glass and plastic against tile.

"To what? Simon, please!"

"Please what?" It was impossible to gain evidence by simple investigation. He slams the medicine cabinet shut.

"Please tell me what's going on."

He opens the door. The bathroom floor is a chaos of glass, plastic, labels that have come loose and will never again identify the correct drug. Simon is sweating; his armpits feel sticky, King Kong after rampage.

"Sarah, what pills do you take and what for?"

"Who mentioned pills?"

"Your father."

"He's an old man."

"There are too many things I can't figure out."

"Let's not figure each other out. My God, everyone does that. Let's just be happy with each other."

But he is implacable now. After all the heavy surprises, the dramatic confusions, her one light reference to having made love to a woman had pushed him over the line. He pulls her by the hand into the living room; past mementos of Vienna, of India, to the more recent memory: the brown couch on which he'd surprised her night mouth with his prolonged attention.

"What is it?" he asks.

She looks fuzzy around the edges; vertigo gazes out of her eyes.

"Let's clear up at least one thing," he says. His face feels like granite; where minutes before melting mouth had been, now is stone. "What about the pills?"

"S-S-S-Simon . . ."

Another surprise; when pushed to the extreme, Sarah

stammers. But pity is as forbidden as tenderness for the moment.

"Tell me!"

"It's d-d-depression."

"What is?"

"I have a kind of illness."

"What kind?"

"You could call it an infirmity of the happiness glands."

"Sarah . . ." What might have charmed him before now makes him impatient.

"No, it's true in a way. Don't be a different Simon now. . . . Nothing I said could make you angry. Now everything does. I'm trying to tell you that I've got a recurring cycle of misery."

"How long a cycle—I mean, the rhythm?"

"It's not exact. Comes and goes. My family seems to have it. Not my father—the women in my family. My mother, her two sisters . . . I can't call it depression. I *won't* call it that. Too damned clinical. It's a deep, deep sadness. I don't stay in bed, I don't collapse, I don't check into hospitals. I don't make bad business mistakes at the agency. I'm just filled with a terrible sadness. Sometimes I don't have it for a year at a time. Other times I need the pills for three or four months straight."

She sits on the edge of the couch. Her full skirt is half rumpled around her thighs.

"They don't make me different," she says. "I get to be different and they make me myself again, happy." She is plaintive. A new note for Sarah.

"Are you on the pills now?"

She nods. "I was in a bad funk a few months before I met you."

Without thinking, he says, "You have to stop!"

"You can't just stop. You have to taper off."

"Is it connected with a special experience—or just random?"

"Random."

"Psychiatrists?"

83

"That's where I got the pills."

"Why do you have to taper off? Why not just stop?"

"You can't. Something in the pills. If you do it all at once you get jaundice." She tries to smile; a convalescent smile. "You wouldn't love me if I turned yellow, would you?"

"I thought you said we weren't doing love—we were doing happiness."

"Ah," Sarah says, "that's right. Could you handle it, Simon? If it comes on again?"

"Give me a vodka."

She makes the drinks for both of them; plaintiveness is now in her expression, mouth down, eyes vague; in shock, perhaps. Simon, too, is in recovery. They sip in silence.

Then: "What was that line from a philosopher, Simon —about help?"

"Aristotle?"

"About the size of cities."

"Oh. That no city should be so large that a cry for help could not be heard at the outer gates."

"How is your city built, Simon?"

"I can handle it if it happens again," he says, surprising himself. "Don't worry. I'll handle it."

15

THWACK, CRASH, ECHOING boom-boom-boom of balls and walls and feet and racquet gut. Stark, hospital-white cubicle, save only the two red lines on the front wall and one on the back (to determine service faults and fouls). Spare white-and-red surreal environment known as squash court, a court without judgment, scores settled on the spot.

Linc serves, Simon lunges; small black ball evades him. Linc's point.

"What's happening with that girl?"

"Sarah?"

"The one you brought to the studio."

84

Smash. Simon finds the strength of wrist; ball hits corner and dies before Linc can move. Simon's point.

"What about her?"

"Something's wrong with her and you."

Dash for the forecourt. Linc hits and stands, dominating midcourt with his tall frame. Simon cannot reach the ball. A let. Simon serves.

"Is that why you called?"

"No. Wanted to see you. Haven't played with you for four years. But I get bad vibrations."

Fault. Service too high. A second's rest.

"Linc, we're too old to get vibrations. We have ideas or impressions. Not 'vibes.' "

"Okay. She seems like trouble."

Sarah's father knew it, Linc sensed it, Sarah admitted it; only Simon had not noticed.

"It's just a . . . thing."

"You and Alex in trouble?"

"I'm in trouble."

"Is there a difference?"

"I don't know."

"This stuff is not for you. You were never Don Juan."

"One 'thing' isn't exactly Don Juan."

A long, slow serve; the black ball slides down the wall; Linc scrapes it off and hurls it at the white wall. Simon returns it, too lightly; Linc puts it away. Fifteen–twelve. Linc's game. Simon has been playing a cautious game, favoring the right hand. Pause between games. Sweat and handkerchiefs. (There are no corners for towels in squash courts.)

"I'm off to Venice. Come along and see what needs to be done."

"No, thanks."

"I need you."

"I don't know what *I* need."

"Greer?"

"Maybe."

Game resumes. Simon is seized by an unthinking rage:

no basis, no conscious idea; just fury. Stops favoring the right hand. Slams ball . . . misses ball; slams into wall, hitting hand. Ignores flush of pain. He plays like a lunatic. Between games Linc says, "Don't mind what I said about the girl."

"Sarah—her name is Sarah."

"Don't take it wrong."

"I won't take it at all. Your serve."

Simon wins the next two games by playing recklessly and risking wall crashes on every point. Finally, he aims a tough slam, misses the ball, smashes to the wall with the racket; the pain that flashes through his right hand forces him to drop the racket and fall. Sitting on the floor of the bare white cell, Simon weeps.

Linc is gone. Simon has no remembrance of how they said goodbye.

He stands up, shaky, dizzy at first, then clear. A peculiar certainty takes him: *No one is going to operate on his hand!* He knows this is a foolish thought. But the sense of certainty stands, consoling in its stubbornness. Suddenly, he feels strange, alone in a small white cubicle, dressed in white—like a lunatic in an asylum of whiteness. Simon feels a sense of possibility not felt for months. In spite of Linc's bad "vibrations" about Sarah; in spite of his own misgivings about her; in spite of the no man's land in which he and Alex and Matthew live these days; in spite of it all, he feels a swift, irrational sense of the possibility of change. He lifts his racket carefully with his left hand. It is time to go home.

16

ANOTHER HOSPITAL-WHITE CUBICLE: rectangular; long, white-sheeted table, small white Formica table in corner; on top, instruments simmering softly. Dr. Rowan, in white smock, appears.

"Arthritis," Dr. Rowan says.

He clips the moist x-rays to the light box. "What we call traumatic arthritis." He traces the map of Simon's pain with a fingernail, then switches off the light.

"Actually, you're lucky. There's an operation for this. For most arthritis, there's nothing. These joint mice have become inflamed—that's all arthritis means in this case. We can go in and remove them. I did a lot of it in 'Nam."

Simon is surprised. One does not meet doctors who had been in Vietnam.

"Three years." His smile is gone. "We should've stayed and blasted the hell out of them. But . . ." The professional smile is back. "Have you been taking the pills for pain?"

"No."

"No pain?"

"I don't want to get hung up on pills."

"Mr. Shafer, I'm always leary about suggesting elective surgery. But as the pain gets stronger, it gets less and less elective."

"What are my other electives?"

"You'll have to restrict the use of that hand more and more, to avoid the danger of more trauma and more chips. Enough of them and elective surgery turns into emergency. And that's always less attractive. Do you find this interfering with your work?"

"I haven't been doing much work lately."

"I'd recommend an operation."

"You're calling it traumatic arthritis now. Last time I was here you were positive it couldn't come from one shock. I told you about being pinned against that rock with my hand, and you said no. I mean, what the hell."

"Take it easy, Mr. Shafer—"

"*Doctor* Shafer!"

"Oh?"

"Ph.D. The mind, not the body."

"I see." Dr. Rowan fiddles with Simon's chart.

"Doctor of cities, actually. You know—the body politic. Oh, forget it! I just don't—"

"What I said, originally, was: the joint mice came from repeated activity and wear over a period of years. *Then* inflammation of those chips can set in. That's what we call arthritis. Traumatic osteoarthritis, as opposed to rheumatoid, which is *in* the bone—and for which there is no cure, and no operation. There *is* an operation for what you've got! I'm not pushing it. But I'm a doctor of the body, not the mind. How much pain you can take and how much use you need from your right hand is up to you. So is the operation. End of lecture!"

Alone in white space again. Nurse appears, white-capped, white smile. "Well, Mr. Shafer," she says.

A moist, muggy Saturday; it rains for an hour, then a thick gray light hovers between strips of clouds, leaking weak sunshine. Simon arrives at Sarah's apartment for one of their briefer rendezvous. He is to pick up Matthew from nursery school in an hour and a half. All the more reason for him to grow nervous when he finds the apartment empty, and after fifteen minutes of fiddling with the hi-fi and checking his watch, Sarah still hasn't arrived or called.

He calls her agency and gets no answer. The less time available for each encounter with Sarah, the more anxiety. Feeling foolish, he plunges into the cloudy streets and arrives, finally, in front of G & D Travel. (What does the D stand for?) There is a shade drawn over the milk glass. A travel agency closed at 2 P.M. on a Saturday afternoon? More mystery!

Simon raps on the door and waits. He hears the phone ring, then stop, then footsteps. Sarah stands in the doorway. She looks distraught; her gray eyes are bleary; she squints at him and makes a vague pass at her loose, rumpled hair.

"Oh, Simon," she says. "Were we supposed to meet here?"

"No. At your place—an hour ago."

"Come in."

"It's almost time for me to go."

"Oh, God, I'm sorry. Please, please don't go yet."

"What is it, Sarah? Has something happened?"

"Nothing really. I sent everybody home—even a client —and I just closed the office."

"What is it?"

"Simon, come home with me, just for a few minutes, okay?"

They have a glass of wine at her apartment. He sits, a spectator at a mystery play; she paces, glass in hand, poking at herself.

"So dumb, closing the place, not answering the phone . . ."

"Everybody has bad days," Simon says.

She kneels on the couch, looking over him; her face is unfamiliar in its grimace of anxiety. "Do you know I almost called you at home?" she says.

"I see," he says lamely, seeing less each moment.

"Do you ever feel that before you can grab hold of your life, it drifts away from you? Do you ever feel as if everything is a dream? As if I'm dreaming you and you're dreaming me?"

Confused in the face of this torn-up Sarah, still he senses that she does not really want straight answers, confirmations that her questions were real. He touches her face very lightly, as if it might break if his touch were any heavier. "Listen," he says. "At least one lover has to be real. It's a state law."

She sleeps for a few moments, on his shoulder, worn out by sadness and self-reproach. He sits quite still, happy to be her sleeping pad. He is oblivious for the moment to lateness, more concerned about Sarah's misery, trying not to think about her almost calling him at home . . . trying not to think of the obscure relationship between Sarah and happiness and sadness and pills and himself. He isn't certain what might be required of him by this new dazed and troubled Sarah. The idea that anything at all would be required of him—this would have to be dealt with, too.

Finally, he wakes her. Time has run out. Bleary, shaken, she does not let him leave yet. "Did this, all this today, throw you?" she asks.

"Do I look thrown?"

"I'm not sure. I don't know you well enough to know how you look when you're thrown."

"You keep saying you don't know me well enough. When do you think you'll know me well enough?"

"Soon, Simon," she says. "I think soon."

He was ten minutes late in picking up Matthew, who was irritated and teary at being kept waiting. For different reasons, Simon felt the same way.

17

"CAN I COME IN? I know I'm soaking wet . . . must look like a lunatic . . . I should have called first. It's hard to explain . . . I'm sorry just to appear like this. No, I can't sit down on the couch . . . well, if you don't mind wet furniture. I just stopped off at home long enough to drop off Matthew . . . Alex must think I've gone crazy. I didn't explain . . . just rushed off here. . . . Where? . . . Today—as you must know by heart from how many times I've talked about it—is Greer day. Friday . . . May first . . . 1971. The big decision . . . I suppose that's why I'm here. No, not a drink, but I'd love some coffee . . . clear my head. . . . You know we've never stood in this kitchen together? I like watching you boil water and play with coffee filters and cinnamon. . . . My God, look at me . . . the victim of an attack of vertigo and spring rain. . . . Change? . . . Well, what could I wear? Can't walk around your apartment

naked—suppose your mother comes in again unan-
nounced, just like I did? Great. I love your red velvet robe:
how do I look? . . . I can smell your perfume on it. The
new androgyny—the magazines are full of it. If I can
make bad jokes, maybe my sanity is returning. . . . Of
course I'm going to tell you what happened—except that
it's hard to tell. . . . We met at the site of the New Town
he's planning: it's going to be north of the city, above
Woodlawn. . . . I took Matthew, for a lark . . . to show him
his first city site, and just to be with his father for a change.
It was sunny and hot. . . . I thought it would be nice. . . .
   "Subway train to the last stop, then an uphill walk . . .
just walking up a dumb hill, tracks beneath me and a
greasy spoon along the way . . . scraggled bushes and
empty lots above. It made me feel back in harness again,
(even though I was half dragging, half carrying in my
arms poor little Matthew: he wasn't poor—he loved it.
Greer was there with his enthusiasm—great salesman,
Greer—and his two lieutenants carrying blueprints. Oh,
they came in a limousine, but I declined, chose the subway
instead, not to be obligated, to keep my decision clean.
. . . By the time I got to the top of the hill I was practically
decided. I could see the Bronx spread out on my right; on
my left, City Island, little pleasure boats bobbing around
in the water, as if they didn't know they weren't at New-
port, just the poor little Bronx. But water magics everything . . . and this New Town would have water at its feet.
Elevation magics, too: the idea of manufacturing a place
for people to live in seems grubby at sea level, but high in
the air it all seems possible . . . at least for a moment. That
coffee is good, cinnamon taste. I haven't eaten anything
since I vomited . . . yes, I threw up. I'll get to that. The
spring sun turned into a summer sun the closer we got to
it—but that's not it. Greer began to pitch . . . quick alter-
nations between philosophy and logistics: On the one
hand, we can house four hundred thousand people of
various incomes . . . race no issue, just like Columbia City
in Maryland. (Greer didn't build *that* one, but it's sort of a

success). On the other hand, the cost of sewage disposal is low because you can *plan* it not to be at the mercy of chaos. Conurbation, he threw in—remembering that I'm supposed to be a little bit in love with the urban theory—conurbation is the enemy of human happiness . . . or something like that. Maybe he didn't mention happiness, not being as obsessed by the notion as I am these days. . . . Conurbation? In one sense it just means the growth of cities. But Abrams uses it to mean the unplanned condition . . . sprawl, et cetera. But there's no need to tell you all this urban planning bullshit. You *want* to hear? . . . Dear Sarah . . . you want to hear about the growth of the square grid pattern in nineteenth-century cities and how differently Greer was going to make it . . . how the street patterns would conform to the occupational and social movements of the people living there? And about this man of Greer's named Lautenbach, an apparatchik of planning . . . a soulless son of a bitch who dreams of moving populations into the right environments the way the Nazis dreamed of deporting populations to the right environments? Oh, I'm not being fair. . . .

Enough. The important thing is how I went from sudden sunny possibility to instant black impossibility. Maybe it was a change in the slant of the sun; maybe it was Matthew getting tired. . . . Shit! I know exactly what it was—or at least I know *when* it was. Greer was talking about something or other and he just casually pointed out Woodlawn Cemetery—famous old Woodlawn Cemetery—and said that all or part of it might have to be moved . . . but that somebody in the mayor's office told him there'd be no trouble. And I looked down—you could see the cemetery from where we were standing. Talk about square grid patterns . . . and no conurbation—oh, no, none at all. Nothing's as *planned* as a cemetery . . . though sometimes the planning's faulty and they have to expand: people keep dying as if there was no tomorrow. . . . And suddenly I knew, absolutely knew, that I didn't want anything to do with the whole thing: not just the gruesome idea of coolly moving bodies out; it was more the relationship . . . moving bodies out from under the ground so you could move in bodies to walk around above the ground. . . . You don't have to listen to this morbid shit, Sarah, just because I fall in on you soaking wet and raving. . . . I mean, what the hell *was* I thinking about? Bodies are above the ground for a while and beneath the ground the rest of the time: what the hell does that have to do with anything, least of all whether I should join up with Maestro Greer and build his New Town? Bodies are what we have; the soul may be around, too, but it doesn't *need* city space. . . . I just saw myself, for one sun-blinded instant, as a disturber of cemeteries . . . and a builder of cemeteries. I just wanted to get away from there. . . . By that time Lautenbach was onto traffic flow and the garden city concept in relation to the central core of shopping centers; but I was gone . . . in my head, that is. Then it clouded over and spring rain came down as sudden as my negative decision . . . and everything came together: mainly the idea that I am fit for nothing more complicated these days than the absolutely firm decision that I wanted *not* to be on that hill with them and I wanted to *be* with you right here. . . . I didn't know if you'd be here or not . . . and I didn't even want to telephone. I just wanted us to *be* here in this space as swiftly as it could be arranged . . . and here I am. . . ."

This the spoken. What Simon does not tell Sarah is how the image had come to him: image of himself lying between Sarah's legs, the wide V before his eyes, an opening road to Sarah, the parts greater than the whole, for the moment. For some odd reason Sarah had become a place: an area of beauty, frailty, reconstruction. . . . It is part of the craziness of the hot day: only moments before he is to turn away from Greer and his two associates and express his decision by vomiting against the rented Cadillac limousine—in that instant he registers the picture of Sarah spread before him on the couch in her apartment, arm flung over her eyes; pink cave of her deepest self.

He knows that he wants to save her; that his challenges,

his precious career, all have shrunk to one problem: building a city so small that Sarah's cry for help can be heard at the outer gates. He waits for Ben Demos's mocking voice: it was the perfect Demos opportunity.

He does not tell her any of this, or that he *will* go away with her. Instead, he finishes his coffee and they sit on the couch, carefully not touching each other.

"What will you tell your wife?" Sarah asks.

"I don't know. Have you told your husband about us?"

"Ah, my husband . . ."

"Have you?"

"No."

"Then tell me about *him*."

"His name is Marcus. His family owns an ironworks in Belgium. But he lives in Venice."

"I thought Monaco."

"He has a place in Monaco, too. That's where he called from. He calls himself a junkman—because that's the family business. But he's a sculptor and he works in Italy a lot."

("She'll tell you," Sarah's father had said. "She's different with you than with her junkman.")

"And *is* he your husband?"

"We're together about four months of the year."

Information flowed smoothly. It was as if by his wearing her robe, lightly scented with flowery perfume, they had exchanged roles for the moment; his questions are not his usual ferocious probes; her responses are not the usual evasions.

Still, he says, "That doesn't answer my question."

She stretched out against him, without warning. "Since I told you about the pills, everything seems different," she says.

"Different good or different bad?"

"Different."

She put her hand inside his (her) robe and caressed his shoulder and chest. It was friendly, not sensual.

"I keep Marcus separate. It's good for me. I've always

94

kept things separate. Marcus says I'm like a man; that I think there are men you sleep with and men you love."

"Have you slept with many men?"

"Yes."

"No big deal?"

"Airline pilots seemed the answer for a long time."

"But you didn't love them."

"No. That's exactly what I didn't do. I didn't love them. I loved Marcus."

"And sex with you and Marcus?"

Something lunatic in the nature of the early evening, of the unexpected arrival, the change in his head, made it suddenly possible to ask things that he knew would have been turned aside before. She obliged his fantasy.

"It's not much. Distance does not lend enchantment. Maybe it dulls. Maybe it's irrelevant. He's not so good that way." She paused. "I mean, we're not so good that way, Marcus and I. But we're not supposed to be."

"Hence—me?"

"Ah, you, Simon. You're still happening. We're still happening."

"Why do you stay married? If you're not really—"

"I didn't say I was not really anything. You're not with your wife now, at this moment, are you? Is it a question of moments; of arithmetic?"

"Maybe you do better with airline pilots."

Sarah leaned down and took off her shoes. She moved slowly, as if pushing through water; dreamy.

"Maybe," she said, reflecting. "In a funny way it's the idea of travel that's saved me there, too."

"How do you mean?"

"When you're with somebody who doesn't matter, the travel experience is useful. It all comes down to the clock —to whom you spend what minutes and what hours with. Lying in a man's arms at three-thirty in the afternoon, I know that it's nine-thirty in Paris; that the poor people of Paris are strolling along the Rue de Rivoli toward the amusements of the Bastille. I know that while the man I'm with is dozing off, it's ten-thirty in Rome, and middle-class Italians have finished their dinners and are walking along the Via Bocca di Leone toward the Via Margutta and closed shops with elegant window displays, or the Piazza di Spagna. And when the man—the lover, if that's what he's called—wakes up and wants more intensity than I want to give, it helps me to remember that in Libya it is four A.M. and the faithful are rising to hear the muezzin call them to prayer; in Ischia, fishermen are drinking thick black coffee before starting their day . . . and the tourists are still asleep in the luxury hotels (to which I've sent them) across the bay."

Sarah's voice and mood had grown low-key. "With you it's tricky," she said. "You're the only man I've ever asked to go away with me. I don't want to lie next to you thinking travel thoughts to make you less real. I want to go *with* you. Together, not separate; in the flesh, not the imagination. But I don't want to think about what it might mean."

Neither does Simon. Thinking into things is not for this day; nor is feeling. What was needed here was detached professional instinct. If Sarah was to be his project, the question was where and how it would be done. The where is growing clearer. The how is less clear.

He decides not to go home. He will stay and have dinner with Sarah. Delighted, she offers to cook for him; the first time. The time has come, Simon thinks, to become a fictional character: to lie to his wife and have dinner with his mistress. The time has come for new categories; to take risks. He surprises himself with his calm.

He takes a hot shower, while Sarah performs sleight of hand with steaks and garlic. On the glass wall of the shower he writes his name. The steamy letters help him focus his day. SIMON. Then he wipes them off and writes SARAH. He dresses again: Sarah's perfume has been washed off and must be left safely in her robe. He is practicing caution; it is like a statement to himself, of serious intent.

Calling Alex, Simon learns something about successful lying. It must contain some truth.

"I was very upset."

"That was easy to see. Where are you?"

"With Linc. The Greer thing scared me."

"And Linc?"

"We're talking about Venice. I might have to go with him for a week or so. Is Matthew all right?"

"He had a wonderful time. He said you threw up, but I guessed it was him—the poor kid."

"It was me, poor kid."

"Oh. Are you coming home?"

"I'll have dinner with Linc."

"You could bring him. I have enough."

"No. I want to kick some things around with him first."

"Okay. Listen . . ."

"Yes?"

"Once you decide something—anything—you'll feel better. It's been a bad winter."

"Today was like spring. I'm sorry, Alex. About acting like a maniac."

"We take turns apologizing. Why don't we skip all that? I love you."

"Me, too."

"You mean Linc is standing there and he's not supposed to know you love your wife."

"Something like that."

Sarah asks nothing, pleased to have him to herself at home of an evening for once. She has changed costume, too. She had been wearing a black sweater and black pants when he'd burst in. While he showered, she'd put on a long yellow robe, hooded like the red one she'd given him to wear earlier. She seemed to have an endless supply of monk's robes to wear for different occasions. In this bright, sunny robe, she cooks their dinner. She assigns

97

him to the setting of the table. He stands in the middle of the dining room area, hands full of silverware, mind drawing the customary blank. When Sarah arrives with the steak platters, he is still standing there.

"What is it?"

"My wife and I had a fight over this just before I met you. It's an old argument."

"Over table settings?"

"I always forget which goes where. Alex is convinced it's willful."

"A kind of marriage civil disobedience?"

"I don't know. Some infantile interplay between husband and wife. I never know how *much* you know about what goes on in a marriage."

Sarah takes the silverware from him. "Look," she says. "The fork always goes on the left, so think of a word like, oh, fork-lift. The knife on the right; think of a rhyme—knife/rife. The spoon next to the knife. You don't need a word there. An idea—because spoons mean coffee and dessert and you know they come last." She goes to a cupboard under the record cabinet and kneels. Simon observes her calf, the curve of her neck under straying hairs. Her recital is like gibberish; still, he knows that the lesson will stay. He is learning something he will not forget. Something classical; an ethics of the dinner table.

"The wineglass goes here," Sarah says, "with the knife pointing at it—*accusingly.* Sometimes an adverb will do the trick." His heart turns over for no reason. He had not counted on any such moments of peculiar intimacy. And over something so trivial. They seem to have traveled a great distance in the hour or so since he'd arrived, soaking wet, at her door.

He says, "Sarah, let's go away, together. Now, soon, tomorrow, the day after tomorrow. As soon as you can do it!"

She stands there, caught in the act of pointing a knife at a wineglass. Caught up in the internal chaos, the heart that turned over, the way a stomach turns over when an airplane dips too suddenly, kicks at his chest. Simon wants to tell her everything he will do. He will go with her to Les Baux, to Paris . . . anywhere. He will lie, plot, endanger his marriage by the chance of being seen. (Ninety-nine to one, Sarah had told him; one is all you need, Simon had said.) He wants to tell her what he had decided at Woodlawn, standing high above the movable cemetery, at Woodlawn where her father had lived a generation before; wants to tell her about Project Sarah. If he told her all this the moment could have become a moral moment, something about their lives.

Instead, the moment becomes, by turns, erotic and comic. Sarah's excitement catches, ignites from his own. Leaving steaks to cool, coffee to boil, knives to point accusingly at wineglasses, she pulls him into the bedroom. There the feather comforter enfolds them; she sits upon him, rides him, by turns tender and vigorous, as if they were already on their way, the coupling of their bodies a means of transportation. Measuring his joy, for once careless of her own pleasure, Sarah says murmurous absurd things, lovely to hear.

"There's nothing I wouldn't do with you" (though their love-making is daring only in its suddenness, its passion, not in gymnastics or fantasies). She comes in a strangely silent shiver.

When she dismounts they lie still. She switches on the bedside lamp, rises, walks softly on carpet feet and opens the bedroom closet where, weeks before, she had placed the secret package brought home from the agency. Rising on one elbow, Simon sees beyond the gray velvet naked shoulder into the dim closet where sits not one but two packages.

"What?"

"Something else," Sarah says. "Last week. People keep forgetting."

"What is it?"

"Shh-h-h."

She brings the package back with her to the enormous

bed and places it amid the tangle of comforter and sheets. Simon allows himself to wonder at this great arena for love and sleep. Why *so* great, he thinks, and feels the inbite of incipient jealousy. Airline pilots and a 747 for a bed.

Sarah sheds the sheaf of brown wrapping papers and string and holds up, in comic triumph, a large white conical object. Its sides are ridged; its tip is a miniature cone that forms a head of uncertain gender: an idol in the form of a sexual artifact. It gleams in the semidark room; a dug-up god from an ancient civilization. The erotic moment has turned comic.

"So that's your skeleton in the closet. A forgotten object, like Brahms serenades; like Rameau."

"Someone showed it to me, after getting back from the Yucatán; then they forgot it at the office and never came back. It was used in some sort of religious ceremony. Isn't it pretty?"

"The anthropological technology of love. Did you hide it from me out of shame?"

"Out of . . . shyness. It's such a weird thing."

"Are you shy?"

"I told you I'd show it to you when I knew you better."

"Do you know me better?"

"Not much. But I think I'm about to. When you travel with someone—"

"You know less, I would think. Shipboard romances and all that."

"We'll find out, won't we?"

"Your face . . ."

"Yes?"

"Just now, as you turned your head sideways, looking at that instrument of pleasure in your hands, I half remembered a line of poetry."

"That's *my* game."

"Hold it: 'Your face is like a chamber . . .' "

"Yes . . ."

" 'Your face is like a chamber, where . . .' I've lost it. I don't even know the poet."

100

She comes and lies on her stomach next to him, the dildo in her hand between their two side-turned faces.

"Since you're so interested in my face, I thought I'd bring it a little closer."

"That was kind of you. The least I can do, then, is kiss it."

"You don't kiss *it,* you kiss me. I'm not parts."

"Then what are you holding in your hand?"

"Ah, that's a toy."

"Okay, let's play."

"That's silly."

"We'll see . . ."

"Oh . . ."

"Like this."

"Strange."

"More?"

"Just play."

"Okay . . ."

Simon leans on his elbow, playing with Sarah and their new toy. He likes the idea of detaching himself from the action on the bed. Something new was happening. In their days or nights of play and sex they had not been especially inventive or experimental. They had little time; the thing was to be together. Touching, doing, all that followed— what happened was allowed to happen. Gradually it had become different. Perhaps it had to do with Sarah separating men into love and sex compartments. Apparently, at least for the moment, he was in the sex compartment. In the dark, he probed; but he had no sense of how he felt about that. And thought: O brave new world, that has such women in it . . .

It seems a terrible intimacy, this playing with hidden flesh and artificial matter; silly, too, it seems, and erotic in a way he did not entirely trust. Angry with himself at this, he thinks, why was trust at issue? He was here to be happy, not safe. Or was that Alex speaking in him? Alex looking over his shoulder, as she had at Ariel, his first, poor, mad, occasionally sane wife. "It seemed like sensual adventure,

101

but it was only her craziness that excited you. It wasn't
D. H. Lawrence, you poor sap, it was Krafft-Ebing."

"Simon . . ."

"Yes."

"I'm afraid."

"Why?"

"The equalizer . . ."

"What?"

"Too deep . . . the coil . . . careful . . ."

A moment later, Sarah turns on her stomach, he takes
her from behind, using the dildo very gently and carefully
in front. Afterward, together, they trip to the bathroom
and gravely wash the extra instrument of pleasure with
soap and water (we'll get lazy, Sarah jokes), like good children taking proper care of their toys. Then they go back
to bed and reverse the procedure.

When breath is regular again, Sarah murmurs, "You
haven't asked what's in the other package."

"No."

"It's even stranger than this one."

"Oh?"

But he is sated, happy; happiness is the enemy of curiosity. For the moment Simon has no interest in unwrap-
ping secret packages. Sarah is almost asleep. She takes his
right hand and squeezes it. Simon braces himself, afraid
there will be pain, not wanting her to feel him flinch. He
will not tell her about his hand. It is his secret package, not
to be unwrapped. By the time Simon realizes there will be
no pain this time, her hand has fallen open, releasing his.
Sarah is asleep. He turns and looks at Sarah sleeping. Her
face lies half turned toward him; her head has fallen off
the pillow and he can only see a profile. She turns in her
sleep and he sees her perfect oval face, cheeks rounded,
dark luminescent skin, eyes lightly closed, lids fluttering
slightly in sleep or dream; there is a sadness in her repose.
"Your face is like a chamber"—it arrived in his mind all at
once—"where a king dies, alone, untended of his
wounds." That was an unpleasant note; he could have

102

done without thinking of that particular poem. His stomach trembles.

He must remember not to fall asleep; must get home at an explainable hour. Now, he thought, now surely Ben Demos will speak. What ammunition he has! His friend Simon lying here with a young woman asleep on his tingling arm: a young woman who is, or is not, married to a junkman/sculptor in Europe . . . a young woman who is subject to vast fits of sadness and is hooked on happiness pills of some sort; who has made love to many men and at least one woman; for whose sake Simon is going to Europe, leaving behind the unresolved questions of a job . . . of an operation on a hurting hand . . . and a suspended marriage dangling an unsuspecting child from its strings. Project Simon: suspended. Project Sarah: begun! Unfunded, only half planned, but infinitely more promising than Greer and the living dead of his new cities, more exciting than joining forces in nostalgia with Linc to save Venice.

Sarah's father, a generation ago, gave sleep to one patient instead of saving the world. Now, instead of extending his hand to the people, Simon would give happiness to Sarah. Not a word from Ben.

The pain woke Simon a few minutes before the telephone rang. He lay still, hurting, in the darkness, listening to Sarah breathe.

18

A FAVORITE WRITER of Simon's youth had written: You had better plan for your pleasures. Everything else will take care of itself, but if you do not plan your pleasures, they will not happen. It sounded simple; it was not. There was the simple planning of an itinerary with Sarah.

But then there was the not so simple planning of lies to Alexandria. The story was: he is to go to Venice to confer, on the spot, with Linc. There is also the matter of Paris and Les Baux; the first to pick up a car for the drive to Provence, the second for the essential purpose of the trip: the exploration of happiness in a dead city.

Telephone numbers, names of hotels, dates of arrivals and departures—even for a week these present a problem. Alex is nervous. To the guilty, nerves resemble suspicions. Unable to deal with this, impatient, Simon decides on audacity.

"I'll probably stay at the Danieli, but Linc is staying with friends—I could end up guesting with them. I'll call you when I arrive. And I may stop off in Paris—it's included on the ticket—just for half a day, maybe. Settle my nerves. Paris is a great nerve settler." He knows he is talking too much.

Absent-minded, her own nerves quiet for the moment, Alex had said, "Okay; I get Montreal in April, you get Paris in May. No arrangement is perfectly equal." It is the humor of desperation. They had been bad with each other, the sex infrequent, undependable; the social fabric frayed, ready to tear. The kind of time together when Alex would turn to him, suddenly, over a crossword puzzle or while drying her hair after a shower, and say, "Maybe I should have stayed away."

"Why?"

"Because *you* have."

"I'm distracted. Between projects is bad for me."

"Is that what you are? Between projects?"

"What else?"

"I don't know. Something more radical. Not just with me." She meant the night before: a gathering of their friends, the first attempt at an invocation of the old magic of friendship since they had gone away the year before. The magic failed. He'd seen them all with the clarity of detachment, the pseudosociological typing understandable with strangers; with friends, inexcusable.

104

Still, he'd suddenly seen himself surrounded by middle-class debris of the sixties. There was a storefront lawyer turned corporation counsel; there was an activist playwright now teaching screenwriting at Columbia; there was a golden-haired German architect who spent most of his time on planes to and from Teheran. "The best-kept secret in New York," Dieter had said, "is the fact that oil money is gobbling up the best of the professional class in New York: Saudi Arabia, Iran, Libya—they're the only people doing any real building or rebuilding." To Simon's expression of dismay he'd responded, "Ja, it's weird how far we've come." He'd been married three times, each time to a Jewish woman.

"That was as close as I came to rapport with a friend that night," Simon complains to Sarah.

"Were they all old friends?"

"A mixture. Pretty *good* friends; some old, some more recent. But it was like watching them through gauze. Their motivations were mysterious to me. Their lives were like the stories by a talented avant-garde writer. I appreciated them; but I didn't really understand them."

They must have thought you were crazy," Alex said afterward.

"Oh?"

"You kept asking everybody if they were happy and why they were and why they weren't."

"They all seemed to be talking about tennis. Did everybody used to talk about tennis?"

"No. But they didn't talk about happiness, either. Are you very unhappy, Simon?"

A post-party post-mortem of truth? Simon declines. Alex does not press.

Expected obstacles often do not appear. The actual departure is surprisingly smooth. His heart pounding (but his hand free of pain), Simon picks up Sarah in a taxi in front of her building. She looks different. A sophisticated, travel-poster version of Sarah: black turtleneck, tweed skirt; one medium-sized bag. Simon helps her with the bag. He keeps his eyes lowered, as if this will make him invisible. One friend passing by, he thinks, and *finis*. His audacity had lasted about five minutes. "You look absolutely terrific," he says at last.

"I cut down on the pills today," Sarah says. "Two a day instead of three." She gives him the words like a present and holds up a hand with fingers crossed.

The cab edges into crosstown traffic toward Kennedy Airport.

Part Two

PROJECT SARAH

We haven't the time to be ourselves. All we have time for is happiness.
                    —*Albert Camus*
                     Notebooks

1

FROM SIMON SHAFER's master's thesis: *The Rebuilding of Paris Under the Second Empire* (Columbia University, 1953).

No great city is the product of one age or regime; it is the work of many centuries and many minds. Paris is no exception. It has grown from a village on an island in the Seine to the great capital of today, reflecting the influences of a wide variety of thought. But the age that left the greatest mark is the Second Empire. The grand boulevards, l'Opera, the Bois de Boulogne, are all the work of Napoleon III and his Prefect of the Seine, Baron Georges Haussmann. From the artistic and logistical standpoint, the great radial avenues of Paris, as developed by Baron Haussmann, created a modern metropolis from the medieval conglomeration. Generations of lovers no less than city planners have been awed by—and felt welcomed by—the open embrace of these magnificent avenues.

To save a day, they take a night flight. ("The old red-eye, we call it in the business," Sarah says.) They leave New York at 7 P.M. and are in Paris at 9 A.M. Paris time.

"Let's go to the hotel," Sarah says, "take a bath and have breakfast at La Coupole."

"But it's really three A.M. in our heads," Simon says.

"The trick is to switch automatically to Paris time." She clenches a round, red-knuckled fist. "Don't give in to jet lag. The triumph of the will!"

She looks comic standing in the baggage claim section, passport in one hand, the other hand clenched in a salute to the will. It seemed, to Simon, to sum up, in a picture, why they were there.

At the Hotel Madison—a small, clean, inexpensive hotel in St. Germain des Prés, chosen by Sarah—there is a message waiting for her. The name is unreadable to Simon.

"It's from Marcus," Sarah says. "He called from Zurich." It has the logic of dreams. Simon had assumed they might meet the mysterious junkman in Europe. But there was an aggression hidden in the swiftness of that first phone call that was startling. Was Marcus Sarah's husband, after all? An outraged one, perhaps, demanding explanations? While Sarah steams in her bath, Simon strolls the bedroom, opens the wall-length windows and stands on the tiny balcony overlooking the Boulevard St. Germain. The statue of Diderot stands, back to his gaze; on the other side of the street, toward the Seine, is the Church of St. Germain. Above, the clouds of Paris, thick and dark gray, ride the sky. The clouds are Paris, Simon thinks. More than the café on the corner, more than the roofs of M. Mansard, more than the stately poise of the inevitable public buildings, those gray, puffed clouds that perpetually hide the sun are Paris.

Simon feels, quite simply, free. He had not known how caged he'd been feeling; a glimpse of it on the hill above Woodlawn, yes. But here, at the intersection of past and future, he feels foolishly free.

Breakfast (or something) at La Coupole. Croissants and eggs and steak tartare, as mixed as clock time and body time. The fluorescent glow is appropriately neutral in the great dining hall. There are not more than three or four hundred people, all making a grand din beneath the vaulted, chandeliered ceiling. Somebody is popping flash bulbs at a group in the center of the room. Simon and Sarah eat and drink their café au lait at a table against the wall. Sarah faces the wall, letting Simon take in the local sights. But her head jumps from side to side as she watches arrivals and departures.

"Alone at last," Simon says.

Sarah gazes at him from over the rim of a flowered coffee cup as big as a bowl. She wears a long flowered skirt and a yellow blouse; ready, she has told him while dressing, for the Paris parks to which she will be taking him. Parks and gardens, it seems, are first on the agenda.

"I can't believe we're here," she says. "That you don't have to get dressed and go home."

"No," he says. "It's a date; just like real people. What shall we talk about?"

A skinny woman with black-painted pits under her eyes strolls by their table, stares directly at Sarah, then moves on. Simon finishes his coffee.

"Garçon," he says.

"They're not garçons anymore," Sarah says.

"It's been six years since I've been here. Paris needs no urban planners; Baron Haussmann did it all just fine."

"Six years ago they were garçons. Now, it's just 'S'il vous plaît.' Don't you travel for pleasure?"

"I do now."

A square-shaped man in a pin-striped suit moved their way. In a sea of turtlenecks and sport shirts he stood out. He left a sullen girl with heavy blue eye shadow standing near the doorway and came to their table. The man in the suit looked familiar to Simon. But not like someone one has met or known; rather like a character in a movie, a play, or in a photograph once seen and remembered for some particular characteristic: avarice, cynicism, the moral life expressed in a style. He leaned across the table and kissed Sarah on the cheek. It was as formal as if he had kissed her hand.

"I knew you were in town. I left a message for you at the Madison."

"Oh," Sarah said. "It said 'Marcus.' "

"Yes, Marcus asked me to stop by. He wants to see you."

"I thought you were leaving Marcus," Sarah said. "Going to work for what's-his-name, that financier . . ."

"He went bust."

"I heard. Oh, Cappy Kaprow, this is Simon Shafer."

"We've met," Simon said. "You were working for the President."

"I got your letter and passed it on. You'll be hearing something. I thought it was terrific."

Sarah was smiling. Simon knew why, immediately; or thought he did. For the first time their lives had crossed: trivially, an incident she couldn't even know about. But it sufficed. It connected.

"You change jobs quickly," Simon said. And then thought about his own changes and felt foolish. "So have I," he added. "You can tell the President there's no rush."

"You can tell Marcus the same thing," Sarah said, paying special attention to the coffee cup in her hand. "I'll only be in town for a day or so."

Kaprow ignored Sarah gently. To Simon, he said, "I've gone private. I don't speak to Presidents anymore." To Sarah, he said, "Jimmy's having an opening. The Rue des Beaux Arts, eight o'clock."

Sarah shook her head firmly; it was like some sort of code, rather than a simple negative. "Got to go," Kaprow said. "I'll have Marcus call you at the hotel later. *A bientôt.*" He kissed a rigid Sarah on the cheek again and was gone into the bustle of arrivals looking for tables under the brilliant neon lights, toward the girl with painted eyes. For the next few moments Simon and Sarah both struggled to keep something private from being ruptured.

"We have a friend in common," Simon said.

"He's not my friend."

114

"That's okay. I only met him once for five minutes about six months ago. What does he do for Marcus?"

"Let's not talk about him. We're traveling for pleasure?"

"Absolutely," Simon said. He reached over and kissed her on the same cheek Kaprow had, as if to wipe his kiss away.

Simon had not counted on any encounters. But he had not counted on anything. The idea had been to do it: to go, without thinking or counting. The thinking could come later.

"Simon," Sarah said. "If the phone rings in the hotel, let's not answer it, either one of us."

2

IN THE TAXI that drove them to a secret destination of Sarah's, a German shepherd shared the driver's seat, staring over his long snout at Simon and Sarah. Sarah asked the driver if the dog was for protection or company. Protection was the answer. There had been several robberies in the suburbs. The driver patted the dog, whose snout then disappeared below the seat.

"Paris is getting rough," Sarah said. "We might as well be in New York."

"Not quite," Simon said. "Let's go to that opening. I can meet all your friends."

"Ah, Simon; we only have two days in Paris. Can't we improvise?"

What the hell, Simon thought. Why am I making trouble so quickly? He kissed her ear, lightly. "You're some travel agent."

"This trip is simple. Two days in Paris, then perfect peace in Les Baux, a few days in Venice to cover your tracks, then back to New York. And those aren't my friends. They're Marcus's."

115

They entered through wrought-iron gates: a park or a forest; there was no way of telling at first. There were wooded flats and great crags of rocks surrounded by overgrown paths; across one of them, a rabbit dashed and was gone.

"This is my delight," Sarah says. "Anyone can take you to the Luxembourg gardens or the Parc Monceau."

"Where are we?"

"Buttes Chaumont." It sounded something like "beauty charmant." "I don't know who put it here or why, but isn't it nice? This is the nineteenth; hopelessly bourgeois. And hopelessly beautiful."

They sat on a bench next to a nurse reading a newspaper while a small boy at her feet tormented a cat. Then they walked farther, past two little white temples made out of something like bamboo. ("Don't ask me to explain. I have no idea what anything here is.")

They climbed rocks and finally stood overlooking a rolling formal lawn, with red and yellow flowers massed trimly in rows.

"Ah," Simon says. "We're in France again."

Just beyond the formal gardens is a small lake. Ducks and swans swim, ignoring each other in regal calm. Simon stretches out by the lakeside, Sarah's head in his lap. "I wanted someplace that you'd never been," she says. "My Aunt Leona brought me here first. Years ago. She called it a medicine for melancholy. Leona has the family's woman's curse, too. She's an internist—saddest woman I know. Anyway, I'm on my second day of down to two pills."

"And feeling . . . ?"

"Then two pills tomorrow. In Les Baux I take a deep breath and drop to one pill a day for two days. Then in Venice—zero! That's the program."

"And if you start to feel wiped out?"

"You said you could handle it."

"I can! So much for family curses."

"I don't know," Sarah says. "I've known those pills and

116

my sadness a lot longer than I've known you. Probably, I'm afraid of a letdown. How long have I been after you to come away with me?"

"I've always had a very vague sense of time and how it passes," Simon says. "Except when I'm on a job."

"And I know every day, month and year; all charted. I lead a seasonal life. We've known each other since February fifth, 1971, and today is May third. I started making little jokes about trips by—oh, let's see—February twenty-first. That makes it more than two months."

He grasps her head and turns it toward him. But she cheats him for the moment; her wide gray eyes are closed.

"There will be no letdown," he says firmly. "By the time we leave Venice you will be off everything—clean—and still happy. How many people get what they want after only two months or so of trying? Spoiled brat!"

Her eyes stay closed and he releases her. Simon closes his own eyes against the warm morning sun. He feels placeless—he, whose sense of place was constant—an instant and continuing assessment of ground-sky measurement and local rhythms. He could be anywhere with Sarah —who was, apparently, happy. That was the key notion to hold on to. Happy with him—and only two pills a day. Someone was playing a guitar and a child's voice was calling *"Attends, Maman . . . attends, s'il vous plaît."* So they were in France, after all. The pressure of Sarah's head shifting slightly on his chest was more real than the thought. Something was opening and closing in Simon, preparing him for change. Drowsily he contemplated it. Jet lag? Fatigue? The aftermath of a swift, dramatic departure? He raised his hand to touch Sarah's hair; the bite of pain surprised him. It had been absent for almost two days. He lowered it gently to the grass and rested it there. The return of the pain was peculiarly reassuring. Something he'd brought with him that would not change simply because children spoke a different language, or Sarah's "husband" was trying to find them. The anxiety that usually accompanied it did not arrive. Other concerns lurked in the half doze.

Something in the sullen closure of Sarah's eyes under his lecture evoked a move toward sullenness in him. He decided to push her a little harder.

"I want to meet Marcus," he says.

"No."

"Yes. I don't want to hang out at art galleries with his friends, but I have to meet him."

"It would spoil the whole trip. Please, Simon."

He lets it drop for the moment. He will find a way.

It is an aesthetic knowledge, like the rightness or wrongness of a blueprint; he knows that Project Sarah cannot be completed without his meeting the junkman.

"You know you're a little crazy?" he says to Sarah.

"Ah, why?"

"Playing disconnected games with husbands and lovers." He stops just short of adding: airline pilots.

"Who says they're games?"

"You—are—rootless." He measures his words carefully. "A—grown—woman—and—rootless."

"Not now. I'm rooted right here with you."

"Playing games with me, too. You're willing to toss me in a bit with *his* friends, but he stays invisible."

"Okay, forget them. I just want to be with you."

He relents. "Even though I'm so hard on you?"

"You're not so hard on me. You didn't hit me. I once had a man hit me."

"You're pretty big."

"That wasn't the problem. It was my fault. We were in bed and I got very excited and . . . something took me—I don't know what—but I said, 'Hit me, hit me,' and he did. And I got so mad I pushed him out of bed onto the floor. I laugh whenever I think of it." And she does laugh, her long body shaking on his chest; she turns her face toward him, eyes open now. Her face has a way of quickly and brilliantly brightening with a smile or laugh; when that is over, sadness rules again.

"I think," she says seriously, "that such crazy moments

118

come from not knowing exactly who I am. That's what you're seeing as a little crazy."

Simon remembers all the New York nights when Sarah fenced with him, refusing to open up her life—as if she had no life to open, no past to share with a lover: only present passions. It was too easy to assume that Sarah lived behind a shield of ambiguity because there were terrible things to be concealed.

The truth might be better and worse at the same time. And it might be that what he most enjoyed in Sarah was this quality of being not yet fully created. You couldn't have it both ways: enjoy the possibilities in an unfinished Sarah and berate her for the murky soup that seemed to be her soul.

"Does it concern you much, who you are?" he asks.

"Not when I'm with you. My sister Jephtha and I talked about it a lot. It tortured me, those days. Not her. She said: be a rock, a tree, a cloud. She got that from a story."

"I know the story. It's Carson McCullers. Carson Mc-Cullers was very big when you were a kid. Look, it might actually rain."

There was one great black cloud hovering on the edge of the lake. Sarah turned over and lay sideways in his arms. "Do people have to be one thing, Simon? I feel most like one thing when I'm alone with you. That might be why I wanted you to come away with me. Your buddy Linc thought he had *you* down pat."

"Down pat is too damned pat."

"You're a hero without heroics. Or some such."

"From now on my heroism begins right here."

He cups her breast, then lightly slides his hand down to the V between her legs. Gently she opens and closes her legs, then lies still, imprisoning his hand. He waits for a jab of hurt; nothing. Is it possible that the whole hand business might be a creation of mind? How would that thought sit with the white-on-white fanatic of bone? The mind, Dr. Rowan, has cliffs of bone. . . .

119

"It was strange," he says, "seeing you with that fellow from Washington, Kaprow, a friend of Marcus's. Puts you in a sort of . . . world."

"I'm in a test tube in New York. Waiting for my married lover to come and uncork the tube and take me out to play."

"Not fair."

"But true?"

"A little true."

"A little?"

"Okay, a lot. I'm rooted in one place, don't forget. I pull myself up each time to get to you."

"Sounds painful."

"I love Alex. You're not her fault."

"Ah, love," Sarah says. "Fault . . . Fault me no faults. And nobody around here is doing love, remember?"

"She's not around here."

Sarah flips over, first hands and knees on the grass; then jumps up, slapping grasslets from her skirt.

"All too much she is," Sarah says. "All too much."

3

Le Drugstore has the precise hand lotion Sarah requires.

"No more sandpaper," she sighs. Back in their hotel room she undresses, rubs lotion into her hands and yawns. It is now 3:30 P.M., Paris time. Neither of them is thinking or speaking of what time it is in their heads. They are for the moment in the present. Perhaps because of the hand-rubbing business, Simon has a twinge in *his* hand; the second since arriving in France. He closes his eyes and waits for it to be gone. In less than a minute or so there is only the memory of a dull ache. When he opens his eyes again Sarah is lying on the bed, asleep. So much, Simon thinks, for the triumph of the will. Warmed by half a bottle of wine, he is tempted to join her for a nap. Instead, he takes the phone into the bathroom and calls Linc Aaron in Venice.

"Hello."

"I can't hear you."

"It's Simon . . . Shafer."

"Simon—are you here in Venice? Speak a little louder."

"I can't. Somebody's sleeping."

"Alex?"

"No. Somebody else."

"Aha."

"Never mind the ahas. I'm in Paris. I want you to do a favor for me."

"Have you run away from home?"

"Sort of. But just for a week or so. Be a friend, Linc. I've been in trouble for months now. I need your help."

"I got your cryptic letter. I won't say a word about anything."

"I need more than that. First of all, can you find out about a sculptor for me—a man named Marcus."

"Marcus who?"

"That's all I know. He works in metal. Junk sculpture of some kind. In Venice."

"What do you want to know?"

"Whatever you can find out. His last name. His address and phone number. How he lives. Is he married?"

"Oh . . ."

"And to whom."

"I see."

"You don't see anything. Please, Linc, try not to see anything except that your old friend and pupil is fucked up in the middle of his life and trying to find his way out."

"Christ, you sound a wreck. Have you taken a job yet?"

"I'm supposed to be coming to Venice to see you about that in three or four days."

"I got your letter. What do you mean, supposed to?"

"For Alex's sake, that's the story. I'd like to see what

you're doing there. But I'm in no shape to work for anybody right now."

"Love?"

"Misery. And peculiar happiness."

"Like I said—love?"

"I don't know anything about such fancy matters as love. I'm trying to save my life."

"Listen," Linc said. "Listen to me, Simon. Are you in the kind of trouble where, like, you don't exactly know what you're doing?"

"You mean am I off my head?"

"That's putting it a little strongly."

"But that's the idea."

"Could you use some professional help?"

"I called *you* for help."

"That was lousy, okay. It wasn't my idea."

"Who told you I was going crazy?"

"Alex called me."

"Oh . . ."

"Today, in fact. She carried on about you taking some kind of fit in the train with Greer and his people; stuff about throwing up and running away. Talking to yourself a lot . . . It wasn't exactly crystal clear, but it didn't sound so great."

So this is how it all looks from the outside, Simon thinks: vomiting, running away, conversing aloud with a dead friend. . . . He'd thought Alex was just waiting in the wings for him to straighten things out. No suspicions, no questions. When all the while she was lying next to him late at night, thinking thoughts of mad husbands, of unhinged middle-aged men coming apart like badly glued model airplanes.

"Yeah, I threw up. Didn't you ever want to throw up?"

"All the time." Linc eases pressure off. "Come to Venice and throw up in a canal. They've promised me a storm and me and my gang are ready for it—Galileo proving his theories. Bring the tall drink of water."

The tall drink of water lies sprawled across the bed. The

room floats in a pearly, early evening Parisian light. Brass knobs on the bed glint strangely. The bed is like a boat, drifting; Sarah's arm lies over the edge. One lotion-smeared hand almost touches the floor. A snore troubles her nose and subsides in soft sibilance. It is nonsense, Simon thinks. He is not mad. He's at work: she is his Venice to be saved from future storms; his New Town to be planned for happiness: his small but grand experiment.

She dominates the bed, lying aslant, one long leg half bent, the other stretched straight. Simon surveys the site of his efforts as if he has never seen her before: the strangeness of the situation, perhaps; or simple jet lag. It feels very important at this moment to look at Sarah's body objectively. He kneels by the bed and gazes at her.

She is long, about five feet, nine inches. She has black hair and gray eyes now closed. Her legs are stocky but her waist is slim and her breasts are small, the nipples also small but surrounded by large pink aureoles, slightly stippled. Simon notes that the small breasts on a tall woman are a striking effect. Her nose is small and straight. Her color is darkish—but she flushes easily when moved or upset. There seems to be a readily available river of blood just under the mottled skin, so that her skin, chameleon-like, appears to be changing shade all the time. She smiles quickly and clouds over quickly. Her hair is very long, down to below her waist when loose; she wears it in different ways: sometimes straight, sometimes in buns on either side à la Russe; or piled on top and pushed to the side in a kind of "rat" effect. When she does this at work she often wears a pencil stuck in it.

Her mouth is full; almost a rosebud. And the lower lip is divided by little vertical striations, like neat chap marks. She often moistens her mouth with leaping tongue—could this be related to the famous dryness that torments her hands all winter? The upper lip, too, has several vertical dividing lines, but not so many. Below the mouth, the chin becomes full, round; it gives an effect of naïveté after the gravity of the long dark hair, the often watery ambiguous gray eyes and the simple straight nose. Her teeth are pale white, the front two slightly longer than the others; it makes her smile emphatic. Her throat is long but not thin; like mouth and chin, it is full. Simon discerns a pulse halfway between her chin and collarbone on the right side. The collarbone itself is prominent. Blue veins rise to the surface like tributaries of a river, surfacing, briefly, between her breast and collarbone, and then disappearing.

She has the classic bikini band of white around her breasts and hips. Her waist indents but not sharply; a kind of lazy moving inward around her middle. The stomach is a round white puff; below it the statement of very dark black pubic hair is startling to see. Her torso is not long for such a tall woman. Her legs add the length, though not slim and tapered; rather, full and stocky when the knee is passed and the calves begin: like a taller, slimmer Malliol sculpture.

Her ankles are narrow, surprisingly delicate. Her toes are painted a pale rose. She wears no polish of any kind on her fingernails.

Sarah is lying, now, half on her side. Viewed from the back, she curves inward and then her buttocks flare out beneath the waist. Sarah is very sensitive in the rear. A few times Simon has parted her buttocks and pressed the little mushroom of her anus and heard the thrum of excited murmurs rise intensely.

Simon reaches across the bed and turns her toward him. One leg flops sideways. Her groin is covered with rich, black hair. When her legs are parted the contrast of revealed rose flesh is arresting. Her clitoris is prominent, enormously sensitive; especially, oddly, when approached from behind. She has described her clitoris to Simon as the center of her self. Not in images; just: "That's me." Or almost silly-sounding, as: "When I was a teen-ager I called it my friend. I never told anyone except my sister." Or: "When you touch me there, you touch *me*." She is very personal about that part of her body, impatient with women who claim to have orgasms through the vagina.

"They're lying," she has said, simply. "It feels wonderful inside but this is everything," touching herself lightly on the tip of the clitoris, for emphasis. It is not a political statement. He has not told her that Alexandria has her full pleasure only deep inside the vagina. And Alex does not lie.

Simon kneels beside the bed and spreads Sarah's legs. A plan has occurred to him; it is also an impulse. He obeys both.

He touches Sarah gently. The whole idea is to achieve the maximum of effect with the minimum of means.

"Oh," she murmurs. "Oh, God, Simon. Oh, I was asleep. . . ."

"Hush. You're still asleep. Just let me do this. . . ."

"Yes, oh . . . please . . . ahh . . ."

The bite of pain that had surprised him by its absence when Sarah squeezed his hand between her legs in the park an hour ago bit sharply between his thumb and forefinger. He stopped his caress and dangled his hand in midair. Sarah, unaware of what had happened, her eyes still closed, turned back again onto her left haunch, her right leg slung over her left, opening a channel. Simon continued as if there had been no interruption. Except he used his left hand to caress Sarah.

At first it felt only slightly strange to be using his left hand for this intimate work. Then gradually it became almost hallucinatory. People with a wounded right arm in a sling who open doors, eat food and put on clothing with their left hand know how disorienting it feels.

"Oh, please . . ."

"Yes."

"Oh, so good . . . Do you want to . . ."

"I just want to do this."

"Yes. Will you make me come?"

His left hand seemed not to belong to him. It belonged to the movements it was making, to the arc it was describing, to Sarah's crinkled black hair wet with her excitement. His right hand was his, but it dangled, useless, impotent with hurt, while the other one pursued Sarah's joy and his own vicarious pleasure.

Sarah's legs moved steadily like trembling parentheses around his hand. Teasing, Simon whispered into her ear: "Why? It's just a finger touching your friend. It could be your own finger." She shook her head desperately.

"Why not?"

"Because you're here," she murmured. "It's you and you're going to make me come."

"Not me; my hand, my finger . . ."

"No, no," she said. "You."

He kept his own breathing as steady as he could. An edge crept into Sarah's sounds: a heightened sound— pleasure so keen that it touched on pain.

Simon stopped.

"Oh . . . why?"

"Will you take me to see Marcus?"

"Don't . . ."

"Will you?"

She lies still; silent. He touches her again; her trembling resumes. He stops again; he wonders: Will she explode in rage instead of the pleasure he's withholding? She would have every right, he thinks. But Sarah continues to lie passively, cupping his hand.

"Will you?"

"Ohhhh . . . bastard."

"Yes."

"Blackmail."

"Yes."

He grazes the surface of her flesh as lightly as he can. Her breathing tells him when to increase the pressure, when to slip inside Sarah for a second, then out again and back to her center. Involuntarily, she guides him. Simon feels as if it is not he who is doing this: he is still dressed, while Sarah is naked; the left-handed love completes the sense of unreality, allows him to play at sensual blackmail. He thinks perhaps it is a necessary shifting of balance be-

126

tween them; not power, but the sense of molding, of making, could begin with the hands, even with a single finger touching the most vulnerable point in the body. Games prefigure real plans; the blueprints could come later. He is delighted with her for staying somnolent and heavy, trembling and ready under his hand; for playing a fantasy the only good way: as if it were real.

She crouches forward more and more, like a fetus, he thinks—and then is startled to see that a finger has crept into her mouth as she moans murmurously and almost comes. He slows his movements, preparing to stop. Sensing what he is going to do. she whispers, "Yes, Simon, yes, I promise." A moment later, curling up around her pillow, finger in her mouth like a baby, she shivers and cries out and is still.

Simon's heart was beating fast, as if he'd been running. His left hand felt stiff and tired, his right one limp and now without pain. Part of him was afraid of her, he realized; afraid of the power he'd given her by running away with her. It was why he wanted so much to see Marcus. Information, any information, could give him more control. And, strangely, by not coming himself, by measuring and teasing and pausing and blackmailing, by using Sarah's "friend" to get to Marcus, he felt more in control of their destinies; even the poor, temporary destinies of the next week or so.

Sarah turned back to him and laid her head on his shoulder. She smiled a sleepy smile.

"Ah," she said. "When my friend is really alive it has no conscience. I would have promised you anything."

At 7 P.M., Paris time, they are both wide awake. The air conditioning is not doing its job and it feels like summer in the room. Sarah showers while Simon thinks about calling home. There is a floor-to-ceiling mirror against one wall. Sarah turns around, carefully, in front of it, checking her complexion.

127

"Not yellow yet," she says softly to herself.

"We left New York twenty-four hours ago," Simon says. "It's too early, isn't it?"

"Once when I almost cold-turkeyed it, I went saffron-colored instantly."

"Paris is full of Vietnamese. I read about it in the *Herald Tribune*. You'll never be noticed."

"Then I'll stay in the room with you all day. You'll notice me."

A second—a twilight—breakfast comes with a rose in a thin curved vase and coffee so black and bitter the hot milk barely lightens its color to beige. A dark, solemn young woman sets up a table for them in front of the tiny balcony overlooking the square of St. Germain and the half-hidden spires of the church of St. Germain and they eat the buttery croissants and bitter, dark marmalade amid the honks and swooshes of the evening traffic.

Across the boulevard the church bells rang the hour. The alien taste of the thick coffee, the pleasantly foreign odor of gasoline from the street, the sight of Sarah in a blue hooded robe—these needed only the sound of bells to give Simon a sweet feeling of happiness. Well, it was what he'd started all this for, after all. He wondered exactly when he'd started to associate happiness with the sound of bells. He vaguely remembered bells, somewhere, somehow, the day he entered Sarah's travel agency. But he had been reading Huizinga's *The Waning of the Middle Ages*, and he might have been musing about that wonderful opening passage about bells and the way they measured every moment, every hour of the day in the Middle Ages.

He had told Sarah this one night and then read her the passage from the paperback. They had become great readers to each other; with a fine, foolish sense of newness, as if lovers had never read favorite poems and books to each other before. Sarah had listened and then said, "In Les Baux they ring bells—but at odd times." (It was early in her campaign to get him to go away with her somewhere—and Les Baux was mentioned often.) "I could never figure out what the bells were for. I told Marcus that. He laughed." Annoyed, Simon had said, "What does *that* mean: Marcus laughed?"

"Nothing. He laughs a lot. In fact, it's one of the things he does best, laugh."

Damn Marcus, fucking Marcus. Simon salved his irritation by remembering the all-important thing Marcus did *not* do well. If he could believe Sarah.

"Does he make a living from sculpture?"

"He makes money, but not a living. Marcus moves around a lot; he needs a lot. There's the family business. And he makes money in other ways."

"What ways?"

"He's there and I'm here. I can't keep track."

In desperation Simon held on to Sarah's words about Marcus's poor performance as a lover. The last laugh. Simon and Sarah rang bells together. That's what bells meant!

"Does he love sculpture? Is it his life? Why is he there and you here so you can't keep track? What *can* you keep?" Sarah stopped his questions with an open mouth on his. Tongues touched happily. In the distance, a tiny tintinnabulation.

Now she sat across a table from him on a balcony in Paris; he had come away "somewhere" at last (*"Married men can't just go away somewhere"*) and he had teased her into delivering Marcus. Or at least into standing still long enough for the mysterious Marcus to catch up with them.

"Crépuscule," Simon murmurs, gazing out at the bluing sky.

"What?"

"One of my favorite words . . . *Crépuscule*—twilight. It's when interesting things happen in cities."

As if the bells had been a signal, the mild May twilight gathered its energies. Beneath the rocking singsong Simon heard a chanting of voices. And beneath that, the menacing thwang-thwang, up and down, of a police siren. Still

129

somnolent from their bed-and-blackmail embrace, Sarah and Simon took only mild notice at first. She leaned back in her chair and holding her half-open robe together with one hand, tried to peer over the balcony's edge. When the noise grew so loud that it demanded more attention, Simon walked to the balustrade.

A ragged marching line of young people carrying signs was spilling down from the wider part of the Boulevard St. Germain past the little square which interrupted the avenue's progress. Alongside them rode two gray police vans, windows ominously shut and shaded. The words being chanted were the same, over and over again: "*À bas la guerre américaine* . . ." with a precise rhythm: *À bas la guerre a*mér*-i-caine*!

"What is it?" Sarah asked.

"A demonstration—Vietnam."

"Is *that* what they're saying: *guerre?* I couldn't hear it."

"You sound like a Frenchman. The pronunciation is more important than the thing itself." He was disappointed, irritated that there should still be such things as antiwar demonstrations even though he and Sarah had run away for a week.

She smiled sleepily over a crumbling croissant. "I'm a chameleon," she said. "Where I am is . . . where I am."

"It was my bad joke. I hadn't expected this."

"Expected what?"

He gestured toward the street. "Reality," he said. "The public. My constituency." He wondered if Sarah knew he was mocking himself. The wide gray eyes gave no hint. The shouting grew louder.

"I was here in '68," Sarah said, "when all hell broke loose. Marcus and I were practically trapped in our hotel for three days. Are those all students out there?" She made no move to get up and look.

"Yes. Plus the usual police."

"Marcus thought they'd actually make it then. Take power and all that."

"You didn't."

130

"You met my father. When you grow up in Washington Heights with a perpetual Party meeting going on—and nothing ever really happens—you don't trust any of it."

"Yes, you're a kind of private party all to yourself."

The sirens split the air as if the police cars were coming into the room. Simon turned back to see. The line of students had broken. Two girls stumbled over each other; one fell and was helped to her feet; then they were both pushed down again. As in speeded-up frames from a film comedy, one of the gray police vans was suddenly on its side and from the upside-down door came policeman after policeman, struggling to his feet and running toward the vanishing students. No one was yelling "*À bas la guerre*" or anything organized, though there was a lot of yelling under the hysteria of the sirens.

Sarah got up and before she could get far, Simon pushed her back into the room.

"I've been in these things. Stuff goes flying; in France the cops might even shoot. It's our first night in Paris. Let's survive it." Sarah retrieved her coffee cup and sat on the bed. "My God," she said. "Is it our first night here, still?"

Simon had gone back to the terrace, peculiarly drawn to the sight below. He took it personally that this should happen his first night away with Sarah. It was like running into Cappy Kaprow; unlooked-for, unwanted. The world was supposed to take a breather while he and Sarah ran away.

Just below, a group of young people was being chased by police. One of them was a black man wearing a torn red T-shirt and jeans. He and a blond girl in black leather pants were running from a policeman who waved a club. They ran toward the little *tabac café* to the right of the hotel. No one seemed to be hurt and the cop appeared to be waving the short blunt club mainly to get rid of them.

Simon turned back to Sarah; he started to close the French doors that connected the room with the terrace and with the scene below.

"Is anyone hurt down there, Simon?"

"Doesn't seem to be. Just scattering everybody."

The phone rang, loud in the room against the distant sirens. At the same time Simon saw someone struggling half onto the balcony, slipping back, then getting both hands more firmly on the edge and shifting his body farther up. Simon opened the doors again, knelt down and grabbed the one hand that flailed in the air, and pulled. It was the young black man who had been racing for shelter in the café. He landed on his knees and then stood erect on swaying legs. Simon opened the doors again and the man stumbled into the room. He was badly out of breath and he brought a metallic stench of sweat with him. Simon couldn't figure out how he'd managed to even reach the balcony; perhaps a jump from the top of a parked car. He stood in front of Simon as if waiting for him to do something. His T-shirt was ripped and his eyes were half-shut. He mumbled something; even the language was unclear —it could have been French, English or an African tongue.

Sarah sat on the bed with the phone against her ear; she was murmuring into the mouthpiece and also watching the intruder closely. She made no move to draw her robe more tightly around her legs.

"What do you want?" Simon said stupidly. Then: *"Que voulez-vous?"* He remembered absurdly and too late that the French always add *Monsieur* to such a question.

The black said nothing. Breath was his only form of speech and Simon could hear him struggling to regain control over it. Suddenly this presence, this otherness in the room, this startling arrival from the street world, this reminder of public turmoil in the flesh—one bloodshot eye smaller than the other, Simon noticed—suddenly it was too much. Simon grabbed the man by the arms, dragged him quickly to the doorway, pushed him out into the hall and slammed the door.

For no good reason, he was out of breath, too. He leaned against the door feeling a little mad. Something had raged up in him far in excess of the cause: a perfectly natural, if dramatic, attempt of a demonstrator to get away from the police. Probably all the man had wanted was the exit—which he'd got from Simon, swiftly and too roughly. It had nothing to do with politics; they were on the same side, for whatever that was worth.

"Not much," Ben Demos said. Simon, it's 1971 and you're still extending your hand to the people. Don't you ever learn?"

4

"WHAT IS AWFUL," Simon said, "and what I don't understand, is that I wanted to hit that guy."

"Who are you talking to?" Ben Demos asked. "Me or her?"

"Whoever. I didn't just want to get him out of there. I wanted violence, fury."

"Aha," Ben said. "You wanted to make a personal statement. Nothing worse! You have to watch that stuff."

The baroque gas-style lamps of the Pont Alexandre III shimmered against the yellow light illuminating the Palais de Justice. They crossed toward the right bank. "We're heading toward the Île de la Cité," Sarah said, "where Paris began. It was just called the Cité then, and a tribe called the Parisii lived here."

"I thought it was called Lutetia," Ben said. He'd lived in France on the G.I. Bill after the Korean War and studied with Casadesus; courses at the Sorbonne in French history had also been good for government checks. Sarah did not seem to be aware that Simon was speaking to his dead friend. For a moment he considered telling her about Ben. It would be a nice thing to do—a gift—like Sarah's cutting down to two pills a day for him. They could be like children taking spoonfuls at the dinner table: "One for Simon, now one for Sarah." But he said nothing; partly because he did not know why Ben was so real, so precise in his utterance—more than just the sense of a friend you missed more than you'd realized, and who was invoked, or invoked himself, apparently, when you were sick, troubled or confused. A dead foul-weather friend. No, he would not discuss Ben Demos with Sarah, yet.

That decision banished his friend. At least for the moment, he was gone. Simon held Sarah against the railing of the ornate bridge.

"This bridge is called Alexandre Trois because it was built in honor of a visit of Czar Alexander—"

"Do any of your clients ever make passes at you while you're instructing them?"

"Not on bridges."

"But bridges are perfect places for shows of affection or lust. They're called trystoriums in the textbooks. Places to meet, for lovers."

"We were talking about clients, not lovers."

He kissed her so hard, so furiously, that it was bruising.

"What . . . ?"

"I'm still in a rage about that man in our room."

"That was an adventure," Sarah said. *"Une vraie aventure."*

"Not so *vraie*," Simon said. "I feel foolish."

"Why did you throw him out like that? Protecting my honor?"

"I don't exactly know. It wasn't about you."

"Why'd you help him up in the first place if you felt that way?"

"That was automatic. But once I'd done it, I didn't want him in there; not for one more second. So . . ."

"Maybe it was because I was on the phone to Marcus. Displaced rage."

"Please don't be a psychoanalyst's daughter."

"I'm not much good at that stuff. I'm better at feeling what you say without words."

"Oh?"

134

"Like what you were telling me with your hand—your finger, a while ago."

"Telling you what?"

"Something about feeling and sex. About detachment."

"Yours or mine?"

"Mine. You were telling me something."

"The hell I was, anyway. I was trying to please you by touching you. Then I got the idea of teasing you to make you give in on Marcus." But he was surprised: some archaeologist of the spirit in her had got an iron, a critical edge to the sexual blackmail. Perhaps a kind of clarity was granted to someone in whom sex and love led different lives.

"I gave in," she said. "We have an appointment at midnight at Marcus's studio in the Marais. Can you last till midnight? I'm keeping my promise."

"I'm not tired; I'm angry. And I think I know why."

"Tell me why," Sarah said solemnly. "I've never seen you so angry." Which was not true, of course; he'd shaken her like a puppy when she'd turned elusive—how long ago?

"Listen," he said. "I'll tell you about it over dinner. If we're meeting Marcus at midnight, we've got three and a half hours. Is there a dinner included on this tour?"

5

THERE WAS, as it turned out, dinner at Lapérouse included on this tour. Sarah led him along the river's side to the Quai des Grands Augustins. Simon's precious *crépuscule* had given way to absolute night, softened by a warm breeze fragrant with the odors of river water and gasoline and lit by the underglow of an invisible moon and hundreds of visible stars. Across the Seine on their left, the low towers of the Louvre shone in careful spotlighting.

Turning right, he could see the taller towers of the Notre Dame, the gargoyles, also lit, gaping at them harmlessly. Straight in front of them, before they turned to the entrance of the restaurant, was the dull, squat Palais de Justice.

"This is one of the oldest *quais*," Sarah said. "Thirteen thirteen; there was a monastery—"

"Sarah . . ."

"Yes?"

He told her that this was one city in the world in which the senses took care of information. He did not remind her that he'd written his thesis on the rebuilding of Paris under Baron Haussmann.

"Okay," she said. "We call that unassigned time in the travel business. You," she added, "are clearly ready for unassigned time."

Unassigned time was to be spent in a small room with low ceilings and tiled walls that made it feel like a kitchen. The owner, a short, plump rooster of a man with twirled mustaches and shiny red cheeks, kissed Sarah's hand. He wished to know all about how her agency was doing, how M. Marcus was, and he wished to order a special dinner for them.

Sarah to Simon: "My last word of travel advice—easy on the wine or we'll both collapse." She was a quieter Sarah. Perhaps, Simon thought, she was hiding some growing mood behind the travel talk.

But, somehow, there was a musty Montrachet with the *oeufs brouillés bergères*. And the mustaches were busily selecting a Burgundy for the next course. In the meantime Simon siphoned off what remained of his anger by telling her how he'd brought all his passion and skills to Chicago, convinced that he could break up the killing monolith into living neighborhoods. He even told her about his meeting with Cappy Kaprow and the mad letter to the President. But as he spoke, the words rustled dryly in his ears; something veiled in Sarah's solemn gray eyes, something sad, perhaps, distracted him. He listened to himself, too; he was curious to know what this new, small-scale Simon thought . . . about the larger implications (if such terms still applied) . . . about the idea that he, Simon Shafer, had wanted to reverse the helplessness of people in cities, the political paralysis, all by a systematic humanization—contradictory but necessary—neighborhood by neighborhood. But like certain flawed moments of sexual potency, the passion, the fantasy necessary to sustain it all, was not there.

"I've never had eggs as an appetizer before. I'm more than a decade older than you, but when we're traveling I feel younger. What's wrong, Sarah?"

She shook her head from side to side as if to say that nothing was wrong, and then said, "I had a terrible dream. Before—just before you woke me up by touching me."

"No," he said. "We will not tell each other our dreams. That's only in bad movies and novels."

But he could see that her eyes were on the verge of filling.

"It was about your wife."

"You've never seen her," he said quickly. "How could you tell it was her?" It was a foolish, delaying question. He didn't want to talk about Alex; especially with the heaviness of such a dream. The mood had been so good. A mood heightened by the anticipation of meeting Marcus. Instead, he was meeting Alexandria; his earnest Alex, whom he'd never before betrayed; Alex, with whom sex had always been involving, satisfying without being wild; inventive and intimate but somehow more than merely "personal," an enterprise of two, connecting them up to the world of people and strategies, of buildings and flaws, coffee cups, future plans, past mistakes. It had been that way even the first time, on a cot in Erving Goffman's office at the University of Michigan, after a late-night conference on Role Theory and Street Life. Simon had lingered, attracted by the way she'd responded to one question or another (the ground outside was covered with seven inches of snow and street life was, for the moment, impossible). She'd answered with cool passion; a kind of aristocratic commitment; a style of address that had never changed. Their love-making had been a kind of passionate postscript to the conference.

Alex had been raised first on an island off the coast of Maine and then all over the world, by Quaker parents— brought up in the tradition that nothing was entirely personal. The social contract lurked everywhere. Behind every encounter was hidden the notion of potential service; obligation was built into the structure of the universe. Making love implied permanence, permanence implied family life, families implied the body politic.

This was only slightly diluted in the grown-up Alex. After Vassar, after the Pratt Institute of Design, after a desperate love affair with an intern who committed suicide, after serving as secretary to Erving Goffman and Lewis Mumford—after all that, the tradition was considerably watered down by irony and easy laughter at her own quirky upbringing and obsessions.

Still, she had written a paper on Role Playing and Sexual Ethics for Goffman and one on Male-Female Ethics in Urban Design for Mumford. (What would she have said about tonight's tiny experiment in sexual blackmail?)

The sex with Sarah was, in contrast, a completely private matter; body curled into body as if trying to make one simple form out of several complex forms; trying to reduce all those limbs, fingers, orifices, wet membranes, entrances and exits, intentions and impulses, to a simpler statement; no concern with overall meaning, no future implied. The contrary, in fact: the future annihilated in the intense, anxious sexuality of the moment. Logos-free sex; two people hiding in each other, using pleasure, like certain kinds of art, to give each other tender, passionate sensual information, but information that was not extendable; no extrapolation; a delicious knowledge that was quite useless—and had to be renewed from scratch each time: with the exception of certain technical knowledge; the hows and whens of making love, not the whys or whats.

138

Simon wondered, some days, whether it was the furtive nature of the affair that was the reason for this—or was it something private, something closed and enclosing, something unpublic, in Sarah herself?

After the Chicago experience the sex between Alex and Simon had gone "off." The result of angry words (*"you're really a politician and a businessman"*), the result of his depression, of her anger at having interrupted her own career for what had turned out to be nothing after all, the result of his anger at her anger; the Chinese boxes of marriage clattering inside each other. In this atmosphere sex had grown tentative, unreliable; a threat of disappointment instead of a promise of pleasure. They began to play it safe as lovers for the first time; the style of passion became restricted. His erections grew chancy and it took Alex much longer to reach that orgasm, deep inside, beyond the vagina: the ones Sarah believed were lies certain women told men and themselves. When she did reach one, sometimes it was as if she were returning from a distant place and had to find her way back by unaccustomed roads.

Simon could not tell any of this to Sarah. But Alex had been invoked. And something in Sarah's heavy-lidded gaze at him over the rim of her wineglass told him that this time she could not be dismissed with the easy, teasing rhetoric he'd used before.

"I've never seen her," Sarah said. "But I have a sense of what she's like. Besides, in dreams you just *know* who somebody is. Knowing what they look like doesn't matter so much."

"Well," Simon said gravely, "she's quite petite—"

"You haven't asked me what the dream was."

He ignored the remark.

"She's named Alexandria because she was born in Egypt. Her parents ran the Quaker mission in Alexandria. Like the city, she is sometimes called Alex."

"I don't think I want to talk about her. Pour me some more Montrachet. It's supposed to be the most complex of all French wines. I've decided I'm in the mood for a complex wine."

"You said we'd collapse unless we go easy on the wine."

"Ah, Simon, Simon, you said you could handle it if I collapsed."

"I was speaking of the soul, not the knees."

The waiter brought the *langouste Grands Augustins,* all herbs and savory odors. Not certain of where the evening was heading, they were grateful for the interruption, eating with careful attention and appreciation. The distraction of tastes seemed to bring the color back to Sarah's face. She had literally paled when telling him that she'd dreamed of his wife in some terrible way. She was the only woman he'd ever known whose skin behaved like the skin of women in novels. It flushed, paled, mottled, darkened. Beneath the normally dark complexion ran a river of response that sent messages to the surface regularly—and these visual signals touched him as much as anything about Sarah: as much as her sudden spurts of passion, as much as her swift fluctuations between independence and need.

"This lobster was worth a detour," Simon said.

Sarah sat back and wiped her chin with her napkin. She said, "Are we on a detour?"

Then quickly, before it could turn to trouble, she relented. "Detours can be the best part."

They drank to detours with the last of the Montrachet. The evening seemed to gallop with the serving of the rest of dinner. Perhaps it was the bottle of Clos Vougeot which followed the "complex" white wine, perhaps fatigue catching up with them. Alexandria was still present, but muted by the flow of blood from their heads to their stomachs. Woozy with wine, they speak of selves.

"Am I different?" she asks.

"From what?"

"From your other women."

"Yes."

140

"How?"

"You're more—enclosed. When you reach out, you reach out from all the way in somewhere. I mean, your lovely soul curves inward somehow—not outward."

"Everybody's does."

"Probably. Sometimes. But I think yours does more often than most."

"Is it why you like being with me?"

One of the reasons. Are you surprised that I like your lovely soul and not just your lovely body?"

"Just where, old urban planner, would you locate that soul?"

"A little south of that mouth, with the raw little vertical lines that attract me to it so often, and somewhat north of what you call your friend, who is so sensitive to the touch."

"That's a large territory. Includes the heart, the liver, the lungs." Sarah looks thoughtful for a silent moment. "Maybe," she says, "it's only that my soul is disconnected. Isn't it amazing—you and me sitting in Paris, drunk on no sleep—"

"*You* slept some."

"—and wine, talking about souls? We were supposed to take our unassigned time here and talk about why you were so angry about our visiting demonstrator."

Simon has a flash of insight, It comes in the form of Linc's face: bony, cracked nose with a piece of cartilage standing up in the middle. "Linc would know," he says. "We spent close to six years marching, sitting in, demonstrating; he did the more dramatic stuff—he's got more guts. Things like chaining yourself to draft resisters. Foley Square courthouse, the Pentagon, the Sheep Meadow in Central Park: that was our territory for years. Alex, too; she's been arrested more often than Linc. So when our hotel room is invaded by a young black it just got to be too much past tense. That's why Linc would understand. He's through with all that. Dead cities like Venice are safe."

But there were correspondences too buried to be immediately available even to Simon himself. The black man with the bandanna around his head, bandit style, rocks crushing against Simon's hand—both faces black, the one a fugitive from the French police, the other an enemy of Simon's project, for unstated reasons. The confusion of motives behind faces of similar color in circumstances of similar violence . . . It was too much for Simon to sort out. He changed the subject.

"Did I tell you that Alex and Linc had been lovers before we met? He arranged our blind date."

Pissing away some of the wine a moment later, he was sorry he'd told her that. It was the kind of detail they could have done without. At least he hadn't asked her how or why her sister Jephtha had died, though he almost had. They'd drunk a lot of wine.

When he got back to the table she was gone. Forcing himself to stay calm, he paid with traveler's checks, waited for change, and did not ask the mustache what had become of Sarah. Outside, on the *quai,* she sat on a bench waiting for him, without explanation, all gaiety gone: the starry but moonless night gave just enough light for him to see that in the slump of her shoulders, in the droop of her mouth. He sat down next to her and waited. If he was to do his job, he could see a certain patience would be required.

"I dreamt that she was dead," Sarah said. "In a car crash. I killed her in a car crash, your Alex."

"I see," he said lamely. A cool breeze blew from the river.

"There was blood and she was dead."

Patience, he thought again. You are a teacher as well; patience and the reminder of reality.

"Sarah," he said, "it's only a dream."

"That's no help," she said.

And mercurial as ever, she smiled at him, stood up, tucked her arm in his and said: "Everything is."

142

6

THE WEATHER DROPPED upon their evening like a
blessing. A cool breeze with enough memory of the day's
warmth in it blew from the Seine; it carried with it that
odor of nameless flowers mixed with car smells and something distant fragrantly burning and the special smell of
being a very old city that Paris breezes bear.

Dry air and dark-blue night skies instead of the expected wet and overcast. Shops were open late in the Fau-
bourg St. Germain. Women in long dresses carried
packages in their arms. The Champs Élysées seemed enormous under its protective coating of stately chestnut trees,
its daunting expanse of boulevard and busyness of cafés,
young people taking, or leaving, the soft evening air,
young men wearing their narrow, severe-looking French
suits, boys their tight-contoured sweaters, the young girls
their equally tight sweaters and long skirts or pants. Even
in the sophistication of tourists staring at the windows of
Air France, in the overheard babble of German and English words ("*Bitte,*" one man kept repeating—as if something were terribly bitter)—even here some squat woman,
accompanied by her square-shouldered, blue-jawed man,
carried a sack from which protruded a *baguette;* perhaps
deeper in the sack lurked fragrant cheeses.

At the end of every lazy gaze lay the arc-lighted, fake-
looking Arc de Triomphe. Bloated with four courses and
two bottles of wine, Simon and Sarah floated down the
Elysian Fields. At the Rond-Point, Simon pointed out how
Baron Haussmann had planned this approach so that the
mobs of Paris could never again threaten to take control
of the city from the ruling class. Simon was taking control
of the evening again. Having lost control of the rest of his
life, he knew it was very important that he keep control of

Project Sarah. In spite of dreams of violence, in spite of black intruders, in spite of an unpredictably sad or happy Sarah. They were approaching the midnight tryst with Marcus; control was more important than ever before. Contrary to what Sarah thought, everything must *not* be allowed to be a dream.

She had dressed up for the evening: long red skirt trailing the sidewalks, white turtleneck sweater against her dark skin. Her hair, too, was "dressed": piled on top of her head, with two braids, one on each side, which she'd twisted in a surprisingly short time, perhaps five minutes. Instead of placing a call to Alex, as he should have, he'd watched her dress, a luxury never taken in New York. Then he'd let her take a clear pleasure in choosing his clothes: gray slacks, a lightweight navy-blue blazer and an open-necked red-checked sport shirt. Playing house with wardrobes, harmless sport.

"Actually," Sarah said, "I shouldn't have come to Paris with *you.*"

"Oh, with who, then?"

"With Edmund—with my father. He's old, and he's sick."

"I didn't know. He didn't seem sick on his birthday."

"He had an operation last year. That's why Mother is with him again . . . sort of. But he'll be all right."

"It was not a friendly divorce?"

"It was not a friendly divorce. But when he got sick and then his friend Blau got sick she relented. He would enjoy all this."

He touched her shoulder. "Sarah," he said. "I'm enjoying all this, too. Enjoying is a foolish word. I'm sorry about your father being sick. I like Edmund."

The look on her face tells him she is following some agenda which is hidden from him. Simon wasn't sure exactly what he expected from this impulsive trip; but it was possible that Sarah expected something all her own from it. Something which, from moment to moment, might be frustrated, fulfilled or held in suspension. Music filtered toward them from a radio in a café; the eternal Parisian accordion accompanied their walk for a few moments. Some strain full of the automatic, familiar regret such songs trade on; it made Simon sad, as if the trip were already over instead of just begun.

"I'm not sure," he said, "that your father would be as eager as I am to see Marcus. He kept calling him the junkman. Not altogether friendly, as I remember."

"They're not a good combination. You did better with Edmund in five minutes than Marcus in five years."

"Even though he knew I was a married man . . . ?"

"Edmund is more complicated than that."

"He said you seemed happy with me."

"Ah, anybody can see that."

"Happier than with the junkman."

It's okay for Edmund; don't *you* call him that."

Simon leans against her, still shaky with wine and exhaustion. Sarah giggles; alcohol or giddiness pushes her breath.

The Rue de Rivoli runs in stately elegance for a while: the Louvre sits on its border; Smith's English Tea Shop graces a long arcade, as does Smith's English-language bookshop and a row of high-plumed trees. But move down past Châtelet toward where the Rue de Rivoli, without warning and without a break, becomes the Rue St. Antoine and you arrive at the poor and very old quarter in which Marcus has his studio.

Here sidewalks are obstacle courses with pushcarts extending the width of the street; children who would have been in bed at this hour in other quarters run between their elders' legs. They have round dark pits of eyes and look to Simon as if they are Tunisian or even African. But many of them wear gold Stars of David around their necks. Short, blunt men grin at the passing Sarah; gold teeth flash. When Sarah led Simon across the avenue to the five-story house in which Marcus had his studio, lettuce leaves clogged the curbstone.

145

It was a five-story walk-up. Marcus clearly had stamina. As Simon paused to catch his breath, he realized how little he knew about the man. Was he old? Did he creep up these stairs? Young and dash up? Middle-aged, a cautious pacer of his steps and breath? The hallway was dark, even when the light stayed on, which was about ten seconds for each floor. The massive staircase, thick to the hand, was coated with dust. Rags lay in corners. It reminded Simon of the Lower East Side dance rehearsal studios of his first marriage; poverty fed by hope and ignoring filth. Was Marcus living the junkman's life deliberately? Sarah had said his family had money.

Surprise upon surprise: the studio is unlocked. The enormous black paneled door swings open at Sarah's touch.

"Isn't he afraid of thieves?"

"What could they steal?"

The studio is magnificent. One enormous floor-through beneath a vaulted skylight. An eerie blue light, half sky, half starlight, shows forth an assortment of giant sculptures. They seem to be mostly plaster casts or clay. But here and there a bronze casts a darker tone. Some are figures: a nude woman with a great torso and disproportionately tiny breasts; a family group: mother, father and child entwined; an abstract plaster model, all smooth, bird-like upward movements. There are ladders of various sizes everywhere. In one corner a scaffolding hangs loosely. There are absolutely no amenities. It is a space for work. Sarah was right. Thieves would need a derrick to cart away even the smallest piece. Strangest of all, in a corner near the broad windows that front the studio is a large tent. The entrance flap is half turned back.

"He doesn't seem to be here yet."

"Let's see," Sarah says, stooping and entering the tent. Simon follows. The amenities, of sorts, are here: a mattress covered by a blue-flowered sheet; and a small table on which is a tottering lamp, which works. Not always, apparently, because there are also two candles set on wax-gnarled dishes. On the table is a bronze ashtray, a bottle of Armagnac and a collection of wine and brandy glasses. Next to the table is a green Buddha—porcelain—on a stand of its own.

"No," Sarah says. "Not yet."

There is also a sink, a water closet complete with bidet, a bar of soap, a clean white towel and shaving soap and a brush.

"God," Simon murmurs, "I don't know when I've seen shaving soap and brushes. How old is Marcus?"

"It's not a matter of old," Sarah says. "He has his own ways."

The moon must have risen during their ascent; the studio is milky as well as blue with night light.

"There's a switch here somewhere," Sarah murmurs. But when she finds it, there isn't that much more light. French economy; they make the tour of artworks as best they can.

"Who buys pieces like this?" Simon asks. "Who can afford the sizes?"

"Banks, companies," Sarah says. "This one"—she runs her hand over a Brancusi-like bronze curvature that slices the air almost up to the ceiling—" is for a city square in Belgium; Liège, I think."

What was striking was the range of styles. There were centuries represented here; and a dozen national styles. The effect, as the eye swept over the clutter of completed and unfinished pieces, was of some universal European style, rather than any one epoch or country. There were blank-eyed beauties who suggested Grecian serenity; and tormented twists of rusted metal parts that called up an automotive civilization in collision with itself.

The scope was impressive and confusing. How many Marcuses were there?

Simon feels the wine buzz begin to go; a sagging in the bones. He thought: Whoever made these sculptures is formidable. Suddenly it is very important that the buzz be kept going. Inside the tent, in the dim lamplight, he pours

Armagnac for them both. On the tiny table next to the mattress a book lies open, face down. It is the essays of Montaigne. Simon turns it up. There is a passage underlined. Before he knows precisely what he is reading, he reads aloud, for himself and Sarah, a passage that has been underlined in red.

"You and one companion are an adequate theater for each other, or you for yourself. Let the people be one to you, and let one be a whole people to you."

"That's funny," Simon says, "for someone making sculpture for the city of Brussels."

"Liège," Sarah says, "not Brussels. Brussels has that silly fountain of the little boy peeing."

He thinks: it might have been Sarah who underlined that passage; there was no knowing. Or Ben Demos. "It is a dangerous thing to extend your hand to the people": how far was that from "Let the people be one to you, and let one be a whole people to you"?

"That's the essay on solitude," Sarah says. "There should be one on being punctual; it's after midnight." She sips from her glass. They are sitting on the large square mattress. Why are all mattresses associated with Sarah so large? Simon wonders.

"That part"—his finger traces the line in the dim light —"that's like a definition of marriage." Damn fool; why bring that up now?

" 'Let one be a whole people to you . . .' " Sarah muses. "Is that the way it is, Simon? You've been married twice." She left the question of whether she was married at all dangling, but present. "Is that possible?"

He stretches out on his stomach, places the glass of brandy on the floor and pulls the book down next to them. "I know more about the second part," he says. "For the last ten years I've been busy with people. I never *thought* much about marriage until the trouble in Chicago. I just did it."

Sarah sat next to him on the mattress, one leg tucked

under the other; her long red skirt covered part of his right arm. He wondered at the picture they would make if Marcus entered quietly, standing in the flap doorway of the tent. There was, after all, no lock on the studio door. Speaking of husbands . . .

"It depends a lot on who that 'one' is," Simon says. "My first wife was never just one. She was so many that she finally went—off."

"Was that when you fell asleep for nine years?"

"That was me—the Rip Van Winkle of marriage."

Simon's skin is beginning to prickle. Waiting for the missing Marcus is bad enough without a marathon on forbidden subjects.

Sarah stands up and tosses off the rest of her Armagnac. "Brandy makes my pulse pound. I can actually hear my heart." She bends over Simon and presses her turtle-necked breast against his ear.

"Can you hear?"

"Yes. But I can't quite make out what it's saying."

"Ah," Sarah says. "I think I'm a little drunk and it feels nice and I hope you are, too, because I don't want to be drunk alone and what it's saying is that I don't see any reason for people to get married, unless to have a baby."

Simon is now a little easier in his skin. "I'm not quite sure why I got married," Simon said. "Not the first time or the second."

"Let's play a game."

"Okay."

"It's called If." She smiled and settled down on a corner of the mattress like a child who has been given permission to do something silly. A cloud of dust arrives in the air. When has Marcus been here last?

"The game is simply: If. Example: If we were married, where would we live?"

Prickling on the back of Simon's neck. Wine was rocking him; his pulse felt deliciously slow.

149

"This game could be dangerous," he said. "You're sure you want to play?"

"A game of chance," Sarah said. "If there's nothing to lose, there's nothing to win."

"Okay," Simon sighed. "Where would we live, if . . . ?"

"You could move in with me."

"Too small. I need a separate study. I work late—you get up early to go to the agency."

"I meant at first. We'd need more room later." Ominous note sounded. Sarah moves in strongly.

Simon defends: "Have you ever lived with a man continuously? Do you know what it's like?"

"How long is 'continuously'?"

"Let's say a year."

"No. You make it sound so oppressive."

How, he wondered, did Marcus sleep in that enormous bed of Sarah's in New York? Like a baby, no doubt.

"It can be terrific," he said. "But men and women living together is different."

"We need space," she said. "A co-op smack in midtown."

"Right. I can't live in the suburbs. It's like the owner of a restaurant not eating at his own place. The city is my place." He paused and pressed forward. "But they're expensive, co-ops. How much do you make a year? Don't look at me like that. It's your game."

She looked so stricken that he relented. "Do you realize," he said, winding a handful of black hair in his hand, "that you're talking about a subject I know better than most? Apparently I was born to be married, because I've always *been* married. When I was twenty, to Ariel—I tend to marry women with flowery names. With her I fell asleep for nine years."

"What do you mean, asleep?"

"That was a long time ago. I don't think much about those years. They put me a little behind. Instead of designing cities, I spent them designing stage sets for her dance troupe—dropped out of college, just like you. You were a divorce dropout; I was a marriage dropout. I followed her

from Merce Cunningham to Jean Erdman to Katie Litz.
. . . I was asleep, but she was quite mad, and then I woke
up and went to graduate school ten years after everybody
else."

"Like an army veteran," she said.

"Like an army veteran. So I worked ten times as hard
and married Alexandria and became a grand success and
then a grand failure and here I am, having run away with
you."

"You haven't run away with me; I've run away with
you."

"It's nice we both think that. Eases up on the guilt."

"Do you feel guilty?"

"I should call Alex, sooner or later."

"For my sake . . ."

"Yes . . . ?" He pressed his face into the tangled hair. It
smelled like spice; she must have shampooed it at the
hotel.

"Make it later," she said. "Me, I've always felt I was born
not to be married. I was always involved with men—starting at age four: his name was Ronald and he had red hair
—but it never occurred to me that continuity was part of
it all. It seemed to me that planning things, structuring
futures—all that could be death to the emotions." She
laughs. "You could have seen me any Tuesday or Wednes-
day in the halls of the Dalton School, explaining to boys
why I didn't want to see them anymore. Then, when I got
more heavily into a sexual life, I wanted it to be a kind of
anarchy."

"That's the closest thing to a political statement I've
heard you make."

"I don't make statements, I don't talk about politics. And
I'm talking about sex."

"It's the same thing. Everything is some kind of politics."

"Not to me. And I'm talking about a freedom that you
can't get unless you're born *not* to be married."

"But how do you sustain that?"

"Ah, silly Simon, with all your degrees. The whole idea

151

is, you don't sustain anything. That's where Marcus came in."

Simon said nothing. He has been waiting for Marcus to come in.

"He's like me," Sarah says. "He improvises a lot. He doesn't stay in one place, he never talks about having children. . . ." She smiles and waves her glass at him: a mock toast. "To anarchy."

Suddenly, very serious, as if something very important were being challenged, Simon asks: "Why, Sarah?"

"Because you can feel more that way. That makes now terrific and later on a game: like the If game. Can we play some more?"

Don't be a hypocrite, Simon thinks. She moved you because of this anarchy; anarchy was what you wanted from her—and perhaps still want.

"Play on," he says.

"Who would be our friends, if . . ." she said.

He thinks, eyes closed, for a moment.

"What usually happens is, some of my friends would stay and some would drop—and vice versa. Linc would stay. I don't see him often, but when I do, we just pick up —it can be after months or even a year."

"My friends might not have that much in common with you," she said.

"Oh?"

"They're mostly in business. Not scholars or intellectuals. One of them gave up everything to follow a man to Italy—she's sort of in the hotel business."

"I have some of those. I wouldn't worry. Besides, how many close friends can people have?"

"But would we have a gregarious life or a quiet one?"

"I need both. I have to be alone for long stretches. Then, suddenly, it's 'Where is everybody?' "

"I'm not so good at parties."

"I love them. Jane Austen said everything happens at parties."

152

The tempo was picking up. Sarah's eyes were bright; her laugh was even brighter, forced.

"I have a million ifs," she says. "What would the sex be like if . . . ? Day after day, week after week. Would we do it every night? Probably not. And what happens to your sense of your body? I *am* my body," she says. "Would that change, I wonder?"

"I've never been my body that much," he says. "I've always been the part that thinks and plans."

"And where would we spend weekends, and how—and how do you arrange about closets and about who says I'm sorry first if there's trouble?"

Simon has a fleeting sense of impending success. Something in the sound and rhythm of Sarah's speculations gives him the feeling that whatever was supposed to work in this crazy experiment of his was starting to work. Was it simply that she was letting the idea of a future into her head—wined, jet-lagged, brandied or not? It was like that moment Simon had experiences with students when a student passes the point of engagement with a problem—and the teacher knows that a solution, of one kind or another, is on the way.

Sarah is changing.

Simon holds the changing Sarah in his arms. His breathing regulates hers, evening out their rhythm, thinning out the tension of their waiting. They doze away as easily as if they were in her apartment in New York, with nothing more to worry about than his usual deadline for tiptoeing home.

Simon wakes to a faint rose light in the corners of the room.

"Sarah . . ."

"Ummm . . . what?"

"It's morning."

"What time . . . ?"

"Not morning, exactly. It's five o'clock. I guess Marcus isn't coming, after all."

153

"I guess not. I don't feel as if I was asleep," she says. "We were playing a game."

"The If game."

"Yes." She stretches up toward him. "And what if," she says languidly, "what if we had a baby?"

He felt a surge of blood to his face. Was he catching Sarah's style; were blood tides so readable in the varying shades of complexion visible in him, too? He didn't want to spoil things; selfishly, he didn't want to have to give up the odd premonition of success he'd had before they'd fallen asleep—even though the terms of that success were undefined. Don't let it get too heavy, he thinks. It's only an if. He is groping for something light to say that will treat the idea of having a baby with respect but without too much reality. When suddenly Sarah lightens it all in her own wild way. She pulls up her white turtleneck sweater; all at once he is staring into her small round breasts, elegant little white cups with tiny nipples.

"Would I be able to breast-feed the baby, I wonder?" she says. "What do you think, Simon, are my breasts too small to suckle a baby?" She kneels on the mattress, knees close together, and lowers her breasts to an inch above Simon's mouth. The perfume from her breasts confused him and she was pulling her sweater over her head, sprinkling him with hairpins, and one of the carefully woven braids spilled down into his eyes and he shook it away while she took his head in both hands and pressed his mouth over her breast, lowering her voice to a whisper, as if she were afraid of being overheard, saying, "Will I be able to breast-feed, Simon—tell me, can I?"

And he nursed her nipple, feeling how much fuller her little breasts were when she leaned over him feeding him like this, actually sensing that instant as nursing, the act of taking from her body, and it excited him as much as her sudden craziness in taking off her clothes while they waited for Marcus. And precisely at the same time, he was making the decision to stop this, to make Sarah put her sweater back on, braid her hair up as neatly as she could, sit on the chair next to Marcus's mattress; behave as the circumstances demanded.

But the circumstances had changed. Simon stood up and pulled Sarah with him.

"Simon . . ."

"Not here. Not on that. His . . ."

"I don't care. Anywhere . . ."

Anywhere was the floor; but in reaching it Simon brushed the green Buddha from its stand; it shattered around them. Shards were everywhere while Sarah released him from his clothes.

"Be careful."

"Shh-h-h."

"Suckle me while you do that . . . please . . ."

Their making of love was slow and measured; as if, once being mad enough to act out nursing child and erotic carelessness with open doors, they might as well make love long and lingeringly. To comply with Sarah's desire that he be simultaneously lover and child, Simon hovers in and above her, arching, curved, like one of Marcus's birdlike forms, feeling her draw at him while he draws at her breasts. He plays with a nipple, as he has seen Matthew play with Alexandria—barely enclosing it—then takes it in his mouth and grazes his teeth lightly over it. Sarah gasps and holds his head tightly. Still playing the infant, he holds on to the other breast: they both wait for him to transfer his sucking/kiss from one to the other. Uncharacteristically, her mouth is entirely neglected. Something else is happening here: mouths speak out, mouth on mouth implies some kind of discourse, no matter how mute; mouth on breast, breast in mouth, is downflowing, ingoing, a self-sustaining, self-enclosing language of bodies and selves. The coming is long and agonizing for both of them; Sarah makes small, sweet sounds and will not let his head leave her breast afterward.

"So much," Sarah murmurs.

"I may never come again," Simon says.

"I'm getting mystical."

"How?"

"I think if I didn't have the equalizer in, I'd have your child now."

The time has come to be ruthless. A weak, false note can ruin everything. At such a moment, Simon knows it is a risk. Bluntly, he says, "I already have my child." The only reaction is: the hand that holds his head to her breast lightens its pressure. He is free to raise his head.

Simon looks at Sarah's gray-eyed gaze. Afraid of what he will see, he sees an alert gleam, no despair or anger; the ifs are over; his premonition of success stays alive in his chest. He remembers running to her apartment in the rain, the taste of vomit in his mouth, the shocked look on Greer's face, the cemetery city below them, remembers the unexpected decision to come away with her, the genesis of Project Sarah. It was for this.

She surprised him when she spoke.

"Tell me about Matthew." It was the first time she'd spoken his name.

"I'm not a good father," he said. "I have no real gift for it. He's a bright, energetic three-year-old, with lots of words, and he's afraid of a lot of things, and I'm no real help. Alex bought him a puppy in Canada. I wouldn't have thought to do it. I love him very much. Something jumps in my chest when I see him and I guess that means love. But I don't have the patience to talk to him in ways that interest him. I forget to make time to be with him and then I'm surprised when he sulks. I forget to bring him presents. But worst of all, I'm as awkward with him as if he were a nephew, not a son; or the child of a friend, a child I don't know very well. I think he knows I'm not a very good father."

Simon stood up. "But he's my child," he said, "and I think he's enough." He adds, with careful coolness: "We seem to have broken an object. I hope it wasn't valuable."

Instead of weeping or looking hurt, Sarah looked up at him from the debris of green Buddha fragments in which she lay, and said:

"*Why* do you think you don't make a good father?"

Her way of asking sudden, clear questions surprised him into thought, into a quick glimpse of a truth.

"Maybe it's because a child, any child, is *the* essential self. A little animal self, no groupness, no structure. Oh, we try to lay the family structure on it. Drop off at an aunt—Alex has a sister—pick up at school. Be like Daddy, be like Mother. But essentially it's still a little monster. I love him and he's *my* monster, but I'm the self subordinated to—oh, call it anything, call it civilization, cities. A child, any child, is pre-city, pre-anything."

Sarah half rose, crouched in front of him. Her eyes had a kind of excited stare; she had not subsided into calm after making love. There were times when fulfillment seemed to arouse her as much as it satisfied her. Physical passion fed other passions. She touched his knee, tentatively.

"I'm a little like that," she said. "I'm not civilized, not really. You have to stay in one place for that. I never have. Nomads don't build civilizations."

"Then I can practice on you, and learn how to be with my kid."

She ignored his words, his light tone. "Look at me," she said. "I don't live with one man all the time . . . I didn't finish college . . . I don't have a child . . . my business is seasonal . . . my only sister is dead . . . my mother and father have split and my father is awfully sick. . . ." She was kneeling before him again; it was a familiar gesture for her: each time it had been for emphasis, as if this was her stance, her physical way to communicate strong conviction, mixed with an imploring style. "Simon, I exist here with you. . . ." The rhythm and pace began to speed up. "Right here and now . . . with you touching my body . . . and touching any other part of me my body touches . . ." He was steadying his gaze on her face and trying to follow what she was saying; the pace and the intensity, even the sense, made it difficult to stay with. "Simon, I'm just an animal soul. . . . I'm only interested in you and me in this crazy cave. . . . You extend me. . . . You finish me. . . . I'm happy with you."

He bent toward her to stop the flow of words. He used his mouth. Project Sarah was beginning to work. But he would have felt more prepared for some desperate lapse into misery than this intense, isolated, isolating happiness. Even as he held his mouth to hers and felt her hand between his legs he thought: suppose he succeeded after all? What would he *do* with Sarah's happiness if he *could* create it?

The thought was blocked off by the sight of Sarah suddenly kneeling on all fours amid the scattered shards of statuary, grasping for him first with her hands, then her mouth, murmuring crazily around him, still wet from herself: "In my mouth . . . come . . . if I can make you come now . . . we won't wait anymore . . . I don't care what I promised . . . I don't want a baby . . . I don't want anything . . . I just want us . . . let's *be* our bodies, Simon . . . come. . . ."

Now it was Sarah who nursed; as desperate as any infant blindly searching for satisfaction with its open mouth, tongue; she enclosed him completely, held him for what seemed whole moments, then returned to the eager suckling. With one hand she held him to and in her moving mouth; the other hand disappeared from view. The murmurous, muffled sounds she made were all mixed up with giving and receiving pleasure, the nourishment of surprise given freely, of simultaneously touching herself, her "friend." She was being her body and he was being his and when it ended it was impossible to know who was getting and who was giving; it did not matter.

Simon felt dizzy, lost in surprised, soft sensation, but lost, too, in a kind of anxious, sensuous falling. Was this being happy?

Afterward she cradled him, loose and wet, against her face, whispering—as if now she was afraid of being overheard: "Let's do everything and if we think about it let's only think how happy we are to be doing what we're doing.

158

Every time I do anything the least bit sudden or inventive or crazy, I think of all the times I've done things, even exciting things, cold-heartedly, cold-bloodedly. Simon, it never occurred to me that you could do those things and love somebody, too. . . ." Her voice was hoarser and hoarser, hard to hear. "I've been doing all this without love—and loving without doing all this—for so long. But to have both together . . ."

The wetness changed, grew thick and warm. Simon felt —then saw—a red splotch on his thigh. Her nose was bleeding. Great gobs began to soak down from her face to his flesh and to the floor.

"Simon," she said, "I—L—L—" Her stammer on the word melted into the clutch of the blood at her nose and throat. But it didn't matter, he thought, as he turned her head toward him and pressed a folded handkerchief tightly against her left nostril.

"I'm sorry. . . ."

"Shh-h-h."

It didn't matter. He'd learned more than he'd bargained for. A stammered *L* on a sea of blood. Sarah had confessed that she was not merely doing happiness. She was doing love. He should have known it was coming. The dream should have told him. Violence was a message that happiness was being transformed to something else: for the moment it went by the name of love. Simon pressed hard and waited for fear, for the sickening fall of anxiety into the stomach. Nothing happened. Information had been exchanged, that was all.

"I—L—L" Nothing Marcus could have told him about Sarah could compare to that as information, past or present.

Beyond her he saw, through the half-opened tent flap, the silhouette of one of Marcus's standing forms: a sphere with extensions—like arms—reaching out on all sides. Simon saw himself, with a rush of unexpected pleasure, standing in a square, like the one he'd worked on in Kyoto, supervising the placement of such an object in a public

159

space: measuring how people could pass by it with ease and joy in viewing; looking out of a window forty floors above, to see how it blocked or opened the vista for the thousands of eyes that would see it; opposing it with the splash of a fountain or the elegant austerity of a line of thin trees on either side; with benches, perhaps, so the public need not always keep moving past, but could linger: could take a private moment, alone or together, in a public space occasionally, a little, he supposed, like the moment he and Sarah had just taken in Marcus's public space, in which they still lingered, exhausted. He had escaped from the intensity of that moment and the information it had given him. Now he was back. He held her, bloody and silent, as they rocked together on the studio floor. He didn't care if Marcus was imaginary, real, dead, alive—was coming up the stairs or would never arrive. For the time being there was nothing more he needed to know about Sarah.

7

THE NEXT DAY they flew to Avignon. They rented a little red Ford and drove to Aigues-Mortes, arriving in time for lunch at the inn near the Romanesque church. It was a damp spring in Provence and the sun glowed through alternating gray clouds and patches of brilliant blue sky. "Ambivalent spring," Sarah called it. "It doesn't know if it's happy or not." She would take it, as long as it didn't rain. She wanted clear weather until they got to Les Baux by early evening. The mysterious tranquillity of Les Baux had been the original motive for the trip. It was something they were to experience together; it must not be spoiled.

But first came other surprises. There were nightingales on the walls at Tarascon. The strange, hesitant melody had a peculiar loveliness. It was too sad for Simon.

"How do you know they're nightingales?"

"They are. Tarascon is famous for them. They used to cover the city walls; now there are only a few."

"I don't think I've ever heard a nightingale before."

"There are no nightingales in America."

"Poor America."

"Lucky us."

The day was cool, chilly, and Sarah sat close to him in the car.

8

HE WAS AS UNPREPARED for the desolation of the Camargue country as he had been for the strange, unbroken line of the nightingale melody. Long, flat stretches of salt marshes ranged on either side of the car. Coarse, spiky grasses were intersected by shallow streams and canals. Here and there on the white and shimmering horizon there hulked farmhouses, flanked by a short line of black cypresses, bending in the wind.

When they saw the herd of wild white horses, he stopped the car and they got out to look. The horses were small: not quite full-sized but not ponies, either.

"They're called *manades,*" Sarah said.

"What does that mean?"

"I don't know. Sometimes you see the local men riding them."

Against the bleak landscape the miniature horses appeared like some Japanese etching; one of them leaped, nervously, and sent the others scampering. They made a noise like steel strings.

She whispered, as if there were anyone to overhear them, "Aren't they the wildest possible things you could imagine? Like child horses who stopped growing."

Ten minutes later, crossing a shaky bridge toward Saint-Rémy, they saw a herd of white bulls. The animals were in a broad field, but they crowded close together, moaning nasally and shoving each other with their short horns and milky flanks.

"God," Sarah said. "Every time you think you've found the wildest thing possible, something wilder comes along."

"Would you be jealous if I took another lover?"

"Yes," he said.

"Ah, what would you do?"

" 'His limbs I'd tear . . . and throw all pity on the burning air.' "

"That sounds like Blake."

"How'd you know?"

"It sounded like 'Tyger! Tyger! burning bright' . . . which is the only Blake I remember."

"Where did you go to school?"

"Hampshire. A little experimental school in New England where you didn't *have* to read Blake. But I read a lot of him. He was so full of lines about desire. I was an art history major: that's how I found him—first the pictures, then the poems. . . . But now I've forgotten. I've forgotten everything from college."

They had stopped, as per Sarah's plan, to have lunch at Saintes-Maries. The Rhone, which had joined them a few miles back, murky blue and twisting, fed here into the sea. First had come lizards whisking under the wheels of the car; then a startled flight of what Sarah assured him were ravens. ("I studied up on the local flora and fauna," she said. "I knew I'd get you here and I wanted to do it right.") Then the few shrubs on the hard white surface of the plains thinned down to none—and against the horizon had appeared the rough, strange tower of a fortress which Sarah assured Simon was no fortress but a church.

It was noon, but the wind had blown a mass of clouds together and the sun was a vague coin shape pressed against a gray foil of sky: it gave little light, no heat and not much comfort. On the left a few pine trees appeared and beyond them the cool glimmer of the sea. Sarah's

162

special reason for stopping here for lunch was not the local cuisine or the fact that the body of Mary Magdalene was supposed to be buried in the church. They had, in fact, stocked up a picnic basket with cheeses a crusty bread and a bottle of the local rosé. And neither of them was interested in sacred relics. ("That's why I'm *not* going to work for Linc in Venice," he'd told her, while they'd planned the itinerary. "No relics.")

They sat on the dusty shore of a lagoon, under a line of umbrella pines, eating cheese, drinking wine and talking about Blake; they were waiting for flamingos.

"The Camargue is famous for all sorts of odd birds: flamingos, the ibis, egrets. I want to see them all with you," she said, "But I'll settle for a flight of flamingos. And Saintes-Maries is the best bet."

For the time being they had to make do with mosquitoes and gnats.

"I taught a course in Blake. He's my baby," Simon said.

"What's he got to do with cities?"

"I didn't come out here to discuss the poets of the industrial revolution, which gave us the cities from which I am fleeing with you. More wine, please."

"Why *did* you come? To avoid making decisions?"

"In part."

"The other parts?"

He grazed a hand over her mouth, her eyes, down to her breasts, her stomach. He was on her thighs when she murmured, "I'm not parts. I'm me."

"Do you know that's the second time you've said that? When people start saying things for the second time, that's heavy stuff. Like an old married couple."

They were logy with travel fatigue and wine. They spoke slowly, sighing between sentences. "There will be no flamingos," he said. "This place is flat as a pancake. Where would they come from?"

"Let's wait and hope. I'm *not* jealous," she said. "Except I commit murder in my dreams. And you can't hold people responsible for their dreams."

163

"Can you not," Simon said.

"Anyway, it's part of nature," Sarah said solemnly.

"You mean jealousy is part of love, naturally?"

She rolled over onto her stomach, on the picnic cloth, her face lying in a scatter of bread and cheese crumbs. The curve of her slender buttocks drew his eye and his hand. He felt a bite of desire for her; it stirred in his stomach and below.

From where her arm muffled her mouth she mumbled, "Being jealous is part of desire."

Something perverse, self-protective, stirred in Simon. He couldn't just respond and float toward her, in and out of her, as before. Not now that she'd made her stumbling declaration of love. He had to keep some distance, some control, or the project would go down the drain. He didn't know exactly what he had in mind by this need for protective maneuvering. He just knew it had to be done. Not enough, he hoped, to spoil the pleasure for either of them. Just enough to satisfy some network of nerves in him that called for more control.

"Do you think I'm jealous of Marcus?" he asked.

"Dunno . . ." she said sleepily.

"I would guess the other way around."

"Could be."

"Maybe that's why he didn't show up."

"He'll show up yet. God knows what people have told him about us."

"What people?"

"Cappy Kaprow . . . Edmund . . ."

"And where will he show up?"

"Maybe Venice. He's often in Venice."

Simon runs his hand down her spine.

"Tell me about your course," Sarah says. "I wish I'd studied with you."

"It was a very 1960's course; you know, 'Eros and Apocalypse in Blake.' Everybody thought apocalypse was around the corner in the sixties—and so did Blake. He thought the apocalypse would come about by an improve-

164

ment in sexual desire. Doesn't it sound familiar? The New Jerusalem through sexual freedom? Down with middle-class puritanism. Up with the revolutionary orgasm."

"Must have been a popular course."

"A smash. The only trouble is: it left out love. Do you want some more wine?"

"No. I'm too sleepy now. I want to be awake for the flamingos. What about love?"

"Well, love brings in possessiveness . . . jealousy. Things pure desire has nothing to do with."

He was waiting for her to sit up; to realize that there was a game of distance and control being played. You needed two players for the game. But her cheek stayed pressed against his thigh, her eyes closed. He would have to escalate.

"You start with desire and energy—which Blake locates in the body—and constitute a kind of heaven."

"Mmmmm."

"But you end with love—which for Blake is a kind of hell."

Small reaction: she turns over on her back, eyes still closed. She says nothing at first. Then: "Sounds to me like he's making a big mistake."

"Oh?"

"Separating the body and the—whatever—the heart, the soul, love. I'm just getting them together. Can't we please, please keep them together?"

He looked at the dark flush over her closed eyes. That was something, he thought. Bringing body and soul together in someone else was no small matter.

He'd thought his foolish little game was ended; they were packing the remnants of food into a basket, wrapping silver foil over the mouth of the bottle of Gigondas, having lost the cork, when he felt some unbearable urge to hold her off, to warn them both about what she'd blurted out in Marcus's studio. It masqueraded in his mind as an urge toward honesty, caution; but he sensed that it might mask even more complex feelings: pressures and

165

angers he had not isolated yet. Perhaps because of this he did not have the nerve to speak out straight. He hid behind the poet of the day.

"I never told you the lines about love."

She looked up from what she was doing, a small squint of apprehension around her eyes.

He quoted:

> "Love seeketh only Self to please,
> To bind another to its delight;
> Joys in another's loss of ease,
> And builds a Hell in Heaven's despite."

"Oh, Simon," she said quietly. For a second she seemed to be considering a number of actions: weeping was possible, in her sudden way, and her eyes might be on the edge; or just a grave disappointment—her voice hinted at that.

He regrets his words, his gambit. Why take a lovely, irresponsible flight and turn it into the usual: misunderstandings, fights, partings?

But again Sarah surprises him. She refuses the gambit, chooses instead to smile, to become again the travel teacher.

"Oh, no," she says, "not here in Provence. Not a few miles from where the troubadours invented the whole idea of romantic love. See up there, those mountains—the Alpilles. There used to be a court that sat there—a court that examined and sat in judgment on the nature of love."

"In general?"

"No. In specific cases—like any other court. It was at Roumanille; we don't have time to go there, this trip. But they would have convicted your poet of false love or some such." Simon is relieved. He does not have the courage of his fears. He will just have to risk Sarah's being in love. Whatever her love was, it did not, yet, seek only self to please.

When they have finished loading the car, she says, "I remember one case, a marvelous one, of a woman who was convinced that her lover was so absolutely perfect that she had taken other lovers to make sure, by comparison, that she wasn't wrong about him being perfect. The question for the court was: is she guilty of infidelity?"

"What was the verdict?"

"Innocent. She had only paid her lover the highest of tributes."

"That's how the court ruled, How about the lover?"

"That's not recorded."

"It's nice I'm not perfect. They were subtle types, those judges," Simon says.

"No." Sarah gazes at Simon over the picnic clutter and the open trunk of the car. "I think they were innocents. The woman was the subtle one. She was testing her lover in some funny way. The court was only a pawn. The way people sometimes use divorce courts for their own weird personal games. And you're testing me."

He feels caught in some crime he hasn't yet had time to fully conceive or execute.

"Just by quoting some lines of a poem?" he says lamely.

"I would have thought," she says, "that desire is what seeks only to please itself; not love."

"I'm not an expert on either one. And I'm not testing anything."

She stood hesitant; he waited. There was a strong wind blowing from the marshes behind them. Strands of Sarah's hair were caught in her lips. Suddenly, from some seclusion of reedy marshes, from one of the canals hidden from their view, behind the town, perhaps, came a flight of birds. They were big, their flight slow and awkward, wide wings beating the still air like pulses. Their beaks were bent, hooked; there must have been easily twenty of them, flying in a triangular formation. The necks were long, long sweeps and the birds were blazing red against that pallid landscape.

"Look," Sarah said, running around the car, her head craned upward. "Look, Simon—I told you." She stood behind him, clasping his waist, excited, following the flight of the flamingos. First nightingales, now flamingos, Simon thought. Some court of love and desire was in session here —but neither the case nor the rules of law were clear. Better to ease off and just feel the quick breathing of a happy Sarah behind him. She stirred against him, crouching low; she was like one of those tense white abbreviated horses they'd seen as they drove down from Avignon, huddling together, nervously nuzzling each other's flanks and necks, even though they had all the wide plains to wander in.

9

THE RAIN WAS SUDDEN, a whipping, windy rain that shook the cypresses along the road and made lines in the sky. It caught them just outside Saint-Rémy: a place composed of not much more than a crumbling Roman arch, the remains of a Roman city and a café. They chose the café, a smoky, seedy place, full of yellow artificial light though it was early afternoon. An unlikely poster announced a boxing match at Arles on Sunday. He drank more of the local wine. Sarah drank tea with lemon leaves. Some people at the bar were discussing the wind. That was all Simon could get, *le vent*.

"They always talk about the wind in Provence," Sarah said. "Sometimes the mistral, sometimes just the plain old wind. But the wind is big stuff down here."

"Same thing where I come from," Simon said.

"Where is that?"

"You don't know?"

"You've never mentioned it."

"My God," Simon said. "Chicago. The Windy City. What did you think?"

"I thought New York, I don't know why. No accent."

"I left when I was a teen-ager."

He gazed at the reverse imprint of the boxing poster in the window. "I fought in the Golden Gloves, too," he said.

"I thought Golden Gloves was for very poor kids."

"I was a very poor kid. Chicago was full of very poor kids. So they had us fight each other for everybody else's entertainment."

The wind threw a wild wash of rain at the window. The sound was startling.

"Simon, Simon, Simon . . . the things people don't know about each other."

"That's not how you learn about people," he said. The sense that he was reversing himself buzzed in the back of his mind. He remembered shaking information out of Sarah on Revelation Sunday. Still . . . "For example: I haven't hit one single person in my adult life."

"In the ancient Roman town of Saint-Rémy I found out about you being born in Chicago," Sarah whispered to herself, "and the Golden Gloves. Travel!"

"Some gladiator. I lost eight out of ten fights. Quick, Sarah, move your head, this way—yes, don't move, now. There's somebody I don't want to see. My God, they're everywhere."

"Who?"

"That's Lautenbach. The one with the purple shirt and dark glasses; he was with us at Woodlawn that day. God-dam apparatchik. Let's get out of here!"

"It's pouring."

"Run . . ."

10

SARAH KNEW THE WAY; she drove and all during the approach to Les Baux Simon was full of restless anger. He wanted to call Alex; he wanted to speak to Matthew and apologize for everything he's said about being a rotten father; he wanted to know why Marcus had promised to show up and had not; he wanted to know if Sarah had lied about exacting the promise. He was not exempt from his own stifled rage. He wanted to know why he had teased, tormented, "tested" Sarah at Sainte-Marie with Blake and eroticism . . . and all because of a man in a purple shirt and dark glasses who made him feel as if he'd run away and hid in Sarah's body. He wanted to choke his own questioning. What was wrong with hiding in Sarah's body? Her body was not only places you could thrust into. What was this bullshit about bodies and souls being separated and brought together? He was not fit to be with.

Recognizing this, he encouraged Sarah to be a tour guide and deliberately registered only fragments of what she told him. The rain stopped about ten minutes out of Saint-Rémy, as suddenly as it had begun. A gray sunlight washed the air. Simon rolled down the windows of the car. The road to Les Baux led through avenues bordered with trees and flower beds. For the first mile or two there was a sweet perfume on the wind from the flowers of Saint-Rémy. Gradually the countryside grew rocky, bleak: the road wound around the Alpilles, the little Alps, Sarah told him—between tales of the House of Les Baux, the warlike Eagles. Their rebellion was not clearly defined. But even from a distance, the punishment could be glimpsed, since the plain was, for long stretches, entirely flat.

The remains of the village clung to the lip of a cliff. The valley through which they drove was called Val d'Enfer: the Valley of Hell. He did not ask her about the name. As they got closer to Les Baux itself, Sarah said less and less.

"The princes of Les Baux were supposed to have been descended from Balthasar, one of the Three Kings, the Magi."

That was the last remark Simon heard her make. He fell asleep and was astonished to realize it when he woke as Sarah turned off the motor. They had arrived at the hotel: Les Baumanière. She grinned at him as if a joke were being shared. His mouth felt fuzzy with wine and sleep.

The anger was gone. In the grand room with its ornate wood carvings in ceiling corners and its king-sized bed, he fell asleep again, to uneasy dreams.

11

"IT FEELS LIKE you've been away for months."

"I keep running into people on their way to the big conference. It doesn't feel as if I'm away at all."

"Where are you calling from?"

"Paris." From the window he can see down past the cliff's edge to a long gray plain and a curl of river as well. It is an amazing sweep to the eye and it makes lying more difficult. "What shall I bring you?"

"Be conventional. Bring me perfume."

"I'll bring you perfume."

"I'm in the mood to be romantic. Don't you think it's time?" There is an edge to Alex's voice.

"Yes," he says, irritable. "When I get back it will be time. It's a little hard on the phone. Can I say hello to Matthew?"

"He's asleep. Just bring him something, too. He's in his acquisitive phase." She relents a touch. "We're having a heat wave in New York. What's it like in Paris?"

"A perfect spring. I owe you one, Alex."

"That's nice. That's a little romantic, even on the long-distance telephone."

"Tell me what you've been up to," Simon says. He is also listening for footsteps that will announce Sarah.

"The usual: Design Group meeting, free-lance possibility for me there, I think . . . a competition in New Orleans . . . pediatrician with Matthew . . . Jerry and Ruth are giving a fund-raiser for Louise. I had a session this morning at Rutgers about the grant proposal . . . money's tightening up . . . it doesn't look good. That's about it."

He is thinking: Council meetings . . . fund-raisers . . .

171

pediatricians . . . When did our lives become so institutional? Or is it only that since Chicago, the personal has shrunk, day by day, leaving the public commitments more visible? Or only since Sarah? He visualizes Alex, small, slender, slicing the air gracefully in a small body's arc; broad forehead and close-cropped hair: her combination of intelligence and high style. With the picture comes a wish to be with her: a wish for the comfort of her strong, straight, clear vision of things, her reasonableness. Alexandria would not raise a glass to anarchy, ever.

"I miss you," he says, glad not to have to lie, or be silent.

"Do you?" Alex says. "I was wondering. It's not mandatory on such a short trip. But it's nice. When you come back, let's leave Matthew with Jerry and Ruth or my mother for a whole Saturday, lock the door, turn off the phone, take off our clothes and make good use of some of that perfume you're going to bring me and a bottle of wine and each other. Is this illegal talk over the transatlantic line?"

The door opens. It is Sarah, gay and voluble. "Damn," she says, laughing. "I'm menstruating. Would you believe it? Bleeding like a stuck pig and all I have is one tampon. If that's room service, I could use a martini."

Simon has covered the mouthpiece with his hand. There is no way to know what Alex has heard. He shakes his head and raises his eyes in a plea for quiet.

"Sorry," he says. "That was room service. No, it's not illegal. I'm sure the operator wishes us well. And I think it's a grand idea. Life can't be all meetings."

"In that case I promise not to ask you about Greer or Linc or anything. This must be costing you a fortune. Call me from Venice. Oh, I forgot: you got a letter you might be interested in. From the President of the United States."

He remembers with clarity of dreams the small room in Chicago, the conversations with Ben Demos, the feverish writing of the letter to the President. Institutions . . . Cappy Kaprow . . . Sarah . . . They are all coming too close to each other. He has a strong desire *not* to know

172

what is in that letter. For the moment, humanizing cities interests him not at all.

"It's nothing," he says. Out of the corner of one eye he sees Sarah, no longer gay and not at all voluble, doing something in the bathroom. As he watches she closes the door very softly. "It's just a questionnaire. Speaking of Presidents, there was a wild anti-Vietnam demonstration right near the hotel. It seemed strange here somehow. Don't bother with the questionnaire. I'll open it when that son of a bitch is out of the White House. Put it with the rest of the mail." There is no danger in this particular lie. Alex would never open a letter addressed to someone else.

"I—"

He interrupts her. "I love you," he says, wanting to say it before she does. He feels quietly triumphant.

12

ONLY A FEW HOURS after telling Sarah he'd never struck a person in his adult life, Simon almost hit Lautenbach in the hotel dining room. The plan was to have a drink before dinner and then walk to the top of Les Baux at the precise pre-twilight hour recommended by the *Guide Michelin* and by Sarah, for the full effect of the ruined city.

They'd walked, first, past a pool in which swam ducks, so tame after red flamingo flights. Sarah, too, was all in red: long crimson skirt covering a matching leotard and only a black semiprecious stone on a silver chain to break the monochrome. Something somber and lovely hovered in her face. Simon was sharpening an interior edge—for what, he had no idea. Both of them were pausing in their individual landscapes, rhythms slowed. Each of them had the sense that something—some sequel—was expected of them. For the first time in days, the sense of being in flight was diminished.

173

"Was that your wife on the phone?" Sarah asked.

"Yes."

"I'm glad."

"Oh?"

"It means she's still alive."

"Sarah, dreams don't kill."

"Ah, don't they?"

"Not those kind."

(*"Everything,"* he remembered Sarah saying, gaily, on the Paris sidewalk outside Lapérouse, *"is a dream."* It was an idea he hated.)

"I hope she didn't hear that about my bleeding."

13

M. THULIER WAS as delighted to see Sarah as the mustache had been at Lapérouse. Clean-shaven, M. Thulier, but his adornments were his paintings and his dining room. Simon and Sarah stood a few moments in the center of the main room, which, M. Thulier told them, had formerly been part of an olive mill. A well in the middle was where the olives were washed before being pressed for oil. Now it was a lovely confusion of flowers: red, yellow, blue and a strange large purple flower, like something out of Gauguin, reminding Simon that they were in the south after all.

They sat in a corner in large, thronelike chairs before a gigantic fireplace that took half the wall; in it one log flickered lightly; the evening was cool. M. Thulier had the courtesy not to ask how M. Marcus was.

As if to celebrate having arrived at their primary destination, they ordered champagne. M. Thulier made more of a fuss than Simon cared for. But then, as if to ransom himself, unexpectedly he advised them not to have a grand wine with their spring lamb, if that was to be their choice; he suggested a bottle of the local rosé, Gigondas, and left them, at last, to their champagne.

It was early, not yet seven, and they were the only ones in the drinking alcove. Then an invasion: five Americans —three men and two women—the men middle-aged, one woman quite young, the other elegant and white-haired. They were in the middle of a chaotic and fervent discussion. Simon had an idea that drinks had been served in their rooms before the round they ordered now. One of them, Simon saw with a sick feeling in his stomach, was the man from Saint-Rémy, sans purple shirt and sans dark glasses; Lautenbach. He was Greer's "theoretician"—the academic front for the New Town operation. The champagne moment was shattered.

". . . The city is *always* falling apart, in the consciousness of the people who live in it."

". . . But the history is not *in* the city but in the *loss* of a city—the inevitable loss of relationships."

". . . Joyce is the great example . . . son, father, mother, lover, searching for each other through a myth and a history."

"Let's get out of here," Simon says softly. "I can't stand hearing this awful stuff."

Sarah's eyes are full of fascination. "That's the man we ran away from at Saint Rémy, isn't it?"

". . . It's no accident that the great city novel gave us the stream of consciousness. Each individual is conscious of himself, but no people are conscious of themselves collectively."

Simon sips his champagne and tries to shut out as much as he can.

". . . That's not the way it felt a few years ago. Big change was in the air."

"Kennedy, then Johnson. Nixon and Cambodia . . ."

"Disfranchised blacks . . . anxious middle class who have no home place."

"Kids playing death games with drugs only blacks used to use."

175

"No sense of community . . . how do you do anything in cities without a sense of community?"

"I can't believe," Simon says, pouring more champagne, "that only this afternoon I heard nightingales singing at Tarascon."

There is a trickle of diners in the doorway. Three Frenchmen in their inevitable dark, narrow suits and white shirts. Simon gathers his courage.

"Sarah," he says, "do exactly what I say. This has probably never been done at Les Baumanière, three stars and all, at least not cold sober—"

"You're not *cold* sober. There's only half the bottle left."

"Stand up. First finish your glass. Right. Now stand up and follow me. Take your glass and don't flinch."

He reaches down, grasps the bottle, wraps it securely in the napkin lying athwart the cooling stand and rises. As they pass the Americans' table en route to the door, glasses and sweating bottle in hand, en route to facing M. Thulier at the doorway, Lautenbach sees Simon.

"Shafer?"

Simon stops. Sarah, just behind him, also stops.

"I beg your pardon?" Simon says.

Lautenbach senses Simon's coolness immediately. He flushes but does not know how to stop now.

"Aren't you Simon Shafer?"

"Yes."

"I'm Conrad Lautenbach: I work for Bill Greer. Wood-lawn, about a month ago . . ."

"I'm sorry," Simon says. He shrugs.

Lautenbach's companions look uncomfortable. Lautenbach addresses them. "This is Simon Shafer, one of the best city planners we have . . . the man who almost changed the face of Chicago."

That "we" and that "almost," Simon thinks. Someone has to pay for that "we" and that "almost." He feels a surge of movement from his waist to his hands. He realizes, with a surreal surprise, that he is about to smash his fist into

176

Lautenbach's nervous smile. It is a touchy moment, but he breathes deeply and it passes. Instead, he bends forward in a bow. "No," he says. "You must mean some other Simon Shafer." And leads Sarah out of the room in their glass-and-bottle parade.

14

ON THE WAY UP to the top of Les Baux, the mood is now merry.

"Thank God M. Thulier was seating somebody when we got to the door," Sarah says. "I never could have carried it off."

"You were superb."

"But how will we ever go back for dinner?"

"I've ruined your career," Simon says.

"The world well lost for love," Sarah says. They stop for a sip of champagne on their rocky route. "I'll send all my clients to the Côte d'Azur instead."

"It could have been worse. I was about to take a sock at him."

"With your golden gloves. Why? Are you hungry to hit somebody—or was it him?"

"Right now," Simon says, "not Lautenbach or Greer or anybody should kill this moment. Isn't that why we're drinking champagne?" They are back in flight. Simon registers this with pleasure.

"The last time I saw you this angry," Sarah says, "was when that black fellow broke into our room in Paris, after the demonstration."

"He didn't break in. I helped him into the room."

"Don't evade. You weren't even mad when Marcus didn't show up as promised. You only get mad when the outside breaks in on us. Or was it because he mentioned what happened in Chicago?"

He kisses her and says, "Dear God, let me not be mad. . . ."

"That's another quote," she says, suspicious but happy.

They are halfway up the road to the summit of Les Baux. On the left the mountain becomes only a hill sloping down to the plain. The day's clouds have scattered and the fading spring sun now gives a clear, glassy light. But it is fading quickly. If they are to be at the top with some light to see by, they have to start moving.

"*Crépuscule* . . ." he intones. "Repeat after me: *Crépuscule*. . . ."

Behind them, as they turned right toward the top of the cliff, the sun hovered above the horizon.

"Ten minutes of light, *crépuscule* or not," Sarah said. "Maybe fifteen, if we're lucky."

It was a steep, narrow lane that turned onto a larger plateau; on the left, space for cars to park; on the right, a superb view of the valley. But it was not the top. The street was paved with rock and there was rock all around them; a bare stone wall with holes where there had been windows; the insides of buildings had been scooped out like cheese from rind. Windows and doorways, in fact, opened everywhere onto their own emptiness. A Protestant temple was a shambles of miscellaneous stones; cats nested in debris not far from a souvenir shop with picture postcards and posters for sale. What a picture of desolation! There was something outrageous about the fact that no one had ever tried to restore the town. Old ladies in black dresses carried sacks of groceries from a store somewhere above, but it was all dead and presented proudly to the tourist as dead. Some of the houses seemed to be growing out of the cliffs themselves.

"Weird," Simon muttered.

"Wait," Sarah counseled. "We're not at the top yet."

"These buildings are Renaissance. I'm not sure exactly when. Shall we buy a guidebook?"

"No. More champagne."

They leaned against a wall and drank, ignoring a group of tourists complete with guide and camera.

"What's eerie is that everything is rock—the street, the ruins, everything backed from the mountain. Look at the rut of that wheel actually *in* the street. Centuries . . ."

Almost at the top, at the crag, they veered off to the right, past a naked wall with holes for windows and doors. Above them they could see a broad, grassy platform with huge pieces of rock cut into towers and battlements: parts of a giant's castle in a fairy tale or a dream.

Their detour was to a small cemetery. There was enough light, still, to read names, dates and even inscriptions.

"Ismail Ibrahim, 1236–1290."

"Muhammed El-Moran. I can't read the date."

"Why would there be a Muslim cemetery here?"

"I don't know. I'm not your guide anymore, I'm your lover."

He poured more champagne for each of them, carefully reserving some for the ascent to the top.

"You are full of elegant information. I would much rather be here with you than down below listening to the living dead talk about the drug-torn youth of our cities."

"My sister, Jephtha, was their drug-torn youth; she was on speed by the time she was eleven. That's amphetamine."

"I know what speed is. My friend Ben Demos used to be on it for diets. Then he got to like it because it kept him from being depressed." He wavered for a moment and decided not to tell her about Ben's presence, his visits. "He was the first of my gang of friends to die. That always gives a special place."

"Jephtha was mine," Sarah said. "People who took speed all seem to be dead." She rested her glass on a tilting gravestone with a flat top. "But Jephtha didn't just do speed. After a while she did everything."

"Poor Edmund."

"You do like my father, don't you?"

"How do you know?"

"You picked up my habit of calling him by his first name, instead of referring to 'your father.' "

"How about your mother?"

"Ah, Mother was—and is—Mother. She refused to believe what was happening to Jephtha. Edmund had to bail her out of everything. I was still a kid when I saw my first jail. She was busted, our first summer on Nantucket. But Nantucket had kind of a sweet jail. They didn't stay so sweet. The drugs got harder and the jails got tougher. That was *our* sixties."

"How did she die?" Where, Simon wondered, had he got the courage to ask that question? Was he looking for some turning point to which he could press Sarah; some soft spot in the stone all around them that could give way into some part of Sarah he was still locked out of?

"She died . . ." Sarah paused. Simon waited carefully. The light was dark rose now; the air was colder but without wind. The pause extended itself. Simon could wait until infinity.

"She died," Sarah said with unexpected passion, "of Zen, of meditation, of communes, of grass, of peace, of heroin overdose, of love, of Reichian orgasms, of speed, of androgyny, of getting into her own head and staying there. She died," Sarah said, "of who she was, and of when she lived."

It was not a turning point. There was nothing he could press. He took a quick sounding and knew that he didn't have the guts, not there in this old Muslim cemetery with the rose light failing, not now.

"Did she look like you?"

"She wasn't as tall. Otherwise, yes."

"Nobody is as tall as you."

He touches her mouth with his hand and kisses her. Here in France, among the exotic nightingales on the walls of Tarascon, among the fluttering of the flamingos on the plains of the Camargue, amid these deserted rocky streets,

180

the vagueness of their earlier lives is becoming more concrete. Details are exchanged, at odd times and places. Lovers, having inferred tastes, sensuality and needs, they are, at last, learning biography. Except it still had some of the ambiguity of fiction; perhaps all biography did. More so, he guessed, because the pressure of time was still there. How to understand things without the benefit of repetition that marriage allows for?

Still, Simon felt his own biography pulling him back. It was part of his rage at Lautenbach. Europe should have been sterilized of any connection with his past before Sarah and he arrived. This was Project Sarah. Concentration was needed, not distraction and least of all anger.

It's hopeless, he thought suddenly. Perhaps he should go home. What was he doing, trying to paste Sarah together among these ruins? These were just the rocks that hadn't hit him as hard as they might have in Chicago. Learning about Sarah's sister and her death wasn't going to help. And Marcus receded whenever they approached.

"Everything is a dream," Sarah had said.

"Everything is politics," he'd told her another time.

Did either of them intend what they'd said to hold up under scrutiny?

In any case, there was no time now for scrutiny.

15

THE SUMMIT WAS as striking as promised. Before they arrived at the castle itself, or what was left of it, they came across small dwellings that were actually kinds of caves now. Inside there were hints of former lives—squared chambers with chimney places still showing blackened parts where fires once burned. The entrances were mostly blocked with debris.

High up in the rock were stone stairs and galleries. The stairs led nowhere and the galleries were unreachable.

"The best view is from the top of the castle," Sarah said.

From there they saw the magnificent view of the great plain to the south. There was a sort of Saracen-like tower that made the Muslim cemetery seem logical even without knowledge of the precise history of the place. And the plain over which they'd driven was stretched out before them, barren and dry. Still, Simon could see threads of canals running through it and a glimmer of silvers, blues and purples mingled with dry brown shades. All the way at the edge of the horizon you could catch a gleam of the edge of the sea.

He was hypnotized: could do or say nothing, just stare. Sarah grasped his arm and turned him halfway around.

From the eastern side the castle looked across the lower Alps; Simon could actually make out what looked like vineyards and olive groves and here and there lines of cypresses. Far down in the valley the olive trees were arranged in orderly squares, beyond them little spurs of the Alpilles, pale and pink in the dying light.

But nearer, just below, was a crazy-looking plain of just rocks of different sizes and shapes. Confusion and order. "Look," Sarah said. The sun was almost below the horizon and in the adjacent quadrant of the sky the moon had risen, pale and almost full. He could make out, from his crowning vantage point, the extraordinary order, now fractured, the once exquisitely arranged contiguity of street to rising street to residence to place of worship, and finally to the now mostly demolished tower from which the deep well of the surrounding countryside was surveyed, was controlled. The entire plan, so practical in origin (the Eagles, l'Aiglons, had to rule their aerie to avoid being destroyed), so eloquent in execution, moved Simon passionately.

Human minds had conceived this amazing place; had planned how the eye would perceive vistas, angles, even colors—long since turned into gray rock. Now, centuries later, the audacity of that vision was still clear, even under the dust of disorder and entropy.

Sarah was saying something. Simon wished, at the moment, that he were not there with her. What was he doing foolishly playing metaphoric reconstruction games with Sarah in this environment, in which every curve, every corner was a reproach to him for bad faith. What would remain of Project Sarah in a month, in a year, in (this is crazy, he thought) a century? How could you compare flesh with stone? And that was exactly what made his stomach tremble at what he was doing with his days and nights.

In a moment the sunlight was entirely gone and only a light wash of moonlight colored the ground and sky. The fall from the plain was almost immediate. Simon was dizzy as they walked around the broken battlements. Heights, or cosmic self-disgust; or a combination of both?

"Well," Sarah said. "What do you think?"

"You can see why they felt so powerful. It's the height. Nobody could get up here without their knowing it."

"That didn't save them. They were too proud and independent, and the old Cardinal what's-his-name . . ."

"Richelieu?"

"He did them in."

Some residue of resentment carried over from the moment before made him ask, "Why did you want us to be here together, almost from the start?"

"I don't really know."

The reply didn't satisfy him, but he let it pass.

They finished the champagne; he held the empty bottle and placed the glasses on a nearby ledge. He said, "It gets dark so quickly."

"We're lucky we have a moon. But then, I think we're just lucky," Sarah said.

"Aren't we lucky," he said.

"Look," Sarah said.

She held up a vial of pills. The modern look of the plastic, the blurry typed words, were strange on that mountaintop.

"I'm down to two a day. Tomorrow could be one. And then . . ."

183

And then, Simon thought. It had an ominous sound. Did she imply regression or completion? But no—the yellow glow of the moonrise and Sarah's small champagne bursts of laughter: happiness, not regression, was in the air. "Things change so fast," Sarah said.

"Nothing's really changed," Simon said carefully.

"Don't be afraid," she said. "I'm not asking for anything. Just because I'm doing love doesn't mean I have to stop doing happiness."

She stepped to the edge of the crumbling cliff and threw the vial of pills over the edge. Without thinking, Simon scrambled forward in a cloud of rock dust and pebbles, trying to catch it before it was completely lost. But he knew it was crazy as he stumbled and slipped in a shifting slide of rocks and earth and felt again the scraping rock edge against his hand and the absolutely unyielding pain.

16

It's all right . . . I mean it's not all right. It hurts like hell. . . but I'll live. It's right there . . . my wrist. I'll get up in a minute . . . not yet. Yes, that's where it hurts . . . yes, oh, there. . . . The pain is so overwhelming, so burning bone deep, so like that first awful instant when it happened in Chicago, that Simon is convinced everything is finished.

He sees it all at once: the arrival at the local hospital (perhaps at Arles, his hand bandaged like Van Gogh's ear) . . . the transfer to the American hospital in Paris . . . the aborted trip . . . the phone call to Alex (by whom: Sarah?) . . . the swift return home . . . Dr. Rowan, the white fanatic of bone. . . . The absolute end of Project Sarah. Even the unthinkable, the unavoidable operation . . . isolated convalescence, being unable to see or speak to Sarah at all.

His eyes have been closed all this time. He opens them

and sees her: dark face, suddenly pale, one gray eye caught by the moonlight, gazing at him. She looks absurdly elegant among the stones, her long red dress like a flag. He is in a half crouch, cradling his wounded hand; her moist hand covers his.

They were sheltered in a slide, a declivity, partly natural, partly created by his slipping body. Others had been there since the seventeenth century. There are candy wrappers, a half-blackened marshmallow and, most astonishingly, a condom, scuffed and dirty, probably used. Tourists, Simon thinks, under the blanket of pain, tourists make cities alike. Renaissance ruins or the New Jersey palisades.

"I'm sorry," he says.

"No . . ."

"So stupid . . ."

"Yes—of me."

"You didn't know I'd be a jackass and run after the pills."

"Why did you?"

"Can you . . . do without them?"

"I don't really know. I thought I'd find out. It was a vote of confidence."

She takes her hand away, delicately, and says something more. He does not hear the words because the pain has become so intense it fills his attention completely. But in some available space beneath this, he is aware of Sarah's face, one gray eye flooded with moonlight, staring at him in concern.

How it moved him! How oddly familiar it looked; as if she'd been looking at him that way for years, standing quite tall, above him in his pain crouch. In some feverish corner of consciousness still open to thought, he decided he would rather continue to feel the pain than to leave Sarah now, than to stop it all in the middle. Whoever had planned the awesome stylings of Les Baux was forgotten; the past and the questions of enduring, of futures, were equally irrelevant.

It meant, of course, that he loved her. That was obvious

185

now. He had probably loved her since that moment in New York when she'd taught him how to set the table (*"the fork on the left, think of . . . fork-lift"*). He had not let himself know it. It was a wisdom he could have done without; one which could carry obligations, demand decisions. What would happen to their precious anarchy now? Could they still *be* their bodies?

The first decision is—not to tell Sarah. He didn't stammer, his nose did not bleed under stress; there was no way for him to tell her that he, too, was now doing love. Strangely, all this made him feel reconnected to his life; was a potential enemy to the situation at hand. There was no figuring that paradox. In the wake of his tumbling revelation he felt a crowd of memories pressing in on him. He wanted none of them. If Sarah could throw her pills away, Simon could throw something away, too. But he would not tell her.

The pain was gone. It was as quick and easy as that. No lingering aftereffect, just—nothing. He'd not thought it could happen this time. But there were surprises still possible. There would be no hospitals at Arles or elsewhere; no phone calls to Alex, no ambulances, no operations; most important of all, no separation from Sarah. It was simple: it was the way he'd realized he loved Sarah, because he couldn't bear not to be with her. He could have felt tricked by the pain. Instead, he felt relieved that it had come, done its work and vanished.

17

THEY DECIDED TO SKIP dinner. Later they would have something light sent to the room. M. Thulier's advice about lamb and wine would go unheeded for the night.

The assumption was: Simon needed rest after his fall. But the real danger was not fatigue or even, apparently, return of pain. It was panic! Simply not telling Sarah what he felt was not the answer. The calm with which he'd received his news felt fragile. How vulnerable would he be? What would be required of him? Not telling Sarah was very different from not telling himself—and he had been told. The famous twilight of Les Baux had come and gone without the promised tranquillity. A black night was pasted against the broad window of their room now. Sarah, dressed still in a half slip, sat in front of a dressing table unthreading her long hair. Simon undressed, gazed at her; brooded. She looked groggy, yawned and murmured something inaudible.

For a travel agent, she was so vulnerable to the exigencies of travel, Simon thought: fatigue, jet lag, alcohol. It was odd, too, he thought, that she'd made no calls to her agency; made no reference to who might be minding the store in her absence. And when he'd asked her how much money she earned, in the If game, she'd shied off. But these were only the small change of anxiety. A larger sense of concern lingered beneath them.

It came encased in, of all things, his father's voice. "Don't get trapped by life," Boris Shafer had said. By life he'd meant women. "You're the kind that gets caught." Boris had, himself, been caught and spent thirty-four years of marriage breaking up and joining together with Simon's mother. In the middle of the night: "I can't take this anymore. So long, Simon . . . sonny." Then the inevitable return, followed by another move: New Jersey, Ohio, Nevada. Anyplace Boris could work out his unworkable automotive inventions and carry on his complicated love affairs under the deliberately blank gaze of Simon's mother. "You're soft when it comes to girls," he'd told Simon. "Don't get trapped. You lose yourself."

Remembering that Chicago-accented Jewish-Russian voice here in southern France made the night, the scrambling plunge into love, even stranger, more troubling. Trapped? Was that it? Losing yourself? Sarah stood up, combing her long black hair.

"Do you think my hair is silly?"

"How can hair be silly?"

"Too long for my age . . ."

"You've never told me your precise age."

"Thirty."

"Too long. But don't change it."

"Marcus says people don't take you seriously if you have long hair." She turned around, her back toward him. Her hair came exactly to the top of her buttocks. He held her around the waist.

"I'm not people." She disengaged and held his bad hand next to her cheek. "How's your poor hand?"

He is aware that she is dressed in a half slip and he is naked. A reversal. He wonders if she is wearing the slip because of some shyness about menstruating? Her usual bedroom costume is absolute nakedness, or one of her many hooded robes of various colors.

By way of reply he takes the hand in question and slides it under the half slip. For once she appears unresponsive. In any case, she slips away from him. Her small breasts tremble as she moves.

There is something she has forgotten to tell him. She hopes it will be all right. They will not be staying at the Gritti Palace. She has a friend, Margaretta Goldoni, who runs a *pensione*. It will be more fun to stay there. Will he mind? He is, please, not to mind.

"Margaretta is a friend from college. A Boston girl. She married an Italian. You'll enjoy her."

"No I won't."

Sarah's eyes turn cloudy. "Why not?"

"I'll probably like her. But I *enjoy* you."

She kisses him on the forehead. "You are such a damned schoolteacher." He admits to the charge.

"Then it's all right?"

Simon says it will be fine. He will call Alex and tell her there was no room at the Gritti. Sarah turns the overhead lights off, leaving only a small light over the bed.

"Does her husband run the *pensione* with her?"

"He ran off without her. A couple of years ago."

"All these absent husbands."

"Sergio is permanently absent. But Margaretta will make us comfortable. And I haven't seen her in a year. God, she was so ambitious—and now running a *pensione*."

Sarah produces a pair of yellow pajamas. They are the first nightclothes he has ever seen her wear. While she puts them on, he calls the restaurant and orders some cold lamb and a half bottle of the Gigondas. He does not ask her why she is wearing pajamas this particular evening. Over the pajamas she wears one of her hooded robes, also yellow, gives him her red one, and they eat their private supper on a table set up on the terrace outside the room. A level below them, the pool winks blankly; no one is out but them, everyone probably still at dinner.

"She actually produced four documentaries before running off with Sergio. One for the Canadian Broadcasting Corporation. What a comedown." Sarah sighs. Life plays tricks.

What about Sarah's ambitions? She surprises him. She spreads mustard on a piece of pink lamb and tells him there are moments when she feels she has missed the boat. The boat, he wonders; he'd thought it was precisely the boat she'd been on all these years.

"I could have had," she says, looking directly across the tiny table at his eyes, the way people look when they want to be sure they're listened to, "a kind of size. Do you know there are days," she adds, "when I think about going back to school and getting a Ph.D. Not that a degree gives you size, but . . ."

"A degree in . . . ?"

"Art history, my aborted major. Edmund always wanted me to go back." Simon pictures the upstairs room in New York, a clutter of *objets,* reproductions, originals, curios; an uncreated montage of taste, as if waiting to be arranged in some order.

"Margaretta and I were going to do a film on the Giottos in Assisi." Her hair hangs down long and straight, below

189

the table. It makes her seem young indeed; an odd mixture: youthful yearnings mixed with regrets, opportunities
for "size" not taken. "We'd done the treatment, ready to
go, when she ran off like that. And now—a *pensione*."

"I think I once saw a film on that subject," he says,
lamely.

"Ah, yes. If you stand still, the world moves on. Somebody else always does it."

"But you've *been* moving on."

Sarah, a quieter, chastened, pajamaed, menstruating
Sarah, raises a glass of rosé and holds it against her cool
cheek.

"Just another way of standing still. Or it seems that way
sometimes."

"Tonight?"

"It's different. You're here with me. But there were
some years—not too long ago—which I'm not too damned
sure about."

Startling, and unfair. People should not threaten to
change during a love affair. It was disconcerting. Love
affairs, by definition, were to be temporary lives, held in
suspension. No one expected lovers to grow and change
with each other. That was for marriage. It was all a confusion of categories.

"What's stopping you from going back to school?"

"It's a silly idea. I've got to make a living."

"There should be a way." Simon realizes, as he speaks,
that he likes the idea of a Sarah concerned with size. It is
not a thought that would have occurred to him before
today. Is this falling in love? Or has Sarah's nostalgia and
the impending Margaretta provided the occasion?"

"It's complicated," Sarah says. She yawns, makes no
move to smother it.

"You are complicated indeed."

"I said *it,* not me."

"Do you separate what you do from what you are?"

"I used to. I used to do a lot of things, Simon. If I wasn't

190

so tired and wine-sleepy, I might be frightened at the things I used to do."

He sits opposite her in his own wine-dazed astonishment. In one day she has gone from flinging away pills in a high-spirits bet on happiness all the way to this touchy tour of a past full of unsuspected dissatisfactions. Giving happiness to Sarah, instead of extending his hand to the people, building a city small enough so that Sarah's cry for help could be heard at the outer gates—this could turn out to be steady work.

In bed, she is ready, for the first time, to go to sleep without making love. Simon is not. He would like to offer her something: a surprise, something in the line of surprises she has brought him.

"I'm nervous about—" she starts.

"Yes . . ."

"—about my bleeding."

How nicely nineteenth-century, he thinks, and kisses her. She responds, licking his lips and mouth wildly. The signals are all confused. On impulse, he goes into the bathroom, brings back a bath towel and spreads it out next to Sarah.

In the dim light from above the bed she seems to be asleep. Her eyes are closed, one arm is thrown across her forehead. Her legs seem enormously long on that great bed. (He has never been in a small bed with Sarah. She seems to live in large beds.) Her breast rises and falls regularly. Yet Simon knows she is not asleep.

He reaches in and removes the tampon. It comes out easily and lies in his hand so naturally. He places it on the towel. A small bubble of frothy blood flickers at the V of Sarah's legs. The V widens, hairs black and finely pink with blood. It feels erotic and tender at the same time. This was Sarah in process, Sarah happening in a secret way—yet right before his eyes. Sarah being her body and he joining in the event by seeing the usually unseen—by

191

reaching a hand forward and touching this new wetness. There could be nothing less social, more personal. It involved no one else, could lead nowhere except to ovulation —and the possible life of that baby she had been toying with and as quickly giving up—and to bleeding again in the regular course of a cycle.

It was an elegant process in its use of secrecy and flow, social only, perhaps, in the odd shame Sarah seemed to feel, and was trying to hide under her arm flung across her eyes. If they were going to play hide-and-seek with selves, if he was going to hide himself in Sarah, this was the way.

"No, please . . ." she says.

"Yes . . ."

"It makes me feel funny."

"You said: let's do everything."

"That's not what I meant."

"Meant? Shh-h-h."

He leans forward. His mouth trails red lines up across the bell of her stomach toward her lips.

"Simon, please."

The signals grow more confused.

18

"So now you're in love."

"I thought you'd be here." Simon had woken unexpectedly in the dark, as if imperiously called. He'd dressed quickly, quietly, and walked up the empty road in the moonlight to the top of the cliff. Everything was still except the cool wind. Ben Demos was waiting, sitting on an overturned piece of flat rock. He was in a rage. Life had made him a specialist in irony and bitterness; death had apparently broadened his range.

"My God, what do you think you were doing—gazing at her menstrual flow and thinking you're one with the movement of life. The *chutzpah!*"

"It looks different to you, on the outside. . . ."

"Touching her quick . . . You schmuck! She's a human being—a woman with a life that started long before she met you, and full of complications that have nothing to do with you."

"That's the way it seemed before. It's different now."

"Because you're in love?"

"No. Because we've been alone together."

"Bullshit. It's because you have the illusion you're re-making her."

"Did you see her throw away those pills? Were you there?"

"I saw, I saw. And what about this talk about 'size,' big-shot planner? She's not a public plaza, or a housing cluster."

"She spoke of 'size,' not me. But people have been known to help each other, Ben."

"Ah, sweet memories of the sixties. We were all helping each other all the time: some of us in public, some in private. I helped you when that cop was trying to break your head in Chicago, in '68. *That's* help. But *size?* Listen, Simon, it's getting out of hand, isn't it?"

"No."

"Then what are you doing up here, a tourist of ruins at four in the morning?"

"I couldn't sleep again after I woke up."

"Why not?"

"How do I know? Sleep is a mystery."

But he knew. He'd woken wondering about the letter from the White House. More mixed signals. The last thing Simon wanted to think about was new projects. Let someone else humanize the cities. He was at work elsewhere.

"You're losing yourself," Ben said.

"If I am, it feels good."

"Feels good is relative. Feels good now, feels bad later."

"Not necessarily. My God, Ben, death doesn't seem to have relieved your pessimism much."

They both faced down toward the dim plain below.

"It's not *my* pessimism we have to talk about. I was born with mine; with me it's a style, like hair growing curly or straight. You've developed yours lately. It's more like a fever. I don't recognize you without your optimism."

"I've still got it, Ben. It's just shifted. I'm making some kind of difference for her."

"Kyoto, Cleveland, Port Said, Chicago . . . and now Sarah Geist. The descent of Simon Shafer—from the body politic to the body."

"Not just the body."

"Call it the personal, the private, the intimate. It's not your field."

"Alex and I—"

"Marriage is different. Especially yours. You're not equipped to handle this kind of project. You were never much good at the self business."

"So I can start now."

"Why? You're good at large stuff. You need a big idea."

"You keep telling me it's 1970—that I should stop extending my hand to the people. Everybody keeps giving me conflicting signals. And look what happened in Chicago. I like the smallness of this; a way of behaving in private. I'm trying something new."

"What you're trying is not exactly new, old friend. Been around awhile." Ben laughed dirtily. It made Simon uncomfortable."

"Wrong, old friend," Simon said. "This is new for me. Besides, it's just for a while. You've only been dead a few years, Ben. Vietnam isn't over . . . the kids talk about ending pollution . . . everybody is breathing very quietly in their own corner . . . trying to get jobs. My students torture me about cities and race and drugs and all kinds of tough bullshit, but they treat it all like just that—some distant bullshit. Nothing to do with them personally. Now,

194

Ben, I've got Sarah to do with, very personally. Why should you come here in the middle of the night and try to take it away from me?"

The moon was gone, hidden behind black clouds; blackness was total, not a glimmer of light anywhere. It was like having your eyes closed. Simon said nothing. He was waiting for Ben to go away.

"Look," Ben's voice said, "you don't know what you're really doing. You think you're here to rebuild Sarah? But suppose she's only a young, pretty woman with some unconventional life arrangements—suppose some sadness and a few pills were only excuses you seized on to run away with her."

"Why would I do that?"

"Because it's *your* city that's a shambles. The project is for you!"

"I've done some good already."

"Have you?"

"Started to bring body and soul together, in a living being. Sex and love, or so she says."

"You may have to be the cement that holds it together."

"She's not making any demands."

"She dreams of killed wives."

"And I dream of my father—his car engines that would run on water, his crashproof plastic fenders. . . . Did he send you?" The moon returned with a burst of yellow. But Ben was still only a voice.

"It was never Project Sarah," Ben said.

"Listen, I've got other directions," Simon said. "There's a letter from the White House waiting for me at home."

"She may need help. Who doesn't? That doesn't change anything. It was your cry for help."

Running downhill in the Renaissance moonlight, Simon wakes Sarah and tells her he loves her. She turns her face toward him. Her breath comes at him, warm with sleep; it carries flavors of acid wine, a wisp of garlic and something like flowers. He bends down and presses his lips onto her mouth. It is an ambitious kiss. He has an insane wish to take from those lips the whole meaning of the silent, sleeping world.

She mumbles something and turns on her side. She does not weep; her nose does not bleed; a fleck of dried snot clings to one nostril. In a second she is asleep again. Simon holds her, uncertain if she has heard him, uncertain if she knows what he wanted her to know; uncertain of everything except that he is happy.

Part Three

PROJECT
SIMON/SARAH

. . . for happiness consists in action, and the supreme good, itself, the very end of life, is action of a certain kind—not quality. Now the manners of men constitute only their quality or characters; but it is by their actions that they are happy, or the contrary.

—Aristotle
Poetics

1

IT WAS EARLY SPRING. Venice was not quite ready to happen. In the gray damp air pieces of boats were being painted, varnished, hung out on walls to dry—a purple-and-gold figurehead, cloth cushions, wood paneling. Simon and Sarah arrived via vaporetto, Sarah sick at her stomach and below, Simon excited, concerned that Sarah should be well; they had so little time.

"Will you make love to me in a gondola?"

"I've never ridden in a gondola. Is it possible?"

"Make it possible," Sarah said.

"Done," Simon said.

Only to find the gondoliers were on strike. On the landing bearing the sign: HERE THE GONDOLA SERVICE, someone had pasted a big NON SERVIZIO. Someone else had tried to tear it off, leaving only strips of paper.

"Would you care to make love on the steamer?" Simon said.

Sarah said, "Please find Margaretta and get me to the *pensione* quickly, or God help me."

Under a light drizzle, Margaretta found them and they walked first, then half ran to the *pensione,* which was a few streets behind the old wooden Accademia Bridge. As

Sarah ran, intent on bathrooms, a sailor on a barge passing under the Accademia called out something raucous, clearly sexual. Margaretta gave him the cuckold's forked sign and helped Sarah into the Pensione Goldoni. They were in Italy.

2

THE ROOM WAS LARGE, blessed with light; Margaretta threw open the shutters and let in more. Predictably, the bed was more than double; vast.

"Can you believe it—a gondolier's strike in Venice? What am I doing in this country?"

"I'm used to strikes."

"Sarah said you're in politics or something."

"Or something . . . urban planning."

"Ah, yes. Well, you'll be able to get a ride—not all the gondoliers are going along with the strike." Margaretta sighed. "In Italy there's always something to hold you up." She looked younger than Sarah, but she was plain: a long, mournful face, sharp nose, small brown eyes and neat, short-cut brown hair.

"The vaporetto picked us up at the station without any trouble."

"Those are different people, the vaporettos." She plumped up pillows and threw open closets, this former maker of documentaries, as if she'd been welcoming guests, professionally, for years. Bleak, gray light filtered into the room. The weather had turned chilly; rain threatened.

"Your friend Mr. Aaron called. You're to meet at Harry's Bar for lunch at one."

Sarah had been queasy on the plane: travel was not all an affirmation of the imagination. She'd headed for the bathroom the minute Margaretta opened the door to their room.

Simon asked Margaretta if she would join them for lunch. He was conscious of her disapproving gaze. She would have to be won over or neutralized. Lunch could be the start.

"I don't know," Margaretta said.

"I would like it if you'd come. Sarah would, too."

"Sarah can speak for herself, if she gets off the bloody pot in time."

"It would be important."

"Oh, come off it, Mr. Shafer. I'm not important to you."

"You're Sarah's friend. That makes you important."

"Why?"

"You know a lot about her I can't know."

"And you think I'll tell you?"

"You might."

"Why should I?"

Simon lightened the tone. "Because I'm nice."

"You're married, aren't you?"

"Yes."

"Then you're not so bloody nice."

"I didn't dream you'd use words like 'bloody.' "

"Oh . . . this is Italy. Most of the people at the *pensione* are British. One picks up the lingo."

"Sarah thinks I'm nice. Doesn't that help?"

"All the worse. What does Marcus think?"

"No one seems to know. He was supposed to show up in Paris, but he never did."

"Sounds like him. What sort of things do you want me to tell you about Sarah?"

"I'm not quite sure."

"Are you sure it's not Marcus you want to find out about?"

"Also."

"I'm not going to tell you anything Sarah won't."

"I'm not out to hurt her."

"What *are* you out for? Or is that a bloody dumb question?"

"Happiness."

From the moment they hit Venice, Simon found himself living on some edge of his nerves he hadn't visited in a while: the kind of edge in which he functioned triple strength at every moment. His attention was focused on every detail of his project: Was Sarah's skin a touch sallow, hinting at yellowness to come? If so, could the pills be got in Europe? How could he get a moment alone with Linc to get a report on Marcus? Could Margaretta add something to the brew of instinct, information and action that made up his intense awareness of Sarah?

He was relieved to learn that falling in love had not dulled the edge of energy and observation. At the same time, he reserved space to enjoy the pleasures of unreality —otherwise known as Venice, otherwise known as being in the strangest city in the world, surrounding himself with water and with Sarah.

It was the kind of nerve-edge alertness he was accustomed to from his best days at work. And though it was intimately connected to the Sarah/Simon relation, it was different from the old Ariel/Simon days: those days of passive following from rehearsal to rehearsal, from one emotional crisis to another. Though something in it had called up the memory—if only to contrast it favorably with the past. The combination of the passivity of the extremely personal and the activity of the professional. It was a delicate balancing act, performed on the thin edge of salvation, pleasure and anxiety.

"I hate pigeons," he said to Sarah. "What am I doing in Venice?"

"There's always business," she said, pointing to the red banner hung across the entrance to the Fenice. It read: CONGRESSO INTERNAZIONALE URBANISTICA.

3

"YOU LOOK DIFFERENT," was the first thing Linc said to him.

"How?"

"Happy."

"It's not hard to be happy in Venice." Simon stalled any serious discussion. It was not yet clear to which party Linc would belong. It was impossible to forget that he had been Alex's friend first.

"It's hard for me," Linc said. "I'm building and waiting for a proper storm."

Simon gazed up at the mottled noon sky. "You may get it."

"It's been this way for days. I need a real change in the structure of the universe to get the storm I need." He laughed. "I'm going a little bonkers. Actually, all I need is a little bit of rough sea—and I'll get it. After lunch I'll give you a demo at the studio. They have computers on this: my weather is scheduled sometime tomorrow, toward evening." Linc crinkled a joint between his fingers and prepared to light it.

"You smoking when you work these days?"

"My dear friend," Linc said from around the ignited joint. "Grass is the least of what's going down these days. Your friend Marcus seems to be involved with lady."

"Lady?"

"Cocaine. What the pulp magazines used to call snow. It's the latest thing."

"You found out something about him?"

"A little. He's a sculptor—"

"I told you that. I saw his stuff in Paris."

"There's a new big piece of his here in Venice. You should see it. It's near the Santa Maria Zobenigo."

In the steady drizzle, gondoliers parade up and down the quay. Some of them carry signs with slogans. All of them wear the traditional yellow straw hat with the blue ribbon.

"He seems to be a European, perhaps Swiss, perhaps French . . . older . . ."

"Older than who?" Simon is impatient.

"Than Sarah. Not like you or me; a lot older. He may be sixty or so. He seems to be connected with some not-so-legitimate elements."

"What elements?"

"Well, for one, there's the matter of cocaine."

Simon is considering whether he's learning more than he wanted to know. Cocaine! Was that why they called him the junkman? Was junk the name for heroin only? Simon's knowledge of drug matters was extremely sketchy. Linc could tell him—but it was not a question he was prepared to ask Linc. He wasn't sure how ready he was for such heavy waters. What was Sarah's hidden life like, after all? He allows Linc to continue at his own pace as they walk in the cool rain toward Harry's Bar, where the others are to meet them for lunch. Linc's report continues: It is not known if Marcus is married or not. He is not in the Venice telephone directory. Linc has been unable to learn where he stays when he is in Venice. Marcus is his given name; his surname is Delmarco. His family is wealthy; scrap metal is the source.

Linc is suntanned, bright with health. The sun has ruled Venice until two days ago. He is glad to see Simon. They pick up some pulse of understanding—an interrupted rhythm that needs only a few moments to reestablish itself between them. Simon has this ease and depth with few. In the past with Ben Demos . . . in the present with Alexandria. He does not have it with his own son. Linc is silent on Sarah. This is part of the subtle second sense of friendship. He offers Simon a toke. Simon declines and asks, instead, if Linc can arrange a meeting with Marcus.

They are almost at Harry's Bar and it is raining slightly. Simon feels sorry for the poor picketing gondoliers.

Linc asks, "What's the connection with Marcus and the girl?"

"The girl's name is Sarah."

"Sarah Delmarco?"

"I'm not sure."

Linc squints at him. "Not sure if she's his wife?"

"That's right."

"You are in a very ambiguous situation, my friend."

"I'm not so sure it's important."

"You're acting as if *he's* damned important."

"That's not the same thing. The things I want to find out may have nothing to do with whether they're married or not."

"Do you really believe that?"

"I've given up believing for the moment."

"In exchange for . . . ?"

"Feeling."

Linc whistles a long, descending whistle. He pulls on the tiny joint, sweetening the moist air between them, and flips the few remaining scraps of marijuana into the canal.

4

"OH, OH, OH, I am exhausted," the Indian said. He was a big chunk of a man, bearded and turbaned. He waved his arms around; clearly one of life's inadvertent comedians. He had got into an argument with one of the striking gondoliers, he told them; not having understood that there were some scabs offering rides, he had been ready to book a ride. The uproar was astonishing to him.

"Italians get quite excited," he said, "though I do not wish to make any national or racial generalizations. You see, I am a Sikh, and in India the Sikhs are considered stupid, thick, you understand; they tell jokes about us, like your Polish jokes. So forgive me."

He sat down and smiled at the group, which had no idea what they were to forgive him for.

"Ram Singh is my associate," Linc said. "He's going to do wonderful things in India someday. In the meantime he's helping me get a storm going here."

"One of the gondoliers struck another one. I cannot stand violence, though my ancestors were fierce warriors."

The tiny shrimp are served, hot with garlic. Sarah finds her stomach again. Harry's Bar is noisy, crowded and as steamy inside as if it were winter, not merely a damp, chill spring. A white Chianti is poured, lemony, then warming. Linc proposes a toast: To Sarah, he says, whose gray eyes and black hair will confound the Italians.

He is flirting with her, Simon thinks. And wonders, sipping Chianti, doesn't he know?

Know what?

That Simon and Sarah were lovers? Of course he knows that. And they are in love?

Ah—a big difference; another matter altogether.

But Linc could not know that. Simon had just found out himself, had hardly assimilated the information; had no idea what to do with it.

Linc has finished with his wine toast and his tiny shrimp. He is completing the rolling of a spectacular joint of what he calls fine old Venetian hash and is offering it to Sarah. She gazes at him for a moment and says, "I'd like to, but I never know if it's going to bring me all the way down." Simon is alert, watching the scene closely. Sarah glances at him; she smiles shyly as if he were a loving parent who might disapprove her naughty behavior. Then she takes a deep toke and holds it down with the assuredness of a long-time smoker. It could be, Simon thinks, an interesting lunch. The pills are resting safely in the canyons of Provence. If Sarah takes a tumble here in Venice . . .

Margaretta passes the hash to Ram Singh without tast-

208

ing. The Indian smokes noisily, like a locomotive, spurting the smoke back out at once. It is Simon's turn. He mimics Sarah's smoking style. No effect, he thinks and thinks it again the second time around. By this time an enormous poached salmon is being served and Margaretta, who is sitting opposite him, is staring at him weepily.

"Is something wrong?" he asks, stupid with helpless courtesy.

"Do you have children?" Margaretta says.

"A son; three years old."

"Do you have a picture of him?"

It would have seemed like a perfectly natural conversation, if it weren't for the eyes full of unshed tears; and Margaretta had not smoked, had drunk only a glass or so of wine. Amazed at what is taking place, Simon finds himself extracting a photograph from his wallet; he is astonished that he has not simply denied having one. It is the only one he carries: a shot of Alex in a white summer dress holding Matthew by the hand, more like a governess than a mother—perhaps because of the white dress, perhaps because she is quite small—Simon standing a little behind them. It was taken at a friend's home, a breezy site a year ago in Chicago, on the lakefront, lovely with summer green. As if it is a matter of simple social grace, Margaretta passes the snapshot around the table and in a matter of seconds Simon is treated to the sight of Sarah carefully examining Alexandria.

Oddly, his first thought is not concern over Sarah's re-action, her state of mind, tumbling, climbing or stable. He is conscious only of an unpleasant sense of having been tricked into a kind of disloyalty. A few admiring remarks about size for age and looking like father and the photograph is back in Simon's wallet. Sarah's face has not changed color. That was key for Sarah. Her blood had signaled no change, no pain.

Over the disorder of coffee, pastry cart and the bill, their table becomes the stopping place for an Israeli urban designer, two architects from Los Angeles accompanied by a poet, and two urban designers who are fresh from mounting a show in San Francisco dealing with imaginary cities. All are in Venice for the Congresso Internazionale Urbanistico at the Fenice, which is to open that evening.

Outside, Simon confronts the dour Margaretta. He is careful to speak to her while Sarah is chatting with Linc and Ram Singh in the doorway.

"What was that tearful children business?" he asks.

Her eyes are dry now. They have a hard glister; they look through and past him.

"Sarah is my friend, even if we don't see each other much. I worry for her."

"What's that got to do with children?"

"Are *you* going to give her a baby?"

"What do you know about Sarah and babies?"

"She wants one."

"Then why hasn't she gone and had one?"

"Fear—maybe."

"Of what?"

"She had a bad abortion once, a long time ago. Left her a bit bloody."

"I know."

"She told you that?"

"You're surprised."

"Sort of."

"Why? Is Sarah so secretive? Even with a lover?"

"She used to be. Not secretive exactly; intensely private."

"But that's what being a lover is—being very private with each other—isn't it?"

Margaretta drew a scarf around her shoulders against the wind. She looked suddenly like an old maid.

"I wouldn't know," she said. "I've been too busy to screw around with married men. I'm trying to make a living." She lowers her voice to a hissing whisper. "Listen," she says. "You be careful with Sarah. Don't make a bloody mess of it. If you kill what she has with Marcus, can you give her something better?"

Ram Singh interrupts, blithely insensitive to tensions between people.

"We will all see each other tonight at the congress, is it not? I am here partly because it is off season and the prices can be afforded for my government. A curiosity, that I am here at all. If you can do anything for a city like Calcutta or Bombay you can save the world. So many of our people live and die in our streets. The slightest improvement in an Indian city one could say will be totally invisible. Or one could say the contrary: that any improvement is an astounding achievement because of the impossible obstacles."

Margaretta shrugs. "One could also say goodbye. And we will not all see each other tonight."

"Goodbye, dear lady," Ram Singh says, bowing so low only his turban is visible. Simon observes how intricate the folds are and wonders if it is hand folded or machine made.

Sarah appears at his side. Her eyes are shining: With anticipation? With apprehension? With the combined effects of wine and hash? With happiness?

5

"THINK OF THIS as a job interview."

"Not in the market."

"I am applying," Linc said, "for a job as your boss. You are the one thing missing from my outfit."

He laughed and yelled something inaudible at Simon over the hideous burr of motors and air vents. A demonstration was in preparation. The air of the floor-through was full of red, acrid smoke. Sarah sat quietly on a cushion provided by a young Indian woman wearing overalls instead of a sari; presumably this was Mrs. Ram Singh.

211

"Get a blower, will you?" Linc called out. A whoosh and the air was clear enough for Simon to see the great circular table on which stood a model made of strange, apparently functionless geometric forms.

"What's this?" Simon asked.

The Indian woman was brooding over the setup of the model. Ram Singh, with a pipe growing out of his clenched teeth, now poked at the plastic dividers that separated the three channels. In each of these channels rested a container. On the farther edge of the table there was a large water tank. It was all very mysterious.

"Santha," Linc said, "let's give our friends a demo, shall we? Ram Singh, give a hand."

"Demo of what, exactly?" Simon asked.

"Of how I'm going to save Venice."

Sarah rose and treading soft as smoke, stood beside Simon. Bald, intense, Linc towered over the project, over everyone.

He pointed to a broad section of the table in front of the tabletop water tank. "Behold," he said. "The Venetian Lagoon. It connects Venice with the sea. But the sea level has been rising, inch by inch, year by year. Venice is actually sinking into the sea. So when a storm comes up over the Adriatic, you get flooding. Like in the disaster of '66. That's the opening gambit—the problem."

Excited, Linc pulled Simon over around to the side for a view of the three furrows.

"These channels link Venice with the sea. Okay—a storm comes up. Ram Singh, the storm!"

Apparently used to these demonstrations, the Indian removed his pipe and whooped up an imitation of an Adriatic storm.

"Santha!"

The young woman threw a switch that opened a gate in the water tank. Sluices of water filled the three channels.

"Now," Linc cried out, "Aaron's defense: end game!" He pressed a switch on the floor with his foot. Compressed air hissed and the containers in each furrow inflated, swiftly, and rose to the top of the channel, blocking the flow of water.

Like a god of the sea, Linc touched the cradle of the lagoon here, touched the equipment of salvation there, talking trancelike all the while about the coastal integrity of cities, of the myth of Venice haunting the imagination —gold, trade, cruelty and love. It was a new Linc, the old Linc without irony, and without a weed to support his dreaming. For a few moments, years vanished into water and it was the Linc who had first entranced Simon at Yale, when wit did not cancel hope, when detachment did not last more than hours, when involvement was as natural as breath. Though he was hovering over miniaturized mechanical objects, still it was an innocent moment, a "before" moment: before disillusion, before violence. Watching him made Simon ache for something not named, something vanished.

Sarah watched them both, intently.

Linc's two assistants put the miniature world back in its natural state: before Linc the Creator ordered the flood and saved the world. It seemed that the central device was the caisson—one of which would lie at the bottom of each of the three channels. When flooding threatened they would inflate with air, rise and block the danger of a submerged Venice. The Italian government had authorized their placement; they were in the lagoon now, awaiting only the proper turbulent weather for a live demonstration.

"It will cost," a sober Ram Singh stated, "seventy million dollars."

"How much of that will be your fee?"

"About four hundred thousand over two years, plus salaries and expenses," Linc said.

"You can't get that in city planning today. Don't you feel guilty?"

"I've paid my dues," Linc said, grinning suddenly. "It's time to collect."

As they are about to leave, a brief noisy thunderstorm

213

breaks out. They linger in the doorway; they can see the whipping waves of the canal. The rain smells cold and fishy. Linc turns to Sarah.

Linc: "How come you've run away with my friend Simon?"

Sarah: "Why do you think?"

Linc: "It's a religious problem."

Sarah: "Religious?

Linc: "At Harry's Bar he told me he was trading believing for feeling. This, my dear Sarah, is a grave responsibility."

Sarah turns and stares inquiringly at Simon.

6

THE RIALTO WAS BUSTLING. The work of the world apparently went on independent of questions of feeling and belief. Goods were bought and sold; money changed hands. The rain had stopped and Sarah, dressed in a blue wraparound dress with a hood, was, once again, the tour guide. Perhaps it was the mercantile atmosphere of the Rialto Bridge; Simon wondered whether you could find a dress like that with a hood ready-made or, if you were addicted to hoods, as Sarah demonstrably was, you had to have them custom made. The unthought question that followed had to do with where Sarah's money might come from, with her seeming unconcern for such questions and with the shadow of Marcus. "The east end of the Rialto used to be the banking center," Sarah intoned. "But money has been replaced by gold—mostly at the western end—and fish and vegetables around the corner. . . . In fact," Sarah continued, "that's where Marcus's family got its original name: Delbanco—later changed to Delmarco."

Simon's nerves tingled. For no good reason, revelations impended.

"He's a Venetian?"

"His family was. A long time ago. Sometimes, when he's high, he jokes about being descended from Shylock."

"Then he's Jewish."

"Yes. Very Jewish, actually. More than most people I know."

"You mean he looks or acts . . . ?"

"It's how he thinks and feels. You'll see. Your Linc smokes a lot, doesn't he?"

Simon pondered the "You'll see." Under the bridge an oarsman poled a barge full of mysterious goods; mysterious because covered by canvas against the rotting spring rain. Simon already "saw" a bit more. Marcus's name was fuller: Marcus Delmarco. That gave a fullness. It went, somehow, with his being sixty years old, with his invisibility. Perhaps it was the historical dimension that granted permission for all fantasy. The Cocaine Merchant of Venice. He decided to answer to the present only—for the present.

"Linc smokes too much, I think. When I first met him, in 1961, he had a short haircut, wore three-button suits and smoked a pipe with straight tobacco."

"What changed him?"

"The pressure of the time. Teaching at Yale, especially in urban policy, he was on the firing line. The students and the newspapers held him responsible for Vietnam—so he began to look into it. It ended up in a peculiar paradox: the up activity of becoming an activist—the words tell you a lot—combined with the down of smoking. At the same time Linc turned into a radical, he turned into a head."

Sarah stepped aside to let a man push a wheelbarrow loaded with cartons past her. She clung to Simon suddenly. "I am delighted to be in Venice with you," she said. "In fact, I want to buy a present."

215

"Margaretta is not so delighted that you're here with me," Simon said.

"She's down on men. I'm the one buying you a present anyway. . . . What did she say?"

"Warned me to treat you right."

"You're treating me fine," Sarah said, and kissed Simon hard on the lips. The Italian shoppers were delighted. "Do you realize," Sarah said, pulling him by the hand toward some shop she had in mind, "that your friend Linc warned me about my responsibility to you, too? Don't they think we can take care of ourselves?"

Sarah browsed among the jewelry boutiques, murmuring about the problems of buying gifts for married men: no monogrammed cigarette lighters, nothing conspicuous. She hung a leather carrying case over his shoulder and gazed, critically. At a little counter within a jewelry bazaar she toyed with a silver ballpoint pen. This, too, was rejected.

Outside, in the gray haze that still covered Venice, she ran her hand over Simon's face and lips, startling him. "Look," she said. "My skin isn't dry anymore. Summer is coming. . . . I feel better having seen your wife's picture."

"Why?"

"Oh, she's pretty. But at least I've seen her."

"I still don't understand why that helps."

"Well"—Sarah groped for the idea—"after all, she's only . . . real."

Unable to find the proper gift, Sarah led the way through the Erberia, around the corner, beside the Grand Canal, to the fish market of Venice. The sea, here, was chopped with whitecaps; there was a wind blowing from the lagoon. The stalls were lined with wet green ferns; there were little red fish, something Simon guessed were eels, shellfish and a stall with only the innards of fish.

At the corner, near the landing, a tall, husky man wearing a blue-striped crew-neck sweater stared at him. He had wild gray hair, brushed it away from his eyes and turned quickly when Simon's gaze caught his own.

"My God," Sarah murmured. She smiled.

Simon knew at once. It was the Marcus of dreams. There was no question.

"That's him, isn't it?"

"Yes."

"Let's go talk to him."

She smiled and shook her head. "I'm going back to find you a present." Marcus allowed himself a backward glance. Simon raised a hand and began to approach him. Marcus turned away and walked with a long, loping stride.

Surprising himself, Simon started to run. Marcus heard —or felt—the pursuit. Without looking back, he began to run, also. Not letting himself think about what he was doing, Simon chased Marcus along the waterfront of Venice. Marcus was fast, a gray wraith weaving in and out of obstacles: vendors, parked bicycles; unlikely ones—a young nun carrying a set of oars, an old man with maps for tourists who had not yet arrived. Marcus kept a lead, though Simon had the sense that he was closing the ground between them. His heart was clumping in his chest louder than his feet on the cobblestones, his breath was shorter and shorter. How did Marcus stay in such good condition? He turned a corner past an enormous hotel, past waiters grabbing a smoke, joking with the hotel porter, decked out in full uniform. Simon almost knocked down the porter, heard an explosion of invective from behind him, but could not stop now even if he had decided it would be best. This was his chance to find Marcus at last.

The older man never looked behind him to see if Simon had given up, or if he'd lost him. He loped steadily, a slim gazelle in the streets of Venice, determined to keep his secrets from Simon. They were in a tiny side street now; a child pumped water from an iron pump. Simon had no idea how long he'd been running. A stitch had appeared in his side which took all his attention. The pain was excruciating; it felt as if he didn't have more than another second or two of running at this pace in him. But he noticed the smallness of the street and saw, for the first time, Marcus looking back at him. Simon could not see clearly, but it seemed as if there was some kind of wall ahead, blocking the street. A dead end? Perhaps, but for the moment Marcus did not slow up, nor did Simon. He was nauseated: the stitch widened its inner track, bit at his stomach; his feet felt like lead; he no longer had any sensation in his chest, but his temples were beating as if each of them contained a heart that was about to burst.

Marcus whirled, darted toward Simon's right; but it was only a feint, because when Simon lunged right to block him, Marcus spurted to the left. He would have made it past Simon, back the way they'd come, except, desperate to end the crazy chase, Simon threw himself headfirst at the older man. He landed with his head butting Marcus's stomach. They both went down: two blocks of stone tumbling on a Venetian street. They rolled in each other's wrestling grasp for a moment or two and ended up against a stained and ancient wall. A blue-and-white sign read: OSPEDALE SS. GIOV. E PAOLO.

They lay in the street like exhausted lovers, Simon's head somehow resting on Marcus's stomach. Marcus looked down at Simon. His stomach heaving, he could barely get out the words.

"I've—got—you," he said. "Are you—sleeping with my wife?" And burst into a spasm of laughing and coughing, coughing and laughing.

7

"I STINK!"

"I beg your pardon," Simon gasps.

"Sweat. I have not—run so hard since—I was a—"

"Yes?"

"A schoolboy. I played soccer at Cambridge—before the war. I mean—the Second World War."

218

"I knew what you meant."

"I could not be sure. We are three generations, really: Sarah is about thirty, you are about forty and I am fifty-five."

"You run like twenty."

"I keep in shape. Let us have a drink here."

A tiny *trattoria* offers some protection from the wind. It is late afternoon and chilly. Now, over a half bottle of Verdicchio, they have to face each other. Simon feels caught in a dream: the glimmer of water opposite his gaze, the exhaustion after the chase . . . the strangeness of sitting opposite Marcus, who has been a sort of dream since Simon answered Sarah's phone one night. *("It was my husband. He lives in Monaco.")* He wonders where Sarah is; has no idea how much time has passed since he took off like a madman after Marcus. Ten minutes? Half an hour?

"Why did you run away from me?" Simon asks.

"Why did you run after me?"

"I've been trying to catch you for some time."

"Yes," Marcus says. "You broke a little keepsake of mine in Paris. Was that in a temper because I was late?"

"You mean you showed up?"

"About six o'clock in the morning."

"Why so late?"

"I didn't really want to see you. I hoped you and Sarah would be gone."

"The Buddha was broken by accident. Why did you tell Sarah you'd come, at all?" Simon hurried on; he remembered quite well how the Buddha had been broken.

"She asked me to," Marcus says simply.

Something in his gaze is sealed; the blue eyes drop, unwilling to confront Simon.

Tired, dusty, still unable to take a deep breath without hurting, Simon looks at the man from whom he'd wanted an encyclopedia of information about Sarah. Some hair falls over his eyes; he stretches his arms. "I ache," he says. "Too old for this hide-and-seek." He throws the hair out of his eyes. Simon sees, now, that the right eye has a sort

219

of cast; it wanders. Simon forces himself to watch only the left eye. Gulls wheel past the table, the sun makes a brief appearance, glints on Marcus's good eye, shines on the bright-blue stripes of his sailor's sweater, then disappears.

"Why, Mr. Shafer," Marcus asks, "was it so important to find me that you tackled me in the streets of Venice?"

All the questions Simon has been nursing tremble in his mind; but Simon says nothing. He realizes how impossible it is to explain Project Sarah. When faced with a stranger —let alone Sarah's husband—it seems an insanely complicated idea; at best unclear, at worst presumptuous.

There is absolutely no question he can ask. Somewhere along the way, the project has changed.

Once that is out of the way—once Simon wants nothing from Marcus—they are like brothers. Marcus takes his arm and they go to see a piece he's just completed at the Church of San Trovaso. It is a Madonna and Child under a tree, created from fragments of junk metal, twisted and rusting, placed in the square facing the church. They are abstract, as much Giacometti birds as they are mother and child.

"The sculpture I do is a public art. This was a big scandal, but I won. In fact, this piece is a little like the group in front of the city hall in Pittsburgh—where you redesigned the downtown part of the city."

Marcus notes Simon's stare of surprise. "The third time Sarah mentioned you, I began to do some homework."

Simon is surprised again; Marcus takes his arm. In a few moments Simon is confiding in the older man. Astonishing information pours out. Not just Chicago and its sudden trauma; old wordless doubts, concerns buried in the past decade, arrive and find words.

Marcus is understanding. Almost too understanding; a touch of the mind reader. He speaks of the problem of the great private values—decency, concern for the individual, the problem of scale.

"But," Marcus says, "personal feelings do not allow for compromise. Example: I was put in a French concentration camp in 1944. I got stuck—bad timing. Arresting political prisoners is a public idea; not so nice, but not so terrible, after all. Gassing Jews—now, that is a private idea. It is, after all, a passion. That is why passions do not belong in public life. At least not to that degree. The very essence of public life is compromise." He sits comically, on the outstretched hand of his "child sculpture"; it seems to be part of an ancient car.

Of course, he understands Simon's situation, he says; has he not made a Madonna and Child out of junk? The individual is so much technological debris; the job is to find the humanity in that debris; Marcus's family business is a living reproach to Simon's profession. Junk, so much junk. To make art out of junk is to understand the extreme position of city life. It takes tremendous energy to fight the public battle. A private respite is understandable.

Simon experiences an extraordinary calm. Walking arm in arm with Sarah's betrayed husband, being consoled by his gray-haired wisdom: perhaps this was why he had wanted to find the man all these past weeks. Not to talk about Sarah; to listen about himself.

Marcus says, "I can be of help. I've been playing games with history longer than you." And he tells Simon of playing soldier of fortune in the Spanish Civil War, of more adventures in the Second World War, where he'd almost lost the sight of an eye. He'd become an American citizen in the forties, had returned to Europe in the fifties and taught sculpture in France in the sixties—had led a student cadre in a strike in May of '68. All of it without political ideology. "All I had was passion and energy; not a shaped idea in my head. I met Sarah in 1965; the timing was perfect. I was ready to give up all that—and she needed someone like me."

Simon prepares himself to finesse the reference to Sarah. But there's no need. Marcus is launching a speech. Standing on the top of a flight of steps behind the Bridge of Fists, around the corner from the Alley of Haste, Marcus declaims: " 'Cities are loved, not so much for their natural and architectural splendors as for the variety and intensity of the spectacles that the ordinary events of human life generate in the streets, the malls, the squares, the parks and other public places. The human as against the economic success of a city is measured by the opportunities that it gives its citizens and its visitors to participate in its collective life.' " Marcus bows low. His floppy gray hair falls into his eyes.

My God, Simon thinks, it sounds like a foreign language. One of the beliefs exchanged for feeling?

"Where . . . ?"

"I have my sources."

Light breaks. "Cappy Kaprow. He works for you."

"For my uncles, in Zurich. He gave me your article."

"What does he do for your uncles, now that he's out of government?"

"Public relations."

"Junk needs public relations?"

"Perhaps most of all."

"But why did you memorize that?"

"It has become important that I involve myself in your thinking and in your plans."

This is getting dangerously close to what Simon wishes to avoid. "Why?"

"I would like us all to dine together tomorrow night."

"It's our last evening in Venice. I don't know. . . ."

"It's important," Marcus says. He sits down on the steps and stretches out his legs wearily. He rubs his bad eye. Now he looks like a man of an older generation. In spite of his caution, Simon cannot resist asking, "You're easy about getting together now; why did you avoid it so carefully before?" Marcus looks up at Simon. For once, just by standing, Simon is the taller one.

"I was afraid."

"Of me?"

"I can't lose her. Give me your hand."

222

Simon extends a hand and helps Marcus to rise. The simple act has the feel of a commitment that has yet to be explained.

8

"DID YOU CATCH HIM?"

"I had to tackle him. He runs fast. I'm a wreck! Why didn't you come with me?"

"I told you. I was buying a present. Look what I found."

It is a white jump suit with a hood. Sarah's hood passion has extended itself to him; when walking together they will look like twins. In the meantime Sarah has no interest in what may have passed between Marcus and Simon.

"I knew you'd meet sooner or later," she says.

"He wants to have dinner with us tomorrow night."

"No," Sarah says. "Let's not do that. Let's have dinner alone somewhere. Just you and me, wearing our hoods."

"I was surprised at how old he is."

"Not *so* old. Try the jump suit on. I have to go out and I want to see if it fits."

The jump suit fits, though Simon barely has the energy to change clothes. Sarah pulls the hood up over his head and poses him before the floor-length mirror on a closet door.

"No one would know who you are," she says, delighted. "Isn't that good? You're always worried about being recognized when we're out together."

The present she'd bought him is . . . a disguise.

"You mean I can wear this in the streets of New York for safety when we stroll the sidewalks—the day after tomorrow, say?"

Her eyes turn vague, unfocused. Without warning she asks him not to go back to New York just yet. Another few

223

days in Venice together—perhaps a week—to extend this happy time.

She does not wait for his reply. "This is the first time I've actually seen you among a lot of people," she says, adjusting the hood so that he can see himself in the mirror.

"Is that good?"

"They're all taken with you. The Indian man who's so funny wants you to go back with him to save India. Linc wants you to save Venice. . . . When we get back to New York . . ."

"Yes . . . ?"

"I'll lose you in a way. I go back into the test tube."

"Not necessarily," he jokes nervously. "I've got my hood now. I didn't know Ram Singh wants me to go to India."

"He's read all about your work for years, he said."

"Indians exaggerate. And India is beyond saving. Almost as bad as New York."

He tells her about Marcus's quoting from his article.

"What did he say about me?" Sarah asked.

"Nothing. It was all about me."

But Sarah is in a hurry. She has no time to stand around musing about Marcus. She has an appointment and must rush if they are to make dinner and then the mass meeting at the Fenice. Who is her appointment? A mysterious friend of Margaretta's. It is raining heavily; the shutters rattle as Sarah dresses for the weather and Simon begins to doze.

Under his exhaustion a strain of thought runs that prevents him from falling asleep at once. The last few hours seem like a poorly remembered dream, Marcus more like a fantasy than Sarah's husband finally encountered. The reverse of the reality Sarah had experienced on seeing the snapshot of Alexandria.

It was all a crazy quilt, upside down. Marcus seemed to have understood perfectly. The chased is the chaser and vice versa. The other wraith, Ben Demos, understood, too. Who and what Sarah was, was not at issue. All the dialogue had been about the question of Simon's size: what it had been, what it might yet be.

Operation Simon? It sounded logical. But his gut still turned over at the thought of Sarah coming back and lying down next to him. Maybe Marcus was merely being diabolical. Afraid of losing Sarah, he listened to Simon's city talk, city fears, city disillusion, with sympathy. Simon in love with tall, sad Sarah. Was that so? Was she sad? He must check her, he thinks sleepily, for signs of yellowing. So it had all been lies and bullshit. History is the last refuge of a city planner in love with another man's wife . . . though he hadn't asked Marcus if they *were* married; oddly, it didn't matter so much anymore. . . . His thoughts splintered and broke down under the weight of fatigue and confusion. Still, something in him had the crazy wish to bring out the hidden in Sarah. Alex was so completely herself; what had looked like stability and responsibility, compared to Sarah now seemed like engraving on stone. . . . Sarah was engraved in water. . . . Her toast to anarchy . . . But the mobile seemed to be turning into a stabile . . . her wish for him to stay on . . . Marcus's wish to "work things out." Simon does not want to know anything about what there might be to "work out." He is sweating in the chill air of the room. Off go the blankets. All he wants is for Sarah to come back and lie next to him. . . . Things are galloping too fast. . . . Simon is not in control. . . . He wants them to go back to New York, to be as they were . . . only with Sarah happy, Sarah connected up in some better way to her life. . . . As for himself . . .

A pigeon appears on the ledge, visible in the thin crack where the shutters do not completely close. In his half doze Simon watches its beak bobbing up and down, grayish green, sharp, like a mask worn by children in a school play.

Something in Simon recoiled from pigeons. They were uninvited presences; uninvited except by old eccentrics or children. Birds should be distant chirps of lovely sound, eloquent rustlings in trees overhead. Pigeons were domesticated, city birds, despoilers of statues in parks, carriers of disease. . . . Alexandria was fearless with animals, easy with birds, whether in parks or in cages in friends' homes.

Three weeks after Simon and Alex were married, a young sculptor friend fell ill: pneumonia, except she did not respond to the usual antibiotics. She was newly divorced and her ex-husband, a colleague of Simon's on a project for the city of Cleveland, was eager to win her back. He had given her a parrot and after her death—apparently from pneumonia—it was discovered that she'd contracted psittacosis, probably from the bird-gift.

The incident threw a sense of gloom over Simon and Alex's happiness. It also reinforced Simon's dislike of pigeons. Alex had thrown off both unpleasant traces; but she was more resilient than Simon. "Apollonian is what I am," she used to say. And maintained that Simon was Dionysian. "Your goat festivals and orgies are your work," she'd said. "The twentieth-century American version."

The pigeon at the window had brought back incidents he'd not thought of in years . . . feelings of bird anxiety, memory-feelings of Alex: how she'd wept over the young sculptor's death, but then decided that she wanted her own happiness, her newlywed joy, more than she wanted grief and mourning. . . .

Exchanging belief for feeling . . . God, what a thing to say! What lay behind those four words? What did they say about his past life of feeling? When had he last felt so swamped by desire—so pleasurably overrun by the satisfaction of that desire—which then only kindled more desire so quickly? When he and Alex had first met they'd made love three times in a row, often. But it did not have this feeling of being overwhelmed. It was a passion that existed by virtue of their lives, of the world. This passion took its license in spite of the confusion of Sarah's life, in spite of the anarchy of Simon's feelings . . . in despite of everything.

It suddenly seems to him as if it is only by means of this

desire that he is still in touch with life at all. He is in a mood in which fatigue and despair are hard to separate. For some time now, he thinks, he has been more in touch with death than life. Perhaps that was why Ben Demos was with him so often . . . why he was here in Venice, a dead city, poisoned with pigeons . . . almost as dead as Les Baux. It seemed perfectly logical to be exploring dead cities, half dead himself. Bad, he thinks, trying not to look to see if the pigeon was still at the crack in the shutters. This is bad . . . and tries to recapture the fine moment in Les Baux when he ran down the hill in the moonlight and woke Sarah to tell her that he loved her. But it is impossible . . . not without her presence. . . . Loving Alex was like loving Mozart, America or little Matthew: it didn't matter if they were present. Loving Sarah was very precise; it required Sarah.

Sarah returned home soaking wet. The skies had opened up while she was out seeing Margaretta's friend. In the half light of the shuttered room she bent over the bed to see if Simon was awake. He looked up at her and lost his mood of misery at once. He was delighted with the curve of her dark cheek, the ribbed lower lip, the rounded mouth and the shining of her eyes. Seeing her struck him a kind of blow, so that he was stunned, full of wonder at how beautiful she was; at how she could move him.

Seeing that he was awake, she cupped his cheek, much in the way that he usually cupped hers—a version of the indistinctive mimicry that comes with marriage. Reaching up for her, he told her, yes, he would stay in Venice; for another week, even longer. In her surprise and excitement she began to weep.

Simon's stomach sank.

9

THE TEATRO FENICE was transformed: a United Nations of international cities. Enormous blow-ups of four-color photographs covered the walls: the Île Saint-Louis adjoining downtown Ottawa; downtown Tokyo next to Akron, Ohio. The pictures reeled and moiled with masses of people. Linc moved from aisle to aisle, shaking hands, kissing cheeks.

"He looks like he's running for office," Sarah said.

"He's running *from* office. Linc's an ex-president of this outfit."

"Shouldn't you be mixing, too?"

Sidelong glance from Simon to determine if Sarah is being ironic.

"This visit is your idea. I'm a runaway, remember?"

"I wanted to see some pieces of your world."

"Well, what do you think of it?"

"Who's that. The tall white-haired man?"

"Philip Johnson. He's one of the speakers."

"Oh . . ."

Simon realized his mistake.

"He's an architect. A grand old man. He worked with Mies van der Rohe. But he's doing everything these days."

"I'm so dumb. But that's why I came. I don't want to be dumb about your life."

They huddled together in the back row, inconspicuous: like revolutionaries who were planning to disrupt a meeting. The first speaker was a white-haired professorial man who made quick, rabbitlike gestures with his hands and nose when he spoke. By the time Simon started to pay attention to what he was saying he was well into his thesis. Sarah began to distract Simon almost at once. Her hand crept onto his lap; her head leaned on his shoulder, drifting perfume into his attention.

The rabbit professor was analyzing the poetic style of recent years to understand where the cities had been and where they were going.

> "Great ash and sun of freedom, give
> us this day the warmth to live,
> and face the household fire. We turn
> our backs, and feel the whiskey burn.

This poem by Robert Lowell, so the poet Louis Simpson tells us . . ."

"My God, two poets in one sentence."

"Shh-h-h."

". . . signifies that the sixties and their hope of freedom are at an end. It is the whiskey that burns, not the ghettos. . . ."

"Stop that!"

"We are returning to business as usual . . ."

"Why should I stop?"

". . . and the life of the family. Every man in his house with his wife and child."

"Because this is a public place. And I'm about to have a very private reaction."

"There is nothing the individual can do in the face of the power wielded by government and the great corporations. . . ."

"I've never heard anybody use the word 'wielded.' Do you realize it's been two days since we've made love."

"Listen and learn."

"Urbanists would do well to listen to the poets. . . ."

"Come back to the pensione *with me."*

"Are you bored?"

"Not with you."

"The form of this poetry is the message; iambic pentameter; rhymed. We are in for a period of conservative reaction. The cities would do well to consider what the people want from them. Not what we think they should

229

have in the way of parks, projects and plans. The endless Vietnam War is the last great public project of the decade. . . ."

"I can't stand this."
"I think that woman is watching."
"It doesn't matter."
"Let's get out of here."

Venice trembled in gray, moist air; heavy winds blew from the lagoon. Clothing stuck to the skin and felt crawly. Simon and Sarah stopped at a sidewalk weighing machine.

"I've gained," Simon said.

"I've lost," Sarah said. "But I think I lost it in the bathroom this morning."

"Gain and loss," Simon said. "The trip isn't over. It's too soon to tell."

"Not for me," Sarah said, happily. "I'm ahead."

"My grandmother would spit twice to avert the evil eye."

Sarah spits twice into the canal. A passing priest watches with amazement.

In the great Venetian bed with golden scrolls of worked wood on all four bedposts, a feather comforter enfolding them, they take refuge.

She is different tonight. Demanding, controlling, drawing him out, asking him to be still . . . talkative, her voice hoarse. He is delighted to be used. For the moment he will be her thing. She had ransomed him from his earlier mood of despair . . . and ransomed him again from the dry bones of the conference at the Fenice. Let the tables turn. *("I like the feeling,"* she'd said, *"that I'm being used. Does that surprise you?")* A languor of acquiescence takes him over. Sarah is direct, abrupt. . . . She wants him inside her right away. She is excited enough from the moment they enter the room and has no patience with play. . . . The telephone rings. They ignore it and it stops. Sarah's excitement is not climactic; it is broad, not focused: an atmosphere. When he touches her "friend" to heighten feeling, she surprises him; removes his hand. Climaxes are not at issue. Something else is happening. When he tries to slow down to stretch out his own pleasure, Sarah thrusts her hips high and quick. He is almost there but senses that she is not; still, she urges him: "Come . . . please . . ." Her hair covers the pillow and half of her face. The one visible eye is open, staring wildly. Simon closes his eyes—this is not usual for him—and pours out. Unexpectedly, Sarah cries out and hides her face in its bed of hair.

"Splendid . . ."
"Yes."
"Lovers are so smug."
"When it's that good we're smug. But we mustn't be."
"Why not?"
"We should be grateful."
"I think I'd rather be smug. It feels better."
"But if things go wrong we'll think it was because we were so satisfied with ourselves."
"Then let's not let things go wrong."
"Ah . . ."
Silence. A match scratches. Sarah smokes.
"Things can't go wrong, because we're staying away from things. Things are what was going on in the Teatro Fenice."
"Or in front of the Ospedale Saints Giovanni e Paolo."
"What happened there?"
"That's where I tackled your husband—and then found out I had nothing to ask him."
"Oh?"
"About you, that is. I decided not to find out 'things' about you. An act of faith."
"Death to things," Sarah says.
"Is that a toast? Like . . . to anarchy?"
"My God," she whispers. "you remember everything I say."

"I remember everything and I notice everything. But only about you. I'm an expert on Sarah Geist. Ask me a question."

"All right. Why was that different just now?"

"That . . . ?"

"Yes."

"I noticed, but I was too busy at the time to analyze it. I give up."

"There was something missing."

"Not that I noticed."

"You couldn't. It's too far inside."

Simon leans on an elbow; he looks down at Sarah; an anxious pulse sets a tempo in his head.

"What do you mean?"

Her cigarette glow goes out abruptly.

"The equalizer," she says. "I had it taken out."

"When?"

"Margaretta's friend is a doctor."

"What a dumb thing to do."

"Don't be angry."

"A crazy trick."

"Harmless!"

"What do you think would happen if you got pregnant?"

She sat up. The blanket embraced her knee; she shivered. "I don't know," she said.

He remembered her haste to get him inside her; the lack of languor, her rush to completion instead of extending pleasure.

"Simon, please," Sarah said. "There wasn't much chance of it happening from one time."

"Then for God's sake why do it? And what happens next? You go back to the doctor and have it put back in?"

"Maybe," she said. There was a touch of sulkiness in her voice. "Maybe not."

"Don't bother," he said. Rage came on fast beneath his calm tone. "I'm going back the day after tomorrow on schedule."

"You said you'd stay."

"You said you didn't care about having a child."

"I said—"

"On your knees, holding me in Marcus's studio, damn it, you said all you wanted was you and me. You're right —I do remember everything you say."

He was trying not to look at her face. He felt tricked and sad and stupid.

"It was an impulse," she said. Simon got out of bed. He put on a robe and opened the shutters and the window. The streets outside smelled of damp; the wind was strong and carried a smell of fish. Bells cracked the air. He remembered that he'd first seen Sarah at her agency, also an impulse: looking for a travel idea. And here he was, mysteriously, in Venice; he'd got what he'd asked for.

"I didn't have to tell you," Sarah said.

"Why did you?"

"I thought if you took it well—"

"What does that mean?"

"If you took it well," she persisted, "I might have cut off some from Marcus, from the way we do things."

"Just because I didn't mind playing Russian roulette with getting you pregnant. And what does that mean—the way you and Marcus do things?"

"It doesn't matter," she said. "You didn't take it well." Sarah rolled over and stepped out of the bed. She was naked and still held her cigarette. It was an odd sight, Simon thought, a tall, beautiful woman, without clothes, cold as ice and smoking a cigarette. The telephone rang, that shrill, rattling sound Italian telephones have. Simon answered.

It was Ram Singh, excited, almost incoherent, calling from the police station. He had called earlier but there was no answer. Could Simon be of some assistance so that he could leave the custody of the police? Linc was not to be found. They embraced the Indian's crisis, glad of the chance to sidestep their own.

10

"IT WAS MOST EXCITING, I can assure you," Ram Singh said. "From the moment the meeting began to break into fights, to the arrival of the police. It was very much like a motion picture, oh, yes. And I thank you, Miss Margaretta, for your help, too."

"If you own a hotel or *pensione,* you have to know the police."

Margaretta had, in fact, handled it all. Sarah had pressed her into service at once; she and Simon then were appropriately impressed as the withdrawn, bitter young woman tackled the Italian police in their own language. A sum of money had been exchanged and Ram Singh had been produced, bleary-eyed and full of information.

Now, at a window table in a tiny *trattoria* overlooking the lagoon, the information was being passed along.

"What was the main complaint?" Simon asked.

"It started when the slides were being shown. Slides of sixties—Detroit in 1968, Watts of Los Angeles, I believe. . . . People began to cry out. No, they cried, no—this is not right. . . . Then more slides—of Vietnam. More cries . . ." Ram Singh was on his feet. Two fishermen watched him closely from over the rims of their wineglasses. His wife sat next to Sarah, smiling shyly and nodding at every point made by her agitated husband.

"People stood up, as I do now. Stop, they call, this is not purpose for this meeting. No politics; life of cities and planning, not politics. Then Paolo Soleri is involved. Listen to me, he says, don't listen to them; radicals must remake cities or they will die . . . and so on. . . ." His turban was crooked and his voice hoarse. "Philip Johnson says no radicals and man who worked for President Johnson tries to keep order." He sat down heavily. "Wait a minute," Simon said. "You haven't told us what happened that brought the police."

"Yes, the police. Somebody puts his hand in front of projector so slides cannot be seen; they shout in French. Hands are pulled away from in front of the slide projector and we see on the screen dead children from shootings— students dead from police bullets. Oh, this was terrible . . . that dead children should be shown like this, I think, to make point for conference on city planning. This, I think, is not right. Though, I know from my work in India that politics is our profession, not this, I think, and I say so and somebody says sit down man with turban, but I do not want to sit down; nobody is sitting down at this time anyway . . . and a black man from New York City govern-ment wishes to make statement about black city needs . . . and somebody holds my arms and I hit them and the slide machine has been broken by somebody else and then, I sincerely believe, then was when the police made their entrance. I tried to find Professor Aaron—after all, he is my employer for the moment—but I could not see him and I still do not know where he is. . . ."

"Not at the hotel," Ram Singh's wife said.

The lagoon was choppy with waves and wind. You could hear the wind through the glass of the *trattoria's* windows. Simon could see the towers of the main part of Venice off to the right, over the stepping stones of a number of little islands. It was close to midnight and rain stopped and started every few minutes.

"In India we Sikhs are considered good for nothing ex-cept to be warriors. But"—he grinned beneath his beard —"there is little market for warriors today. My country is not in Vietnam. And I assure you I am innocent of any hurt to anybody tonight."

"I'm sure you are," Sarah said.

"Professor Shafer, I think perhaps I will go back to India with new excitement after this experience. Perhaps you will come, too."

The excited, exhausted Indian used titles as formally as a German.

"What would I do in India, Mr. Singh?" Simon said. The recital of the hysteria at the conference made Simon wish he'd stayed. At the same time it seemed quite distant; it would have been, as Singh had suggested, like a movie; a movie out of the past—as all movies are out of the past, the instant they are made. Conferences, too, he thought, were the material of an instant historical past. He'd attended so many; for every possible constituency there was a conference. They were the church and town meetings of institutional life. They'd been dramatic, from time to time. But rarely as dramatic as the scene described by Ram Singh. Like movies, they had all been out of date almost as soon as they were over.

More wine was being served. Except to Margaretta, who was drinking straight tequila. Margaretta had a seemingly unslakable thirst for the liquor. Mrs. Singh drank nothing; perhaps because of her religious beliefs, Simon thought; but he knew little about India in general and less about Sikhs in particular.

They were standing now, the bearded, bulky Indian nonwarrior and his tiny wife.

"I go to sleep," he said. "With much gratitude. Tomorrow morning I return the moneys you paid to the police. My government will reimburse everything. My government is committed to helping all of our people live like the human being. If you come to help, Professor Shafer, there is a project being constructed for the city of Calcutta which cannot fail. After what I have seen of the planners of the West—tonight—I assure you to come to India, because our politics is our lives and our lives are like hell . . . and to make hell even a little better is the best to do, is it not? Since heaven is so distant?" Without waiting for denial or approval, the two Indians, like some Far Eastern Mutt and Jeff, benign observers of the decline of the West, bowed to all present and made their way out of the *trattoria*.

* * *

236

"What a scene that must have been," Sarah said. "All those Ph.D.s going ape."

Margaretta sighed and drained her glass of tequila.

Simon said, "All that stuff going down about the sixties. That's only a few years ago. Poor Singh. He got caught in the middle of a bunch of trapped intellectuals trying to make sense of their lives and work. They use the idea of decades the way they use T squares or research models."

"They're not all wrong," Margaretta said. She was portentously sober, as only someone getting quite drunk can be. "There are distinguishing characteristics to each period. . . ."

She paused, staring into her glass. Simon was polite: "Yes?"

Margaretta resumed. "The only trouble is, people like you"—she raised her empty glass in reproach to Simon—"pick the wrong characteristics."

Simon glanced at Sarah. He was about to challenge Margaretta and he didn't want Sarah to think he was continuing their private quarrel by means of her friend. Sarah did not meet his eyes.

"And you know the right ones?" he said.

"Listen to that wind," Margaretta said. "There's going to be flooding pretty soon. Yes, I know more than all these professors. I'll tell you what marks the last decade or so from the ones that came before. It's not any of the things they deal with at conferences. It's strictly something that happens between two people. But it's probably the heaviest indication that you could pick out."

She continued, Margaretta with her glass of tequila, standing up and putting on her rain slicker. "It's something hidden from the eye, usually. Sometimes it surfaces. And it's the biggest change I know of." She swayed a bit, a skinny, nervous young woman with torn fingernails; something meager and bitter around the mouth hinted at a criticism of men and women so radical as to make solitude inevitable—not this year or next, but perhaps the year after that. She was trying to make a careful exit, having apparently just become aware that she was drunk enough to have to leave.

"It's sex with strangers, that's all, my dears, sex with strangers. I don't mean the new freedom, or the pill or promiscuity—though all of those are included. I mean something new as a piece of experience for a *lot* of people in the well-brought-up middle class. That's right, kiddies, sex with strangers. Don't tell the nice professors, whatever you do."

When she opened the door to leave, she was almost blown back at Simon and Sarah in a blast of wet wind.

"Well," Simon said, nervous, alone with Sarah and the few fishermen at the bar.

They ordered another drink. It was as if by staying here at this accidental place they could postpone picking up where they'd left off—with recriminations and the danger of saying things neither of them wanted to hear. They drank in silence and then ordered another one. They are preparing for rage.

11

"You've been using me. I can't find the light."

"Here, I've got it. How?"

"Like people use liquor or drugs. Not to think."

"Or to think differently, maybe. You've been using me, too."

"Why'd you turn the light off again?"

"My hand slipped. I'm in a strange country."

"How have I been using *you?*"

"You're testing yourself and Marcus in some way—and I'm in the middle."

"I'm soaked. Help me off."

"Leotards . . ."

"The perfect underwear. Did you know that I spent

years studying ballet—my sister and I—? Starting at six."
She strikes a stance and says, "Plie," moves and says, "First
position," leaps in the air and cries out, "Entrechat," and
then "Damn" as she comes down hard. "I'm not six anymore. Listen to that wind. It's going to tear down Venice."

While she is in the bathroom he reads his messages,
surprised that he should receive messages during his
anonymous flight. One is from Linc. He has arranged a
meeting with the mysterious Marcus, as per Simon's request. The following evening at eight; the Gritti Palace.
No mention of turmoil or police; just a favor for an old
friend. The other note is from Greer: in town for the
congresso, he would like Simon to call him; also at the Gritti.
Linc's note ends: "Don't say I never did anything for you."
Greer's ends: "We have a lot to talk about." The result of
both is to make him welcome Sarah's reentry. His business
is with her; no one else.

They have gotten drunk trying to avoid a fight; now the
fight arrives.

"You used me . . . to run away . . . to avoid . . . to postpone . . ."

"You said that."

"But I don't mind; so why be so angry and cruel when I
use you in a silly, half-assed way?"

"What did you think you were doing?"

"Maybe the *idea* just made the intimacy that much
more—"

"Babies aren't ideas!"

"Yes they are!"

My God, Simon thinks, everything *is* a dream to her. He
wants to rouse Sarah.

"A trick like that's a long way from your precious anarchy."

"No. That is anarchy—no plan—what happens happens. I just wanted the feeling—not necessarily the real
thing."

"It looked more like a plan to me. A visit to a doctor in
a foreign country. Why call it the 'equalizer' anyway? In-

239

trauterine device I think its real name is—right? IUD. Equalizer just means you want to imitate men. Fuck 'em and forget 'em. Sex with strangers, Margaretta called it. Maybe that's what she meant."

"She meant us."

"Us?"

"We were strangers the first time we made it."

"Don't use that dumb jargon." His anger surprised him. Something was being readjusted.

"I'll use anything I want. The first time we fucked. Is that better?"

"We stopped being strangers pretty damned fast."

"Did we? Do you think I know anything about you? The things people who aren't strangers know?"

"That's just information; data. All anybody has to know is what brought the other person there."

Unsteadiness of foot is the only remaining sign of Sarah's overdrinking.

She is, uncharacteristically, choosing nightwear. She stands, long legs apart, like a department store manikin just before being cloaked.

"It's too cold to sleep naked," she murmurs as if being accused.

She slips into a purple hooded robe and turns to Simon, who is sprawled on the bed.

"But I always knew that," she says. She climbs into bed. "What brought you to me."

"Yes?"

"Don't give me that ice-cold 'yes.' I'm not going to give you some rehash of your work troubles; that was only the trigger. The reason you came to me . . . I don't exactly know how you smelled it in me or if I smelled it on you, right away. These things are always masked in one way or another, but you're *like* me—I don't think you've ever really *done* what would pass for love. Not absolutely and completely . . . not the first time you told me about your wild first wife, that Ariel, and not since."

240

She paused as if to gauge if she'd gone to far in her anger; if, in fact, the statement had come from her anger. She'd gentled down in the middle of it. Some larger truth seemed to take the edge off her present rage and allowed her to offer a full, thought-through idea. When it was clear that Simon was not going to say anything, she went on. "I think it was why I kept reminding us both, for so long, that we weren't doing love—and you kept reminding us we were doing happiness. I think we're people who never put the two together. We just got more and more ingenious in inventing ways of doing one or the other."

A series of shivers and shakes took her, uncontrollably. Simon watched her movements as if they were a code— some new way of her telling him something impossible to say in plain words.

"What is it? Don't be so upset," he said lamely.

"Upset! It's so damned cold in here. Something's wrong."

Upon her investigation, something turns out to be quite wrong. The ducts at either end of the room are sending up cold instead of warm air. While Sarah telephones the concierge, Simon marvels at the cool slap of her thought. Sarah had been, for him, a creature of wonderful bits and pieces: a murmur of poetry here, a surprise toast there, or a blurted-out confession. This was the first piece of synthesis. Had she been working this out in her head for weeks, this disturbing haiku of the heart and the head, this three-sentence History of Happiness and Love in the Twentieth Century as Seen Through the Life and Times of Simon Shafer and Sarah Geist? This brief equation: Let X equal Happiness, let Y equal Love . . . two parallel lines that never meet?

The loud silence in the room told them the air conditioning had stopped. And in that silence Simon thought of the anger, the fighting, the shouts he had missed at the meeting—his natural habitat for so many years—and remembered from years before, Linc's superbly absurd

241

statement: "We've been applying a kind of—let's call it what it is, crazy as it sounds—a kind of love to the public world." Some love!

How terrible, he thought, how terrible that Sarah should have become his only continent and then, once he was marooned on her, give him speeches about love and happiness.

He felt torn open by Sarah; shaky and vulnerable to the chill Venetian air. Sarah had opened the windows to replace the stale cold air in the room with fresh wind. It blew wildly around them. Simon slammed the windows shut and latched the shutters. He grasped Sarah. Something sullen and unyielding in her kept her still, passive, in his arms: no escape and no surrender. He tugged at the zipper of her robe.

"No."

"Come on."

"You didn't understand what I do or what I say."

"I don't want to understand. Let's just be us."

"Please, Simon . . ."

"You said, back in New York a million years ago, you said let's not figure each other out the way everybody does —let's just be happy."

She rested her cheek against his shoulder for a moment. "Did I say that?"

"When I was going crazy looking for your pills, you said it. Now the tables are turned. We're on the other side of an ocean and I'm saying the same words to you. Everything's different: I've met Marcus, you're off the pills, we're doing love and letting happiness take care of itself —and I don't give a damn if I understand what you do or say." The robe was off and on the floor, Sarah and he lay across the bed, naked and cold; there was still something ungiving in her flesh. It kept the edge on his anger while he ran his lips over the breasts she'd worried were too small for nursing babies. He'd run away to hide himself in Sarah—if *she* shut him out. He had, for the moment, given

242

up any notion of the project being for Sarah. Ben Demos was right: it had been Simon's cry for help all along.

"Sarah . . ."

"I don't want to now."

"Don't punish me. Here, hold me."

"No."

He opened her to him; it took no force. She trusted him.

"I can't," she said. "I have nothing in—"

"I know. That's what you wanted."

"I'm afraid."

"Nothing will happen."

"Simon."

"Yes . . . ?"

"Before . . ."

"What?"

"What I asked . . . Will you stay?"

Angry at the blackmail, remembering his own, more light-hearted blackmail, he murmurs something indistinguishable. Later, as his pleasure is about to become uncontrollable, Sarah stops, suddenly, and eases him away from her. She kneels, face away from him, and guides him to the little dark button.

Startled, Simon says, "I'll need something . . ."

"I'm wet enough," she says. "Here. Easy. Wait—all right now."

For a second Simon wonders if this is Sarah being careful—anarchy stopping short of getting pregnant—or if she is simply being Sarah: unpredictable, exciting, extending the possibilities of any moment—the Sarah who renewed him with inexhaustible surprise.

Never having been taken into that small, secret place before, he stays there, lying heavily on and in her, half shrunk, damp with pleasure. Sarah makes a move to turn over; he steadies her with a hand in the small of her back; she lies still. She turns her head so that he can see her eyes. Sweaty strands of hair are plastered to her forehead. He

243

recognizes the look. They have been exchanging it for months. A look of desire so strong that it is half satisfied and half rekindled all at once.

He runs a finger lightly down the line of her spine until it touches the channel of her buttocks, touching the beginning of the furrow and himself, resting there, at the same time. The unaccustomed specialness of that particular sensuality, her reluctance to accept him between her long legs and her surprise acceptance of him between her buttocks widens the question of their acceptance of each other; a question which had been narrowing dangerously. The intimacy that had been swamped by anger was back, returned by this magic of body places.

It was, what we had . . . these sensate places . . . these indentations and protuberances . . . these valleys, rivers, hills, levers, tubes, entrances and exits . . . some familiar, some strange . . . this soft, fragrant landscape that offered a thousand private, foreign tours of what was essentially familiar terrain. It was how we encountered each other; one way of noticing where we stopped and others began . . . material for a thousand nervous jokes. The differences in the structures of flesh helped us understand the similarities. The games played in these moist theaters were one way of understanding, for a series of instants, what it's like to be someone else, what it's like to be one's self. He remembers Ben Demos saying, "The descent of Simon Shafer—from the body politic to the body." He reaches beneath them to place his finger between her legs, touching the empty place. She stirs; Simon begins to move again.

Afterward, happy once more, they lie in the tangled bedclothes, unable to sleep.

It is after 1 A.M.

"Marcus is afraid of losing you."

"He doesn't really have me."

"Does he deal in cocaine?"

"Who told you that?"

"Linc."

244

"No. He uses it. He doesn't sell it; he's not an addict. He just uses it a lot, like Linc smokes a lot. He says it helps him with his work. It's hard to get through without using anything."

"He thinks I'm going to take you away from him."

"Are you?"

"How can I, if he doesn't really have you? Besides, married men can't take anybody away from anybody." There is no sense of risk in the remark at this point. They are in a happy moment: encapsulated. "Listen," Sarah says. "What I said before about loving and happiness and separating them and all that—I never got to finish because you were so damned mad. What I mean is: that's how we started; it doesn't have to be how we end up."

She sits up, wearing a portion of yellow sheet like a tousled, long-haired queen; she leans over him for emphasis.

"I may not want to keep on living this way with Marcus."

"You mean without and with at the same time?"

"I feel like I was hit by a train and split into a thousand pieces a long time ago—and you're putting the pieces together."

The project was a success. Simon could think of nothing to say.

"You taught me something," she said.

"I know," he said. He was frightened at last.

"You taught me—" Her face looms over him, large but vague in the darkness of the room. She is shy again. The old stammering Sarah makes a brief return. "You taught me how people—how t-t-to—you know."

He said nothing. If he spoke at all, there was no way of knowing what it might cost him, later—or if he could pay.

Finally she was able to say, simply and clearly, the word that had been such a tongue-twister for her at Marcus's studio in Paris; the word that had not yet been said directly to him: clear, unambiguous.

"Love," she said.

She waited, patiently. Having given him the word, it was as if she was free of it. It was his to deal with now.

12

By 2 A.M. it was clear that neither of them could sleep. It was the storm that shook the shutters, shook the entire *pensione*. No, it wasn't the storm, they agreed. It was their lives. Still, the violence of the wind and the heavy rain was scary. Sarah disappeared into the Byzantine bathroom and returned with pills. Simon examines them with suspicion. Sarah assures him these are simply Valium. They are yellow. But they do not turn anyone yellow when you stop. They will simply let him sleep. They take the pills together, drinking from the same glass of water; they are giddy with fatigue and strain.

A half hour later they are lying next to each other, wide awake. Sarah seems high; Simon's pulses are fast. This is an effect he has heard of: if you didn't sleep with certain pills, they took you up instead of down. It felt strange to be taking pills—after his struggle to get Sarah off hers, after his refusal to take Dr. Rowan's pain pills. Alex took no pills, stoic in the face of all kinds of discomfort. Comfort was not at the center of her life.

They lie next to each other in the dark, not quite touching. He thinks of calling Alexandria. Outside, wind wars with waves. Simon imagines waves tall enough to swamp boats. The poor Italian gondoliers, he thinks: striking, when no one could venture out in a boat anyway.

There is something circling his mind which, if he catches it, will let him sleep. It is elusive as long as he hears Sarah's irregular breath. The moment her breath becomes louder, more regular, and finally metamorphoses into a genuine snore, he seizes the fugitive idea—or it seizes him. Apparently he had to be alone in order to receive it. And until your lover is asleep, you are not alone. Consciousness is all.

Sarah was right. He has never, he realizes, completely

loved Alexandria. It was the secret of their being able to survive bad times. Matthew developing symptoms of a fatal kidney disease proven finally false; Alex's sister Dak, hospitalized with a breakdown. . . . Alex coexisted with his projects. They both knew that without ever having to state it.

With Ariel, on the other hand, there had been an awful, self-annihilating love that comes, perhaps, only at twenty —if you were lucky. But this was not to say that he didn't love Alex: he loved her with the very strength of incompleteness.

There was a power in that understood split; a confidence, something that never theatened because it was instinctively measured; oddly proportionate for anything to do with as volatile a notion as love.

It excited him to think about this. If he and Alex had this split/love, then there were spaces in it which could still be filled. (It could be, of course, that Sarah filled one of those spaces.) Unlike Ariel and him, so much each other that there was no place to go except to emptiness and death.

He remembered all the fallings of his childhood and young manhood. Never had the sensation of falling been so much a part of love. Vertiginous, self-obliterated, he would stagger home those many midnights to throw up: an ecstasy of discovery, his ritual offering to the gods of Total Love. (If it was one of the rare times that his father was home, the light in his parents' bedroom would click on, a murmur of disapproval, then the click off. If his mother was home, alone, as was more usual, just a resigned sigh in the darkness.)

After the first nausea would come the long, slow process of joining and cutting loose. What else could follow such intense identification? Not until he entered the world of obsessive projects was he able to free himself of this way of love. It took an Alexandria to coexist, happily, with projects. Alex, with her sense of the necessary usefulness of things; she was born to be never more than half of a man's life and the man no more than half of hers.

Which was why it was such a disaster for them when his work died in him. It could have thrown him too much into Alex. Instead, it pulled him away from her. It was why they were as close to being estranged as they'd ever been.

But it was also why Sarah had her unique place. Why Sarah—whatever she might think, awake or dreaming—was not in competition with Alex. Sarah was that other half that Alex had been happy to live alongside. Sarah was the replacement for his career; she is—now—his career, his work place; his laboratory in which he is working out his life. Trading belief for feeling is only one way of testing belief. The results of that test were still in question.

He loved Sarah as powerfully as he had at that other moment of falling; when his hand pain had erupted under the rocks of Les Baux, threatening to bury their adventure.

But *it had no claim against his marriage.* He must not stay on, must not seem to endorse any such claim. There was no reason to place this happiness against the rest of his life. It was a moment of cool lucidity. It suggested why, after hunting Marcus down, he'd asked him no questions.

Sleepy at last, he heard Sarah's snore with pleasure. His happiness was centered. It could be counted on again.

At 4 A.M., still awake, he threw the covers from the bed and examined Sarah's body for signs of yellowing. What the hell was he doing? he thought, as he searched; he must be going crazy!

Not a sign. Mottled beige and white as usual. Seeing this, in effect seeing Sarah sleeping and happy, he gazed at her face awhile and fell asleep at last.

13

HE HAD SLEPT until almost three o'clock in the afternoon. Sarah was gone—off with Margaretta, her note said. Back in an hour, her note said: I love you, her note said. Apparently once that word was born it had a life of its own. He'd stared at the four letters until they disappeared into gibberish. A stick, a circle, a cleft and an incomplete circle—that's all love was, he'd thought, from a typographical point of view. But he recognized this reduction as anxiety and went off to Florian's for a large breakfast à l'anglaise. As he walked past the boat dock of the Riva degli Schiavoni, a sudden burst of bright chilly sunshine opened up the sky. A young woman with eyes set wide apart, almost in the Oriental manner, a straight, proud nose and very red lips stepped from a vaporetto. Simon examined her face and remembered observing Sarah's face while she slept the night before, lost in a tangle of bedclothes and hair. Eyes closed, her face had looked different, alien. Then she'd turned and murmured a cluster of meaningless sounds. Something had moved in him.

What was it, he wondered, that gave this particular face the ability to touch him? Why this one at this time? Even stranger, the face that he'd encountered that first day at Sarah's travel agency was not the face he looked at now. Too much had happened. Something public in that face —the cool, expectant, welcoming smile, a smile that expected nothing—had grown to expect a great deal. And something private in that first face— a sealed-off quality masquerading as poise—had become public: more of her was available each time they were joined by people; still poised but less wary.

Yet the face's mysterious attraction remained. It was a

strange solipsism. No change in the face itself could threaten its power; only a change in his eyes. It was not a question of beauty in beholders' eyes; it was not a question of beauty at all. But where *did* it get this power to move him? And why via the eyes: line, color, shape? These shadowy sources of the power of faces made it all the more troubling.

To be at the mercy of one face out of all the faces in the world . . .

At Florian's he ordered orange juice, bacon and eggs and coffee. A nun carrying an enormous green plant struggled across the piazza. It was the right kind of foolish, pleasant image for that moment. It made Simon realize, as he smiled, that he felt fine this morning. Rested, too, in spite of only a few hours sleep and a stormy night.

"Spring," he said to the waiter who was pouring more bitter coffee for him. He pointed to the nun and her plant.

"Signor?"

"Primavera."

"Not yet, Signor." And pulled aside his striped shirt to show Simon the heavy sweater he wore beneath.

"Soon."

"May the fifteenth. In Venezia, never sooner."

On May fifteenth, Simon thinks, they will be in New York, leading their accustomed lives again. He is confident. As for his own "fall": he is not going to throw up. He will manage, control, plan, organize. It is what he was trained for. Walking briskly back to the hotel, he encounters a ragged file of gondoliers, signs dangling from oars slung over their shoulders and singing a song, like gondoliers in a movie. Except, Simon thinks, gondoliers are usually found one by one, not in groups. And these gondoliers are carrying oars slung like weapons and their song is about anger, not love.

As startling as the wind was the sight of cameras on wheels behind the gondoliers. Was it a movie? Or a news program filming the event for Italian television?

Bells broke the air, sending pigeons aloft in broad flights, like gray flags sweeping the air.

"His wife thinks he's gone crazy."

"Sarah doesn't want to talk about my wife."

"No, it's all right now."

"Don't you want any coffee, Simon?" Linc asks. "I drank a potful to help my hangover."

"Why crazy?"

"She called me three or four days ago from New York. She was worried."

"I think maybe I *don't* want to hear this," Sarah says.

Linc has gathered them up from the *pensione* for coffee near the Ca' Rezzonico; they must wait with him until the boats were ready to head for the test run in the lagoon; they must hold his hand and drink coffee and do a little sightseeing on their last day. "It's not the last," Sarah had said. Simon had said nothing. Then, over coffee at a café around the corner from the Rezzonico ("Browning died there; Beerbohm wrote a story about it"), Linc grew manic —and the subject of Simon's madness came up.

"I'm sure there's a reasonable explanation," Linc tells Sarah. "I've known Simon for over ten years and only one of us is crazy."

He describes the nature of Alex's concern: it seems Simon has been observed speaking to someone when no one was there. Sarah gazes at him. Her attention has a new edge.

In the overflow of his confidence Simon tells them about Ben Demos. It seems absolutely natural that a grown man should have an imaginary playmate; should allow his mourning to take the form of "silent" conversations with a dead friend—even if the "silent" words could be heard. Lonely and defeated in Chicago—beginning to feel estranged from Alex and Matthew—Simon had heard Ben Demos speak to him. He'd answered; that was the only difference. The question of Ben's being real was not an issue. He'd been alive, hadn't he? Of course he was real.

251

You didn't stop being real because you died; you only stopped being present.

Such is the mood under the thin rain that Sarah and Linc agree. Sarah asks questions about Ben. What did he look like? Was he married? How did he die? And Linc contributes a consoling anecdote about Freud. Late in his life, in conversation with a colleague, Freud kept referring to a mutual friend who had died as if he were still alive. When this was pointed out to him, Freud had said, "Oh, yes, I know he's dead. I just can't accept it." Encouraged by their laughter, Linc then entertains them with a description of the wild scene at the Teatro Fenice the evening before. Sarah presses Simon's hand beneath the table. And Simon thinks about Alex and how awful it must be for her to fear her husband may be a lunatic. Reason was more important to Alex than to most people. She had not suspected him of adultery; rather of losing his mind.

Simon has a new task waiting for him at home. He will have to convince his wife that he is sane.

"Do you think my hair is silly?" Sarah asks Linc.

"Yes," Linc says, as if he has been thinking of nothing but the appropriateness of Sarah's hair. "It's a little girlish for a grown woman."

"Ah," Sarah says.

"You'd better put it up before you come out on the lagoon."

He is ready to leave them to check on Ram Singh and the state of the upcoming voyage.

"This is my day," he says, peering at the sky. "The computer says so: my storm . . . my demo . . ."

"The wind's died down," Simon says.

"Don't you believe in computers? Sarah, this man is beyond redemption: he doesn't believe in computers. I didn't realize exchanging beliefs for feelings extended so far."

He gazes at Sarah as he speaks, less innocently than Simon would like. His mood seems addressed in some unspecified way to Sarah.

"Anyway," Linc says, "you have to come out with us on the lagoon for the test flight. It's your last day, so you must."

"I told you," Sarah says, "we're staying on. For a few days anyway."

Linc's gaze drops before Sarah's steady stare.

"Smart man," he says to Simon. "Venice beats New Haven. Even in the rain." But he looks at Simon with careful eyes, measuring.

"Classes are out," Simon says. "I wouldn't be in New Haven anyway."

"They're having a heat wave in New York, according to Alex." This second mention of Alex is noted by Simon.

"Sure," he says, "We'll come."

"Great," Linc says. "There'll be a crowd. We've got two boats. You go with Ram Singh and I'll show Sarah the caissons close up."

It is Simon's turn to use eyes to measure.

Back in the *pensione* to change into warmer clothes for the race to the lagoon, and to wait for Linc's phone call, Sarah proposes leaving Venice the next day for a few days in Naples. No rain, the warm sun, and lunch on the slope overlooking the Bay of Naples. Paralyzed, Simon is about to risk the ruin of the trip by saying no. But happily, Margaretta knocks on the door at that moment. He is to call Alexandria at once. Panicked, he places the call and holds on to the phone, even though there is no telling how long it will take to get through. In the bathroom, Sarah, naked and happy, sings what Simon takes to be a Neapolitan melody. She is in Naples already. He will not have to answer yet. Ruin is postponed a moment, an hour, a day. From the bathroom comes the sound of running water interspersed with Sarah's words.

"Let's get away from Linc and his wildness."

"Oh, is that it?"

"It's exciting, but . . ."

"But . . . ?"

253

"Too much, somehow. I liked him that time in New York. But here he's all storms."

"He frightens you?"

"A little. Besides, I've had enough rain."

"It's as if he's trying to will the storm."

"Margaretta says November is the high water time in Venice anyway, not May." She steps out of the bathroom, sweatered and blue-hooded against the cold and rain, smiling at him, phone still in hand.

"If you hang on to that phone, we'll never get the call we're waiting for, and they'll start the storm without us."

"I don't think I'm going to the storm," he says. He had not known he was going to say that. "I have an appointment," he says, "with Marcus."

"Why won't you come with Linc instead?"

"Not," he says, "because you were flirting with him in the Piazza San Marco, and then give his wildness as a reason for dashing off to Naples. Though they might be good reasons for most people."

"Are we going to be most people?" Sarah says. "Is that what's going to happen?"

Simon knows it is perverse of him to insist on keeping a vague appointment with Marcus. Which is, perhaps, why he asks Sarah to join him. That will make it legitimate exploration, the three of them, together at last, deciding where they stand.

"I don't want to have dinner with Marcus tonight," Sarah says. "And I wasn't flirting with Linc. I was listening very closely while he talked about you. Where I stand with you is what I'm interested in. That's all."

"Then come with me."

"Why do you want to talk to Marcus? Do you still have a list of questions?"

No! He wants nothing from Marcus. Which means that now he can find out what the man wants from him. He grabs at Sarah and whispers this information to her.

"Don't be a bastard," she whispers back. "It was you who promised Linc we'd come and watch."

254

"Then I can unpromise."

She runs a finger down his cheek and touches his mouth before he can speak. Her mouth is open against his face, her breath warms the air around them. Simon raises his hand to her eyes and then down to her cheek. He is about to give in. Suddenly his hand goes limp; not quite with pain: pins and needles jab at the juncture of thumb and forefinger. The hand is paralyzed, for the moment entirely without feeling. Simon says nothing, waiting for the disembodied tingling to turn into pain or peace; to become a sign.

14

"HERE IS MY THEORY," Marcus said. "Each decade has a particular quality. But this is not so brilliant a thing to notice. The Roaring Twenties, the Red Thirties, the Mauve Decade a long time before that. No, I mean something more condensed."

"Condensed?" Simon said.

"Simpler, simpler," Marcus said. "Like alternating current: one on, one off."

"On and off—what?"

"One decade is personal, internal, private; the other is public, political. Example: The twenties—personal, individual. The thirties—external, political."

"Too simple," Simon said. "The seeds of that stuff in the thirties—it was all active in the twenties."

"Exactly my point. I don't rule out preparation and delivery. There were, as you say, seeds of social thought in the twenties—everybody from Houston Chamberlain to Eugene Debs—but it did not reach mass proportions until later. And then the forties—the World War makes them public. The fifties—already famous as 'quiet'...ergo, personal. The sixties—"

"—are too complicated for your theory."

"Vietnam."

"The revolution of consciousness."

"Communes."

"Drugs . . . LSD . . . exploration of the interior."

Like teacher and student they disputed happily, turning concept into cliché and vice versa. Except for Simon's sense that Marcus chose his themes from some secret knowledge of his wife's lover and his situation. Had Sarah been involved with someone else, would there have been a different theory?

Marcus was tense, restless; leading nervously through streets, across tiny bridges in their predinner stroll. Simon had the sense that if he had started to run, Marcus would have tackled and toppled him.

"I was disappointed that Sarah didn't come."

"Sarah is a guest at a storm."

"It's all right. We will have dinner at Malamocco. The streets there are paved with sea shells; the wine is powerful. And finally, it is you who can give me what I need, not Sarah."

A soldier steps from a moored barge, carrying a side of beef in one hand and in the other a sleeping baby wrapped in a pink blanket.

Less rain, more wind. In the sudden dry spell, Marcus leads him to a detour: the church of San Giorgio Maggiore. It is elegant standing among lowly convent buildings. The view from the campanile, Marcus says, is extraordinary. A short, fat monk takes them up in a tiny elevator. "Swiss," the monk says proudly. At the top the view of Venice is swathed in rolling clouds of fog.

Downstairs again, Marcus says, "A drink before dinner; how about it?"

They are near the Taverna Fenice. Marcus orders grappa for both of them. He takes a small box out of his coat pocket and opens it gently. "This goes well with grappa."

"I've never tried it."

"It's an honest drug. What you borrow from it you pay back tomorrow. But it can be worth it."

"I don't do much of this kind of thing," Simon says. "I never have."

Marcus looks up from his careful operation. "But tomorrow you are leaving?"

Simon does not answer. As he was leaving the hotel room, Sarah about to be guided toward the crepuscular mists of the lagoon by Ram Singh, the phone had run again. Simon had waved them off and hung on for fifteen minutes; after which the operator told him he had "lost" New York. Instead of placing another call to Alex, he sent a cable, telling her he would be arriving home the next day on schedule. Hurrying out of the *pensione,* he had given a chastened, hung-over Margaretta his plane tickets to New York to be reconfirmed. He said nothing to her about sunshine or lunch above the Bay of Naples.

The powdery white operation has been completed. Simon takes a frigid sniff, then another on the other side. He closes his eyes and wonders at what he is doing. But it is clear that this is the only way the two of them can deal with each other this evening.

"No one notices," Simon says quietly.

"Perhaps and perhaps not. Venetians are not like other Italians. They have a way of being just as observant in public—and very private about what they observe." He breathed deeply and quickly.

Simon's heart is beating quickly; he feels it knocking against his chest. Is this a predictable reaction? Or is he afraid of what the older man is going to ask of him? He should have gone with Sarah and Linc.

Simon called into the wind, "I've had this same feeling before."

"What did you say?"

The wind blew their words away; the motor launch chugged against the current toward the sea gate.

Simon called up more breath. "I used to go to a doctor for injections into my nose. Before he gave it to me, he'd put some stuff on cotton and leave it inside my nose for about ten minutes. In five minutes I was completely up—full of ideas for projects, position papers, everything. I even mapped out a complete book under the influence. In less than ten minutes, I was in a happy high like this."

"It's the same stuff. Deadens pain of injections, too. . . . What was the book you were going to write?"

"It was called " 'Happiness in Cities.' "

"You didn't write it."

"How do you know?"

"I know what you've done."

Before reaching Malamocco they passed two processions. One a solemn, slow parade of garbage scows shaped like gondolas. The other a funeral procession, with a priest standing straight up in the front of the first boat as if he were going to bless the roiling waters.

"We've eaten like madmen," Simon said. "Now let's talk about Sarah and what you want from me."

"Piles of pasta. Pounds. Let's talk about you."

"A whole chicken."

"Don't forget the veal and peppers."

"And the scampi. Why about me?"

"Don't forget the female crabs."

"Were they female?"

"Specialty of the Trattoria Malamocca. About you because I have the impression that your life has put you together with Sarah."

"Are we high—is that why we were so hungry?"

"Doing coke always makes me hungry."

"You sound like Sarah—doing love, doing coke. . . . And the grappa. What is it?"

"A clear brandy," Marcus said, "made of grape husks. Very strong."

"I used to wonder what it would be like to meet you—

back in New York, when you were a distant figure, all shadows and mystery."

"Is it coming apart with you two? Is that why Sarah didn't come tonight?"

"It's coming together, not apart. But Linc Aaron promised Her a storm."

Marcus poured more grappa for them. He proposed a walk in the restaurant's garden, looking out on the lagoon.

They walked, gazing in the water, where, past the Porto di Malamocco, boats—perhaps, Linc's armada—began to swarm. The wind blew leaves in their path; the light was half gray, half golden. It would soon be twilight. Simon knew their chatter had a freakish rhythm. But he was ready for some supreme clarity. The air he breathed, through a fresh nose, was filled with a supernatural buoyance. It was drug-created sensation. Yet he decided to trust it. He had come a long way to walk beside this husky, gray-haired sculptor; it was a moment of revelation he'd been looking for since he'd picked up the phone in Sarah's apartment months—it seemed years—before. Simon in his hooded jump suit and Marcus in his black trousers and heavy black sweater could have been two monks strolling a monastery garden to talk about ultimate matters, instead of the most intimate of concerns.

"I have a sense of what you've been trying to do with Sarah. But I would like for you to tell me."

And as easily as that, Simon told him. It was a relief, like confessing a dark secret no one knew—least of all Sarah and her husband. Project Sarah, presented objectively as a thesis, but sung as lyrically as Simon's doubt and anxiety, as grappa and cocaine, could make it. And he placed this personal song in the setting of his colleagues wandering around Venice—architects, builders, planners, fund raisers—none of them knowing what to do, finally erupting in shoving matches that evoked the police . . . all because no one knew what to do anymore. To this he added personal details he had never told anyone except Alex. His father's

259

periods of violence, destruction of whole rooms of furniture followed by disappearances of as much as six months at a time, leaving Simon shaken and scared, his mother struck silent with misfortune; his rheumatic fever, which had confined him to bed for a year when he was eleven. These eloquent irrelevancies caused a subtle change in the crepuscular confessional—to the spiritual was added the medical. The history was being taken: diagnosis and then prescription would follow—perhaps along with penance? It didn't matter at this point. Nor did it matter that the listener/confessor/doctor might be his lover's husband. He concluded with the disaster at Grant Park—which, it developed, Marcus knew all about already.

Marcus took the case on. He addressed himself to Simon's complaint with careful objectivity. He understood the basic outline of the two parts of what the patient had told him: he'd given up the rebuilding of cities—to help rebuild one woman. But apparently it could not be attacked quite so simply.

Near the waterfront they came upon a group of very old men playing a game in a long, narrow, sandy alley. Marcus brightened up. "Let's play some boccie," he said.

"I don't know how."

"It's simple. The scoring is complicated—but these gentlemen will keep score for us."

He sprayed a stream of Italian phrases at a little spider of a man in a heavy sweater. The man nodded and in a moment Simon and Marcus had divided a dozen balls between them, Simon's red and Marcus's black. There was also a white ball, smaller than the others.

"This little ball," Marcus said, "is called the *principessa*—or the mistress. The aim is to get as many balls as you can closest to the little ball. The loser owes the winner a favor. Here—you throw out the *principessa* first. . . . Good throw."

Marcus knelt and sighted the curve of his toss. "You are suffering," he said to Simon without taking his eyes off the little ball, "from a crisis of legitimacy. People must feel that what they're doing with their lives is legitimate." He threw the first ball. It rolled gently to about half a foot to the side of the *principessa*. There was a ripple of approval from the old men. Pipes were removed from teeth; obscure laughter traveled among the men. "Why do you think kings and popes could rule for so long?"

Feeling as if he had seven fingers on his right hand, Simon half knelt and tossed his ball. It hit a bump and stopped abruptly, about a foot from Marcus's ball. "The people they ruled," Marcus said, "believed in their legitimacy. But that was a long time ago." Marcus smoothly knocked Simon's ball even farther away, his second ball nestling even closer to the little one than the first. There was a snapping of fingers in some ritual of scorekeeping and approval.

Marcus knelt on both knees to assess the lie for his next throw. He had clearly played this game for years. "Now," he said, "they take the smartest people we have—like you, for one—and give them the assignment of saving the world. Behind this, of course, is the assumption that there *is* a world that everyone believes in—and that it can be saved."

He rolled the ball gently; it moved in slow motion to join the other two in a semicircle around the white ball. He dusted his knees. "They hand you the Enlightenment— the hope of human perfectibility—like a lollipop. Not noticing that it doesn't taste as sweet as it used to, and to make things worse—No, wait; grip it hard, like this, but throw it gently; you get more control that way. To make it worse, they hand you the decade of the place when everything is either being burnt down or rebuilt from scratch." This ball actually edges one of Marcus's out of the way and arrives in the magic semicircle. Someone mutters, "*Bravo, americano.*" Simon feels elated and weird at the same time. It must be, he thought, one of the oddest confrontations between lover and husband ever held. Instead of the traditional accusations, he was getting "The Dilemma of Modernism," Section 6: Meets at twilight on the Venetian

Lagoon, over a game of boccie. No paper required: only a change in the way you live.

Contradicting his advice to Simon, Marcus slammed the next ball down the alley. It neatly knocked Simon's one success out of the alley and landed only a few inches from the little ball. "But," Marcus said, "you are being asked to fight a new war with the weapons of the old. We are entering the age of the individual—and if you think the age of social hope gave us terror, wait till you see the new age." He turned and half bowed Simon to his next throw. "The move from being social beings to being"—he paused and searched for the word—"*creatures* is under way."

There was a small opening between two balls. Simon aimed carefully and rolled his ball gently toward it. He was astonished when it delicately separated the other two and rolled to a stop almost immediately. He was concentrating too hard on playing the game to reply to Marcus. More scorekeeping sounds. Marcus holds his ball and turns to Simon. "Listen," he says, and pauses. Simon listened. As if reliving an old dream, he heard faint bells, the swoosh of water against wooden piles; somebody was whistling and motors churned gasoline out on the waters. "It is quiet everywhere. The French and German students are back in school; the American campuses are calm . . . waiting for the war to end . . . waiting for something to happen. You are going to be seen as the enemy."

His throw was wide but curved around with premeditated english to stop on the far side of the *principessa,* only a few inches away. It was an exquisite shot and the audience registered its approval noisily.

"Me?" Simon said. He was not about to try a throw of such subtlety. He chose, instead, a violent attempt at breaking up Marcus's grouping. His ball went completely wide and ended up at the side of the alley, resting against the wooden slat.

"You stand for the city; city hall: the cry will be for the needs of the individual *against* you. Only two balls each left."

Simon gazed at Marcus's eyes. The man was inspired with his statements, but it did not seem to be a result of being high. He was less the drug-inspired prophet now; just a European intellectual who had caught another man sleeping with his wife and was explaining how he saw the matter, in the larger sense.

Marcus turned away and dropped the next-to-last ball in an almost casual toss. It ambled slower and slower, until it looked as if it would leave the point to Simon. But its slow progress took it, finally, into the company of its fellows. The circle was almost closed. Simon would have to blast it open to gain any points. And he did not have the control for that.

"Mann predicted it all. Personal happiness is insatiable; it then becomes the forbidden, which becomes, at last, the demonic. Then there's old Faust . . ."

Simon knelt in instinctive imitation of Marcus's style. He threw the ball hard. One of the old men giggled even before the ball stopped outside the circle. Marcus had won, or was about to.

"Too gentle," Marcus said. "Faust, he starts by asking for wisdom, ultimate knowledge, and how does he end? By seeing the vision of the most beautiful woman who ever lived, Helen of Troy, and all he can say to the passing moment of happiness is: 'Stay, thou art so fair.' " He intoned it in German, for emphasis. " 'Verweil doch, du bist so schön.' "

He rolled the final ball. It closed the protective circle. The game was over. He turned to Simon and smiled. "The remark of a man who has lost all belief in the social order, is afraid of death, adrift in time . . . You played pretty well for a beginner. Now, some coffee."

Their table had been cleared. The coffee was thick and sour.

"Why now?" Simon asked. "And why now . . . to me?"

"Because when politics dies—the idea that we can control our lives together—when that goes, then we turn back

263

to our personal freedom, over which we can at least *feel* a sense of control."

"And can we? Will that work?" Simon assumes they both know he is asking a serious personal question.

"No," Marcus said, abruptly. "It's an illusion. What do we actually have that we can control? Bodies to touch and to be touched? It's an illusion. Sensual satisfaction requires endless repetition. Sex never moves us forward from where we began; only back to the starting point again. Sensuality, not work is the myth of Sisyphus."

"And love?" Simon asked.

"Yes, oh, the heart. But love dies or changes into something else. And the body, which contains the heart as well as all that wonderful apparatus for sensual enjoyment, personal happiness and individual freedom—the body dies, too. It's a losing game! But,"—Marcus's eyes shone like a cat's—"the instant one says no to Eros, everything magnificent in the cities of men and women becomes possible. . . ."

As the theme took a dying fall, so did the high. Marcus leaned back in his chair; Simon slumped forward. The lights began to blink on around the harbor. Simon came down slowly, and remembered Ben Demos reflecting that only the insane notion of enduring as a species, as a group, could justify cities . . . that individual men know the city will outlast them; that they will die with some part of the place they call home unvisited.

Simon's mouth was dry, his eyes tired, wanting to close. The diagnosis was in. It was time for the prescription.

"What's the answer?" he asked. They were getting closer and closer to the particular. Sarah would undoubtedly be discussed by name in a matter of moments.

Marcus had some passion left. He leaned forward, smiled happily, struck the table.

"Give us back an idea. Anything! Any workable myth in which we can join together."

"And if there is none?"

"Give us a public lie, then. I didn't say it had to be true.

Only that we believe in it. This is the first time in generations that the next idea—true or false—has been so long
in coming, leaving everyone to their own devices."

" 'All that believed,' " Simon said, " 'were together and
had all things in common.' "

"What is that?" Marcus asked.

"Sarah said you were fond of quoting it or something
like it."

"I never heard it," he said. "Sounds like the Bible. But
maybe all you have to do is blindly stick it out . . . keep
believing that the coming together of different people—
who don't have all things in common—is as important as
our own whining little selves." Marcus was gathering intensity, or else was about to crash hard. He did something
that startled Simon. He reached across the table and took
Simon's hand in his own larger paw. "Please," he said,
"don't leave us alone with ourselves."

"How do *you* handle it?" Simon asked, embarrassed.

More grappa released the hands for pouring and drinking.

"I make sculptures for public spaces," Marcus said. "And
I live in public spaces. I have no real, no continuous private life—except when Sarah and I meet, en route, in New
York or Venice or Paris or Kenya or Ischia or Copen-
hagen. I live, for the most part, in motion and surrounded
by crowds."

Simon took a breath. Win or lose, a bluff had to be
called.

"I think Sarah's through with all that."

Marcus pushed his wild gray hair back from his forehead. Had he, perhaps, expected to hear this? His eyes
shifted from Simon to his own fingers, then back again.

"She's restless, I know," he said. "It's why you're here.
And it's why I asked you to meet me. I have a favor to ask
of you."

"At last," Simon said.

He closed his eyes. It was a mistake. The world inside
his head proved as unstable as Marcus's description of the

265

private life. Everything whirled. He opened his eyes and breathed deeply. From the direction of the water a voice called out: *"Eh, dolce, per piacere, un pochettino dolce, eh?"* Someone was asking for gentleness. It was that sort of night. Looking away from Marcus because it was impossible not to look away, Simon saw the towers of Venice over to the right, beyond a series of small islands, begin to flicker with lights. Marcus is speaking; he has left the public sphere completely. He speaks for himself only. He is afraid. The word has leaked out to him some time ago (from Sarah? those late night phone calls?) that this one might be serious, that her famous detachment, her elegant separation of heart and body—that parody of what men have done for centuries—might be a casualty of this affair. That love might be rearing its ugly beautiful head.

"And the favor?" Simon asks.

"Sarah and I have a delicate balance. . . ."

"Are you married?"

"Not anymore. We were married for three months, in 1965. Sarah got an annulment—and we began."

"Began?"

"She realized that she did not want to be married, perhaps never. So we have kept each other balanced across oceans, across the years. I have never mixed into what Sarah does; we have been a shining example to a world of tormented, controlling men and women. Together we are fine; apart we are fine."

"Except . . ."

"Except for you."

"And the favor . . . ?"

"Is to leave things . . ."

"As they are."

"Take what she gives you—the part—and leave alone what she can't give you, for me to live on. . . . I can't do without it."

"That's up to Sarah." He does not want to point out that he is married—that he cannot change anything, whether he wants to or not. It would be a betrayal of the project if

266

he endorsed their "delicate balance." In a way, he has come to Europe to tip that balance, to let Sarah fall into some other connection with a life. His remark is a mortal error. Marcus, the gentle, wise teacher, turns savage. Assuming Simon has refused his request, his fair skin flushes, much like Sarah's under stress. His breathing becomes irregular. The steady rhythm of his language breaks down into spasms.

"You think you can just say that . . . you think . . . Do you know what you have there . . . the history? Do you think you know who you're playing love and reconstruction games with? You've seen her with her nice Jewish middle-class analyst-father—comfortable ex-radicalism nesting in lower Manhattan—or dispensing travel advice in midtown. You don't know a thing about Sarah. . . ."

Two pigeons fluttered down and settled at Marcus's feet, as if summoned by his rage. "When I met your darling Sarah she was a basket case. She'd taken every pill there was and was currently on Dexedrine and Quaaludes, spiced up by cocaine. I think there had been some heroin in the days before I met her, but I didn't see that with my own eyes. I held her while she vomited up her various habits—a nice legacy from her big sister."

"Shit!" Simon said. He couldn't summon up the nerve to call Marcus a liar; but he hoped the opposition of the word would slow him down or stop him cold. It did neither.

"By the time you got to her she was just trailing off on some nice tranquilizers. Do you know she had not a penny? Haven't you noticed the casual way she handles the agency . . . the vagueness about money? I set her up in her business—did she tell you that?—and I run a very loose ship, because she mustn't be pressed too hard. . . . You don't know a damned thing."

"I know . . ." Simon murmured. He'd meant to confirm his own ignorance, but it came out as a denial.

"You are under the impression that things are under

control, perhaps. Do you know, have you noticed anything odd about Sarah and the subject of babies . . . children?"

Before Simon can, again, try to confirm, Marcus tells a tale of half-familiar fragments; of Sarah's long-ago botched abortion, after which she is told she can no longer have children. Her response: to be fitted with an IUD. After all, she thinks, it is not a perfectly exact science. There is no guarantee that she can never become pregnant. By wearing the device, she takes control of the situation. She will *decide* not to have a child—until the magical moment arrives when she is certain she can conceive. . . . Wearing the IUD is her mad gesture to hope—a fantasy acted out of a wish and a fear—while she repeated to Marcus, at odd post-midnight hours, "They kept *telling* me it's not an exact science. . . ."

Simon was sick; he felt as if he had crashed all at once. He had shelved the awful stuff about drugs because it was too wild to take; but there was something terribly convincing about this last tale of blind hope and careful control over the uncontrollable. It sounded like Sarah. In a crazy way it sounded like anyone in an extreme situation. If one story was true, were all stories true? A siren sounded close by; the conventional clamor of the waterfront evening was louder now: voices, distant and near, beneath the siren's call.

"What do you think you can know about Sarah that compares to what I know? Even the evidence of your senses. . . . Have you noticed the charming way she holds her head to one side? The abstracted look sometimes?"

Simon said he had noticed.

"She's almost deaf in one ear."

"From what?" Simon asked, stupid with shock. He'd meant to ask—just as stupid-sounding—which ear?

"Measles, when she was three years old . . ."

Dimly aware that the few diners who'd shared the evening with them as well as the waiters were scurrying toward the waterfront, Simon could only wonder: Into which ear had he murmured his declaration in the early morning hours at Les Baux, to a Sarah half asleep but happy? Had she perhaps never heard the news that Simon Shafer was, at last, doing love with Sarah Geist?

Marcus stood next to Simon; his flush was gone and he smoothed his tangle of white hair with quick gestures. His bad eye wandered while he tried to focus his gaze on Simon. He, too, seemed to have crashed.

"There was no way for you to do this job you took on," Marcus said, quietly. "You couldn't know that Sarah, this Sarah of mine, is everything secret, private, ambiguous— with something hidden at the heart of her that is totally disconnected . . . experimental . . . unsettled . . . promiscuous. Antisocial, really . . . Oh, I've tried to socialize her more than once and failed. Even marrying her didn't work. . . . Hasn't she ever told you to stop trying to look inside her? She has her reasons."

The siren became painful to the ears as it passed close by, apparently attached to a boat. Marcus turned toward the sound. Just in time: Simon had become interested in hitting Marcus. He is in a confused rage; he feels enclosed in a cadence, as if the purpose of his affair with Sarah was to lead him to this waterfront restaurant in Venice, to drink powerful grappa, sniff cocaine and hear, at last, a life of Sarah, true or false; complete or incomplete.

The siren stopped and in the sudden silence a wild, distant yelling could be heard. A waiter ran past them. He called out, "*I carabinieri,*" and ran on.

Twilight was finished. It was night. Past the green wet water meadow in the direction of the sea wall, the lights of various boats could be seen; their motors chugged away and the scent of motor oil filled the air. In spite of all this feast for the eyes, ears and nose, it was difficult to perceive exactly what was going on.

In a minute or two they were back in Marcus's boat, and on their way into the lagoon. They passed a small jungle of fishermen's poles sticking up out of the shallow water and made their way past an abandoned lighthouse into deeper waters. It was an unpleasant embarcation; mud clung to the boat and the wind was bitter around their ears. The lagoon seemed a hostile place.

"It's your friend's party," Marcus called out. "Something's going on; those were police sirens."

They were headed toward the cluster of boats beyond the sea wall. The tide pulled against them; it felt like a struggle. A wild wave splashed up a pool of water; a small panicked fish leaped in the unaccustomed air. Simon threw it overboard.

Somewhere beyond the sea wall—Marcus knew where they were, Simon did not—they landed in the middle of a circle of boats. Marcus cut the motor down to a slight rumble. He steered them next to a long, gondolalike craft. Sarah was there, leaning over the side; or at least it appeared to be Sarah: a hood was in evidence. Someone who might be Linc was waving his arms wildly. A searchlight, probably from a police boat, lit up the scene. Two people leaned over the side of the boat, one of them working a pump of sorts. When he straightened out for a moment, Simon caught a glimpse of a turban. It was Ram Singh: the raising of the caissons was in progress; the final rehearsal for the Saving of Venice.

But what was the excitement about? Two power boats, overflowing with people, circled; screams poured into the air. There was no way to understand the dynamics of what was under way. The waves were high, slapping the boats and twisting them around in semicircles; Linc's storm had arrived along with the mysterious, hostile boats. The searchlight snapped off. Simon vomited over the side of the boat. The violent wind blew strands of vomit back into his face. As soon as his stomach heaved he no longer felt sick: purged and clear instead of high.

Marcus cut the motor. Simon wiped his face and wondered at his nausea. It was not ordinary seasickness. He never got motion sickness; not the large quantities of grappa or the cocaine, either. It was a response to either

270

part of Marcus's information: the part about himself or about Sarah.

The moon made a surprise appearance. It threw enough light for Simon to see Linc on the deck of what was really quite a large boat—some kind of steamer—waving his arms in some semaphore of the sea. He looked soaking wet. He nodded his head and yelled something. A hissing sound was added to the mix: then, like some weird creature of the lagoon, a gigantic round object sliced the surface and bobbed around for a moment, before being propelled in the direction of the sea gate. Linc went wild; he was hugging someone—Sarah, Simon thought, though he could see no hood or other identifying marks.

Simon was delighted: Linc's caisson worked. Wild or not, Linc was his friend; he wanted him to succeed in his nostalgia. He had stopped feeling betrayed—especially since, after accusing Linc of deserting, he had organized his own desertion.

All this while Marcus had been maneuvering the boat to get as close as he could to the caisson. Then the moon disappeared again and a wave swept the deck; Simon enjoyed the cold blast of salty wetness on his face. The water in the boat was now up to his knees. Marcus started the motor again. In the absolute blackness the voices were louder, angrier. He heard someone yell, in English, "Oh, my God, no . . ." Then the sound of wood hitting wood.

Sirens split the air again.

He was almost asleep when Sarah fell into bed next to him.

"Sarah . . ."

"Yes. Let's go to sleep."

"Where've you been?"

"There was an accident."

"I know all about that. We were there—in Marcus's boat."

"I took Linc to the hospital. He had to have five stitches."

"Where?"

"They hit him with an oar just above the ear; ripped open the skin."

"The ear . . . Sarah, did you ever have the measles?"

"What?"

"Measles."

"When I was a kid."

"Are you okay now?"

"What are you talking about?"

"I mean—any bad effects from it?"

"I'm hard of hearing in one ear. The left. I told you that."

"No you didn't. Marcus did."

"Those crazy gondoliers thought Linc was using scabs to handle his boats, so they came out to drown everybody. Imagine Linc getting brained in an Italian labor dispute?"

"Is he at the hotel?"

"He has to stay overnight at the hospital. Some dumb insurance thing. But he's a happy man."

"Oh?"

"His caissons work. At least the big models did. I'm wiped out."

"Sarah . . ."

"Yes . . . ?"

"Did you get an annulment from Marcus?"

"Right after we got married. I told you that."

"No you didn't."

She settled into the curve of his back, naked and chilled.

"He was impotent," she murmured. "Amazing. He knows everything, he can do everything, except that."

Her breathing measured itself, first into long sighs, then into snores. Like a machine that could process no more information, Simon's mind closed down. Sarah breathed against his neck. He was happy and slept without dreams.

15

SIMON OPENED the shutters to blinding sunlight. The storm had brought the sun back to Italy. Under the door was a message unnoticed the night before. It was from Madama Shafer and it requested that he telephone a Mr. Morrow at the White House, in Washington, D.C.

When he goes to the closet to dress he finds one of everything: shirt, trousers, underwear. But his suitcase is gone. Simon drags himself downstairs to discuss the theft with Margaretta. He is sluggish, his head hurts and his body feels not quite connected to his mind. Marcus's honest drug is collecting its payment for the energy and sense of illumination lent the night before.

Margaretta is changing traveler's checks at a table in the breakfast room. She is wearing a skirt and blouse and her hair is tied up in a kerchief. She looks like a schoolgirl, instead of the bitter solitary who drank too much tequila and made pronouncements about sex.

She is, in fact, sorry about the pronouncements, she states at once. She has not been in good shape. Sarah's arrival has triggered all sorts of memories and disturbing feelings. Their time together had been the most hopeful days of her life, after all. But the end has been good. She is thinking of selling the *pensione* and returning to the States. She is, after all, still young.

No, his luggage has not been stolen. Sarah had asked the porter to ship it through on the Naples train along with her own. She was at the Ospedale Ss Giovanni e Paolo visiting Linc and would pick up Simon in time to make the train.

A wild dash to the train station puts him in the middle of railway officials, none of whom know anything about his luggage. Does he not have the *biglietti*—luggage tickets? If he waits any longer he will miss his plane. Somehow, it is imperative that he not miss this particular plane. If he, once again, needs a sign, the same one is available to him, only in more dramatic form. His hand is in a perfect spasm of pain. (Emotional stress, Dr. Rowan had cautioned, can exacerbate the effects of the loose bone pressing on the nerve.) He feels pushed by events, by the wishes and needs of others, by bones and nerves. The sun splashes a magnificent pool of light on the sidewalk outside the train station. A buzz of voices fills the morning air. Spring is arriving at last. Naples with Sarah would be warm, sensuous—altogether delightful. But he takes the vaporetto to Marco Polo Airport with only the shirt and jacket on his back, his wallet and passport in his pocket.

Enraged, his right hand in high anguish cradled in a makeshift sling, more in love than ever, Simon boards the plane for home.

Part Four

PROJECT...

*Eald oefenscop, eorium bringe blisse in
burhum. . . . ("Old poet of the evening, I bring
to men happiness in their cities.")*
   *—Old Saxon riddle of the nightingale
    reported by Jorge Luis Borges*

I

New York was a foreign country.

A heat wave held it, like a South American state, for ransom. The streets were choked with victims panting in the shade, seeking out oases: air-conditioned movies, restaurants, drugstores. On upper Broadway, Simon actually saw steam rising from a puddle in the gutter. He waited for a moment to see if a face would emerge from the mist. None did; instead, a scraggly brown dog sat down in the water and then scurried off, wetter and happier. But it told Simon that he was still looking for signs and portents.

He stood there, his hand in a sling which he used when he was alone, breathing short bursts of the hot, damp air. At his feet there was a jagged hole in the concrete where the sidewalk had buckled from the ninety-five-degree heat. Afraid to look down into the hole for some reason, he hailed a cab. His mission was to buy a new dog collar and leash for Matthew's puppy. Something in his Paris conversation with Sarah—his Confessions of a Lousy Father—had focused what little energy he had, since coming home, on Matthew. Perhaps it was easier to handle paternal guilt than the conjugal kind. Matthew seemed not to notice any difference; but Alex had cast odd looks at him as the two of them sat over Robin Hood or a record of *Peter and the Wolf.*

The cabdriver explained at length about the nonfunctioning air-conditioning system of his cab. He turned around and stared sweatily at Simon.

"It ain't as hot as hell," he said.

"Oh?"

"It's hotter'n hell!" he said in triumph. And choked down a little laugh.

Cabdrivers were always experts, Simon thought. Even on hell. He might become one himself. "Stay, thou art so fair": a comic-strip Faust, dripping sweat, afraid to think about what his Marguerite was really like. A freaked-out drug addict on her way back . . . a weird survivor of a botched abortion playing out a contraceptive fantasy . . . He didn't know what to think; was beyond thinking; only waiting. He'd got up the nerve to call Dr. Geist: Sarah was due back tomorrow.

The driver turned on the radio. Con Edison was asking everyone to use less electricity. Blackouts were feared. Before entering the pet shop, Simon carefully removed the hand sling.

At the corner of Eighth Street and Fifth Avenue, street musicians played. They were young, probably students. When Simon had been a kid, in the forties, the street musicians had been old men, playing the violin in the wintertime, with fingertips sticking out through mittens. Now the heat brought out the new kind: the boy who played the oboe was about twenty and the two girls, clarinet and bassoon respectively, were younger. All three were bare from the waist up. The sight of women's breasts in the street, which had given swift political shock in so many street occasions of the sixties, now had a lovely, pastoral tone. If it was a plea for anything, it was a plea for meeting nature—in this case extreme heat—on its own terms. It was as personal a statement as the Haydn woodwind trio they played.

280

He told Alex what he'd seen. She stood in the doorway of the kitchen, waiting for something. He realized that she was waiting for him to fill in the missing sense of what the scene meant to him. He couldn't. All the nuance of contrast between past and present experience, which had been so clear to him on the steaming street as he listened to half-nude Haydn, was gone. He stood, dumb.

After a moment she blinked once or twice, smiled and continued into the kitchen to prepare for guests, with Matthew playing on the floor as she worked.

Simon went to his study and tackled the mail that had piled up during the past week. He carefully placed the letter from the White House on the side of the pile and started to work on the rest. He has not returned the call from Mr. Morrow in Washington. Halfway through the invitations to seminars, requests from graduate students for letters of recommendation, fund-raising requests from anti-Vietnam organizations, he found his throat closing and his insides turning over in the awful way they do when an airplane makes a sudden drop. But when the sensation came now, it stayed.

He had been happy for a long time. Then he'd tried to extend the scope of that happiness. Now it was gone. In its place had come a kind of permanent vertigo.

At least until tomorrow, when Sarah returned.

2

IT WAS A GOOD dinner party. Except that Simon felt thousands of miles away. It was a good party, lively and witty; except that Simon's hand was in agony and he had to act as if it were not. He wondered for a moment why he could not tell Alex about it.

It was as if he must keep all secrets or he could keep none. Shaking hands was a problem, solved by a lot of hugging. The occasion was a visit from Alex's sister and her husband, Max Rosengarden, en route from their home in St. Louis to Ankara and then Cairo. Max was a presence: all jowls and girth. Dak was a delicate woman and, unlike Alex, was an active Quaker. The Quaker movement, along with her husband and her little boy, Seth, was her whole life.

Max was a bull: loud, coarse and likable. He carried his five-year-old son on his shoulders for much of the evening, even after sleep had struck the child down and he drooped over his father's shoulder.

Jerry and Ruth Meskin: Jerry was Simon's oldest friend, older than Linc, first a storefront lawyer and now working at Warner Brothers. Ruth Meskin was a sociologist at Columbia (sociology, she told Dak: that's anthropology using white people). And there was Dieter Lantz, an architect who developed projects with Alexandria and flirted with her in a mild, vaguely homosexual way.

The talk moved lightly, laughter burst out every few moments; a sprinkling of shop talk, which Simon used to enjoy, salted the conversation.

Except that Simon listened to it all with an awful detachment. It was as if he had died of a mysteriously wounded hand, and had returned to his own home and friends to find that *they* were ghosts. He was visible to them; but they were not quite real to him. His attention was fixed on the absent Sarah—and on the absent Simon who floated through recent scenes, like a replay of forbidden home movies. It was unbearable to him that he might be condemned forever to be not quite alive, not quite present in his own daily life. Heat did not alone make hell. To be not present where you were—a new definition of hell the cabdriver had doubtless not thought of. As they stood up from the table, the buzz of interested conversation in the air, he could only wonder where Sarah was, what she was doing, and whether the flirtation with Linc had flowered into something heavier. With the little detachment he

282

could muster, he thought: My God, I am about to enter the world of popular songs: jealousy, yearning . . .

Max Rosengarden cornered him. It was like being cornered by a tank carrying a small boy around its turret.

"You look terrible," Max said.

"I do?"

"You're putting on weight. I know, I'm a horse, but I'm always that way. Besides, you're floating around like you didn't know where you were."

"Is this your own observation, Max, or is it from Alex?"

"I've got eyes. But she's been telling Dak for over a month that you're a mess. Why don't you come with me?"

"Where?"

"Turkey. I'm going to fix a bridge—and then I'm going to help them widen the harbor at Port Said. I could work you in."

"I think not, Max. Tell me, do you get along with Seth?" He indicated the drowsing child folded around Max's neck.

"Kids have to get along with us, not the other way around."

"I mean, do you have a lot in common?"

Max stared blankly. "He's my son."

"I see," Simon said.

"Listen, give it some thought. You need a new start at something . . . you need—"

"I'm sort of sick of people telling me what I need, Max. There seems to be a lot of it going around these days."

"You schmuck, didn't they give you any psychology courses at Berkeley, or wherever the hell you went? If you walk around looking like you have a headache, people offer you aspirin. I'm the intellectual dregs of this family —don't deny it: it doesn't bother me anymore; Dak would deny it and Seth wouldn't believe it, but I know—and I'm smart enough to know that there is a look in your eye, a way of holding your head as if you're listening to someone speak who may not even be there . . . but you're listening

because you want to be told something. So don't be surprised if everybody you know harangues you or gives you
the truth in ten words or less. The truth is: you're on the
verge of doing something crazy—anybody can tell that.
And I'm married to your wife's sister and I'd like to stop
you. So how about it?"

"No, thanks, Max."

Max shook his head, unwound Seth and lowered him
gently to the floor.

"Need some money?"

"I did my total assets this afternoon. With no income
except one course at Yale and six thousand dollars in the
bank, I may call you in Turkey or Egypt."

"Call collect!"

He undressed with a surprisingly light feeling. Max
thought he was going to do something crazy. Did that
mean leaving Alex and Matthew and marrying Sarah and
living happily ever after? And what had become of his
sense that Sarah had no claim against his marriage? Ah,
when he'd thought that he was in the throes of happiness.
Other throes were in progress.

"I think I like Max," Simon said.

"In spite of—"

"Yes, with Max it has to be in spite of."

"Did he—"

"Try to save my soul? Yes. But these days that's like
going into a bakery. You have to take a number."

"That means you're not going."

"That means I'm not going to Turkey or Egypt with
Max. Let's forget about my soul for now."

"Simon . . . What is it?"

"Nothing. Go back to sleep."

"You made such awful sounds."

"Bad dream. Rub my forehead."

"Like this?"

"Yes. What made you get a harpsichord again?"

284

"I felt this tremendous urge to play."

"After all these years?"

"It's a slow year. My husband was away in Europe; I can't seem to get the grants I need—the world is holding its breath; so I thought I'd make some music in the meantime. Matthew says it sounds like his music box. Are you worried because of the cost?"

"No. We'll be stone broke in three months anyway—unless something happens."

"It's so hot in here. Are you sure the air conditioner is working?"

"It's just working too hard."

"Are you all right, Simon?"

When had the dialogue of marriage that had once included everything from sexual gossip about friends to why Matisse had been overlooked in favor of Picasso for so many years—when and why had it been reduced to being —or not being—"all right"?

Misery began with specifics, but if it went on too long it became an abstraction. Happiness was exact, specific: remember the day we stumbled on the raspberry field outside Stamford while checking a house site, and stopped working and got drunk on raspberries? Remember the first time I realized you liked to be touched there, or here? Remember the day we ate three dozen oysters and drank a bottle and a half of Montrachet at La Coupole?

But prolonged misery cancels memories: except for the obsessive dwelling on defeats. Leading, finally, to such rich, resonant conversational gems as: "Are you all right?"

They have been circling since Simon's return. He has been waiting for some change in the mood, in the language between them; a change that would trigger a move toward each other—bodies first, hearts and minds later. Now, when he replies, wearily, "I'm all right," she turns to him, raises herself on an elbow and says with slow sadness: "It's very hard to live with someone who feels his life has come to nothing."

It is the trigger. The clarity of the statement allows him

to turn to her. The restraint of the phrase is meant to convey pain without a sentimental hitting below the belt. They make love awkwardly.

3

THIS TIME it was Sarah who was "just back." Just back from Venice, from Naples, perhaps having shared lunch on the hill overlooking the bay with a recuperating Linc. Simon let himself into the apartment with the key Sarah had given him a month after they'd met. She'd arrived and gone out again; Simon's missing suitcase stood in the foyer, with Sarah's raincoat draped over it.

The great bed does not seem as large as he'd remembered. On impulse, even though it is only three in the afternoon, he undresses and waits for Sarah's return, trying to nap in the cool sheets. For the first time, somehow, his presence in that bed feels illicit. It makes him too alert; he cannot sleep. He looks forward to the first sight of Sarah, framed in the bedroom doorway. Then he is aware that a naked, sweaty body is pressing against his back. The blinds have been drawn. He had fallen asleep, after all, and missed Sarah's entrance.

"It wasn't this hot in Naples," Sarah says.

He turns and lets his eyes grow accustomed to the darkness. He wants to see her face. But Sarah does not wait. She kisses him, becoming a blur in the process.

"I missed you," she says. "You tend to leave places very suddenly. Does not make for a feeling of security."

"Then you went south?"

"I just followed the luggage."

"I never realized how impulsive you were."

"Didn't you, Simon?"

"I take it back. Maybe stubborn is the word I want."

"Ah, don't you remember how long ago I started talking about going away—"

"Somewhere . . ."

"And you kept saying—"

"Married men can't just 'go away somewhere.' "

"But you did. That shows you how stubborn I am."

"Were you surprised when I came back alone, on schedule?"

"With no luggage. I have your suitcase. Only partly surprised."

"Partly?"

"Well, I didn't know what Marcus might have told you."

But he is not ready for such exploration.

Instead he begins to touch her. She responds; but he proceeds in a way that leaves some distance between them. It is not something that Sarah can notice. But Simon wonders at it. He is wary. The journey has left him cautious. There are, apparently, several Sarahs. It is not clear which one he is with now. He is anxious at how glad he is to be with her. She murmurs, "That was a fine trip. Think of the memories we'll have." At which Simon strikes her mouth a blow with his own and words stop. What follows is, for Simon, some crazy attempt to establish a total possession of Sarah. He is sure, afterward, that she has no idea of what has been happening; but for him, he is living out what he predicted in France by singing for Sarah Blake's sad song of human love. One of them, he knows, is going to possess the other. It marks an end of one phase of their being together. He consciously tries to be brutal, controlling, moving her heavily and harshly one way and another to satisfy his desire. But, innocently, she simply responds, makes her own implied or murmured desires known, happily moaning out her satisfaction a few seconds before he comes: he is far too conscious of what he has been doing to be completely satisfied.

He has been acting out of fear; he knows this immediately afterward. If anyone is to possess anyone, he knows it will not be him. He is now possessed. He knows that even if Sarah has become involved with Linc it will not change anything.

At least, not for Simon.

He rests his head on her breast, feeling his head rise and fall with her breath. It is a nice unity. He is sad sensing that the two of them have just had different experiences —at the same time.

Other people's lives always escape us, he thinks. Marcus's version, Simon's perception or, finally, Sarah's version—if it existed: it would still be impossible to grasp, to fix as a truth. It was why he'd been happy with Alex for so long. Her way was to deny the contour of their lives in exchange for density. The specific, not the general.

"What memories did you have in mind?" he asks.

"The horses in the Camargue . . ."

"I remember. Wonderful short, tense little animals . . ."

"The flamingos . . ."

"Which I said would never show up. . . . Did you know that I did cocaine with Marcus?"

"Was it good?"

"It opened things up. He needs you badly enough to make a plea."

"Did you grant it?" She could be a little nasty, even after making love.

"It's complicated. We were playing boccie at the time."

"Who won?"

"I think nobody."

He is aware of a different kind of rhythm in their conversation; a hesitancy on her part, every few exchanges. Is it, he wonders, because of hearing difficulty? And why has he never noticed it before?

But a second later she settles herself against Simon and says, "I want the whole thing, Simon. Let's do it. Let's be married: let's live together and do what the rest of the world does. I want it!"

"What happened to blessed anarchy?"

"I've done anarchy. I need *you*."

288

"What happened to continuity being death to the emotions?"

"Don't keep asking 'what happened?' You happened. We happened. It's all different now."

"And Marcus?"

"That's different, too. I had a dream on the plane," she says. "I'd seen the movie, so I turned off the light and dozed. It was a nightmare. I dreamt there were hands choking me."

"You have violent dreams. The last one was—"

"I know what the last one was. But this was me—my breath was going. Then I woke up. The hands were Marcus, I think."

"That's strange: it's such a hands-off life with him."

"It's up to you now, Simon. I love you and I always will love you."

There was a shiver for him in the words; but also a terror and a sense of foolishness. He laughs, nervously. "How can you say always?"

"I'll put it in writing," she says. "Here." She reaches across him and switches on the bedside lamp, takes a piece of notepaper and a ballpoint pen and writes: "I, Sarah Geist, love Simon Shafer and I always will." She signs her name, folds the sheet and hands it to Simon. "Okay," she says. "The rest is up to you."

He thinks of Marcus, boccie ball in hand, pointing out that love changes, that the body with its handy apparatus of pleasure decays and dies—all in the service of convincing Simon to return to the outside world again. And here was Sarah's neat refutation.

"Are you sleeping with Linc?" he asks.

She does not blink. "Are you sleeping with Alexandria?"

"That's not fair."

The phone rings. Simon almost reaches out for it, but Sarah hastily grabs it from across his chest. "Yes," she says. "Okay, I'll meet you there. Fifteen minutes." Then she is out of bed and dressing swiftly. "I have to go to the hospital," she says. "New York Hospital."

"Why?"

"My father's in for tests."

"I'll come with you."

She pauses in the act of pulling on her skirt. "No," she says. "Please don't."

"Why?" he asks, feeling childish, but compelled to ask. It is related to the swift grab for the phone before he could pick it up.

"Not this time, okay?"

At the door she kisses him goodbye. She is dressed with dash for New York: blue pants, silver blouse, a scarf loosely knotted around her throat; he is naked and shivering in the air-conditioned room.

"Sarah," he says.

"Yes?"

"Suppose I can't do it? Can't leave and be with you? That was never in the cards."

"You needn't worry about one thing—the equalizer is back in." She kisses him again. She is gone. It is an unfamiliar sensation, a reversal: she dressed and gone, he naked and left behind.

4

THE PAIN WAS SO BAD that he hailed a cab and gave the driver Dr. Rowan's address without even calling for an appointment. About five blocks short of the office, he stopped the cab and got out. He walked in the steaming wet air toward the corner of Seventy-ninth and Lexington.

When he got to the door and saw the metal nameplate — R. T. ROWAN, M.D.—he hesitated. He let his arm dangle, but the pain was steady. The door opened and a man encased in a body cast from the waist up was helped out by a gray-haired woman, with a little girl trailing behind. Simon fled.

290

Now there were no taxis to be had—it was almost noon —and he took the subway at Seventy-ninth Street. The heat underground was drenching, the air foul. Simon was so enmeshed in his thoughts—why was he so insistent on not seeing the man in white? and was it connected with the despair that filled his chest cavity as if that were precisely where his soul or heart was located?—that he rode past his stop and found himself in Brooklyn. In the subway car riding back he found himself staring at a travel poster which featured a calendar. The date May 1 jumped out at him. The Greer deadline. It seemed as distant as a movie title: *The Greer Deadline*—like *The Ipcress File*—full of menace and as fictional. But the newer deadline, although it had not yet been set, was more disturbing: Sarah's Deadline.

At home he took two of Dr. Rowan's yellow pain pills and lay down. He was in a sweat not entirely related to the weather or the hurt in his hand. Well, he had taken the pills he'd been avoiding for so long. He wondered if Sarah was entirely off hers. He'd forgotten to ask her the day before; and he was through checking her for signs of yellowness. Project Sarah was a success. A success he now had to deal with. Alex had taken Matthew out and the phone must have rung four or five times before he felt able to answer it. A crisp operator's voice informed him that the White House was calling for Mr. Shafer.

"I'm sorry," Simon said. "You have the wrong number."

"Please forgive," the operator said. "Have a nice day."

It rang a dozen times or so before it stopped. Simon forgave. Everyone except himself. He was sick of the unreality of past months. Sick of having provoked from Alex her remark about living with someone who feels his life has come to nothing. Was he that someone? What kind of insanity was it to push happiness so far that it turned into this kind of misery? Was it Sarah he had wanted? Or was she right when she'd said he was using her as a distraction? Some distraction! Because of her he couldn't enter a doctor's office or get off at the right subway stop or take a

291

phone call from the White House. He was not impressed with the source of the phone call. He knew that, grandiosity aside, he was what they referred to at staff meetings as a "supplier." He meant to change the face of the world; but they thought of him as supplying planning services . . . pacifying certain urban constituencies. . . . Or were these the thoughts of despair? Once you turned yourself over to someone else in exchange for happiness, you couldn't trust anything you did or thought. It wasn't even the politics of the phone call. Behind that operator's voice lay the invisible sons of bitches against whom he'd been demonstrating, it seemed, for centuries—actually, almost a decade. The week they'd bombed Cambodia and shot the students at Kent State University, Alex and he had done nothing but send telegrams and round up signatures for petitions: it all seemed like a distant childhood—all of a year ago. At four in the morning, Alex had regained her poise and humor. Lying across the bed half alseep, she'd sung Gilbert and Sullivan's description of the whole problem:

> Every little boy and girl
> Born into this world alive
> Is either a little liberal,
> Or else a little conservative [rhymes with *dive*] . . .

They'd grown used to the fact that the people who controlled the money and had the power didn't have to be nice, let alone good. No, he wasn't impressed with his own paralysis.

He found himself living Sarah's past life; it was easier than living his own. In the supermarket, buying eggs and cocktail napkins, he suddenly envisioned the abortion scene: the Cuban nurse, the fat doctor asking her about her father, a German accent adding to the horror. Then the bloody sequence, the afterpains and, finally, the verdict: "Never!"

Sarah: "No children, ever?"

Fat Doctor: "Never!"

292

Sarah: "I wasn't sure if I wanted children, but—"
Fat Doctor: "Never!"

It was as if he had to extend Project Sarah backward; to participate in her past suffering; to deal himself in from the start, or as far back as he could get. It could lead him to the moment of her decision to refute her destiny. The birth of the IUD decision. "If I wear an IUD I must be able to conceive; otherwise why would I wear an IUD?" A triumph of tautology. A tautology as sad as a Schubert *lied*.

To save his sanity he allows himself, at 4 A.M., to fantasize: How would it be if Sarah were his wife? The If game: only played with more desperation.

They would live on the East Side. He could not bear running into Alex with Matthew, shopping for toys. He tortures himself with the extra weapon of sentimentality. They would travel, because his work demanded travel. So did hers. But if Marcus had told the truth, her business was only window dressing for an ex-addict. But if Marcus had told the truth, the whole fantasy was insanity—because she was a wreck, held together only by Marcus's backing in business and his loose arrangement in personal life. Impossible to conceive! Simon groaned at the ugly pun.

"What . . . ?" Alex said in her sleep.

"Nothing," Simon said. "Go to sleep." And added, crazily, "Maybe my life will *not* come to nothing."

"That's all right," Alex exhaled. "I'm your best friend."

Simon couldn't believe what he'd heard. "What did you say?"

She said nothing; her breath said sleep; riding on a faint whiff of atypical alcohol.

"New York Hospital."

"I'd like to inquire about the condition of a Dr. Geist."

"One moment, please . . . Are you a member of the family?"

"Yes."

"That's Room 785, Dr. Geist. Dr. Geist's condition is serious."

Why did he call? What *right* did he have to call?

For the first time, she cannot see him when he asks.

"Why not?"

"I just can't tonight. Couldn't you give me a little more warning?"

"You know how it is."

"But I can't tonight. And I can't handle how it is."

"Let's go out to dinner tomorrow night?"

"Out?"

"I have this jump suit with a hood; no one will recognize me."

"I'll wear mine, too. It's a little hot for jump suits."

"We'll stroll on the street together, hand in hand."

"What's going on?"

"Maybe a movie?"

"We've never been to a movie together, In public?"

"How about this picture *Summer of '42?* It's really about us. An older person and a kid, sexes reversed. I miss you, Sarah. I wish we were still in Europe."

"Let's go back. No; we'd better try the movie."

He says nothing about her father. It is a dangerous subject. Going to dinner and the movies is dangerous enough. He has a longing to tell all he's going through to a friend. Naturally, that friend would be Linc.

As he is preparing to pick up Sarah for their "date," Alex appears.

"I had a super session with the Women's Design Group." She takes off her hat and sits down. Alex is one of the few women in America who can still wear a hat with a sense of style, not looking out of date.

"And," she says, "I am drunk."

Startled, all he can think of to say is, "Matthew is asleep and I'm off to dinner with Jack Jackson."

"Who's that?"

"The black guy from New Haven—wants me to do a textbook with him."

"Have a drink with me first, for old time's sake. Then I'll hit the sack."

It is the first time in five years that he has seen Alex high on anything.

"Here's to Alexandria," she says.

"I'll drink to that."

"I mean the city of my birth, not me. At the meeting, Rose Ruder was telling me about her trip to Egypt and it all came back to me—about the frogs."

"You've never told me about frogs."

"Legs," she said. "They hunted frogs in Alexandria, for their legs—*grenouilles*. Decadent, my dad called them, and my mom couldn't eat them."

He sips his drink, starting to feel sad. He cannot recall if Alex always called her parents Dad and Mom.

"It strikes me"—Alex drained her glass—"that they had an answer that sustained them through all sorts of terrible questions." He tries to follow her from frogs to her parents.

"I mean, they knew that other people were the answer —that yourself is only a terrible question."

"How do the frogs come in?"

"This was Alex in the palmy days—before Farouk's revolution. I was only about four or five; Dak was ten or so. But I remember going on a frog hunt at night. They had big searchlights. Bang, they turn it on and there sits the poor slimy thing, heart going thump-thump, transfixed by the light, and then one of the servants throws a spear— *thunk*—right in the heart. Then off come the legs. God— all for the sake of *haute cuisine.*"

He undresses her and puts her to bed, feeling as if some awful thing he has said or done has pushed her into drink.

"My father had a sense of humor. He said, 'Quakers have no position on the killing of frogs.' And my mother joined in by saying that all that garlic sweats out of you for days and makes you unfit company. But I knew what they meant. They meant don't shine lights into anybody's eyes and scare them and then kill them and cut their legs off. . . . They thought everybody could be good; all they had to do was try. . . . Do you love me, Simon?"

"Yes," he says seriously, and kisses her.

"Good," she says drowsily. "They had bats in the movie theaters, too, and one got in my hair and everyone said I was very brave because I didn't scream, but I had nightmares for years and never told anyone until now. Greer called—I forgot to tell you. Good night. Feed the puppy."

"How could you do that?"

"There was nothing else to do."

"It was disgusting."

"I had no choice."

"I don't want to hear that."

"It was all planned to be a nice evening out—"

"Just like real people . . . only real people don't run the three-minute mile from a theater lobby to the subway station and then hide until the train comes."

"They were friends of Alexandria's. In her Design Group."

"My God, remember the days when you were not even supposed to mention her name!"

Simon said he remembered.

"I was better off when I was in the test tube and you just took me out and put me back in."

At home, he vomited into the toilet bowl. Ben Demos held his head.

"Not so loud," Ben cautioned. "You'll wake Alex."

"Matthew, maybe; not Alex. She went to sleep drunk."

"Alex?"

"This is not drunk-throwing-up; this is just me."

"Why is Prometheus upchucking? It's hard work giving fire to mankind. . . ."

296

"Womankind . . . Hand me that towel. Alex thinks I'm crazy because I talk to you."

"Sometimes I think I'm crazy because *I* talk to *you*. You don't listen. I warned you you'd get your ass in a sling trying to make and mold."

"I only tried to help her be happy."

"You want to be a saint, then suffer!"

"I don't want to be any such thing. I want to be happy."

"Then suffer!"

Suffer was what he did best these days.

Anodynes escaped him. Liquor left him destroyed. It was not an "honest" drug; it took back more than it gave. He would have liked to try cocaine again; an "up" was needed. The greatest escape of all was becoming problematical. The immersion into Sarah's body and self was now complicated. That simple, profound joining which took place outside of time, place and responsibilities was just another part of life: tied to waiting on a father's death, complete possession, otherwise known as marriage—which meant divorce—which meant the introduction of lawyers and children and puppies and parents and all the machinery of day-to-day life. Like everything else, it had become political. If Sarah was sleeping with Linc, was that adultery? Of course not; neither was married. But was it a betrayal? Of whom? Linc was his friend, but Simon didn't own Sarah. Should Linc have asked his permission? It all led to more suffering.

5

HE WALKED THE STREETS like a wild man, full of hate. The crowds pouring out of the subway exit on Thirty-third and Park Avenue South drove him into a fury. A woman carrying an umbrella jabbed him with the tip as she brushed past; three black teen-agers, laughing and innocent of malice, gave him a thrill of false danger —and the skies were clear. The absolute irrationality of all these people with their varied concerns squashed into this vertical life, breeding ground for paranoia. Nature red in tooth and claw. Bullshit! The city was the greatest animal cage ever invented—and its inhabitants the animals. No wonder ground-level apartments all had bars.

By the time he reached the Battery, stopping off to stare like a demented thief into the windows of the jewelry stores on Canal Street and to wander briefly among the slower-moving, more-at-home-appearing Chinese on Mott Street, he was soaking with sweat and contempt. How had he ever let himself get trapped into this lunatic life? A cage-builder—worse, even, than an architect: the planner of the Great Cage. If so, what was the big fuss about whether he built new cages or helped make old cages more humane places to live in.

Standing on the dock at Peck Slip, he watched a Dutch freighter load and unload unmarked crates: feeding the hot city what it needed to live on while extracting other substances to be sent to other cities. The whole process was like some enactment of a mystery play. He was sick of it. And sick of the polyglot flow of nationalities, races: cheek-bones bespeaking certain parts of Asia, intonations that sang of Eastern Europe, straight blond hair and clear blue eyes from northern Europe. There was a time when the people in a town all had the same last name. That was when place meant home.

When he was good and angry his hand hurt less. He sat on a bench in Union Square Park, just he and a few other derelicts who found city life too demanding to manage. It was very important to him to deal with the fear that kept him from the doctor's office. Physical courage had been a strong point, starting when he was eight years old and getting pounded around in prize fights for which he'd always volunteered, continuing to silly things like forgetting to wear a hard hat on construction sites. Lack of imagination, he'd called it. A distraction of mind that went so deep as to prevent the idle fantasies of death and destruction that cross most normal minds and make for careful behavior, even cowardice.

No. it was something else. The idea of his right hand being tampered with was so connected to the doing of work—the work he was not *doing*—that it was too terrifying to consider. It was as if Dr. Rowan was a demonic angel in white sent to administer the final punishment. *If I forget thee, O Jerusalem, may my right hand forget her cunning. . . .*

"Do you know where I can get some cocaine?"

"Are you putting me on?"

"Why?"

"I just don't think of you that way."

"How do you think of me, Jack?"

Jack Jackson was not only an alibi Simon had used for his disastrous night out at the movies with Sarah; he was real, a black colleague at Yale who had shared some of the wildest days of student-faculty demonstrations with Simon and Linc. A letter from him proposing a textbook project had been waiting when Simon returned from Venice.

"I think of you as the ideal man to write a textbook about urban reform. But I don't like the way you think about me."

"Why?"

"You've got this white motherfucking idea that every black man can score drugs for you."

"Can't you?"

Jackson smiled. "Of course," he said. "Now let's order lunch and talk about life."

"How are your students these days?"

"Students? Ain't no students no more, man," Jackson mocked. "They're all back in the woodwork waiting for the war to end and thinking about getting jobs. Hence our textbook. Do you know how much bread there is in textbooks?"

299

"Never mind bread or students—how are you doing these days?"

"Tired, man, I am bone tired. I am tired of moral rage, I am tired of mystical experiences, I am tired of spontaneous political action, I am tired of this endless war, I am tired of being Yale's black; I am just weary. Hence, as I have just pointed out, our textbook. I am ready for a rest. And I have a gut feeling that this whole country is ready for a rest. There is usually heavy money in doing what the country feels like."

"I'm not sure I am," Simon said. "Ready for a rest, I mean."

Suddenly he is not sure he can get through an ordinary, pleasant lunch with this bright, serious, charming black colleague. Such simple rituals may be beyond him. With growing panic, he watches Jackson study the menu. God, he thinks, don't let me get up and run. His wife thought he was crazy. She was probably right. But perhaps it could be kept from the rest of the world a little while longer.

"This is the second time you've ever cooked dinner for me."

"I don't think I want to risk fleeing from a restaurant. One hide-and-go-seek game a month is all I can stand."

Before he can assume from her tone that it is going to be a grim evening, Sarah turns from the refrigerator, where she has been searching out arcane fragments of food, and kisses him.

"I miss you when you're away from me," she murmurs, "even more than when you're here."

"But you've been staying away."

"I have to," she says. "Let's duplicate that first dinner I made for us. It ended so nicely. It was the night you said 'yes' to going away. Steaks . . . endive salad, I think . . ."

"It's tricky," he says to her as he sets out the wineglasses, "to repeat anything. Marx says everything in history happens twice. The first time it's serious—the second it's farce."

"That's history," she says. "This is love."

How easily the word flows from her now. Just a matter of practice.

As she is sitting down he stands over her and pulls her to her feet.

"If you recall, we never got to eat that dinner." But their kiss does not move from the table to the bedroom. Instead, they eat, and drink the Gigondas Simon has brought as a remembrance of Les Baux.

"What's wrong with this wine?"

"It's the same stuff M. Thulier served us."

"It doesn't travel well. Like us."

She tells him how her father's illness frightens her.

"I've always been a D.G."

"What's that?"

"Daddy's Girl."

"Oh."

"It might explain Marcus. If he needs explaining."

"I called the hospital the other day. Just because I'm barred from visiting doesn't mean I'm not concerned. He liked me. In fact, he warned me about your skin: trusted me on sight."

"My skin?"

"Apparently he knew about those pills, and what happens when you stop suddenly."

"It didn't happen."

"Are you off, still?"

"Clean as can be. I have some grass for after dinner, if you'd like."

It is an unpleasant reminder of the impingement of Linc, of Marcus's accusations. But the wine flows into glasses and mouths so smoothly during dinner that other highs are not in question.

Then, desperate to repeat the experience of happiness, he kneels before her chair and spreads her legs. Sarah lets her head fall back, sideways, against the chair, her fall of hair dark against the polished wood. Simon pauses and looks long; the wet, rose-colored special skin that never

301

ceased being at the same time something lovely—a thing to contemplate—and something magnetic, which drew him hypnotically to touching and kissing.

In that moment of sight before touch, Sarah, her eyes closed, murmured, "I love it when you look first, for a long time, and then hold your mouth there." He feels himself sinking with the familiar, drowning delight that has ransomed him from hopelessness in the past month. For a long moment he gazes in familiar fascination, then moves forward. But before he can touch her, she vanishes.

The lights have gone out. Disconcerted, he presses forward anyway—and feels her shaking with laughter. The erotic weight of the moment has become weightless; funny. He on his knees in the dark, after being passionately exhorted on to intimate looking. Marx has won: the repetition is farce.

"You and your cities," she chokes. "Nothing works."

"It's a heat wave. I warned them in the nineteenth century—this city wasn't built for more than a hundred thousand people."

"There are candles in the kitchen."

They sip cold coffee on the living room couch by candlelight, naked now not to make love, but because the air conditioning has stopped working. Sarah rests her head on Simon's shoulder and says, "You're not coming to me, Simon, not ever, are you?"

"I'm here," he says. "Let's go on the way we were doing. Was it so bad?"

She cannot, she says. She knows it sounds like something out of *Alice in Wonderland,* but he has given her so much, she has to have more.

"Is it Linc? Is that a big thing now? Either—or?"

"Ask him. He's your friend."

"If it's Linc, you just picked some kind of a Xerox—an unmarried Xerox." He is angry and near tears. A terrible reversal has taken effect. She is not crying anymore these days, but he is on the verge of tears for hours at a time. What he gets is silence as well as darkness and oppressive heat. He recalls Marcus saying something about Sarah being essentially secret . . . ambiguous . . . private. . . . He stands up, shakily, making his way toward his scattered clothing through the shadowy candlelit obstacles.

"Simon," Sarah says. "Give me back my key. Please. I want it back!"

"I must have sounded like an idiot," Simon said. " 'Is it Linc? Is it Linc?' My God . . ."

"What did she say?" Linc asked.

"She said: Ask Linc."

They were lunching in the solemn precincts of the Century Club. Simon had chosen the occasion: lunch—early enough for Linc to be entirely unstoned. He wanted as much clarity as possible. Linc had chosen the place. The old-fashioned, 1900's look, the elegant sweep of the enormous marble staircase, the hushed atmosphere; the only visible blacks, servants. It was not the kind of place they had ever met in before. The people who ran the Venice Foundation had proposed Linc for membership; in the meantime he enjoyed having lunch in the same room as a large painting of Henry James as a young man.

"Are you going to ask Linc?"

"Not just yet—if ever. How was Naples?"

"Great place to recuperate from a lacerated scalp. What a comedy of errors."

"I was a witness. Sarah's ex-husband and I were on one of those small boats milling around. But your mechanical stuff works."

"That's what I'm doing in New York, Presenting my report and getting the okay on the next steps. I left Santha Singh to mind the store; Ram and I are here on and off for about a month."

"I notice you haven't mentioned my joining up with you to restore the wonders of the past."

Linc occupied himself with his *omelette fines herbes.* "It does not," he said, "seem particularly appropriate just at this moment. Are you going to leave Alex?"

303

"No!"

"Simple as that?"

"As complicated as that. But still: no! Are you going to marry Sarah?"

"Yes. Once she gives up for good on you."

"Simple as that?"

"She makes me less angry; less cynical about women, about myself. I'm happy with her. I'm even smoking less —maybe because she smokes with me. Laura used to just sulk—and I'd end up smoking more."

A noiseless waiter filled their glasses with wine. The quiet was hard on Simon's nerves.

"If it's of any help, she made the first move. Not very manly of me to admit it—but maybe more friendly."

"Are you saying you're sorry?"

"Something like . . . I know what a lousy time you've been having."

I am not, he thought, going to sit here in this posh club and be pitied. He knew he might be able to throw Linc into a funk by the same methods Marcus had used with him. A simple recital of the litany: starting with drugs and ending with a fairy tale about a contraceptive device. At the least he could regain an advantage of balance; at the most he might cause heavy trouble. As with any foreign object tossed into smoothly working machinery, there was no predicting exactly what damage would be done. It might be interesting to watch.

But it quickly became an important point for Simon *not* to repeat any of Marcus's description of Sarah. It was still not clear whether Marcus had not simply shown him "his" Sarah; the way someone shows "his" Paris or Rome or Venice. But more important, it would be a cheap, weak shot. Right at that moment Simon needed every piece of strength he could rouse and hold; even the appearance of strength.

"Did you find out what you wanted from Sarah's junkman?" Linc asked.

By not attacking, Simon felt stronger already.

"It's all between Sarah and me," he said. "Marcus is an irrelevance. You are, too; a distraction. She and I have to fight it out. She asked me to give back her key."

"Oh . . . ?"

"I didn't. I told her I'd left it at home."

"She could always have the lock changed."

"She won't. That would be a defeat."

Simon's patience vanished. He wasn't ready to throw a punch at Linc, but he couldn't maintain the civilized style for another moment.

"What the hell," he said in a voice calculated to be too loud for the comfort of anyone in the room, Linc included, "are we doing, you and me, lunching in a place which undoubtedly keeps out women, blacks and all Jews except the rich or famous?"

There was the anticipated number of turned heads and stares.

"Cut it out," Linc said quietly. "You and I don't have to talk in code. If you're pissed off, you're pissed off. But Sarah's father is dying; did you know? This may be the wrong time to make a fuss about keys and lovers."

"People always die at the wrong time," Simon said. "If Ben Demos had died in the fullness of years, I wouldn't have thrown poor Alex into a panic by talking to him."

"Do you still speak with him?" Linc asked.

"Only when spoken to," Simon said, and signaled for the check. Enough was enough!

6

COMING IN FROM a downpour that doesn't cool, only steams, Simon spies on Sarah. He is beyond shame. He had spent the day before almost completely paralyzed, lying on his bed for twelve hours, forcing himself not to call her. Alexandria and Matthew walked around him, quietly, as if he were ill. Thus, today, action of any kind, even this disgusting, furtive and probably pointless surveillance, was better than being not quite alive, not quite dead.

Behind the glass door on which is lettered G & D TRAVEL AGENCY (Geist & Delmarco?) Simon lingers unobtrusively. Or so he hopes. It is the end of the day, but Sarah appears busy. An assistant, a slight, bony young man with hair tied in a ponytail, stands arranging brochures in a wall rack. Sarah alternately tends to customers and the phone, which rings three times during the first five minutes of Simon's spy mission.

He is testing one of Marcus's hypotheses: that Sarah's business life is a cardboard front, backed by Marcus as a kind of distracting toy. A detoxification tool.

But customers come and go; maps are examined; checks are written as deposits; American Express cards are run through stamping machines. It all bears a striking resemblance to real life. Simon keeps touching the folded piece of paper in his pocket: the one on which Sarah has written a silly guarantee of eternal love. It makes him feel, somehow, less grotesque in his espionage of despair.

Like most amateurs, he is caught. Sarah sees a client to the door and Simon does not duck away fast enough.

Her long hair is piled on top of her head in two small hills, secured with combs. A pencil peeks out from behind one hill. Very businesslike; very put together. Nothing vague, subtle or ambiguous is suggested by her manner.

"Simon! What are you doing here?"

"I thought maybe . . ."

"Yes?"

"Well, it's almost five."

"I have to go to the hospital after work."

"How is he?"

She says nothing.

"I thought we could have a drink."

"And after that," she says, as if continuing her sentence, "I have an appointment."

306

He gazes at that face which he has studied so closely: that rosebud mouth, those gray eyes, those plump, dry lips with the thin lines dividing spaces across the upper lip; and that rounded chin that gave her an extended youth, a little baby fat above the throat and below the slightly protruding front teeth. It was time he saw it for what it was: just another face, of a young woman whom so many men would look at and say: For *this* all that pain? From *this* all that happiness? Just an attractive Jewish young woman in her early thirties, with small breasts and heavy thighs and a personal life that did not bear too much thinking on.

It didn't work.

It was still Sarah. Something stirred in him when he looked at the combination of elements that made up Sarah. It hadn't always; maybe it wouldn't someday; certainly it didn't for everybody. The whole world couldn't be in love with the same woman. It wasn't practical. But for the moment, he was without choice.

Her office is around the corner from Top of the Sixes. She has yielded a little: a drink before she goes to the hospital.

"You were spying on me."

"Yes."

"Why, for God's sake?"

"I don't exactly know. To see you in the world, like an outsider."

"But you're not an outsider."

"I'm not always sure of that."

"Bullshit! We're lovers."

"Are we?"

She smiles, weary; the lips turn down so that fatigue and a touch of contempt are too close to each other to be comfortable.

"Simon, don't hang on to confusion so desperately. I've told you I want you and me and the whole story the way it's usually told. I'm trying to simplify. But if you can't . . ."

The hint of contempt does not escape him. No longer completely the lover, he is still partly the spy. If you aimed directly for happiness, you were not safe from anything.

"If I can't . . ."

"Then leave me alone, please; you have to, have to, have to, have to leave me alone."

"Alone?" he says. He is disgusted with himself for saying it, not even able to blame the one daiquiri still in his hand.

The warm rain has shrouded the famous view of the city in mist. Almost nothing can be distinguished except the distant arcs of one bridge or another toward lower Manhattan.

"I should have been a civil engineer," Simon says. "There's nothing ambiguous about bridges. Everyone needs bridges. Make a bridge and you're on the side of the angels forever. Do you want another drink?"

"I want my key, Simon. Please give it back, now. Don't tell me you don't have it with you. I want it back. It's mine!"

They are the only two people in the elevator. Sarah stares straight ahead. Simon stumbles silently on words that have to be said but will not form themselves decently. Suddenly the lights in the elevator flicker and the whirring sound stops. The elevator slows, then gently stops somewhere between two floors. After a few shudders it is completely still.

"Oh, God," Sarah says. "Another one. This is some summer! I hope the lights don't go out."

The lights did not go out. From above them someone pounded on a door.

"Shout to them, Simon," Sarah says. "Quick before they go away."

Simon shouts. Something unintelligible is shouted back; then silence. In seconds they are both shining with sweat. The heat is thick in the elevator car, pressing in on them.

"Will there be air to breathe?"

Simon points out the vents at the top of the car. There will be air to breathe.

"They'll get it going soon," Simon says. "In fancy buildings like this they always have auxiliary power." He has made that up, but it sounds comforting.

"I have to get to the hospital," she says. "I wish I had a cigarette."

From some reservoir of humor and detachment he finds easing words—about his city failing her again, about cities being made for winter and the country for summer. But beneath these civilized words runs the fantasy of kissing her wildly, of her responsiveness as he remembers it, of making love on the plastic floor of the airless trap of the elevator cage. He curves a hand toward her sweaty cheek; not as a prelude to love—they can barely breathe—but to a necessary truce. She clings to him. He bends her to him. Her forehead smells rancid with sweat near the hairline.

"Make it work," she whispers to him. "I'm afraid. Everything used to work, Simon. Make it work."

Sensing some kind of truce, if not his own, he crumples her to him, both of them wet rags by now, and tells her that he loves her, that he'd told her so late one night in Les Baux but he wasn't sure she'd heard. Somebody is pounding again; a number of voices are sounding in the shaft above them, but Simon cannot make out the words. In spite of his reassurance, he is finding it difficult to breathe. But he feels weirdly exultant just holding Sarah again. The lights are growing dimmer. As if working against a deadline, he proposes to return to the way they'd been: secret Chinatown nights, another trip to Europe. He is soaking in her sweat as well as his own. It must be one hundred degrees in the elevator shaft. When he tries to kiss her she is shaking her head wildly from side to side. She is crying.

"What is it?"

"Please . . . if you only knew . . . that dream was so terrible."

"What dream?"

"The hands . . ."

He remembers. "Marcus's hands . . ."

The words make her wild. "No, no, no, no, no; they were your hands."

The lights flare out and then back on full strength; the elevator starts to move, slowly, then swiftly; the air conditioning hums. Sarah is weeping, shaking her head as if all she can do is say no and cry. There was something in that "no," something dense, so thick and palpable that it had the finality of a death. It freed Simon, for that moment, because of its fatality. He could say anything.

Standing in the steaming twilight mists of Fifth Avenue, he hits her with everything Marcus had told him. He does not state. He asks.

She is ice cold, answering his questions as if he were the police; as if it were essential to tell the truth, but no more than is required to keep from being arrested.

Had she been strung out on drugs like her sister?

"No," she says. "Just what you've seen. I smoked; I dropped acid once—but nothing much happened. That's all."

Had she been dead broke and backed by Marcus as a losing proposition?

"He lent me money to get started and I paid him back; I'm in the black now."

Had she been rendered sterile by an abortion and did she "deny" it by playing at wearing the equalizer?

"I've never gotten pregnant since; but that was my choice. Except for that dream, I've always told you the truth. I don't care what you think, now."

It is clear to him that these questions and their dead, clear, monotone answers, with their simple reasonableness, were a corner they have turned. If he has never quite trusted her life, she now would never quite trust him.

She wipes her face with a soggy handkerchief and asks him, once more, for her key. She asks with the new moral authority of this fragile moment. He reaches into his pocket and for an instant is ready to give in.

At the last moment he hands her the downstairs key to

his own apartment building. He will have to ring the bell and be buzzed in. She does not notice the deception.

"I suppose," she says, "that Marcus told you things about Jephtha and me."

Behind them the lights in the building ripple on, floor after floor, until the glass façade gleams happily against the black wall of rain beginning to fall again.

7

AT HOME, he found Alex packing for a night flight. She was happier, more excited than he'd seen her for a long time.

"Louisiana?"

"New Orleans," Alex recited with delight, "has decided that our design for the mall most meets the goals of modern economy of line and the French traditions of their special city. Rose Ruder and me and Nora—we're on our way. I was waiting for you to get home before I left."

"How long?"

"About five days," Alex said. Would Simon be a help? Would he take care of Matthew? The Swedish au pair they sometimes use will look in and give an assist.

"Aside from it being a break for me, we can use the money."

Simon is too far gone to register a tremor at the reproach.

"I don't like you flying in this weather. The visibility is about zero."

But as usual Alex was without fear. Though not without certain concerns about him. She held up a vial of pills. "What are these for?"

A cue? For complete revelation, using Chicago and the hand injury as the kickoff point? The strength is not there.

"Orthopedic hangover from a while back. Enjoy yourself. Don't eat any frogs' legs. We'll be fine."

He lies on the bed after Alex is gone. It had taken all his available energy to see her off. The bed claims him immediately she is gone. He remembers a phrase read somewhere: "his mattress grave." A bed, alone, is like a grave. . . . What does he think about Alex's success/happiness? That she is a dupe. . . . Having given up belief for feeling, do you end up thinking all who still believe are dupes? fools of conviction? Crazy, to lie in bed, alone, in a world of fools . . . Having buried yourself in one human being, only to be evicted . . . Worse than just renouncing his ambitions, for a while or forever, he has been actively engaged in the pursuit of doubt. At this moment he would give anything to stop feeling and start believing again. (What had Sarah meant: "I suppose that Marcus told you things about Jephtha and me"?) Perhaps the real reason he is not leaving Alex to marry Sarah is his sense that Marcus was right . . . that happiness is a dumb idea, a dead end. Carried to an extreme, it was a horror. You could not pursue happiness . . . only experience it in passing. To have happiness is to not have a destiny. . . . The hum of the air conditioner reminds him of the stalled elevator. What is he going to do now? He has not exchanged belief for feeling: he has exchanged *doing* for *being*. . . . It is a new experience: he has never just *been* before. It is awful . . . a state of permanent anxiety.

8

HE CALLS SARAH. The line is busy; for a minute, for five minutes, for twenty minutes. Now he is frantic. The operator tells him the line is not busy—it is the circuits. The pounding in his chest will not stop. He wants to speak to her; to wipe out things; to explain to her about the deception of the key before she finds out herself; to find some way to reassess everything that's happened. Perhaps they can be friends; perhaps they can set a deadline of a year—less if she insists—during which time he will work things out; anything but this precipitous rush toward loss.

And it must be said not only tonight, but now—at this actual moment, this pyramid of moments piling higher and higher, measured out by the pulse of the busy telephone circuits.

He calls the Swedish au pair and tells her to come at once. He is desperate to run out; it makes him sick to his stomach to wait until she arrives. When she does, he rushes past her into the street. Maybe the circuits from a street phone will not be busy. But the same signal greets him: a faster rhythm than the usual busy signal. The entire district is out, the supervisor tells him.

In the cab rushing toward Sarah's apartment on Fifty-seventh Street, he thinks of just ringing her bell—sees Linc answering the door, Sarah standing behind him, half naked, like some nineteenth-century painting; somber, suggestive with menace.

He disembarks at Fifty-seventh Street and Sixth Avenue and calls again from a corner phone. The booth doors close around him, holding him in a column of hot, wet air. This time the phone rings through. The city's essential services are alive again. On the second ring Linc answers. He does not sound surprised to hear Simon's voice on this particular telephone. Sarah is not there. Her father died a few hours ago; she is staying with her mother for the night. Simon writes down the funeral details on a pocket pad. They are like two members of a family caught by unexpected bereavement, uncertain of what tone to adopt, not knowing how to say goodbye.

9

"... THE VERY SIZE of this gathering tells us more than mere words can tell . . ." Over and through the press of mourners and visitors, Simon searched for a sight of Sarah. Riverside Chapel was filled with people in dark suits and striped or quietly patterned ties, who could only be psychiatrists. A number of older men wore skullcaps. The rabbi was bareheaded. In one of the front rows Simon saw the complex folds of a white turban: Ram Singh was paying his respects to his employer's new-found personal involvement. Next to him a gaunt old lady with blue hair in neat waves bowed her head in her hands. Respect shared the air with quiet grief. The funerals of old men *should* be different than others, Simon thought. He recalled his father's last surprise visit home, sick, coughing blood; and his funeral—Simon had been eight—Simon's mother screaming, restrained from demonstrating her devotion by joining his father in the grave: as if he had not become a stranger over the years; as if this funeral were not merely another unexpected visit from an undomesticable husband and father; his death, his last and least practical scheme.

"... devoted service to the medical profession and the young science of psychiatry . . ."

Here, as elsewhere in the city, the air conditioning was helpless in the face of the temperature and the press of human flesh. Tasting his own salty sweat, Simon thought: Not a word, naturally, of the immigrant revolutionary who came to ensure happiness for all future generations—and stayed to bring happiness to them one by one, starting by bringing sleep to one wakeful woman. He'd given up "the people" for that one woman—and had been full of regrets. Well, Simon thought, as the coffin was rolled up the

314

aisle and Sarah and her mother walked behind it, he'd done the opposite. He'd awakened one woman so thoroughly that he was being left alone with his regrets.

Sarah looked different somehow. Not a death difference; something else. It was her hair; she'd cut it off. Short and trim, it made her seem a young, attractive, sophisticated matron: no longer Daddy's Girl.

10

On the sidewalk as the crowd splintered, Simon caught a glimpse of the top of Marcus's head. He moved toward him, hidden among the chatting mourners and purring limousines. But when he got to the curb, the thick gray thatch was gone.

"Are you going to the cemetery, sir?"

"I . . . don't know. Where is it?"

"Woodlawn. We have room in this car."

Reached by car, the cemetery at Woodlawn looks different. Not at all like the desolate place where he'd confronted Greer and had voted with his stomach for the private life. Still, it was here that Greer and Company had discussed grid theory versus open form. And here was the final grid of all: row upon row, neatly laid out, though the unstable movement of the living hides the perfect symmetry from view. There is some confusion as to the precise location of the plot. Delay, followed by the rabbi and his assistant rounding people up quickly to attend the brief graveside ceremony.

There must have been a thunderstorm while the chapel prayers had been going on. The oppressive heat has broken; a rose flush decorates the afternoon sky and a breeze troubles trees and mourners' hair. A few murmured words, a chant, an amen, and it is over. Simon has been unable to catch a sight of Sarah. As the group breaks into smaller groups heading for their cars, Simon sees her. Her head is on her mother's shoulder as she weeps. Mrs. Geist stares straight ahead; next to them a lost-looking Linc shifts uneasily from foot to foot and smokes something— Simon assumes it is only a cigarette, considering the occasion. Something in Simon is pleased that Linc looks so lost. Let him now enter the jungle of new relations; a lifetime of personalities and entanglements to be understood in a matter of weeks.

Seeing Sarah weep (which, after all, is not an unfamiliar sight) moves him toward action. He would go up to her, right here at the least appropriate time and place, and surprise her tears with the astonishing news that he will do what she asked. Decisions could not be based on large issues, always; sometimes small details, even tiny ones such as the way Sarah's head tilted on her mother's shoulder, her head shaking "no," much as it had in the stalled elevator when Simon had held her; and the cool breeze blowing around her and not ruffling her hair because it was so short now—surely these things were reason enough to leave a wife and child and begin a new life together.

The individuals who had broken apart congeal once again; a group containing Sarah and her mother and about a dozen more people move past Simon. Possessed with purpose, he moves toward Sarah, his right hand stretched out before him. Someone grasps it.

"Professor Shafer, surely you remember me, Ram Singh, the assistant of Professor Aaron." The giant Sikh pumps Simon's hand as if it had been offered in greeting. He presses himself close to Simon and smiles his dazzling teeth at him. His breath smells fragrant, vaguely foreign, as if he had gargled with some Indian aftershave lotion.

"Of course," Simon says.

"I have been going to call you up about our conversation in Venice. Professor Aaron has given me your telephone, but I have been so busy with the success of our project."

Sarah is out of sight; car engines growl. The moment has passed without significant action. He will not leave his family and marry Sarah, apparently. Instead, he will accept a lift back from an Indian gentleman who is obsessed with the idea that he and Simon had reached some meeting of the minds about Simon's coming to India to work on a project. It is hard to say which is crazier: Simon's impulse in the graveyard or this weird insistence on a marriage of principles which had never taken place.

"I did not promise."

"I understand. But you promised to consider."

"I remember no such promise."

"But does one need a promise to merely consider?"

"But you said I *had* promised."

"This is a silly conversation."

"Yes."

"I mean . . . here is my card."

There are about eight telephone numbers neatly inscribed on the card.

"We have the funds. My prime minister is committed to make India's cities fit for human living for everyone. We will begin small. One district in Calcutta."

The card is firmly ensconced in Simon's hand. It would be embarrassing to thrust it back at the man.

Ram Singh utters a sigh and leans back on the limousine's cushioned backrest.

"Sad, even though he was old," he says. "A great man, Professor Aaron told me. A socialist when young."

"No," Simon says. "A communist."

"Yes." Ram Singh beams, as if he and his new colleague can disagree on nothing. "He meant well for the people."

11

HE WAKES in the middle of the night. The blackness in the room extends to every corner of his life and the world; it is total. Knowing this might happen, he had gone to sleep in Matthew's room so as not to be alone when he awoke. But Matthew sleeps in long breaths; not knowing that his father had almost left him to live somewhere else, or that the chance stretching out of a hand by an Indian had saved the boy from abandonment.

Simon switches on the light. Matthew is surrounded in his bed by small stuffed animals and odd pieces of a board game. He is not alone. Outside, the Swedish au pair sleeps in Simon and Alex's bed, her schoolbooks on the floor next to the end table. In Simon's hurting mind, his misery forms itself around one image, which saves him. The key.

He knows why he has stubbornly refused to return Sarah's key; has actually lied and tricked her. It is because this moment was on its way. The black moment that could be lightened only by a visit to the apartment in which he had been so happy—when he was still alive.

The minute he lets himself in he is like a raging maniac. He hurls himself into the bathroom and performs his famous pill-searching routine. But he has never even bothered to learn the medical name. What he wants is an end to feeling. Any anodyne would do. Cocaine only gave him heightened feelings of another kind. He wants to stop it completely. In his present mood he could take any and all of the contents of the medicine chest. How many people, he wonders, have taken their last breath because they'd felt this way? Some saving whiff of sanity arrives in the guise of memory: the second secret package in the closet. At least he could learn what it contained; no one was coming to the apartment that night. Sarah would not surprise him. He is like a child taking revenge on adults. His regression and humiliation are complete; he will not resist them, will rather roll in them until his disgust with himself is complete.

The package is well wrapped; he takes it to the kitchen and uses a kitchen knife to cut the string. Inside is a shiny black revolver, A long way from Brahms and Rameau, forgotten music and forgotten umbrellas, to this frightening object, held so easily in his hand. He thinks, vaguely,

318

that Sarah may have broken some law by keeping this particular found object; and that he may be involved by simply holding and not reporting it. Why would she want to keep *this* toy? The discovery is as effective as pills would have been. He is so distracted by the shock of discovering a gun that he does not even think of using it. Death was not what he had had in mind. There had to be better ways of ending feeling than squeezing this small curved shiny trigger.

Standing in the center of the open kitchen, staring down at the pistol in his hand, he hears a key turn in the lock. From over the top of a bag of groceries, Marcus stares at him.

12

BOTH MEN ARE SILENT. Marcus walks past Simon to the kitchen table. He puts down the bag and turns again to Simon. His eyes are wide; not, Simon thinks, with any fear: they are mocking. In a moment he will speak—will say with eloquence what he thinks of lovers who wait for husbands (ex- or otherwise) with guns in their hands . . . since that is what the scene must look like to him. Simon remembers the eloquence the man had call on in Venice that cold night, during that wet, silly game of boccie in which everything was at stake—and nothing was lost or won. He can date the downward turn of everything from that night, from that eloquence. He is convinced that the reason he cannot take the next step toward Sarah, the reason he has to lose her to Linc, is that Marcus had shaken him. Some nagging sense of being a fake in this new style of being he'd adopted had stayed with him ever since. It was not only what Marcus had told him about Sarah: who she might have been, who she might *not* be. . . . It was what he'd told Simon about himself. That accurate poke at the center of his gut and spirit: "... *love dies or changes into something else* ... *the body dies, too* ... *don't leave us alone with ourselves* ... *any public idea* ... *even a lie* ..."

Something in Simon has always invited peroration, persuasion, harangue. Some sense of the seeker in him seemed to give people permission to tell him how life should be lived. Linc had and before him Alex and before her Ariel, and before her Ben Demos and before him Uncle Jack ... They'd seen Simon as a pilgrim; and pilgrims tend to encounter prophets. Marcus had smelled this out and had used it to try to prevent the loss of his Sarah. That he hadn't was no fault of his. You can't lose what you don't have.

The gun felt unbearably heavy. He shifted it to his left hand, preparatory to setting it down.

Marcus waved a hand at the gun. "Do you think you need that to find out more about Sarah?"

In a kind of answer, Simon threw the revolver onto the couch.

"You only want to know what you think you can handle anyway," Marcus said. "Whatever fits into your neat middle-class picture of men and women and how they behave."

Simon accepted the gambit. "Sarah said you would have told me things about her sister Jephtha and her. What things?"

Immediately he was sorry. Some austere silence would have been a better response. But it was too late.

"Tell you things ..." Marcus said. "You're such a damned stupid fool. Why do you think you know anything about Sarah? When did you earn such an idea?" He raised his voice; not quite a shout but loud enough to be uncomfortable. As if his audience might dismiss what he had to say if it were not said at high volume.

"My wife," he said, "is a drug addict; she is a lesbian; for years she and her sister, they—"

Marcus was taken by surprise, but he turned his head a quarter turn to avoid the blow and Simon's hand struck his upper cheekbone, hard. There was a cracking sound: Simon saw that he was looking down at Marcus, who had fallen to one knee; a kind of mock supplicating position, but with no mockery. It had been a hard punch.

Pain crackled into Simon's hand and arm. He'd not even had a moment to test his feelings: exultation? revenge? remorse? The pain wiped everything else away.

13

"I'M A PATIENT of Dr. Rowan's."

"I'll need your insurance information."

"He's associated with the hospital."

"This is only the emergency room. I'll still need your insurance information."

"Listen . . ."

"I understand that you're in pain. The nurse'll be here in a minute."

Simon felt himself swooning away in wave after wave of pain; they came like electric impulses, with even rhythm and sharp shocks. He was, at last, far beyond questions of turning doorknobs or grasping suitcases; far beyond makeshift slings. It was rapidly becoming a question of losing consciousness or of screaming. Instead, he managed to throw his wallet on the admissions desk. The clerk extracted the appropriate cards.

"How did it happen?"

"What happen?"

"Your hand, the accident . . ."

Alertness was suddenly required. Place of accident? Sarah's apartment . . . the gun . . . Marcus half turned away, fallen on one knee. . . . Hospitals always called the police; police always came to the home. Alex . . .

"There was no accident," he said. "It's a condition I have. Dr. Rowan knows all about it."

And having successfully supported the secrecy of months, he fainted.

A moment later, or so it seemed, he was conscious again, seated in a wheelchair in a small white room. Towering over him was Ram Singh.

"It's me, sir, Singh."

"I know."

"They called me."

"Why you?"

"They found this in your pocket."

It was Ram Singh's card on which the Indian had written eight telephone numbers in hopes that Simon would call one of them.

"Your home number had no reply."

"My wife is in New Orleans. The au pair sleeps like a teen-ager. Nothing can wake her. Thank you for coming."

Simon was neither alert nor befogged now; neither in absolute agony nor free of the pain. The throbbing was now unfocused, systemic. They must have given him a shot. He was aware of hurting, but he felt flat, emptied out.

In this state Ram Singh's presence seemed to impinge far too much. He was always interfering in things he did not understand: striking gondoliers, the violent consequences of a love affair.

As if to prove this, he knelt down next to Simon's wheelchair and said with great solicitude, "Which leg is it, Professor Shafer?"

"Please call me Simon, and it's my hand."

Simon tried to raise his right hand to illustrate his point, but nothing happened. Actually, what happened was that two nurses entered, one wrapped a blood pressure cuff around that particular arm and proceeded to pump away; the other wrote something on a clipboard. Embarrassed at all this activity happening in the presence of the neutral bystander from India, Simon felt the need to explain away his appearance in Ram Singh's life. His body was not under his control, but since awakening from the faint, his mind was; he wanted to take the moment of clarity to shake off the Indian Question for good.

"It was good of you to come down, but I feel badly, because of our misunderstanding the other day."

"Of what misunderstanding?"

"About coming to India to work with you. I'm finished with all that."

"How am I to understand this? You are a planner I am a planner—how can you be finished? You are a young man."

"That's not what I meant." How to say what he meant to someone who believed so strongly? It was like talking to himself two years ago.

"What I mean is, I don't have much hope for the large solutions we were trained for. And I'm stepping out of it. I won't be coming to India or anywhere. I don't know exactly what I'm going to do."

Ram Singh's eyes were wide brown ovals. "But how is this? I have heard about your work for years."

Was there anything as irritating as innocence? Simon thought. In his blurry mental state, he blurted out a mélange of disillusionment: a sixty-second graduate course in urban alienation; an overripe pudding stuffed with bits and pieces of history, politics and public policy of the past two centuries. It was a virtuoso condensation of Simon's public misery, sung in the service of his private grief. By the end of it, seeing Ram Singh's uncomprehending stare, he could only summon the energy to say. "Look, cities are politics and politics is crap. Everybody alive knows that now."

The Punjabi stood up quickly. Simon had forgotten how tall he was; the turban seemed to add another foot. He was sputtering like a giant bearded fuse.

"Oh, sir, this is a bad thing. I do not mean to make a

323

fuss when you are ill with pain, but this is very wrong. I can hardly know what to say to this, but it makes me very angry to hear this."

Basic rule of life: never make a six-foot-four Sikh angry with you when you are confined to a wheelchair and the painkiller that has been administered to you is rapidly wearing off.

"This, of course," the Indian said, "is a very special, very wonderful option, as you call it, open only to a few million white males with incomes."

The blood pressure ritual was finished. Now he was being asked to make a fist while blood was drawn from his arm into a vial.

Ram Singh was oblivious to the delicacy of this process. "Everybody else," he continued, "blacks, browns, poor, which is already most of the entire world, sir, I respectfully suggest, and not least of all, not at all, sir"—that repeated "sir" told Simon how angry Ram Singh actually was—"is the *Jews!* Now, you of all people should know that! Oh, I know everybody, the poorest of the miserable pariahs in Calcutta streets or the most lost soul black in New York half dead from heroin—snack, I think they call it—"

"Smack," Simon offered helplessly as his blood silently filled the glass tube.

"He too, they too, have a part-private, part-public life and undoubtedly some of his suffering is a personal matter—but how about the rest? How can a Jewish person like yourself not know that this is a fancy fantasy of yours? Are you aware, sir, that many of the six million Jews murdered by Hitler refused to believe that this purely 'political,' silly 'public' matter had anything at all to do with them? And how about the Jews who were killed at York in the seventeenth—"

"Sixteenth," Simon corrected again, helpless as before.

"And shall we perhaps go backwards in time and ask one of your ancestors who is waiting for Cossacks on horses to come and slice at his five-year-old child and rape his wife and daughters—shall we ask him if the public life

324

is exhausted, meaningless, and we may all now turn to the pursuit of happiness?"

They were wheeling him to x-ray, with Ram Singh dancing his dance of rage as they went. What did the nurses make of this, Simon thought, or the bleary-eyed young doctors in their stained whites, filling out forms in the glass cubicle they passed?

They arrived and waited at x-ray. Two people were ahead of them. Ram Singh was now towering over Simon, Simon confined to the wheelchair by the nurse's edict; he shook a fist in Simon's face, a Sikh warrior once more, a touch of parody present since he was menacing a proto-cripple, but alive with rage and righteous human fury. For a moment Simon thought the man might actually punch him in the face.

"Did you know, sir, that Mr. Marcus Delmarco, a gentleman I understand is somewhat involved in your nonpolitical happiness, was captured and tortured by the Nazi Party in France, and that they almost blinded him by inserting a pin in the corner of an eye? And he had committed the double sin of being political and being a Jew. . . ."

"I didn't mean . . ."

"So perhaps we may not completely blame Mr. Delmarco for his unusual life with the young lady Sarah—neither married nor unmarried, according to Dr. Aaron—for his games with drugs. . . . It is possible that the private sense of life, of being one's self—which may be one of the great reasons for existence—can be poisoned, perhaps permanently, by participating in the public parade of the century's despicable life. . . ."

Simon was sprinkled by Ram Singh's furious spittle. All those *p*'s popping at him, climaxed by the final "despicable." It was a kind of anointing; the saliva of an outraged brown-skinned man who was committed to the salvation of life in cities, sprinkled over Simon in the hope of bringing him back to what Ram Singh undoubtedly thought of as his sacred task.

* * *

The pain returned immediately following the x-rays; this time it was accompanied by nausea. Simon concentrated on not throwing up. Back in the white-on-white cubicle, they were to wait for Dr. Rowan. But Ram Singh was not through; only more controlled. There was no longer a clear and present danger of assault in a wheelchair. But he had points to make that were still pressing. His arm was lowered, but his voice was not. In the corridor outside, a wide-eyed Puerto Rican boy put down his transistor radio and followed the action; a pregnant blonde who had been dozing on the handlebars of her bicycle woke up and gazed uncomprehendingly at the angry dance of the Indian.

"You will forgive me for telling private secrets I have heard about. But to justify my bad behavior, let me tell you a story. It is a story about someone whose life confounds all categories. A life of a boy named Zachar. He was born in a gutter in Calcutta; he has never in his life seen the inside of a building. All of your precious history, all of your magnificent Western—or Eastern, for that matter—culture, is lost on him and to him. Because he is prehistory, nonhistory. He is a creature of need and place. Only think of this: *he has never been alone in his life.* This makes him at once the most private and the most public of beings who has ever lived. Oh, perhaps at four in the morning if he wakes from his stinking straw in the alley where he lives, and everyone else is asleep, except perhaps a cat looking for a scrap of food, I suppose you might say he is alone at that moment. But the physical presence of the other breathing bodies acts against the kind of solitude the poorest white American has. . . . So much for the distinctions between public and private. Your Thoreau did not write for him; his love story will forever be a dirty film. . . .

"It is quite extraordinary, but Zachar grows up with a sense of what is right and what is not . . . but what are we to do with him? I do not say that he is your responsibility —like an advertisement in an American magazine with a

326

coupon for money. No! I only mention him because his existence may make these questions you have been torturing yourself with seem not so easy . . . if they ever did, and I respectfully suggest that you are not showing to me—who am, after all, almost a stranger—all the pain that attends with those questions; only the answers you would like to think you have arrived at."

He wiped his forehead with an enormous flowered silk handkerchief, straightened his turban and dabbed at his moistened beard. He produced the suggestion of a bow, from the waist up; it was as if some form of politesse was needed to restore the natural order of things between them.

"I am going to offer an apology for my emotions. But first I must add that it seems to me that of all the people in the world, a Jew should understand this."

Before Simon could elaborate on how poor a Jew he was, how little he was entitled to this special intellectual consideration the Indian was offering him, Dr. Rowan filled the doorway. There was only time for a quick change of roles for Ram Singh: from angry prophet to messenger. He is to look in on Matthew, he is to call Alex, at once, at this number. He is *not* to tell Linc or Sarah.

As Dr. Rowan is talking to the first nurse, and the second nurse wheels him toward the elevator, Simon smiles at Ram Singh: a smile designed as a temporary bridge over the chasm between them. Without thinking, he extends his wounded hand in a gesture of friendship. Ram Singh takes it in his paw and squeezes it warmly.

It is a point of pride with Simon not to cry out; he concentrates all his attention and force of being on not fainting again. He succeeds. It is going to be an interesting relationship.

Jabbed with anesthetic, groggy with Demerol, sheeted, draped, painted with red, pink and violet antiseptic, Simon lay behind a sheeted screen while Dr. Rowan carved out joint mice from his right hand. Only the hand was present, extended through an opening in the screen; Simon, himself, was absent, at last entirely public—an object to be sliced to perfection.

Afterward he was wheeled to the recovery room and slid from the table into a wheelchair. Two young nurses, commanded by an older nurse with masses of bright blond hair piled on her head, rigged up an intravenous feeding unit to his left arm. "It's only glucose, honey," the head nurse said. "You don't really belong here. Are you all right? Answer me?"

"Oh . . . ?"

"You're a come-and-go. These others are real post-ops."

The others were all breathing deeply in what appeared their final comas. Simon was pleased to be a come-and-go.

"You've had local. But we have to keep you here to make sure you don't go into shock. Just a couple of hours, maybe. C'mon, let's take a look at the doubtful case."

Simon's right hand was wrapped in layer upon layer of bandage until it resembled a giant white boxing glove. He'd been looking for a fight since Les Baux. He'd gotten the fight and the glove had come after the fact. Poor Marcus. He might never know Simon had hit him just to keep him silent; just to avoid hearing the truth one time too many. A long way from the Golden Gloves to this white sterile arena, with a giant glove growing around his hand.

Monitoring machines were in every corner of the room. Simon sat in his chair in the room's very center. To his left a young boy breathed noisily; an old shrunken brown man in the bed next to him seemed not to breathe at all; but the screen next to his bed had a healthy beep popping rhythmically.

The nurses were bustling quietly around the bed of the doubtful case. He was screened off, so Simon could see only activity, not details. At one point he heard the head nurse say, "May have to go back . . ." Did one, then, go back so soon after surgery? A mistake; an object left inside in error. Something in the awful futility of the idea reached Simon through the cloud of tranquilizer in his head and he was suddenly filled with longing to see Sarah. He saw her slightly rounded chin and gray eyes. He had never intended to be so at the mercy of a face; all he'd wanted was to be quite happy for a time. And now he was filled with unhappiness and probably on his way to India. As soon as you were occupied with happiness, everything got away from you.

"Nobody said you had to make a project out of it."

"Ben!"

"So it's going to be India this time."

"How did you know?"

"It figured—from the minute the guy with the turban started talking about the kid in the streets."

"I think it might be a little more serious than that."

"Nothing's more serious than sentiment."

"You know what I mean, Ben."

"Sure. 'Every little boy and girl/Born into this world alive/Is either a little liberal/Or else a little conservative.' "

"Sometimes it's more than a bleeding heart, Ben. Sometimes your mind bleeds."

"I wouldn't know. There's no blood where *I* am."

"Listen, Ben . . . since you're dead, can you see what's going to happen?"

"Sure."

"Really?"

"Absolutely."

"You never mentioned it."

"You never asked."

"Can you tell me what's going to happen?"

"Yes. But not what's going to happen about you."

"Tell me about Sarah."

"Just the immediate future, okay?"

"Right."

Ben sketched for Simon the coming years of Sarah's life: the impossible would soon take place. The agitation, the mystery and anarchy of Sarah's days would disappear into the bourgeois regularity of a known life; she would be a married woman, with projects of her own: her marriage to

Linc—women often marry, Ben commented, after the death of a father—her agency (renamed G & A Travel); she would make a documentary about the saving of Venice, with Margaretta; and there would be her child, a girl named Jephtha. Sarah would have her size.

Then came the part that was hardest for Simon to hear and to bear: she would look back on this year with Simon, and the years before it, as a distant time of confusion, a dizzy preparation for her present order—a necessary prelude to a "real" life. She would remember that Simon had been an earthquake in the life of her feelings. But Simon's project—what he had perceived as a passionate and permanent rebuilding of her life, demanding heroic measures from a lover—would be recalled only as a bad dream of a long time ago.

"And me . . . ?"

"I said not about you. I wish you luck if not happiness. You'll never be the Jewish Christopher Wren—but you're okay!" Ben winked.

It all had the sound of farewell. But it left behind a flood of information—a life in miniature—so difficult to assimilate. Sarah whole: a child . . . a film . . . a husband; connected to the world with all those invisible threads that held ordinary people. Sarah calm, pill-free; Sarah centered, with a self so well focused that she would rewrite their time together as an adolescent love poem: intense, overheated, but essentially a story without point, as any story rewritten from the point of view of happiness must be without point.

The project had been a success. It was absolutely clear to him, dizzy with Demerol as he was, shaky with surgical shock from having had his hand carved and recarved like faulty sculpture; in spite of the derangement of time and place, the sense of being floated through his mind, his boxing-glove hand raised in a frozen gesture of benediction: still, the sense of success invaded him like some exhilarating anti-anesthetic.

The whole crazy idea had worked, after all. And in ways

330

he could not have foreseen. An accidental success; a Prince of Serendip, he had made his blueprints and something else had happened. The impossible idea of remaking a human being—because he, the Maker, was in despair over the possibility of making *anything*—was not so impossible after all.

He had not known that the *means* would be so awful, so painful, so foolish. Characters from a puppet show: the Husband and the Lover fighting over the Beloved while the Best Friend casually scooped her up and ran off with her to live happily ever after. He wished Sarah and Linc well. Their pulling it off made everything possible. Simon remembered the most fantastic of projects: Cleveland in 1967, Bogotá in 1968. It seemed now, in retrospect, that any success that clung to those projects had been accidental, the results of random connections, chance developments, some silly: They were about to be booted out of Bogotá at one point when the minister of the interior discovered that Simon had taught his nephew urban history at Yale. A half bottle of wine later, the project was back in motion. Some accidents were more grand: a zero added to a preliminary estimate of necessary funds by accident, in Cleveland, allowed for the hiring of extra staff for six months, which made everything work. By the time it was discovered, the recommended changes in Cleveland's central city had been approved by the mayor and the governor and the error was validated after the fact.

Success justified all effort; as failure placed all energies and invention in question.

Marcus may have been right about history. But he had been wrong about Simon and Sarah. And he had suffered loss because of it. But so had Simon. The very success of Project Sarah had, unexpectedly, dealt both of them out.

An odd sense of the rightness of things settled over him; odd because it mixed with his missing Sarah, wishing she were there.

He rested his head in his good hand and thought about the accidental plunge into India.

331

It was going to be awful and he knew it. Behind the fancy rhetoric of Ram Singh lay generations of smug, corrupt government shenanigans, learned, perhaps, from the English masters. It would be enough to make Alderman Murphy seem like Lincoln Steffens.

Simon could see ahead: not to the nobility of saving Ram Singh's young boy, Zachar, from a deadly public life lived and died in the streets. No, it was to be lies about ends and means; it was to be one Indian official denying any knowledge of what another official had agreed to; it was to be the petty contempt of one group of Indians toward another; it was to be that unbearable pseudoknowledgeability about absolutely everything that had made the Indians met in school or traveling in Europe so painful. The window is stuck? "Ah, yes, we Indians know about windows; we have the finest tradition of window-makers in the East, in the world."

Something in him was determined to be relentlessly accurate, post-Sarah; it drove Simon to think out the worst, most ironic, most foolish aspects of the adventure he was letting himself in for. Because it was the next project after Sarah, he must strip it as bare as possible. Let him appear to himself as the worst kind of ethnocentric Western invader, white-man's burden 1970's style. It might at least be some inoculation against the fever that would undoubtedly take him again; he would, he knew, develop the passion, the combination of craft and hope, that Linc had once absurdly called a kind of public love. And where Sarah had received it, now an impossible place would.

But since when did one lavish love only on the so-called worthy? Had Sarah taken him in one hand and weighed him against his marriage and his intentions in the other? Or had she just fallen? It was no accident, he saw again with the suspect clarity of the recovery room and its drugs, that the expression "climbing into love" or "stepping into love" had never developed in any language he could think of. One fell because falling was totally without judgment; a denial of judgment, in fact.

Finally, perhaps, his Indian adventure would be no more silly than his Sarah adventure. Even there, accidental success might be waiting with its cryptic lessons for him to learn.

It was hard for Simon to concentrate because the head nurse with the high-piled hair began to order two other nurses to wheel the doubtful case out of the recovery room. Imagine, Simon thought, if the poor bastard has to go back and be opened up again, just to find a miscounted sponge or a clamp. Science, apparently, was not an exact science. Everyone was a doubtful case.

As they bustled, Simon sat there enthroned in his wheelchair, the i.v. stand at his left arm like a scepter, his right hand swathed in the boxing glove of bandages, like a mace. The king of the recovery room, by virtue of being the only conscious patient present, surrounded by anesthetized post-op sleepers and by screens on which appeared electronic bleeps.

It occurred to him that this might be his last kingdom. Never to be the Jewish Christopher Wren. Ben had seen into his enterprise, from his start to Sarah's finish. He must have known that if the heart is too open to questions of happiness, you had to be content with smaller victories. In that tension between the weight of pain and the flight of happiness, that swift moment in which the decision is made to endure the pain a little longer, to postpone the leap of joy—in that moment of hesitation the cities were born, revised, filled with sculptured images, colors, sounds and spaces: were made livable, cut back again to the human scale.

But Simon had not been able to endure that hesitation. He could handle the pain of bone but not the pain of unhappiness. The long moment had come and gone. He'd used it to create Sarah (and himself) from scratch. And he'd lost them both, along with his joint mice and his conquering march through the cities.

Now he would wait for Alexandria and the future to arrive. He was to be so many things: Alex's friend—so

333

she'd murmured as she fell asleep; Ram Singh's Jew—
which seemed to carry certain permanent obligations;
Linc's failed friend—or was it the other way around?;
Marcus's nemesis—the instrument of his losing Sarah;
Matthew's father—without the gift for fathering; and
Sarah's bad dream of a time when she had to be taught
how to say "love" without stammering.

Two hours later Alex arrived. She searched for him
through the broad glass windows of the recovery room. It
was like peering into a nursery looking for the right baby.

Simon raised his boxing-glove hand in greeting. Alex
was in disarray; she had been frightened; her hair had
been blown about by the winds of airplanes and taxicabs.
She was too nervous to enter the recovery room, uncertain
if it was permitted. In spite of all this she seemed to Simon
in his Demerol haze, as he saw her framed in the glass,
small, elegant in the way a solution to a problem can be
elegant, whole: a completed work.

Even though Alex had probably been terrified by Ram
Singh's midnight call and had scrambled wildly to get back
to New York, he was glad that she chose to be intimidated,
to stay beyond the glass wall of the recovery room, at least
for the moment.

Did that make him a monster? And on what scale? Was
Linc a monster for moving into the space between Sarah
and his friend? And what of the secret life between Sarah
and Jephtha: that long flowing hair splayed out over the
legs of her sister. Was that monstrous? The answer was yes
to all—as well as no. Every private action had its private
value—and its public one; all a terrible confusion of
realms.

It was good to be in this simple place, the recovery room.
The nurses on duty to ensure that he did not become a
doubtful case; Alex standing her uncertain guard duty
outside the glass. He rested his boxing glove on his lap
and slept a few moments.

When he woke he felt as alert as if he'd slept for hours.

He was glad to see that everything was the same as when he'd fallen asleep: machines purring quietly, Alex beyond the glass, a nurse fiddling with a sterilizer.

Everything might not, after all, be politics. But he was glad that everything wasn't a dream either.